THE HELSINKI AFFAIR

A Novel

ANNA PITONIAK

SIMON & SCHUSTER

New York   London   Toronto
Sydney   New Delhi

Simon & Schuster
1230 Avenue of the Americas
New York, NY 10020

SIMON & SCHUSTER and colophon are registered trademarks
of Simon & Schuster, Inc.

Text design by Paul Dippolito

Manufactured in the United States of America

ISBN 978-1-6680-1474-5

For Nellie and Ruth

PART I

THE WALK-IN

CHAPTER ONE

I t wasn't exactly the sensible thing to do, standing outside in the hot noon sun in July in Rome. Semonov paced back and forth, mopping his brow, his handkerchief long since soaked with sweat. No, this wasn't sensible. He ought to have done as the Romans did, escaping the summer heat by stopping at Giolitti for a cone of gelato, or napping in a shuttered bedroom, or fleeing the city altogether for the breezy hills of Umbria. But Konstantin Nikolaievich Semonov was not standing here, pleading to be admitted to the American embassy, insisting that he had urgent information to share, because he was an entirely sensible person.

In his air-conditioned booth, the soldier hung up the phone. "You need to make an appointment. No one can see you today," he said.

"Sir!" Semonov exclaimed, leaning toward the pinprick holes in the glass. "You are a Marine. I am speaking to you as a fellow military man. I am an officer in my nation's army. My nation which is *Russia*." A needless emphasis, as ten minutes earlier he had slid his passport under the bulletproof glass barrier to identify himself. "You must understand. I have information that matters *today*. Not tomorrow, not next week."

In fairness to the soldier, Semonov was a hard man to take seriously. His shirt buttons strained to contain his plump stomach. His pockets jingled with loose change. Behind his round glasses, his eyes were wide and guileless. But when the Marine hesitated for a moment, Semonov's instinct, which was well-honed, told him to seize his opening.

"I am from Moscow." Semonov lowered his voice. "I am here in Rome on holiday with my wife. It would not be possible for me to communicate this information while in Moscow. The nature of my work means that I am closely watched. Do you understand? The nature of my work has also exposed me to certain *information* that I believe your officials will value."

"Even if that's true," the Marine said, "you still need to make an appointment."

The Marine was no more than twenty-four or twenty-five years old. Crew cut, clean shave, trim as a sharpened pencil, a good soldier, a rule follower. To grant exceptions to the rules—to take pity, for instance, on a sweaty stranger with a thick accent—required the seasoning of age, which he didn't have. And so Semonov realized, with some reluctance, that he would have to resort to blunter tactics.

Semonov stood up straight. A change passed over his features, like a shadow passing over the sun. Staring at the Marine, he said: "My information concerns Robert Vogel."

The tiniest flinch in the young man's brow as he registered the name.

"Senator Vogel's flight is due to land in Cairo in one hour," he continued calmly. "His life is in danger."

·   ·   ·

As postings went, Rome was one of the sleepiest. It had its perks, of course. The glamorous garden parties at the Villa Taverna, where the American ambassador plied his guests with crystal flutes of prosecco. The wine-soaked weekends in the hill towns of Tuscany. The simple ability to walk safely home from the embassy without an armed escort. But Amanda Cole would have gladly given up any of those perks for the chance to do her job.

Her *real* job. The job she had trained for. Back in Washington, when she received news of this posting, her boss in the Directorate of Operations only shook his head, both sympathetic to and bemused by her obvious disappointment. "Enjoy it," he'd said. "Try to make some memories, Cole. You'll be glad to have them when you get to the next Third World bunker."

Italian-style lunch breaks were another perk of the posting. On any given day, between the hours of noon and 3 p.m., most of her colleagues were nowhere to be found. They went home to eat and take a midday siesta, or they enjoyed a leisurely meal at one of the city's finer restaurants, entertaining a source on the government's dime. They had learned to take the work for what it was. If they were bored, at least they were bored in comfort.

On that hot July afternoon, Amanda Cole was halfway through her two-year posting as deputy station chief for the Central Intelligence Agency. She was forty years old—though everyone said she looked much younger—which meant that she'd been in this line of work for almost seventeen years. It was the only career she'd ever had, if you didn't count her stints as bartender and dishwasher and au pair. After graduating high school, she had no interest in college. Beyond that surety, her sense of her future was painfully unclear, so she decided to travel the world, paying her way with a series of short-lived jobs. It wasn't until she eventually came home and started at the agency that she learned to channel her restless curiosity to more productive ends. To succeed in the Clandestine Service required an appetite for the world's chaos. Travel had whetted that appetite.

Her success, over time, had made her more disciplined. Amanda knew how to play the game. From the moment her flight landed at Fiumicino, not a single word of complaint had passed her lips. She nodded, smiled, acted the team player. And yet she wasn't *exactly* one of the gang. The ambassador's dinner parties, for instance. They tended to run late, but Amanda always left early. After she had slipped away, when her colleagues were deep into the Montepulciano, they sometimes speculated. Was she running something off-the-books? Was she trying to set an example? In any case, they agreed, among themselves, that there was something obnoxious about her workaholism.

Regardless of her reasoning, the fact was that Amanda was the only person there, in Rome station, to answer the phone on that summer afternoon, and to tell the young Marine *not* to admit this strange Russian man to the building. This was a problem for their embassies around the world. All kinds of people liked to bang on the gates and demand an audience. Ninety-nine percent of the time, they were utter kooks.

After hanging up, Amanda stared at her computer screen, trying to regain her concentration. She was in the midst of approving a spreadsheet of expense reports, which (no one ever warned you of this) comprised a significant portion of her work as deputy station chief.

The phone rang again. She picked it up and said, irritably: "You know, Sergeant, if you want to talk to me so badly, you can just ask me on a date."

"He says he knows something about Senator Vogel," the Marine said. "He has all the details about his trip to Egypt."

"Bob Vogel?" Amanda sat up slightly. "What else did he say?"

"He said . . ." The soldier hesitated. Amanda could imagine the young man's gaze flicking back to the visitor, wondering if repeating the words would make him sound like an idiot. "He said Senator Vogel's life is in danger."

She could have laughed at the melodrama of it. But when she glanced around, taking in the deserted station, the dull windowless chamber with its beige walls and gray carpet, with its lone fiddle-leaf fig plant yellowing in the corner, she found herself thinking, *Anything is better than these spreadsheets.*

"Fine," she sighed. "Send him up."

•　•　•

At least the conference room had a window and made for a change of scenery. Amanda slid a bottle of water across the table. Konstantin Nikolaievich Semonov took it gratefully and gulped it down. Amanda raised an eyebrow and said: "Would you like another?"

"Please," he said. "It is very hot today."

Despite the air-conditioning, Amanda noticed beads of sweat kept gathering on Semonov's brow. She noticed too the wedding ring on his right hand, and the meticulous care with which his shirt had been patched and mended, and the gold watch on his wrist. She folded her hands atop the table. "So," she began. "Mr. Semonov. I understand you have some information you'd like to share with us?"

"I apologize. My English isn't very good," he said.

"It sounds quite good to me. But if you'd rather continue in Russian, we'll have to wait until one of my colleagues returns, because I don't—"

"No," he interrupted. "I am your guest, of course we will speak English. But I say this because I must have misunderstood. You work on economic affairs for the U.S. State Department?"

"That's right. I'm an attaché in the economic section."

"But my information does not concern economic affairs."

"Well." She smiled brightly. "It's July in Italy, Mr. Semonov. The embassy is a little bare-bones at the moment."

"I see." After a long pause, staring at her, he said: "So you are Amanda Clarkson. Amanda Clarkson, the economic attaché."

She could perceive, beneath his sweaty brow, a deeper perception. Something inside her twinged to attention. The detached part of her brain carefully registered it as another data point.

"That's me!" she chirped.

"Very well." Slowly, he nodded to himself. "Very well, Amanda Clarkson. Even if you are the economic attaché, I hope you can help me. I come to you today with information concerning Mr. Robert Vogel. He is a senator in your country, from the state of New York.

A powerful man, I understand. An aging man, too. I have read reports that his health has been declining recently."

Another twinge. "Yes," she said. "I've heard that, too."

"He is part of a delegation en route to Cairo. Yesterday evening, the delegation boarded a plane in Washington. In less than an hour, that plane is due to land. A military convoy of the Egyptian government will escort the Americans from the airport to the Four Seasons, where they are staying. Tonight, at six o'clock, the convoy will escort the Americans to the Heliopolis Palace, where they will be dining as guests of the president."

He could have googled this, though, she told herself. *It would only take a few minutes.*

"The military convoy will accompany the American delegation for the duration of their three-day visit." Semonov spoke with bureaucratic precision. "The Egyptian president is determined that their safety be absolute. He does not want his guests exposed to unstable elements. There will be one exception, though. Tomorrow morning, the delegation will be participating in a review of the Egyptian military. This is the primary purpose of the trip to Cairo. For the American visitors to assess the strength of their ally."

She kept smiling, even as her pulse accelerated. Sure. Nothing unusual about this. Nothing weird about a Russian man walking in with detailed knowledge of the Senate intelligence committee's movements.

"During this review the Americans will, of course, be surrounded by the military," Semonov continued. "It will be the safest place in all Egypt. Therefore, there is no need for the convoy. The Americans will be free to move about, speaking to various generals, examining the artillery, interacting with soldiers. The review will begin at eleven a.m. At that hour, the temperature is typically thirty-seven or thirty-eight degrees centigrade. They will be assembled outdoors. There will be very little shade. The president has ordered that the review last no more than one hour. He is aware that several of his guests are older and may struggle in the heat. Unfortunately, his precaution will not be enough. Just before noon, Senator Robert Vogel will suffer a heat-induced stroke. He will be taken to the nearby hospital, where he will be pronounced dead."

She swallowed. There was no mistaking this internal quiver. But now, right now, it was important not to spook him. "Okay." *Piano, piano*, as a local might say. "Okay. Mr. Semonov. Let me begin with an obvious question. How can you know about a stroke before it happens?"

"I can't. But there are certain chemicals that produce symptoms in the human body that appear very similar to those of a stroke. So similar that there is no reason to question the initial conclusion. Especially when the deceased is eighty-one years old and in frail health."

"I'm sorry, Mr. Semonov. What you're describing sounds like an assassination."

"Yes."

"And how could you know about this assassination before it happens?"

"Because I work with the men who will carry out the assassination."

"And where is that?"

He squeezed the water bottle in agitation, the thin plastic crackling in his hands. "You don't believe me, do you?"

"It's not a question of—"

"Then I should leave. I shouldn't be here!"

He began to stand, but Amanda placed a hand on his arm to stop him. "Mr. Semonov," she said. "I *want* to believe you. I want to take this seriously. But to do that, I'm going to need more information." She paused. "You work with the men who will carry out the assassination. Where do you work?"

The tension in his forehead was visible. "I work for the General Staff of the Armed Forces of the Russian Federation."

"And which division, specifically?"

"The Main Intelligence Directorate," he whispered. "The GRU."

• • •

"Jesus Christ," he said. "Cole, are you drunk?"

Osmond Brown stood behind his desk, hands planted on his hips, narrowing his eyes at Amanda Cole, who had followed him into his office as he returned from lunch. Amanda Cole, who was more than thirty years his junior. Amanda Cole, who worked for *him*, but who never seemed to remember that goddamn fact.

Amanda closed the door and gestured for him to sit down. There was something especially impertinent about this coming from *her*, what with her slight stature and the childish freckles across her nose. He almost snapped at her (this was *his* goddamn office, *he* would decide whether to sit down), but then he shut his mouth and sank into his chair. Over the past year, Osmond had discovered that it was difficult to raise his voice at Amanda. She never flinched, no matter how much he yelled, and this was strangely deflating.

"He's telling the truth," she said.

"And how on God's green earth can you know a thing like that?"

"Because he's scared. He's terrified. It's not the kind of thing you can fake."

"Did you ever stop to consider," Osmond said, in his Mississippi drawl, which often grew exaggerated after a glass or two of wine, "that maybe the man is so goddamn *terrified* because he's being dangled as bait to the Americans?"

"They would never pick a man like him for a dangle."

"Oh yes. My apologies, Ms. Cole. I seem to have forgotten you're a mind reader, too."

"If the Russians were trying to sell us on an agent," she continued, ignoring Osmond's sarcasm, as she always did, "they'd pick someone who looks the part. Someone with an obvious motive. Greed, preferably. Greed is always the most convincing."

Osmond scowled. "Let me guess. Now you're going to tell me that your new friend doesn't have a greedy bone in his body."

She held up her wrist. "His watch. He's wearing a TAG Heuer. So he's well-off, he's comfortable, but his shirt is mended in at least half a dozen places. He clearly isn't materialistic. Not enough to make for a convincing dangle. The Russians only pick people who *look* the part. Semonov doesn't, and he's terrified. That fear is the information we're working with. And in less than twenty-four hours, there's going to be—"

"Whoa," he interrupted. "Whoa! Hold it right there. You're acting like we have to *do* something about this."

"Well, yeah. Of course we have to."

"Says who, Cole?"

"Says the evidence, *sir*."

Across the expanse of his desk, Osmond regarded her. Despite his best intentions, he had allowed himself a glass—okay, two glasses—of Vermentino with lunch. How could he resist when it paired so beautifully with the sweet summer cantaloupe? But now he was tired, and he had a headache, and this whole thing sounded like a boondoggle, and Amanda was possibly the stubbornest person he had ever met. Dealing with this woman was one of the more exhausting parts of the job. And yet, he knew her kryptonite. Amanda Cole did, despite appearances, possess an essential kernel of respect for the Way Things Were Done. She would push back, but she wasn't one to disobey a direct order. At the end of the day, he saw it as his task to remind her of her fealty.

Well, clearly she was all worked up about this. Why not indulge her a few moments longer, before he lowered the boom? So he settled back into his chair, folded his hands on his stomach, and said: "Okay, Cole. Let's talk this one through. Let's say we decide to believe this guy, this what's-his-name—"

"His name is Semonov," she interrupted. "Konstantin Semonov."

"Sure. Okay. Let's say we decide to believe this Semonov, and decide that the threat to Bob Vogel is real, and decide to act on it. We'd need to get word to Senator Vogel about what's happening and tell him to skip the review. How do we do that?"

"Verbally. Send someone to tell him. One of our people in Cairo."

"But when? Where? How? Every minute of the delegation's schedule is accounted for. They have some downtime at the Four Seasons, but you can't just have one of our people waltz in. Everyone in that hotel, from the maids to the managers to the goddamn window-washers, *every* person in that hotel is on someone else's payroll. That hotel is wired six ways to Sunday. So if we send one of our people to deliver the message verbally, what happens when that person arrives at the Four Seasons and beelines straight for Senator Vogel? Hmm?"

The furrow of her brow softened slightly. *I'm a good teacher,* Osmond thought. *No one ever wants to admit it, but I've got a knack for this part.*

"You think they want to blow our network in Cairo," she said.

"Bingo."

Amanda nodded. Osmond was pleased. See, at the end of the day, he just wanted these kids (and yes, they were kids, he was older than most of their fathers) to be a little more *careful.* Not to get themselves *killed* for no good reason.

But instead of thanking him, she said: "I don't buy it."

He sighed. "And why is that?"

"He's telling the truth. I'm *certain* he is. And don't just say he's their useful idiot, that his bosses at the GRU gave him this line to swallow and counted on him feeling guilty and running to the Americans. He's smart. He'd see through it. He saw through my cover in about three seconds flat."

"Look, Amanda, I get it. You're bored out of your mind." He tapped a finger against his temple. "Nothing happens in Rome. This isn't where the action is. And they know that, too. They're trying to use that boredom against you."

"You're really suggesting we do nothing about this?"

"I'm not suggesting. I'm *telling.*"

She shook her head, but her eyes went glassy. She tended to do this, to go quiet and retreat into cool detachment when she was overruled. Osmond respected her for fighting as hard as she did, but he also respected her for knowing when to surrender.

"We're the soft underbelly," he explained, feeling that pleasant flood of paternal benevolence that was, quite frankly, the only aspect of the job that still made him feel good. "Our networks in the Middle East are airtight. It wouldn't work to target them directly. So the Russians try to take the back door. They plant a seed in Rome and hope the tendril reaches Cairo. All they need to do is keep an eye on Senator Vogel. If we send someone to meet Vogel at his hotel, bingo: they've just identified the Cairo network. It's clever, isn't it? So the best response, or actually the *only* response, is to do nothing. You see?"

• • •

But that was the point, Amanda thought. The scheme Osmond had just outlined was too clever by half. It wasn't how the GRU worked. The many moving parts, the subtle contingencies: it lacked their signature bluntness.

Amanda left his office and walked through the bullpen, back toward the door that led to the rest of the embassy. One of her colleagues called after her ("Hey, Cole, that guy in the conference room one of yours? The fat guy with glasses? James Gandolfini past his prime?"), but she didn't hear him.

She buzzed through the unmarked door, walked down a hallway, down a flight of stairs, down another hallway. Through the glassed-in walls of the conference room, she saw what her colleagues would have seen as they returned from lunch. Semonov, pacing back and forth, like a goldfish desperate to escape the confines of his fishbowl.

Amanda had been trying to figure out what to say, how to explain this failure of hers, but as soon as he turned and looked at her, he seemed to know. As she closed the door, Semonov shook his head. She felt a strange gratitude for his perception. It was a terrible feeling, having to deliver this kind of bad news, having to shatter another person's desperate hope. Semonov had just spared her that feeling.

He sat down and dropped his head into his hands. She sat beside him, touched him on the elbow. "I'm sorry," she said. "I'm really, really sorry. I did everything I could."

He was saying something, but his voice was muffled by his hands.

"Mr. Semonov?" she said. "I can't understand you."

When he lifted his head, tears were spilling from his eyes. "My mother died last year," he said. "It was a spring day. The lilacs were in bloom."

"Oh," she said. "I'm, um . . . I'm sorry to hear that."

"Just before she died, she called me to her side, and she said: 'Kostya, you have a soft heart. You must be careful. The world suffers when there are too many soft hearts.' She was right! I've been a fool." He shook his head. "A fool of the worst kind. I knew that this day would come. And what did I think? That I could stop it? Look at what I have done!"

Amanda slid a box of tissues across the table. Semonov looked at her with watery appreciation and blew his nose with a comedic honk.

Your menagerie, her best friend Georgia once called it. *Your strange little petting zoo.*

Bartenders in seedy dives, hostesses in swanky clubs. Taxi drivers with photographic memories. Hairdressers with a knack for gossip. Restaurant owners with private back rooms. Chambermaids and bellboys and window-washers at five-star hotels. They liked making the extra money on the side, and they liked how seriously she took them. They liked to feel that occasional brush with danger. Together they comprised her strange little petting zoo. It was part of the job, collecting people like this, although Amanda tended to hang on to the assets even when they had ceased offering any obvious utility.

Look at what I have done! Semonov had exclaimed. She was curious about what, exactly, he meant by that; what role he played in the Vogel story. The expense reports could wait. So Amanda patted his hand and said: "Tell me about your mother. What was her name?"

. . .

In late July the sun didn't set until 8:30 p.m. As Amanda walked home, a benevolent twilight lit her way. Past the church that housed the famous Bernini carvings; past the imposing marble fountain that marked the terminus of an old Roman aqueduct; past the ancient Baths of Diocletian. The seventeenth century, the sixteenth century, the third century. "It sounds like you're practically tripping over history," her mother once said. And she meant it as a good thing, but history, Amanda knew, was a tricky Janus. History provided important context, but history also exerted a dangerous narrative gravity. If you expected the present to be a continuation of the past, you weren't actually looking at the present through clear eyes.

"It's like this," Amanda once said to Georgia. "Remember how we used to see that old man feeding pigeons outside school every afternoon?"

"Hector? I loved Hector."

"And you could reasonably assume that you'd see Hector every afternoon, right?"

Georgia squinted. "Why do I feel like I'm being set up?"

"But then one afternoon Hector doesn't show up. And everyone is so surprised. Because if Hector does the same thing ninety-nine days in a row, then *obviously* he's going to do the same thing on the hundredth day. But where is it written that the past ever predicts the future?"

"So you can't bank on *anything*? Is that really how you look at the world?"

Amanda shrugged. "I mean, no. Not really. But I try to not be surprised when the pattern gets broken."

But that night, on her walk home, she wasn't engaged in such profound considerations. As Amanda squeezed past a crowd outside the Repubblica metro, she could only think about how hungry she was, having missed lunch thanks to Semonov. The refrigerator in her apartment was bare. For the umpteenth night in a row, she was going to have to stop at her usual stall in the Mercato Centrale. The market was housed in an old wing of the Termini station, just a few blocks from her apartment. Stalls sold colorful heaps of vegetables, creamy orbs of burrata, dimpled sheets of focaccia, blistered rounds of pizza. Her favorite stall sold fresh pasta and premade sauces. Amanda had been pleased to discover that this demanded no more effort than did a box of Kraft macaroni and cheese. And it tasted good and it was cheap. She had decided, a long time ago, that this was the easiest way to feed herself.

During her visit last September, Georgia had been appalled by this habit. "You can't eat the same thing *every night*, Amanda. You know that you're in Rome, right?"

"I just don't care that much."

"This coming from the girl who once ate a scorpion in Bangkok. Who once drank pig's blood in Seoul. Who once—"

Amanda laughed. "Oh, yeah, you mean the girl who was a drunken shitshow and didn't know what she was doing with her life? You mean *that* girl? Should we bring her back?"

"You're not giving her enough credit. She was fun."

"She was crazy."

"Well, she's still in there. I know she is. No amount of Talbots can cover her up."

"This is J.Crew, thank you *very* much. And also, fuck you. I like Talbots."

Georgia laughed. Curled up on the couch in the apartment in Rome, she prodded Amanda with her foot. "I don't understand it. Your mom is so chic. And even your dad, you know, he has *decent* taste, in that boring Waspy way. And you, somehow, have the world's worst style."

"So this is my rebellion. Besides, who am I trying to impress? Other than my bitchy best friend?"

Georgia rolled her eyes. "It's not about *impressing* anyone. It's about a little self-respect."

At the market, Amanda also stopped at the wine stall. She rarely kept wine in the house, but it had been a long day, and she needed it. She unlocked her apartment to find the air inside hot and stale, so she opened the windows in hopes of a breeze. Sometimes she wondered what the neighbors across the courtyard must think of her. This American woman who came and went at strange hours, whose freckles and smile suggested friendliness, but who never offered anything but the smallest of talk.

Ten minutes later, having changed into a ratty old pair of shorts and a T-shirt, she flopped on the couch with her bowl of pasta and a glass of wine. It had been a marathon day. Amanda and Semonov had covered a good deal of his life story. How he had hoped to work as a translator for the GRU, only to be assigned the considerably more boring job of fabricating passports and visas. How his wife, an Italian woman named Chiara, had moved to Moscow for work, which explained his presence in Italy: they were visiting her family. He and Chiara had met in a Moscow metro station. She was lost and disoriented, and Semonov helped her find her way. He couldn't help smiling like a schoolboy when he talked about his wife. As the hours passed, Amanda had felt increasingly certain that he was telling the truth. She didn't know why exactly; she just knew.

She stabbed at the pasta with her fork. Here was the problem, though. She had been wrong before. Maybe Osmond was right, maybe boredom was causing her to jump at the chance for excitement. And she *was* bored. Was this just ego at work? This yearning for motion, for *action*, this desire to prove that she wasn't just sitting around, watching her muscles atrophy from neglect? Besides, she knew the odds. Years ago, during training at the Farm, she learned to be skeptical of walk-ins and defectors. Those things happened in the movies, not in real life. To recruit someone took work. The old-fashioned, time-tested, carrot-and-stick work of psychological manipulation. A Russian walks in and warns of a threat against an American politician? Things like that didn't just *happen*. Not according to the agency. Not according, specifically, to the people at the *top* of the agency, who believed they had earned their way to those positions of power. The idea that the world was random— that the universe was the product of chaos—that just didn't jibe.

But, see, on this particular point, she was stubborn. Like she'd said to Georgia: sometimes the world *was* random. But that look on Osmond's face had kept her from pushing. She knew a losing battle when she saw one.

Semonov had eventually looked at his watch. He had to go; his wife would be waiting for him. "Where are you staying?" Amanda asked. And when he gave her the name of his hotel, near the Piazza del Popolo, she felt a small ping. *Good*, she thought. *If it comes to it, that makes things easier.* She walked him to the lobby and shook his hand. "Enjoy the rest of your time in Rome," she said, in her friendliest *we-know-you-have-a-choice-in-airlines* tone. "And, Mr. Semonov—"

"Please," he interrupted. "Call me Kostya."

"Well, Kostya. Thank you for coming in and talking to me. I know it wasn't easy."

Amanda stood up and carried her bowl and wineglass to the sink. She recorked the wine and placed it in the cupboard. As she climbed into bed and switched off the light, she thought of how his face had darkened at their goodbye. He looked grateful for her sympathy, but mostly he looked sad; her sympathy wouldn't change the course of events.

The night was hot and still. The fan at the foot of her bed did little to help. Amanda's mind traced an endless loop. She should have done more. No. She had done everything she could. She thought of Semonov, at his hotel across town, and wondered if he would lie awake all night, too.

·   ·   ·

Osmond Brown was usually the first to arrive in the station, but that Friday morning, the door to his office remained closed. Amanda stared at it, puzzled, until one of her colleagues noticed. "He's out today," the colleague said. "Frolicking with the ambassador in Capri this weekend."

"Right." She nodded. "Forgot."

She looked at the clock on the wall: 8:47 a.m. Having lain awake all night, she was almost delirious from lack of sleep. The morning stuttered by in minuscule fragments. 9:03 a.m.: writing her contact report. 9:17 a.m.: locking the bathroom door and splashing water on her face. 9:42 a.m.: making a cup of coffee. 9:45 a.m.: finishing the coffee. 9:47 a.m.: considering making another. Amanda wanted to be proven wrong. She had never wanted this so badly. There was a bar on Via Ludovisi, one block from the embassy. At 12:01 p.m., she decided, at the precise moment when Senator Vogel and the rest of the delegation departed the military review and returned safely to the Four Seasons, she would go to that bar and reward herself for her wrongness with a shot of tequila.

11:06 a.m. They would have arrived by now. 11:31 a.m. They would be moving among the troops, examining the artillery, talking to the generals. She turned off her computer screen so she didn't have to look at the time. She gnawed on her thumbnail. She jiggled her knee. One of her colleagues glanced over in mild alarm, but when he noticed the look on her face, he thought better of asking her what was wrong.

Amanda turned her screen back on. 11:57, 11:58, 11:59 a.m. Noon! Noon on the dot! She broke into a giddy smile. "I'm going to lunch!" She jumped up from her desk and reached for her bag. "If the chief calls, tell him I got drunk and went home."

"Uh," her colleague said. "Really? You really want me to—"

But he was interrupted by a sudden, high-pitched chirping. Halfway across the room, Amanda froze. Every computer in the bullpen was emitting that identical electronic chirp. *No*, she thought. *No, no, no.*

"Holy shit," the colleague said. "Holy *shit*. Cole! Did you see this?"

She felt her stomach plummeting.

"It's Bob Vogel," he said. "He's dead."

CHAPTER TWO

At seventy-two years old, Charlie Cole couldn't move like he once did. His forehand was missing its former velocity, and his left knee complained when he tried to pivot too quickly. Sprinting was now out of the question. But when Lovell whaled the ball deep near the baseline, Charlie knew exactly what to do. Cross-court backhand, nice and easy, drop it just over the net. Death and taxes and Lovell's lousy short game. Grunting his way toward victory, Charlie thought: *What I lack in vigor, I make up for in wisdom.*

They stood at the edge of the court, shaded by a small green awning, drinking their water in silence. Eventually, Lovell nodded at him. "Good game," he said graciously. "Nice backhand on that last one."

"Beautiful morning, isn't it?" Charlie said, as they walked back to the clubhouse. It was just shy of 7 a.m., and the July heat wasn't yet oppressive. The courts were busy at this hour, a chorus of rounded *thwack*s echoing from figures in white. The sprinklers shimmered above the emerald lawn. The flag on the flagpole flapped gently in the breeze. The country club on a summer morning was a peaceful and prosperous scene, kept that way by the gate out front and the steep initiation fees. Charlie didn't like to admit that he had turned into one of Those People. Privately, he maintained that this wasn't actually who he was. But he and Lovell and the rest of their group had been playing together for two decades—no, three—and he could no longer fathom life without these thrice-weekly games.

Charlie enacted his clubhouse ritual. Steam room, shower,

shave. Plain white shirt, plain blue tie. Gym bag and tennis racket in the trunk of the car, suit jacket laid across the back seat. "See you next week," Charlie called to Lovell, who was unlocking his Corolla a few spots over. On his lobbyist salary, Lovell could afford a car with a lot more flash than a ten-year-old Toyota, but he drove the Corolla for the same reason Charlie felt so conflicted about the country club membership: because forget the gray hair, forget the potbelly: for a certain kind of aging man, idealism is the hardest vanity to surrender.

With traffic at that hour, it took exactly thirty-one minutes to drive from the country club to the agency. Thirty-six minutes if he decided to stop at Starbucks, which, because it was a Friday, he did. Charlie turned in to the campus, passed the visitors' center, passed the front entrance and the cars parked directly outside that entrance. He kept driving and driving until he finally arrived in his lot. If the parking lot assignments were an accurate reflection of status, then Charlie was squarely at the fiftieth percentile.

Next year would be his last year at the Central Intelligence Agency. Several of his tennis buddies had already retired from their careers as doctors, or judges, or general counsels. They said it wasn't so bad. There were other things to live for: kids and grandkids, travel with their wives, little projects around the house. But his tennis buddies often seemed to forget that Charlie had never remarried, and that his only daughter was (a) uninterested in children, and (b) far too busy to devote herself to her old man. He did, however, derive great pleasure from yardwork. If nothing else, retirement would be his chance to improve the health of his garden.

Besides, when his friends tried to share their wisdom, Charlie felt inwardly defensive. *I'm not like you!* part of him wanted to say. *What I've had is different.* His had been more than a career. It had been a *calling.* And yes, that was true half a century ago, when he first joined the agency. But then there was Helsinki—the disaster that was Helsinki. After that, at the tail end of the Cold War, Charlie was recalled to Langley and assigned to a boring desk job. This had been his life ever since. The brick colonial in Falls Church. The country club in Arlington. Not a calling, then: just the safe sinecure of failure.

He parked the car, draped his jacket over his arm, and walked toward the front entrance, carrying two coffees. Basically, this was a job like any other. Thousands of people passed through that white marble lobby every morning. Most of them, like Charlie, would spend their day engaged in the minor progresses and petty questions of any ordinary bureaucracy. Some people were different— some lived closer to the edge, some put their actual bodies on the line—but Charlie was no longer among their number. He'd spent the last thirty years trying to make his peace with this, but every morning, as he walked through the lobby and caught a glimpse of the stars carved into the marble wall—caught a glimpse of one star in particular—he felt a visceral wave of guilt. There were certain things a person couldn't undo; certain mistakes that could never be forgiven.

"Triple venti soy mocha with whipped cream?" Cherise asked, like always, as Charlie handed her the Starbucks cup with plain black coffee.

He smiled at the security guard and said, like always: "Just the way you like it, Cherise."

Charlie scanned his pass and the turnstile buzzed open. He was joining the stream headed toward the elevators when a voice boomed from behind him: "Cole! Hold up a second."

Charlie turned to see John Gasko attempting to buzz himself through the turnstile. The scanner wouldn't read his badge. Gasko smacked the ID against the scanner again and muttered, "Jesus Christ. Today of all days."

"Sir?" Cherise offered. "If you want, I can—"

"No!" Gasko barked. "Just give me a second, it's just this stupid— *There.* Finally." He strode through the turnstile and clapped a hand on Charlie's shoulder. "I hate those things, don't you? Listen, Cole. Nice work on that speech. I liked that line about unintended consequences."

"Oh. Thank you, sir. I'm glad to hear that."

After leaving the Clandestine Service, Charlie had cycled through a series of jobs in the Directorate of Support, doing the kind of administrative work that no one beyond the CIA ever thought about. After a long stint as a recruiter for HR, he was currently a mid-level flak in the Office of Public Affairs. With his gray hair and white-toothed smile, Charlie projected the kind of official-but-nonthreatening air that played well in the public sphere.

"Might need you to work something up for Vogel if they decide to do a memorial service." Gasko shook his head. "*Such* a loss."

Charlie smiled vaguely. "Vogel?"

"You haven't seen the news?"

"The news?" Charlie began patting his pockets, then remembered his phone was in his briefcase. He'd put it there before his tennis game and hadn't looked at it for over two hours. (Not a habit you wanted in a PR flak, which was probably why he had never progressed beyond that far-flung parking lot.) As Charlie reached into his briefcase, Gasko touched his forearm, steering him toward the hallway that stretched south from the lobby.

"Stroke," he said quietly. "They said it was quick. At least he didn't suffer."

"Bob Vogel had a stroke?" He walked quickly, matching Gasko's gait. The hallway was lined with tall glass windows on one side, presidential portraits on the other. Gasko nodded at each person they passed, conveying a blanket message of *hi-how-are-ya, great-work-keep-it-up.* John Gasko had to be equal parts operator and politician, winning hearts and minds on both sides of the fence that surrounded the Langley campus. It was his second year as director of the agency. The consensus was that he was finally getting the hang of it.

"Two hours ago," Gasko said. "Just before noon in Cairo. A hundred and ten degrees in the shade, and he had those bad lungs. Poor guy. Poor Diane. She's a wonderful woman, you know. Pam and I had dinner with them just last week." He cocked his head. "Come to think of it, Bob didn't look so good, even then. You knew Bob, didn't you?"

"I met him once or twice."

"Great guy. Just a great guy. Such a loss."

Gasko stepped into the elevator and pressed the button for the seventh floor. From his body language, Charlie knew he, the mid-level bureaucrat, was meant to remain here, on the ground, on the other side of the threshold. As the doors closed, the director smiled mournfully. "They don't make them like that anymore, do they?"

· · ·

It was a funny thing. Men like John Gasko loved men like Bob Vogel. It shouldn't have worked—two egos that massive shouldn't have gelled—but Vogel was more than twenty years older than Gasko, and the generation gap allowed them to admire each other without any need for wariness. In the coming days, as the flag-draped coffin made its way across the Atlantic, countless men like John Gasko would grow misty-eyed as they talked about what a legend Bob Vogel had been.

Charlie had only known Senator Vogel in a vague way. Live in Washington long enough and paths were bound to cross: it was a thermodynamic law in the capital. The longest exchange they'd had was in 1995, when Charlie participated in closed-door testimony for the Senate Committee on Foreign Relations. The Taliban was starting to sweep through Afghanistan. The army was holding strong in Kabul, thanks mostly to the forces under Ahmad Baraath's command. The Senate committee was weighing whether to send aid to those forces. And while, by 1995, Charlie was working in the agency backwaters, because of his experience with Baraath a few years prior, he was summoned to Capitol Hill to deliver his personal assessment of Baraath's trustworthiness. The senators grilled him, and he hemmed and hawed—after all, it wasn't like he could tell the *real* story of Ahmad Baraath—and in the end, they seemed palpably unimpressed.

In the years since, he'd seen Vogel at occasional dinner parties in Georgetown, and performances at the Kennedy Center, and black-tie fundraisers at the Newseum. The last time Charlie had spoken with Vogel was three months earlier, at a book party in a brick mansion in Kalorama. At the buffet, while reaching for the shrimp cocktail, their elbows had collided. Charlie stepped aside and said: "Sorry about that, Senator. After you."

Vogel looked up at Charlie. He didn't say anything. He only stared.

"Great party, isn't it?" Charlie tried, faltering.

But Vogel just kept staring. He was notorious for his prickly manners, but this seemed extreme. After what felt like several minutes, Vogel finally said: "Charlie Cole, right? Well. It was good seeing you."

That was the extent of the encounter. Charlie probably would have forgotten about it were it not for the strange fact that Vogel had remembered his name.

·   ·   ·

A couple of days after Bob Vogel's death, on Sunday afternoon, as she was partway through a long-overdue spring-cleaning of her closet, Jenny Navarro's phone rang.

When she found the phone under a pile of sweaters and saw the name of the caller, her stomach twisted. VOGEL HOME. Was this some kind of sick joke? Or had she (please, God) somehow imagined the events of the last forty-eight hours? It took her a moment to remember that, obviously, there was nothing strange about this.

More than one person resided in the Vogel home. *Come on, Jenny*, she told herself. *Pull it together.*

"Diane?" she answered, her voice shaky.

"Oh, Jenny. Oh, honey."

"I'm so . . ." But Jenny couldn't get the words out.

"I know," Diane said. "I know. Me too."

Diane apologized for not calling sooner. And she was sorry to ask this, to be so *businessy* about things, but Bob kept certain important papers in the house—the Georgetown house, that was—and between the funeral arrangements and the press inquiries, she wasn't going to have time to get down to D.C. for a while. "I know it sounds ridiculous, but he wouldn't want things to slow down just because he, you know. *Died.* God forbid some piece of legislation languish on his desk just because he *died.*" Diane sighed. "That sounds crazy, doesn't it?"

Jenny smiled, despite herself. "No. It sounds like him."

"And I know it's the weekend, but I was wondering if you would—"

"Of course," Jenny interrupted. "I'll go right over."

"You really don't mind?"

"Honestly, I'd like to make myself useful right now."

Besides, she wasn't making any progress with her closet, and to do something that needed doing was an immense relief. It didn't seem possible that Bob was actually dead. Bob: her boss, and one of her favorite people in the world. Bob: her unlikeliest friend. A few years back, when Jenny first interviewed for the position, the senator skipped over her résumé (degree in applied math from Stony Brook, two years at McKinsey, degree from the Kennedy School) and zeroed in on her upbringing. Jenny Navarro, born and raised in Central Islip. Oldest of four children, taught her immigrant parents how to speak English, first in her family to go to college. "Interesting," he said. "Tell me more about that."

A certain kind of person loved Jenny's story, loved what it represented. This person was always older, often male, always white. She found this increasingly irritating. Not bothering to conceal her impatience, she said: "You've never hired someone like me."

"No, I haven't. I recognize that this is a problem."

"Okay. Well, I'm not sure I'm interested in fixing that particular problem of yours."

Vogel arched an eyebrow.

"You represent New York State," she continued. "Hempstead. Buffalo. The Bronx. If you've never hired someone like me to run your policy, that means you're not trying very hard."

"But you want this job." He paused. "You're pretty bold for someone who's asking me for a job."

"I'm not a good liar. And if you're planning to use me to check a certain box—like I said, that isn't going to work. So I'd rather just establish that right now."

After a moment, he broke into a grin and asked her when she could start.

Last year, Vogel had promoted her to chief of staff. Jenny knew that her parents and siblings back in Central Islip were proud of her career, but she also knew that they didn't *quite* know what it entailed. Her new position came with an enormous amount of influence, but that influence was really only understood by those who played the game for a living. This, she was learning, was both the pleasure and the pain of life in politics.

Jenny hurried over to the house on N Street. It was a grand building, wide and palatial where most of the houses on the block were narrow and modest. She had once encountered a pair of tourists lingering on the sidewalk, craning their necks at the topiary, the red brick and dark shutters. The woman had whispered to her husband, "That's the French embassy, you know." Jenny, amused, hadn't bothered to correct her.

Jenny unlocked the front door and disarmed the security system (3-7-4-5, Diane's birthday). In the front hall, she paused for a moment. The orchid on the table, fresh and sprightly. The polished wood floors, smelling of lemon Pledge. The air conditioner, keeping the house at a pleasant seventy-four degrees. The rest of the Senate delegation was flying back that afternoon. In an alternate universe, Bob would be walking into this house in a few hours. He would be happy to be home. Like all consummate Washington insiders, Bob claimed to be an outsider, but his love for the house on N Street belied that. Bob had offices in the Capitol, in New York City, in Albany and Buffalo and Rochester and Syracuse, but his office upstairs, Jenny knew, was his favorite. Here he did his best thinking, seated behind a handsome oak desk whose surface was obscured by a messy sprawl of papers.

In the study, Jenny surveyed the mess. Good thing Diane had thought to call her. Who knew what might have gone missing otherwise? She began sorting the documents into stacks. And Diane was right; Bob wouldn't have wanted the work to stop. Drafts of legislation. White papers from think tanks. Schedules, calendars, scribbled notes on legal pads. It was her job to know everything he knew, and then some. "You're just like me," he'd once said to her. "That's why I hired you."

"A workaholic, you mean?" she'd replied.

"Yes. But a smarter, nicer workaholic."

Both of them recognized this addiction for what it was. But they also both agreed that, as addictions went, at least this one might do some good in the world.

Over the next hour, Jenny made steady progress. She could almost see the surface of the desk. Buried beneath a pile of letters from constituents was a plain manila folder. Inside were several pieces of paper covered in the senator's spidery handwriting. She was unsure which pile this belonged in. Sometimes Bob would read about someone in the news, an obscure expert in an obscure subject, and then he would call them up, ask them to dinner, spend hours grilling them, scrawling notes while they spoke. (As he said, what good was being rich and powerful if he couldn't do things like that?) And then he would ask Jenny to read the notes and see what she thought. This was probably just the most recent instance. Probably he just hadn't gotten around to sharing the contents of this folder yet.

She skimmed the first page. *New frontier in markets. Online mania. Day traders moving in tandem.* This wasn't surprising. Having made his fortune at a hedge fund before getting into politics, Bob remained keenly attuned to the world of finance. *Meme stocks. Virality—online forums, social media.* She kept reading. *Algorithm VERY influential. Which posts get clicks. More clicks, more enthusiasm, snowball effect, thesis is self-validating.* Well, sure. Bob was also genuinely fascinated by the behavior-shaping power of social media. He was, despite his age, the only senator who could hold his intellectual own with the tech world's evil geniuses.

Finger on scale of algorithm. Plant idea, create virality, stock goes up. Leverage. Okay. She had never heard of this. *Approach CEO w/ demands. Greed usually sufficient. Don't want music to stop. Other threats if necessary.* Yeah. This was getting a little strange. *No visible patterns. Market movement obscures links to Moscow.* Goose bumps surfaced on her arms. *Gruzdev believes this is next frontier. Business drives geopolitics, not vice versa.* Nikolai Gruzdev, the Russian president? Her heart beat harder. *Keep quiet. Risk of leaks.* "Quiet" was underlined three times.

Jenny was frozen. Diane had asked Jenny to get his papers. Had she known? Was she referring to *these* papers specifically? But no—if Jenny didn't know, then Diane didn't know. The notes on the next page continued along the same lines, but the color of the ink changed. The writing was in blue, then black, then pencil, then back to blue. The paper kept changing, too. Lined yellow sheets, plain white printer paper, smaller pieces of hotel stationery. She flipped back to the beginning. In the top corner of each page were numbers: 1/20, 2/26, 3/12, 3/27, 4/9, 4/23, 5/15, 5/30. These were dates, she realized. These notes were taken at different times, in different places, over the past several months. *Keep quiet. Risk of leaks.* So it wasn't a question of Bob getting around to sharing these notes with her. He had obviously never intended for her to see them.

She held the papers lightly, as if they might scorch her. Jenny knew that whatever this was, if it was important enough for Bob to conceal from her, it was important enough to merit further investigation. And Jenny wasn't an idiot. She knew her limits. She wasn't some crackerjack Nancy Drew. She needed to get these to someone else—someone with expertise—someone equipped to do this the right way.

The last piece of paper in the folder caught her eye. It had no date. Written at the top was a name, and beside the name was scrawled a star. She recognized the name. But from where? Who was this? It hadn't been that long ago. A few months, maybe. A year at most.

Her gaze landed on the bookshelf across the room. Then she remembered.

That pretentious book party in Kalorama. Bob had dragged her along. The Senate was preparing to pass a last-minute budget amendment and he wanted to get work done in the car. During the party, when she was being verbally waterboarded by a lobbyist for Dow Chemical, Jenny noticed Bob at the buffet table talking with a man she didn't recognize. Bob looked unusually wary. Even from a distance, Jenny could perceive the wariness. Later, in the car, he seemed distracted. "Who was that?" she'd asked.

"Who was who?"

"That guy at the buffet."

"Oh. Uh. Just someone from Langley."

She raised an eyebrow. "Langley?"

In retrospect, Jenny could see how uncomfortable these questions made him. He was doing his best to feign nonchalance. "No, no, nothing like that." He shook his head. "That guy, he's, uh, no one. Charlie Cole? He's just one of those glorified paper pushers."

.   .   .

That Sunday, like every Sunday, Charlie kept himself busy with a series of minor household tasks. He walked Lucy, his yellow Labrador. He weeded the bed of zinnias and made a note to buy more fertilizer. He drove to Safeway and bought groceries for the coming week. He flagged a recipe for grilled salmon in the *Times Magazine*. In the domestic sphere, he was far more capable than most men his age.

At first, in the stinging aftermath of the divorce, he resented this growing self-sufficiency. A tidy house, a stocked refrigerator, a respectable meal: he'd learned to do these things because Helen had left him, because he had *failed*. But as time went by, it became clear that, rather than making him pathetic, these skills actually made him more attractive. When he eventually started dating again, the women seemed to appreciate that he wasn't some feral bachelor in need of rehabilitation. Grace, the petite widow whom he was currently seeing, had been impressed when Charlie showed up at their mutual friend's dinner party with homemade brownies for dessert. Impressed enough to say yes when he called and asked if she'd like to go with him to *Rigoletto* at the Kennedy Center.

Charlie and Grace got along well. She, like Charlie, had no interest in remarrying. He always established this at the outset. It wasn't a fear of commitment, as many women seemed to suspect. Rather it was the awareness—sharp, stabbing, omnipresent—of just what a shitty husband he'd been to Helen, and the determination not to subject another person to this shittiness. But this was too complicated to explain, so he let them think whatever they wanted to think.

He and Grace had dinner together a few nights a week, but never on Sundays, because Grace had three children and five grandchildren, and every Sunday her family gathered for dinner at her place in Arlington. Her devotion to her family was one of the things he liked most about her. Charlie hadn't yet attended one of these dinners, but he didn't think an invitation was beyond the realm of possibility.

At 6:30 p.m., Charlie turned on the news and poured himself a glass of wine. Earlier that day, he'd marinated a pork chop in soy sauce and brown sugar. As it sizzled in the skillet, he looked at Lucy, who gazed up at him forlornly. "I know," he said. "I'm sorry."

He would eat his pork chop, he would drink his wine, he would clean up the kitchen, and he would turn off the light by 9 p.m. And then, in the morning, he would wake up with the sun, drink his orange juice with Metamucil, do the crossword, and begin another unremarkable day. Every once in a while, when Charlie recalled the ambitions of his younger self, it struck him how flat and ordinary his life had become. But most of the time, this flat and ordinary life seemed like a miracle, an allotment of tranquility he didn't deserve. Even Helen, in time, had forgiven him.

Toward the end of the nightly news, the anchor said: "We finish tonight with a remembrance of Senator Robert Vogel, who died Friday at age eighty-one. He was in Cairo as part of a Senate delegation and suffered a stroke during their review of the Egyptian military. Over the course of his twenty-five years in the Senate, he served as chair of the Finance Committee, the Foreign Relations Committee, and minority whip. A member of the Democratic Party known for his bipartisan alliances, Vogel began his career in finance. This afternoon, President McAllister released a statement that reads—"

Charlie changed the channel. The Yankees were up 5–3 against the Blue Jays. Lucy lay with her chin on the floor, gaze fixed on Charlie. He'd left the fatty rind of the pork chop on his plate, and now he nudged it over the edge. He only did this on special occasions. Like

Sunday nights. Like Saturday nights, or Tuesday nights, or pretty much, these days, any old night. He found it almost impossible to resist her sweet brown eyes. "Stop looking at me like that," he said, when Lucy finished licking the floor and returned her gaze to Charlie. "No more. I mean it."

As Charlie loaded the dishwasher, the phone rang. The screen showed an unfamiliar Washington number. Sunday evening seemed like an odd time for a stranger to call. He answered: "Hello?"

"Charlie Cole?"

"This is he."

"My name is Jennifer Navarro. I work—worked—for Senator Vogel. I was his chief of staff."

"Oh," he said. "I'm sorry for your loss."

"I'm calling because . . . well, I understand that you and the senator knew each other?"

"Not really. We spoke once or twice." A heavy silence as she waited for him to continue. Charlie was perplexed. "I'm sorry," he said. "Why are you calling?"

"Before he died, Senator Vogel was working on something, something obviously . . . important. But he didn't tell me about it, and I'm guessing it goes beyond my security clearance." A pause. "But I think you probably . . ." Another pause. "I think you'll know what to make of it."

Charlie frowned at the muted TV. The Yankees were now up 7–4. *Security clearance.* Her suggestion was clear enough. But if she had some kind of agency-related inquiry, well, Vogel was friendly with plenty of people at Langley, all of whom outranked Charlie by a mile. Director Gasko not least among them.

"Mr. Cole?" she prompted. "Are you still there?"

"I'm here. I'm just wondering why—"

"I think it would be best to show you in person," she said. "Could we meet tomorrow at the Grant Memorial at seven a.m.?"

CHAPTER THREE

"**D**on't do anything until I get back," Osmond said. "Amanda. Did you hear me?"

It was Friday afternoon, right after the news had broken. On social media and CNN, the stroke narrative was already prevailing. Semonov had been right. Aging man, poor health, hot day: there was no reason for anyone to question the circumstances of Bob Vogel's death.

"When will that be?" Amanda said. The news was everywhere. Semonov would have seen it by now. The longer he went without hearing from her, the more difficult this would be. Her window was narrowing.

"Alitalia just canceled this afternoon's flight," Osmond said. "Don't ask me why. I'll get the first flight tomorrow morning."

She took a deep breath. "I'm sorry, sir. You know I don't like doing this."

"Doing what? Listen to me, Amanda, you can't—"

"I'm the deputy station chief," she interrupted. "When you're not here, I'm officially in charge. Tomorrow could be too late. I'm sorry, Osmond, but I'm going to see him today."

"No. No. If this guy is the real thing, we need to brief the director, we need to get a plan in place, we need—"

"Come *on*. You know this isn't an if."

She could hear him breathing, could imagine his red-cheeked frustration. Many times, their relationship had been stretched thinner than seemed wise. But apparently today wasn't quite the day that it reached a breaking point, because Osmond sighed and said: "Fine. Fine! But don't offer him anything. Make no promises. Understood?"

The walk from the embassy to the hotel took her past the Spanish Steps and the Piazza del Popolo. Both of them were, as she'd been hoping, thronged with tourists. She entered the marble foyer of the hotel and turned into the bar. It was pleasantly dim and cool, with its parquet floor and leafy potted palms. Behind the bar, Tomasso was polishing a glass. "Signora!" he cried when he spotted Amanda. "La bella signora! Where have you been?"

Tomasso, who as bartender at this well-known hotel was privy to any number of interesting conversations, had been one of Amanda's first recruits in Rome. She ordered an espresso and a Pellegrino and slid a piece of paper across the bar. "There's a man named Semonov staying here," she murmured. "Could you slip this under his door?"

Over the next two hours, the bar swelled with the Friday evening crowd. Amanda drank three espressos, pretended to read something on her phone, and kept the door in her peripheral vision. The precautions were excessive. This was Rome, not Moscow. She could have simply picked up the house phone in the lobby and asked Semonov to come downstairs. But after so many years, the habits were too ingrained to shake.

Finally, around 6:45 p.m., he appeared. Following her instructions, he strode through the bar without looking at her, carrying a book beneath his right arm. Amanda left a twenty-euro note on her table and hurried to follow him. Outside the hotel, he turned down the Via della Penna toward the Piazza del Popolo, navigated his way through the crowd, and found a seat on the edge of the Neptune Fountain, which was packed with people seeking relief in the cool mist. After several minutes, when the woman next to Semonov stood up, Amanda walked over to the fountain edge and took her place.

"I'm so sorry," she said.

He shrugged heavily.

"I'm so sorry. This was my fault. I knew you were telling the truth."

Semonov shrugged again. He was too exhausted to feel anything. Two weeks of this high-wire tension had left him spent. He'd told no one of his plan, not even Chiara, because Chiara was entirely too sensible to let him go through with it. She would have pointed out the obvious: the Americans were never going to believe him. He had learned about the assassination through mere happenstance. They would see that his story was full of holes.

But he knew, too, that he didn't *want* to be talked out of it. Even if it was a mistake. Which it probably was. Not because he necessarily thought the GRU would find out about his conversation with this American official—Rome offered a degree of anonymity that was impossible in Moscow—but because, in having tried to stop this terrible deed from happening, he had recognized just how terrible the deed really was. A deed of which, despite being a low-level bureaucrat, he was undoubtedly a part. A deed that was just one of many, many similar deeds. And now he would have to live the rest of his life with that terrible recognition.

But he didn't blame Miss Clarkson for this. Yesterday, in the conference room, she had clearly believed him. She didn't have to, but she had.

"I was reading about his wife," Semonov said. "His children."

"He was a good man."

"A good man. Yes. And now he is dead, and I am his murderer."

Amanda shook her head sharply. "No, you're not. You tried to stop it. Listen to me, Kostya. I've seen how these things go. A lot of people in your position would have done nothing. But you did something. You *tried*. That's the difference."

He blinked, his face crumpling. She could see him teetering on the edge of collapse. If he fell apart now, he would be no use to her. Time to change tack, then. Amanda was sitting beside a GRU agent who (a) was morally repelled by his work, (b) had just been proven to be telling the truth, and (c) was getting on a plane back to Moscow in just a few days. This could be a gold mine, but she had to act fast.

"Look," she said. "I understand. I've been in your shoes, Kostya. I know how painful this is. Right now you have two paths. You can let yourself be sad and depressed, or you can *do* something about it. You can fight back. We weren't able to save Bob Vogel's life. But we might be able to save the next one, if you're willing to help us."

Semonov looked down at the book in his lap. A hardcover copy of Lampedusa's *The Leopard*, which he'd taken from one of the bookshelves in the hotel lobby. He traced his finger over the cover. "I don't know anything else."

"You might think you don't. But you have an important job. Maybe you don't realize just how important it is."

"I didn't even *want* this job!" he cried. "I wanted to be an interpreter. I wanted to travel the world! You know that I attended the Military University of the Ministry of Defense? My mother was so proud. It is the best language program in Russia. But I only made it through the first year of that training. And do you know why? Because of a man named Charles Dickens."

They were getting offtrack, but at the same time, Amanda had noticed how his expression had changed with this last remark. Anything to interrupt his self-flagellation. So she said: "Charles Dickens?"

"I've always loved to read. Chiara does, too. It's one of the reasons we get along. Of course, she reads *everything*. She reads much more than me. During training, I used to read on my lunch breaks. One day, during the first year, the instructor spotted me on my way to lunch. I was holding a copy of *Bleak House*. He sneered and asked why I was reading it. I told him it was useful for improving my English. He said it was subversive. I told him I disagreed. And then I offered to lend him the book when I was finished. Apparently this offended him. The next day he ordered my reassignment to another division of the GRU." He sighed. "I should have kept my mouth shut."

"You were honest. You couldn't help it."

"But it's not very useful to you, is it? If I were an interpreter, I would be meeting people, hearing things, learning things. But I sit in my office and spend my days making passports and visas and bank statements, and I know nothing."

"That's not true. You knew about Senator Vogel."

He shifted his weight uneasily. "It was only that one time."

"What do you mean?"

"Well, you see, I'm never told *why* a thing is needed. Simply I am told to do this or do that. They submit their request, and I fulfill the request, and I am never told what happens next."

She cocked her head. "Then how did you come to learn about Vogel?"

The fountain behind them burbled and splashed; the church bells pealed seven times. Semonov began to blush. Even in the evening light, his embarrassment was obvious. Amanda averted her gaze, giving him time to collect himself. On the horizon were the dark green pine trees of the Borghese Gardens. Above it was the clear blue of evening.

Finally, he took a deep breath. "Okay," he said. "It happened two weeks ago."

• • •

It happened two weeks ago. Most of his colleagues left at 5 p.m., he said, but he often stayed late. He did his best work when the office was quiet, and though he didn't particularly enjoy the work, it would have filled him with shame to do anything less than his best. That night, after everyone else was gone, he went into the kitchen to make a cup of tea. As he waited for the water to boil, two men appeared. He didn't recognize them. They must have been from a different directorate.

"Isn't there anything to eat?" one of them demanded, after finding the refrigerator bare. "Where is the food, hmm?"

This man clutched a bottle of vodka loosely in his hand. The other man swayed slightly. They were drunk, and bored. They looked at Semonov. Then they glanced at each other, reaching silent agreement. "Nothing to eat?" one of them said. "Then at least sit with us and have a drink. Forget the tea. A real drink. Come, comrade."

They wore identical expressions of self-satisfied stupidity. *Tweedledum*, Semonov thought. *And Tweedledee.* They pulled out a chair from the kitchen table and ordered him, the solution to their boredom, to sit. So who was he? What was his name? What did he do? Why was he working so late? Did he not have a nice lady to go home to? See, *they* were working late because their work was extremely dangerous and extremely important. But you, comrade! Tweedledee laughed. With glasses like that, what do you know of danger?

"Hang on." Tweedledum narrowed his eyes. "Now wait just a second. Your name is Semonov? I've heard of this Semonov. You're the one making our passports."

"Semonov!" Tweedledee yelped. "Ah, of course, the famous Semonov!"

Yes, of course, this explained why he was here so late. Surely he was toiling away on their passports right this moment. Wasn't that so? He should be honored to be given this task. Not everyone had the chance to work with their unit. But their superior had requested him specifically. He had a reputation for being the best.

"You've heard of our unit, of course," Tweedledum said. "Unit 29155?"

The kettle came to a screeching boil. Semonov leapt to switch it off. "Ah," he said nervously. "Well. As you said. Your passports. I must get back to them. They're very—"

"Sit down, you're being rude. Oh yes. Yes, you've heard of us." He was clearly amused by Semonov's terror. "You know exactly what Unit 29155 does, don't you?"

"I don't wish to pry."

Tweedledee laughed. "He's a liar! Just look at him. He hasn't been this excited since . . . since . . . since he was a baby sucking at his mother's breast!"

"Well, and are we feeling generous?" Tweedledum said, with a cruel grin. "Shall we tell him why we need those passports?"

"Oh, yes. I'm feeling generous."

"You see, my friend. There is an American. A man named Robert Vogel."

They talked and they talked. Why had they decided to brag in such detail? Something about Semonov's manner filled them with a violent contempt. Striking fear into the heart of this pathetic man was, to them, as darkly gratifying as kicking an injured animal. They egged one another on, adding details, relishing the fear on Semonov's face. The nature of the poison. The method of delivery. The death would look natural, but on the inside would be agony. His muscles would be frozen in pain; his lungs would refuse to breathe. Robert Vogel would know, in his final moments, that he was dying an unnatural death. You understand how it will feel for him? They grinned wickedly. You understand, my friend? He will know that God is not doing this to him. *We* are doing this to him. There will be no grace in this departure.

By the time Semonov finished talking, the sky above Rome was a deep navy blue. The water in the fountain was lit with a pale glow. "That's awful," Amanda said. "I'm sorry you had to go through that."

"It's nothing compared to what happened to him," he said quietly.

"And they didn't . . ." She shook her head. Where to go from here? It was tricky. "You don't know why they were targeting Senator Vogel. They didn't say."

"No."

"But do you think that, maybe, they *did* know? That they knew and just didn't say?"

"No."

"What makes you so certain?"

"I know what kind of men they are." He lifted his shoulders. "Some people learn to make peace with their limited knowledge. Other people find it offensive. It irritates them, the idea that they are missing something. That's how those two men were. Offended. Insecure. They haven't been told the most important thing, which is *why* they are doing what they are doing. They are merely cogs in the machine. They know that, and they hate that. So they boast, they brag. They find people like me, who know even less, and they brag to make themselves feel better."

"Oh," she said.

"Yes," he said. "You see what I mean, don't you?"

•　•　•

Like Semonov said. Some people learn to make peace with their limited knowledge. Other people find it offensive. The world might well be a happier place if there were more of the former than the latter, but this isn't the world we live in.

Charlie Cole, for instance. He, like so many ambitious young officers during the Cold War, had been intoxicated by the notion of the world as a solvable problem. The answers could always be found, if only you worked hard enough. It was energizing, thrilling, capable of lending romance to even the harshest backdrop. He had been fully under this spell when he and Helen moved to Finland in the early 1980s. Their apartment was two blocks from the Baltic Sea. The enemy was just over the border. Blizzards hushed the city into a frozen snowscape. The northern lights shimmered above the road to the safe house. Heavy-browed Russian visitors took their Finnish cousins to dinner while the Americans watched from across the street. These vivid details accrued into righteous-

THE HELSINKI AFFAIR • 43

ness. *I'm doing this for you*, Charlie sometimes thought, as he lifted Amanda from her crib and kissed the top of her head. *I'm making the world a safer place for you.*

Osmond Brown had his own version of this. He'd arrived in Angola in 1976, freshly minted from the Farm, wearing pleated khakis and a clean white shirt and aviator sunglasses, every inch the cinematic hero. Angola was wracked by civil war. Did the Americans know how that war ought to end? Did they know what this country needed? Damn *straight* they did, the young Osmond thought, and sometimes said, in his Mississippi twang. In the Angolan summer it rained every day, the sky bursting violently, the pavement steaming in the heat after the clouds passed. The humidity persisted from November through April. Osmond loved it. The skin-drenching weather reminded him of home. Here in the jungle, he felt charged up with purpose. The work came easy. He was *good* at this. Guns, land mines, aircraft, money, food, water. Life and death. All of it.

And then, he thought to himself, so many years later, as the plane arced high above the Atlantic, *then I got soft.*

It had been a long time since Angola, or Libya, or any of the postings in which Osmond Brown had been required to risk bodily harm. But the older he got, the more he tended to lose himself in those overgrown thickets of memory. Long flights were the worst, with their awful dearth of distractions. He shook his head. It was Monday, a few days after the assassination. Another three hours until they landed. He couldn't focus on the papers he'd brought along, and the TV screen in his seat wasn't working, and he had no one to talk to, because across the aisle Amanda was asleep. Slumped over, her head at a lopsided angle. He reached over, shook her arm. "Amanda. Hey, Amanda, wake up."

She blinked. "What?"

"You're going to get a crick in your neck if you sleep like that."

She grumbled, shifted position, closed her eyes again. "No,

listen," Osmond found himself saying. "We need to go over the plan one more time."

"Why?"

"Why! Because this is a big fucking deal, that's why."

It was never a good sign when the director summoned you back to Langley like this. On Friday afternoon, Osmond called Director Gasko and told him about the walk-in, the strange Russian who had delivered his warning to Amanda, and who now gave them reason to conclude that Senator Vogel had been assassinated by the GRU.

After a beat of silence, Gasko said: "So we had the chance to stop this."

"Well, yes," he said carefully. "But we had no way of verifying the—"

"Jesus Christ, Osmond. You made a mistake. Own the fucking mistake. And go get Amanda. I need to know more about this guy."

"Uh, sure. Okay. I'll ask her to call you right now."

"Just go grab her, would you?"

His face flushed. "Well, you see, I would, except I'm not. Well. I'm not in the station right now. I'm in, um. I'm in Capri. I'm trying to get back to Rome as soon as I can."

"*Capri?*" the director yelped. "You're in fucking *Capri*?"

From there, it only got worse. When Osmond explained that he'd asked Amanda to wait, to hold off on reestablishing contact with her walk-in until they had a strategy, but in his absence she had gone ahead and done it anyway, Gasko snapped: "You said *what*? Of course she needs to get with him. What were you thinking, Osmond? This guy can't be left out in the cold. No. Forget it. Amanda is calling the shots on this. And by the way. I need both of you here in Washington by next week."

Both of them? But surely it would be better for Amanda to stay in Rome, stay close to the situation. Surely he, Osmond, the station chief, could handle the big picture and . . . "Both of you," Gasko barked.

So he and Amanda needed to have a united front. That was the only way to survive this. As Osmond was about to launch into his speech, the flight attendant rolled the cart down the aisle and stopped between them. "Chicken, beef, or pasta?"

"Nothing, nothing." He drummed his fingers against the armrest impatiently. When the cart was finally wheeled away, he looked at Amanda, lifting the foil from her tray of pasta, which somehow looked both gloopy and dry. "*Why* are you eating that?" he asked.

She raised an eyebrow. "Because I'm hungry."

"Well." He sat up straight, trying to project as much dignity as thirty inches of legroom allowed. "Well. *So*. You don't know the director like I do, but I can tell you, Amanda, Gasko is a team player. And he wants the rest of us to be team players. He doesn't tolerate discord. Got it? Infighting, drama, none of that flies. He needs to know, he needs to *trust* that Rome station is running smoothly. So tomorrow morning, when we meet with him, we're going to make it clear that this was a decision we made together."

She poked at her pasta and frowned.

"I mean," he continued, "that we both decided, we *both* decided, that it was imprudent to act on Semonov's information. Right? I know you agreed with me in the end, Amanda. It took a while for you to get there, but in the end, you didn't go raise the alarm in Cairo, did you?"

She stabbed at her pasta in silence. Lifted her fork, considered it, set it back down. "I didn't raise the alarm in Cairo," she said quietly, "because you're my boss. I wasn't going to disobey a direct order. You knew that. I knew that. But that doesn't mean I agreed with you. I did it because you told me to. You're my boss," she repeated. "I have no problem saying that. Is *that* what you mean by a team player?"

She looked up. Her green eyes were blazing.

As he was summoning his response, they hit an air pocket. The plane jolted, and Osmond grabbed for the armrest, and the passengers let out yelps of fear and surprise. The plane shuddered and juddered with unnerving persistence, the kind of violent rattling that caused a person to suddenly reevaluate his relationship with God. But the turbulence didn't faze Amanda. She was staring right at him, without so much as a flinch.

Why on earth had he thought that she, of all people, would compromise herself in order to protect him?

Osmond, you fool, he thought. *Whatever you have coming, you deserve it.*

• • •

The next morning, in Langley. Osmond felt a painful envy, watching the men and women stream into the marble lobby, coffees in hand, badges displayed, happy and unfearful. These normal people. These annoyingly normal people.

As Osmond and Amanda stepped through the turnstiles, he asked himself what he had asked so many times: *What happened to me?* But he knew exactly what happened. What happened was Aisha, the young woman he'd been running in Tripoli in the 1980s. Aisha was the daughter of a high-ranking general, and a member of Gaddafi's entourage. She was a born spy, with an appetite for risk, but also an instinct for when she was pushing it too far. She had warned Osmond that she needed to lay low for a while. Gaddafi was, lest they forget, a violent lunatic. But this was April 1986, and the Berlin nightclub bombing had just happened, and the U.S. was determined to strike. They needed to get to Gaddafi, and Osmond needed her intelligence. *Needed* it. This wasn't optional. Understood?

The airstrike happened. It killed a bunch of Libyans, but not Gaddafi. Not long after this failed strike, Aisha was executed.

There were trade-offs to this work, Osmond told himself. The master he served was bigger than Aisha. What was the value of an individual life when tallied against the greater good? After she was executed, he tried to believe in these old calculations, but Aisha was dead. She was *dead*. When you really got down to it, what was the difference between Osmond and the person who pressed the gun to her forehead?

It wasn't worth it. That was what he'd realized. That realization was his life's great dividing line. From that point forward, part of Osmond had understood that, from here on out, he wasn't going to be very good at this job. That he was simply marking time.

"Osmond?" A light touch on his arm. "It's this way, isn't it?"

He and Amanda were standing in the middle of the seventh-floor hallway, facing the floor-to-ceiling windows with their view of the courtyard. The trees outside were the color of American summer. Bright green, defiantly green. An exquisite overabundance. He shook his head. "Follow me," he said.

They reached the end of the hallway. The phone on the secretary's desk rang. She said: "The director is ready for you."

Behind his desk, Gasko was standing up and striding over. Osmond's heart was racing. He and the director were shaking hands. Before he knew it, he found himself saying:

"Director Gasko, sir, I'm here to offer my resignation. This past week made it clear to me that I'm no longer capable of serving as an effective station chief. It's time for me to step down."

Gasko's eyebrows shot up. "You are."

"Yes, sir. I see no other way forward."

After a moment, Gasko's eyebrows descended into a pleasant expression. "Well. *Well.* Osmond. You're a good man."

"No, sir." He let go of the director's hand. "I'm an old man."

He was flooded with relief. This feeling! This was the best feeling in the world. He should have done this sooner. Much, much sooner.

"Well, how about we just call this retirement?" Gasko said. "That's the only thing we need to say. Don't have to get into the rest of it, right?"

"Really?" Osmond said. "That's, uh. I mean, thank you, sir. That's kind."

"You'll be leaving the station in good hands, anyway." Gasko glanced at Amanda. "Thanks, Osmond. We can take it from here."

. . .

"Not bad," Gasko said. "What are you, thirty-eight? Station chief at age thirty-eight? Not bad at all."

The director gestured for her to sit. Amanda instinctively glanced back at the closed door. That was really it? That had really just . . . *happened*? She shook her head, collecting herself. "I, uh, turned forty in April."

"Cole," he said. "So you're Charlie Cole's kid. Good guy. I'm guessing you always wanted to do this. Like father, like daughter."

"Oh," she said. "Well, actually. No."

"Really?"

Her pulse was gradually settling. This was one of the things that made her good at the job, this rapid absorption of new realities. So she was station chief. So, okay. This wasn't the moment to celebrate. Just take a deep breath and get on with it. "Growing up," she said, "this was the *opposite* of my plan."

Gasko tilted his head, asking the silent why. Not that she was going to tell him the real reason. Amanda's relationship with her father was a particular thing. Her mother she never worried about; her mother had a toughness that permeated to her core. Charlie, though. Her father's gentle nature was what she loved most about him, but it often struck her as a reaction, as a calculation: like his determined contentment was a shield against the dagger of wanting. Even as a child, long before she had the words, she could sense that her father had a sadness about him. The older she got, the more it seemed related to his work. And this, she decided, was never going to happen to her. She was freewheeling, she was *fun*. So she graduated from high school and decided to travel the world. Vaguely she imagined the travel would yield a glamorous outcome:

she would fall in love with a rich foreigner, maybe, or become a writer. She certainly hadn't planned to wind up in Langley, doing exactly, literally *exactly*, what her father had done.

But she didn't feel like explaining that to him. And she doubted that Gasko really *wanted* that explanation. So she used a truth better-suited to the seventh floor. "I saw the cost of it," she said. "Lying for a living. It destroyed my parents' marriage. So now you're wondering, what changed?" She shrugged. "Well, I realized marriage is a scam, so what did it matter?"

A gold wedding ring glinted on his left hand, but Gasko merely smiled. He was the type of man who prided himself on taking nothing personally. "So you met with the source again," he continued. "How did he seem?"

"Calm, actually. Depressed, but calm. He'd always known it was a long shot, that we weren't likely to take him at his word. With his job, he's usually in the dark. This time he got lucky. He happened to learn about the threat to Vogel."

"And this was his guilty conscience at play?"

Amanda nodded. "And despite sounding the alarm, he *still* feels guilty. Complicit. It's kind of amazing. After so many years at the GRU, this guy hasn't lost his moral compass."

"Great. That's great. So you think there's more juice in that lemon?"

"If we play it right." She was careful not to promise anything. "He's not read into much at the GRU. But he might be willing to get creative. *Might*. It could be a way of working through his guilt."

"I assume he wants money."

"Money wouldn't hurt. But he mostly wants a fresh start. He wants to leave Russia and come to America."

"Not Italy? You said his wife was Italian, right?"

"Not Italy. Something about his wife wanting to stay far away from an overbearing mother. But also, if they leave Russia, he imagines that the GRU will eventually put it together and come after them, and he doesn't trust the Italians to keep them safe." She paused. "But he thinks we probably can."

"Well." Gasko grimaced. "I guess it's nice that *someone* still admires our capabilities."

The director's tone contained more than a trace of self-pity. The CIA's reputation was currently in tatters, and a large part of Gasko's job was reweaving the scraps into something serviceable. While President Caine had been in the White House, even their closest allies, MI6 and Mossad and the BND, had stopped trusting them, and stopped sharing intelligence with them. The bosses on the seventh floor liked to moan and groan about the loss of prestige. But Amanda had never understood those complaints. So their allies didn't fully trust them? But they weren't *supposed* to be trustworthy. They were spies, for God's sake.

Again, not that she was going to *say* this to Gasko. Instead she continued: "He'd prefer to leave sooner rather than later. They'd pick up and move to America right now if they could."

"Does his wife know what he's been up to?"

Amanda shook her head. "He's trying to protect her, I think. Or doing the chauvinist thing. Doesn't think this is her turf. Both, maybe. In any case, I told him we couldn't move that fast. We didn't have the authorization, etcetera. I probably bought us six months. Maybe a year, if we're lucky. So they flew back to Moscow yesterday."

"Good. And you've figured out how to maintain contact?"

"Yup."

"This is great, Amanda. Really great stuff. Keep him in play as long as you can." Gasko nodded. "Now. Let's talk about what we're going to tell Diane Vogel."

∙ ∙ ∙

From his perch on the seventh floor, the director had been gradually thinning the ranks of the older generation, gently but firmly urging them toward retirement. The older generation had too much scar tissue for his liking. They had lived through the 1960s and '70s, the agency's era of disrepute: failed coups, botched assassinations, the Church Committee. This didn't enhance the image Gasko wanted to cultivate. (His generation had their *own* failings, of course, but he found it much easier to forgive their faults and flaws.)

So when people heard the news of Osmond Brown's retirement, no one thought much of it. Just another victim of Gasko's geriatric purge. On the same day that Amanda met with the director, Charlie Cole bumped into an old friend from the DO. "Well, I guess I'm allowed to tell *you*, right? You must be so proud of your girl."

His friend shared the news. Charlie wondered whether he had misunderstood. "He retired?" Charlie asked. "Osmond Brown?"

"Guess so."

Charlie wandered away in a daze. Actually, he had been in a daze ever since his conversation with Jenny Navarro the day before, on Monday morning, when she handed him the papers from Bob Vogel's desk. Bob had kept them private from her, she explained, which meant he had kept them private from everyone. So Charlie had nothing to worry about. Jenny's face was creased with anxiety, hoping he understood the subtext. He nodded and said, sure, he understood, he would take it from here. Then he drove away with the manila folder on the passenger seat, glancing over every few seconds, as if expecting it to explode.

At home he placed the folder on the kitchen counter. The longer he stared at it, the more certain he became about what he was looking at. His past, submerged in darkness for so long, now preparing to surface. This moment had always been inevitable.

He might have stood there for hours were it not for Lucy, alarmed by his stupor, barking at him. Charlie jolted back to attention. "Right," he said to her. "Well, shit. So how do we want to play this?"

She lumbered over and shoved her head into his knee. She

hadn't liked the tense silence. It wasn't Charlie's style. "What do you think? Should I turn myself in, just get it over with?" Her tail wagged. "Maybe I shouldn't even read it."

But this idea was obviously ridiculous. Not read it? If he had that kind of self-control, he never would have found himself in this situation to begin with.

So, instead, Charlie poured himself another cup of coffee. An ordinary Monday morning in the suburbs. A moment thirty-odd years in the making. He ought not rush through it. He sat down at the kitchen counter, took a deep breath, and began to read. The first page didn't make much sense to him. Day traders? Meme stocks? The next page was more of the same. And so was the next, and the next. He flipped through the papers faster, searching for familiar words—Helsinki, Särrkä, Ahmad Baraath—but it was in vain. Vogel had uncovered some kind of scheme, but Charlie couldn't see how this was connected to him. That last piece of paper bore his name, but why? What did it mean?

He looked up. The clock on the oven showed that he was already late for work. As he returned the papers to the folder, he felt his chest tightening. *You thought it was over*, a voice said. *But it isn't. Not if you play your cards right.*

If he gave the folder to someone at the agency, they would ask him why his name was in there. Charlie would say that he didn't know, which was the truth. But that person, while carrying forward the investigation, would probably, eventually, manage to answer that question. And in this they would probably, eventually, perceive a certain murkiness surrounding Charlie's departure from Helsinki. Setting this into motion would probably, eventually, lead to his demise. This was one option.

The other option was to keep the folder to himself. Burn it. Destroy it.

The sharp clarity of surrender—not anymore. Now he had to make a choice. He also had to get to work. "Fuck," he muttered, starting the car, backing out of the driveway. "Fuck. Fuck!" Obviously he didn't want to go to jail. But in destroying the papers, he would, in effect, be aiding the other side. *Moscow. Gruzdev.* Did he really want to do that?

Twenty minutes later he pulled into the parking lot without any memory of the drive. That day and night passed in much the same way. His paralyzing panic blocked out the rest of the world. But hearing this news about Osmond Brown on Tuesday afternoon—something pinged in the back of his mind.

Last Christmas, after spending the holiday with her mother in New York, Amanda came down to Virginia to visit Charlie. He took her to lunch at the country club, where the dining room was festooned with pine boughs and red ribbons. When the waiter came over, she said: "Grilled cheese and a chocolate shake, please."

Her old childhood favorite. Charlie smiled. "You're not just indulging me, are you?"

Amanda smiled, too. "Maybe a little."

"So how's Rome treating you?" Charlie asked, even though he knew she couldn't really talk about it. It was the nature of the job.

"Honestly? It feels like death."

"Oh, come on."

"Seriously. I mean, Rome is never going to be the most exciting posting. I know that. But it's not just quiet. It's like, it's *purposely* stagnant. The station chief—Osmond Brown, did you ever know him?—it's like he doesn't want to do *anything*. Nothing. He's allergic to even the smallest, tiniest molecule of risk."

"Well, that can happen. Probably means it's time for him to retire."

Amanda snorted. "That's the problem. He's *never* going to retire. This job is the only thing he has going. He wouldn't know what to do with himself. And honestly, Dad, Rome is such a ghost town that no one in Langley will ever notice what a mediocre job he's doing."

On that Tuesday in July, the memory of this remark came rushing back to him. It had been years since he'd used the old machine.

Decades, really. But it was still in there. The cold, clinical, action-oriented apparatus of logic, unspooling two different threads:

One: If Osmond Brown wasn't planning to retire, that meant something significant had happened. If Amanda had been elevated to station chief, that meant she had been on the right side of that something.

Two: If an old man in poor health collapses under the blazing sun, death by stroke is a reasonable conclusion. But if the old man is revealed to be in possession of papers that outline the tenets of a mysterious conspiracy, then that conclusion must be reexamined.

A shakeup in Rome. A death in Egypt. Coincidences happened. They weren't *necessarily* connected. But Charlie could feel the prickle up his spine. He'd shoved the folder in a kitchen drawer, jumbled up with the whisks and wooden spoons, because he didn't know where else to put it. Even from here, miles away in Langley, he could sense it radiating a white-hot danger.

But maybe—maybe—he had just stumbled upon a way forward.

·   ·   ·

At the end of the day, Charlie stood on the grass outside the main entrance, checking his watch. Amanda was running late. Well, sure. Considering what had just happened, she was probably deluged with new responsibilities. He checked his watch again. This whole thing might be a bad idea, but it was the only idea he had.

"Dad!" she said, emerging at last. "Sorry. I got caught up."

For a few seconds, the sight of his daughter swept away every concern. She was the walking, talking embodiment of his marriage; of the most significant years of his life. Her green eyes, which she'd gotten from her mother; her freckled complexion, which she'd gotten from him. He returned her smile. "Sweetheart!" he said. "I'm so proud of you. This is a big deal."

He saw the blush beneath her shrug. "Yeah, I don't know. It's good. Listen, Dad. I promised I'd stay with Georgia this time. That's cool with you, right?"

"Oh," he said. "Well. Sure. No problem."

"And actually," she said, typing on her phone, "what do you think if she comes to dinner? You probably haven't seen her in forever, right? I bet she'd love to see you."

"Dinner?"

"I'll tell her to bring a bottle of wine. What are we having?"

"You know." He swallowed. "Maybe not this time, honey. There's something . . . There's something I need to talk to you about. Something important."

She looked up, alarmed. "You're not sick, are you?"

"No, no. Nothing like that."

"So, what, then? Hey. Are you and Grace finally getting married?"

He tried to smile. "It's just . . . better to have privacy for this. Tell Georgia I'm sorry. Next time."

On the drive home, Amanda kept glancing over. The atmosphere in the car was thick. "You can't just tell me now?" she pressed. "Dad. You're being so *intense*. What is it?"

"Hey," he said. "So this station chief thing. That's fantastic. That must be why you're in town, right? Is there some kind of rite to mark the occasion? Some secret ceremony?"

"No," she said, although it was unclear which question she was answering.

Fishing, he said: "He's not *really* retiring, is he? Osmond Brown, I mean."

Charlie kept his eyes on the road, but he could sense Amanda staring at him.

Eventually she said: "Well. So. The Yankees swept the Jays, huh?"

Which was code for: *Please don't ask me questions you know I can't answer.*

told me Osmond wasn't planning to retire. So, obviously, there was a reason he left. I won't pretend to know exactly what happened, but I know it had something to do with Bob Vogel."

"Dad, I really . . . I don't know what you're talking about."

"And I was glad to hear about your promotion. Not just because I'm proud of you—and I *am* proud of you, honey, I hope you know that—but because it also makes this . . . I won't say simpler. Definitely not simpler. But more feasible." Charlie was growing calmer. He seemed to be gaining in confidence. "And please, sweetheart. There's no need to look at me like that."

"Like . . . ?"

"Like you're so surprised I still understand these things."

She blinked dumbly. This job required you to lie, even to the people you loved, especially to the people you loved. She knew that, and he knew that, and, oddly, this was why their relationship had strengthened in past years: there was an understanding of the limits. He'd seen through her previous evasions, surely he had, but he had never before been so unkind as to point them out.

Charlie stood up and walked across the kitchen. He opened the drawer next to the stove, withdrew the manila folder, and slid it across the counter to Amanda.

"Dad," she said. "What's going on?"

"The information in there is what got Bob Vogel killed."

"But why are . . ." Her mind was whirring. Konstantin Semonov walks into the embassy with a warning. Five days later, her father hands her a folder taken from the desk of the dead man. Was it some kind of trap? "Dad. What do *you* have to do with this?"

"Nothing."

"But that doesn't make any sense."

"Take a look." He tapped the folder. "You'll see what I mean."

For a second, she hesitated. But who was she kidding? She shoved aside her half-eaten dinner and opened the folder. *Links to Moscow.* Fuck. *Gruzdev.* Fuck fuck. She flipped the pages faster.

This was bad. Well, also, it was good. Because, right away, it was obvious how these papers might fit together with Semonov's story. When she got to the end, to the piece of paper with his name on it, she shook her head. "Obviously you have something to do with this. So, what? Were you talking to Vogel about this?"

His mouth twitched toward a smile. "I'm flattered you think I'm still privy to this kind of thing. I'm just a PR flak. You know that."

"Well, yeah, but you could be lying about that."

The smile vanished.

"It doesn't make any sense," she insisted. "There's some reason your name is in there."

Charlie closed his eyes and rubbed his temple. *Oh, I'm sorry*, she thought, irritation curdling in her chest. *Are you tired? Is this stressing you out? You started it, you jerk!* "Dad," she snapped. "Come on! Just tell me. You're making this worse."

"There are things I'm not proud of," he said. "Things I would rather leave unsaid. But it's . . . It has nothing to do with this. Algorithms? Meme stocks? Amanda. Can you really imagine me understanding *any* of this stuff? Look. I'm not going to stand in the way. Whatever Vogel was uncovering, I want it to continue. I want there to be justice. I'm only asking that you leave me out of it."

"This doesn't make any sense."

"Can I see that?" He plucked the last piece of paper from the folder. Then he stood up, walked over to the stove, and turned the burner on. He held the paper to the flame, where it twisted and curled. When the flames had nearly reached his fingertips, he dropped the remaining fragments in the sink. He turned back to Amanda. "I'm retiring next year. I just want to make it to the end. Then I'll be gone. It won't matter anymore. So. I'm only asking that you leave me out of it."

"I still don't understand."

But he just shook his head wearily, as if explaining himself any further would require energy he didn't have. If this was his exhausted appeal to her tenderness, a plea to take pity on her old man, then it wasn't working. If anything, she felt herself recoiling. Yes, it was true. Her love for her father had sometimes verged on pity. But now? If he asked for her pity, but refused to tell her the truth—then why on earth did he deserve it? "So, what?" she said caustically. "There's some deep, dark secret you don't want anyone to find out. So then what was even the point of showing me that piece of paper? If you're going to ask me to leave you out of it. Why even mention it?"

"I don't know."

"You don't *know*?"

"I don't know. I thought it should be up to you."

She laughed, disbelieving. "Yeah, except you just lit it on fire."

"Well, you could still tell Gasko what you just saw. You could tell him exactly what I just did. Including asking you what I've asked you to do. Including burning that piece of paper. It's up to you, Amanda."

Heat rising in her cheeks, she looked down at the papers. In places the spidery scrawl was hard to decipher. Vogel had never intended for anyone to see this. Amanda felt a sudden desire to be alone with these notes, to start piecing them together without this hovering extra presence of her father. She couldn't think straight. She had to get out of here. (Thank God she was staying with Georgia.) She drew a deep breath and closed the folder. "Okay," she said. "Well. Fine. If you want to be recused from this, I guess we should stop talking about it."

In the taxi back into the city, she considered it. Charlie would only ask Amanda to do this if he had something seriously bad to hide. But what he was asking her to do was a big fucking deal. The choice would come down to this: compromise him or compromise herself. How did he not see the impossibility of that position? Or *did* he see it, and he just didn't give a shit? *Did* he see it, and he was simply banking on her filial obedience?

• • •

The Vogels lived at the corner of Park Avenue and Seventy-First Street. The penthouse, as well as its contents, was a testament to the financial success Bob Vogel had enjoyed before entering politics. The living room alone had a Picasso above the fireplace, a Degas figure on the credenza, a Rembrandt sketch near the bookshelf. He hadn't cared much about the art per se. Mostly he'd enjoyed the reminder of how far he had come from his one-room-apartment childhood in Queens.

The family had done a private burial earlier that morning. In the coming weeks, there would be the requisite memorial service, the military salutes, the flag-draped casket in Washington National Cathedral. This gathering, high up in the Vogel penthouse, was for just a few dozen people, close friends and Senate colleagues, and the occasional luminary like John Gasko. Amanda was most definitely *not* invited, but Gasko had insisted she come along. She'd taken an early Amtrak up from D.C., nursing a hangover with bad coffee from the café car, deeply regretting her decision to have that extra martini with Georgia at the Hay-Adams the night before.

Gasko was waiting for her in the lobby. "Ready?" he asked. "Good. Let's go."

They rode the elevator to the top, which opened directly into the apartment. A waiter whisked over, offering glasses of white wine. A second waiter followed with a tray of tiny cucumber sandwiches. In the living room, Gasko quickly spotted Diane. "Stay here," he said. "I'll go ask if we can speak to her in private."

They talked for a minute, then he turned and nodded at Amanda. Diane nodded in return. Amanda followed them down a hallway to a small book-lined study.

The space was almost unbearably intimate, borderline claustrophobic. Amanda and Gasko squeezed together on the love seat. On the end table, within easy reach of Diane's armchair, sat an old-fashioned landline with a spiral cord. Next to it was an address book, a notepad covered with copperplate script (nothing like her husband's scrawl), a pair of reading glasses, a half-drunk cup of tea. Entering this room was like stepping behind the penthouse's pristine stage set. This was where actual *life* happened.

"So," Diane said to Director Gasko. "You have something to tell me?"

"This isn't easy to say, Mrs. Vogel, but I want to get right to the point. We have reason to believe Senator Vogel didn't die of a stroke."

She blinked at Gasko, once, then twice.

"More specifically," he continued, "we have intelligence suggesting that Russian operatives in Cairo administered a lethal chemical agent, which caused symptoms that are designed to mimic those of a stroke. We are reasonably certain this was an assassination."

She was silent for a while. Then she said: "That makes sense."

Gasko cocked his head. "It does?"

"I knew it wasn't a stroke," Diane said. "It couldn't be a stroke. Just the other week Bob had his physical, and the doctor said he would live another twenty years. You know he quit smoking? He hasn't touched cigarettes in years. He had that scare, and then he turned everything around, and now he is, or he *was*, healthier than ever. Not that you'd know it from reading the newspapers. Poor health. Bad lungs. Bad heart. Good *grief*. You'd think at least *one* of those reporters would check their facts."

Gasko nodded sympathetically. "I see. So, Amanda," he prompted. "How about you tell Mrs. Vogel what's going to happen next."

(They had rehearsed what to say, and what to leave out. It was delicate.)

Amanda offered a redacted version of the last week's events, the timeline left vague at Gasko's behest. "So, we learned from our source that there were GRU operatives in Cairo at the same time as Senator Vogel," Amanda explained. "But our source has limited access. He doesn't know *why* the GRU was targeting the senator. And this is where we're hoping you might be able to help us, Mrs. Vogel. Why the Russians would target him. Does anything come to mind?"

Diane shook her head, but before she did, there was the slightest pause.

"You're sure?" Amanda pressed. "Even the smallest thing. Even if it's just a suspicion, a hunch. It could be helpful to us. You were closer to him than anyone in the world."

"Yes," Diane said crisply. "Yes, Amanda, I am *sure*. And I don't particularly like the implication of what you're saying."

"Of course. I'm so sorry. I didn't mean to suggest that."

Diane offered a cool smile. "I'm sure you didn't."

Gasko stood up and buttoned his suit jacket. "We've kept you long enough, Mrs. Vogel. Let's let you get back to your guests."

•   •   •

While Gasko mingled ("Ah, the distinguished senator from Florida," he said. "Excuse me while I go remind him of the budget currently atrophying on his desk.") Amanda scanned the room. There she was, standing by the buffet, recognizable from the picture in the *Politico* profile. Walking across the room, Amanda nodded at the people she passed, conveying vague sympathy, hoping it tricked them into thinking they knew her. With her resolutely dull wardrobe, she tended to blend into this kind of Northeast Corridor crowd. At the buffet, she selected a crostini with cherry tomatoes. The woman next to her was staring vacantly at the crudité. Quietly, Amanda said: "Jennifer Navarro?"

Jenny startled. Then squinted. "Do I know you?"

"My name is Amanda. I was hoping to talk to you about the papers you found on Senator Vogel's desk. Maybe somewhere more . . . private."

Briefly, terror rearranged Jenny's features. "It's okay," Amanda said reassuringly, touching her on the arm. A gift of her small stature was that no one was ever *that* scared of a woman who stood five feet, two inches. "I'm from Langley. I'm working with Charlie Cole. You did the right thing, by the way. I just wanted to ask a few questions. Standard procedure."

This appeared to calm her down. When Amanda suggested they take a walk, Jenny said: "Yeah. Okay. Actually, I'm kind of dying to get out of here."

Had he known what Amanda was about to do, Gasko would have been furious. But he was too busy working the room to notice her absence. "Nice evening, isn't it?" Amanda said, as they strolled toward Central Park. "The weather, I mean. Much less muggy than D.C. Let's go in this way. We can find a place to sit."

In the park, they found a bench on the Mall. Jenny looked around at the hectic panorama, the tourists with their selfie sticks, drummers and saxophone players with money-filled hats, rollerbladers weaving through pylons. "You don't want to find somewhere a little quieter?"

"This is good," Amanda said. "So. Jennifer. Or do you prefer Jenny?"

"Oh. I guess . . . Jenny, I guess."

"Great. Jenny. As I was saying, I'm glad you called. That was the right thing to do. Senator Vogel was working on something important. We're going to make sure that work continues. What I'm hoping is that you'll agree to do the same thing Senator Vogel was doing, and keep this quiet."

"Yeah. I mean, of course. I'm not going to tell anybody." Jenny shook her head. "It still kind of hurts, though. I thought he trusted me."

"This didn't have anything to do with trust."

Jenny frowned, not seeming to buy it. If she had one shortcoming, Amanda thought, it was the pride she took in her own integrity. The idea that Vogel might have doubted that integrity was clearly torturing her. And so, rationalizing that this was the kindest path forward (although, yes, it was also the path that was going to get her what she wanted), Amanda said: "It wasn't trust. It was to keep you safe. I'm going to tell you something I'm not technically supposed to tell you. Senator Vogel didn't die of a stroke."

"What do you mean?"

"I mean he was assassinated by Russian operatives. For reasons that have to do with those papers you found."

"You're kidding, right? Wait. You're *not* kidding? But that's . . . that's not the kind of thing that actually *happens*, is it?"

"I'm afraid it is."

Jenny blinked at her, mute with shock. This was always the least pleasant part of the job. The Grim Reaper in Talbots: that was what Amanda felt like. When Jenny finally gathered herself, drawing a deep breath, she said: "Does Diane know?"

"About the assassination? Yes. But not about the papers you found. The less she knows, the safer she'll be. The same goes for you. That's what I wanted to say. That's why I would suggest, I would *strongly* suggest, that you don't talk to anyone about what you found. We can leave you out of this entirely. No one needs to know that those papers came from you."

"But *you* know they came from me."

"Well, yes."

"And obviously Charlie Cole knows they came from me."

"Yes."

"But how do I . . ." Jenny shook her head, trying to compose herself. It was impressive, her determination to think clearly while in the grips of an entirely rational fear. "I'm sorry. No offense. But how do I know I can trust you guys?"

"Well, how about this. I haven't yet told you my full name. It's Amanda Cole." She paused. "Charlie Cole is my father."

"What?"

"Charlie Cole is my father," she repeated. "I'm not sure what he led you to believe. Maybe that he was Senator Vogel's source for this intelligence. But that's not the case. The truth is that Charlie is hiding something. He may not be involved directly in this scheme, but he's worried about *something* coming out. He gave me those papers on the condition that I leave him out of it. Which is, obviously, completely stupid. He's asking me to obstruct the investigation of a major assassination. He thought I would agree to it because I'm his daughter."

"And that's . . . I'm sorry, what does that have to do with *trusting* you?"

"Two reasons. One, our incentives are aligned. Just as much as you, I want to keep the origins of the folder as quiet as possible. And another thing. I've just handed you a very sensitive piece of information. So I know the truth about you, but you know the truth about me, too. You have something on me. Do you see?"

Jenny stared at her. Possibly she thought Amanda was spouting nonsense, but the longer she stared, the more it became clear that she could follow this logic. "Huh," she finally said. "Wow. Okay. So did you agree to it, then?"

"I didn't say anything, one way or the other."

"So then what are you going to do?"

For some reason, this question surprised Amanda. She hadn't really considered that there might be more than one path forward. She was struggling with what to say when Jenny added: "Well, in any case. It's pretty fucked up that he's putting you in that position."

They were silent for a while.

"You know," Jenny said. "You didn't need to tell me that stuff about the assassination. I wouldn't have told anyone about the papers anyway."

"I thought you deserved the truth."

"The truth." Jenny sighed. "Yikes."

Amanda cocked her head. "Would you rather have been left in the dark?"

"Honestly? Maybe. That's probably inconceivable to someone like you."

"Well, tell you what. In a few minutes, I'm going to stand up and walk away, and that's it. Tomorrow I'm going back to D.C., and then, after that, I'm going back to where I came from. You'll never see me again. You'll never hear from me again. Nothing."

"You promise?"

"I promise."

"Well, good." Jenny looked grim. "No offense."

PART II

THE OLIGARCH

CHAPTER FIVE

I n the dark moments, Helen reminded herself that she'd always known what she was getting into.

On that late summer afternoon in 1975, they'd been dating for just over two years. The Dennehey family rented the same beach house in Old Lyme every August, and her fiancé, Charlie Cole, was visiting for the week. The house was always too crowded, the shower always ran out of hot water, sand gritted the floor in every room, but even in the chaos, the Dennehey family had certain rules. It didn't matter that Charlie and Helen were now officially engaged. Until they were married, they would sleep in separate rooms. "You can't just go to confession at the end of the week?" Charlie joked. "Isn't that what it's for?"

Because Charlie was their tall, handsome, unmistakably Waspy guest, and because the Irish Catholic clan seemed to retain some weird epigenetic respect for Anglo types, he was given one of the good bedrooms. Helen, meanwhile, was relegated to a bunk bed on the third floor, along with the cadre of younger cousins. During that particular August afternoon, when the rest of the family had trooped down to the beach, Helen was lying on her bunk, reading a James Michener paperback. The floorboards in the hallway creaked. She lowered her book, and there in the doorway was Charlie, grinning his big grin.

They were still at the stage when it was unthinkable that they might go more than twenty-four hours without having sex. Afterward, he lay on his stomach, eyes half-closed, drowsy and content.

Helen traced a finger up and down his naked back. His shoulders were tanned and strong; unlike the fair-skinned Helen, he took to the sun easily. "Mmm," he said. "How am I supposed to live without this?"

"It's only a year," Helen said. "A year is nothing."

Charlie lifted his head. "What if you came with me?"

She laughed. "And do what?"

"This," he said. "For starters."

"This." She smiled. "And what else?"

"Well, whatever you want." He rolled over, propped himself up on his elbow. "That's the thing. You know how far my salary goes in a place like Algiers? You wouldn't even have to worry about working. You could, I don't know. Perfect your French. Write that book you always wanted to write. Helen, I'm serious! Do you really want to spend another year of your life in *Connecticut*?"

It began as a lark. But as he kept talking, Charlie began to wonder out loud why this had never occurred to him. They didn't need to wait a year to get married. They could do it *now*. They were madly in love. What else mattered? She listened with bemusement, knowing that it would never happen. Helen Dennehey, the good girl, the Phi Beta Kappa bookworm, drop out of college for a man? The plan had always been for them to do long distance for the year, and then they would get married after she graduated from Connecticut College, and *then* she would join Charlie in Algeria.

"I know what you're going to say." Charlie held up a hand. "It's irresponsible. Sure. But set aside responsibility for a second. Imagine it, Hel. The whole day writing in cafés. Weekend trips to the desert. The sea. The light." He grinned, took her hand, kissed it. "Not to mention an apartment all to ourselves."

Later, it was obvious. This was what Charlie Cole did. This, in fact, was what he was *trained* to do. To bound into your life and show you how much better, how much more *exciting* that life could be. He wasn't exactly lying. What made people believe him was the fact that he believed it, too. Earlier that summer, after Charlie received news of his posting, Helen was curious to learn more about Algiers, so she read *The Sheltering Sky* by Paul Bowles. Dark as it was, the world of that novel had enchanted her: the cafés, the desert, the sea, the light. And Charlie talked, and he made it sound so *real*. The bunk bed above them, the rusted springs and the sagging mattress, might as well have been the glittering stars of the Sahara.

Words, mere words. How could they be enough to cause her to throw everything overboard? Maybe it was the post-sex haze of pleasure, or the scent of sun and beachgrass, or the dried salt on their skin. Or maybe it was knowing that Charlie was actually right. She *didn't* want to spend another year of her life in Connecticut.

In any case, it worked. Two weeks later, Helen and Charlie were married. Three weeks later, they were boarding a plane for Africa.

• • •

It was during his senior year at Yale that Charlie was approached by the CIA. His father, who had served in the OSS during World War II, suggested to his friends in Langley that his son might be a suitable candidate. During the long courtship, Charlie made up for his middling grades with a well-calibrated demeanor. Just the right amount of interest in the job; just the right blend of optimism and realism. In the end, his performance did the trick.

His decision to accept the offer didn't come as much of a surprise. But it did, to Helen, seem like a mistake. They never exactly *argued* about his decision—she recognized that it was his decision to make—but they did have a series of fraught conversations. Helen asked him, once, if he was joining the agency just to impress his father. Charlie scoffed at this, in fact he seemed deeply offended by the notion, so she never raised it again.

She was still getting used to the sight of the gold band on her finger when they arrived in Algiers in September 1975. Predictably, it wasn't nearly as romantic as either of them were anticipating. But her diligence helped her to pass the time (she learned to cook, she made friends with the expat wives, she read Flaubert and Zola in the original French), and then the posting was over, and it was followed by the posting in Switzerland, and the posting in Germany. Her twenties passed in a blur of packed boxes, currency exchanges, constant goodbyes. Charlie found it simple enough to trade one place for the other—each was merely the next rung on the ladder—but Helen felt the losses acutely. The ancient light of Algiers, the punctual calm of Switzerland, the fairy-tale melancholy of Germany. Eventually she developed a fondness for these places, but the fondness always seemed to happen just before they left.

In 1982, Charlie was assigned to a post in Helsinki. He was overjoyed. Like all the most ambitious officers in those years, he was a Russia specialist, and the opportunities afforded by Finland's proximity to the Soviet Union suited his ambitions. By this time, Helen decided to stop making the same mistake she always made. She wasn't yet using the word *regret*—she was too deeply in love with Charlie for that—but she was beginning to recognize the shortcomings of this life. And Helsinki was drab and lifeless, a cold prison sentence that she would rather just endure than attempt to mask. She wouldn't even bother trying to make friends. But that was before she met Maurice Adler.

One night during that first winter, Charlie brought Maurice home for dinner. Maurice, he explained to Helen, was a Russian native who had moved to the West. Now he was a professor at the University of Helsinki, and one of the agency's most valuable cutouts: an intermediary through which officers like Charlie could communicate with sources. Despite her malaise, Helen felt obligated to be a proper host to their guest—anything less than that would have been rude—so she made coq au vin from Julia Child's cookbook.

The three of them sat at the little pine table in the kitchen. At first she thought Maurice an odd man. He had nice manners, and asked perceptive questions, but he also seemed slightly absent, as if she were getting a convincing performance of the person, but not the person himself. But then Charlie went into the living room to change the music, and Maurice leaned forward and said, "Charlie tells me you're rereading Proust?" That was when something in her, or something in him, or maybe something in both of them—that shy sense of hesitancy—began to evaporate.

The three of them wound up lingering at the table, talking late into the night. When Maurice finally left, he asked Helen if she'd like to have coffee the next week, so they could talk more without (a wry smile) dragging poor Charlie into their literary minutiae, and Charlie (smiling too) said that was a great idea. Later yet, as they were getting ready for bed, Charlie earnestly asked what she'd thought of Maurice, and Helen understood that Charlie had done this for her. He had gone out and found her a friend. He knew that she needed more than just him to stave off the loneliness.

Maurice began what became a ritual of weekly visits. Helen would brew a pot of coffee, and he would bring a box of lingonberry pastries. Over time, their conversations grew more wide-ranging, more personal. He was eleven years older than her, but the age gap didn't matter. She often surprised herself with her candor. Helen wasn't much of a crier, but in the middle of telling a story about the stray cat who lived outside their apartment in Algiers, she found herself, embarrassingly, beginning to tear up.

"I'm sorry." She swiped her knuckles across her eyes. "I don't know why I'm crying. Charlie was the one who fed him, not me. I didn't even like that stupid cat."

"You don't need to apologize. Sometimes it's easier to cry about the small things."

Another kind of friend (a female kind of friend, if she were being honest) might have pressed the question. *Helen, honey. You can tell me. What's* really *the matter?* But this wasn't the nature of their friendship. Their relationship would always be marked with a degree of deference. You could only know so much about another person. They had decided, for whatever reason, to respect those limits.

Although sometimes, within the privacy of their marriage, she couldn't resist trying to find out more. "But what does Maurice *do* for you, exactly?" She and Charlie were walking back from a cocktail party at the British embassy on a frosty night, satin slingbacks dangling from her gloved finger. The winter sidewalks were treacherous, and Helen had adopted the local custom of differentiating between outdoor shoes (her snow boots) and indoor shoes (her high heels). Maurice had been at the party, too, but he'd left early, without saying goodbye.

"He's kind of like a connective tissue," Charlie said. "A Finn might be spooked by an American. But if Maurice does the approach, they might be more receptive."

"Is that what he was doing tonight, do you think? Going to meet someone?"

Charlie shrugged. "Beats me."

"You aren't even curious?"

"Honestly, Hel, it's not always that exciting. He basically spends most of his time doing what he does with you. Visiting, drinking coffee, talking. Getting to know people. Figuring out what makes them tick."

She felt flushed, and slightly queasy. She suddenly regretted bringing this up.

Charlie smiled. "Not that he'd ever try to recruit you. Actually, that's the whole reason I thought you guys would hit it off."

"What do you mean?"

"Well, it's blurry. The boundary between his regular life and what he does for us. He doesn't *really* work for us, but he's also *always* working for us. Does that make sense? And that can get confusing. Point is, he doesn't have to worry about that when he's talking to you. He can't recruit you. Because, you know." He slid his arm down her waist, grabbed playfully at her butt. "I've already taken care of that."

She swatted his hand away and said, "You wish." But as they slipped and skidded home, she felt a lightness, a relief. While there wasn't any physical chemistry between her and Maurice (she adored him, but not like *that*), Helen nonetheless—sometimes— felt guilt about their deepening friendship. Precisely because he never pushed, she was letting him see the parts of her that were quietly dissatisfied, the parts whose existence no one else knew about. It felt—sometimes—like a violation of the primacy of her and Charlie's marriage.

• • •

Many decades later, on that July night in New York City, Helen and Sidney were out at a dinner party. After saying goodbye to Jenny in Central Park, Amanda beelined for her mother and stepfather's apartment. The doorman let her in, and Amanda, exhausted from the last several days, went straight to the guest room and collapsed into a dreamless sleep.

Ten hours later, she opened her eyes. The bedroom was cool and dim from the blackout shades. Helen must have crept in at some point, knowing that Amanda would have forgotten to draw them. She rolled over: there was a note on the nightstand. *Didn't want to wake you. Running errands this morning, I'll be back with breakfast. I'm so glad you're here.*

Amanda lingered in the shower, basking in the hot water, allowing herself to momentarily forget the developments of the past week. She always slept better under her mother's roof. Helen and Sidney had moved to this apartment eight years ago, after Sidney's big promotion at the investment bank, so Amanda had never actually *lived* here, but the doorman always remembered her, and Helen always kept her favorite snacks handy, just in case.

She was in the kitchen, helping herself to coffee, when a voice echoed from the foyer. "Honey? Are you up?"

Helen appeared around the corner. She was dressed for her exercise class, black yoga pants and a black tank top, her gray bob held back with a headband. "You're probably starving," she said. "Sorry, sweetheart. That took longer than I thought. I bumped into Mrs. Markopolous. She told me to tell you to tell Georgia that she needs to visit more often."

They hugged, and Amanda noticed, as she had been noticing over the last several years, that she was now slightly taller than her mother. Helen was diligent about her yoga and Pilates and strength training, but nothing could slow the march of time, or of bone density loss. Amanda said: "I can vouch that Georgia had already called her mother *twice* before I managed to leave her apartment yesterday morning."

"She said Georgia has been picking fights lately."

"Fighting is their love language."

"Well, I'm on her mother's side. *Anyway.* Then I got to Bagelworks and a fresh batch was coming in ten minutes, so I decided to wait. See? Still hot."

Amanda opened the paper bag, the aroma of yeast and malt filling the air. She smiled, feeling a childlike happiness. Bagelworks was a mile away from the apartment, which in Manhattan terms meant it was in another state, but it was the place they had gone every Saturday morning, back when it was just the two of them, back when Helen was still in night school, back when they lived in that dingy walk-up on First Avenue. Bagelworks was her mother's way of making it clear that Amanda's visits, even if they were brief, were a special occasion.

"So," Helen said, as she buttered a sesame bagel. She passed half to Amanda. In return Amanda passed her half of an everything with cream cheese. Neither of them could remember when or why they started this half-and-half habit; they had always just done it. "Tell me. What news from the Eternal City?"

"Well, actually. I just found out I'm getting promoted. Station chief."

"Station chief!" Helen exclaimed. "Honey! That's a big deal."

"I guess," she said. "Yeah. I don't know."

While Amanda looked down and took a big bite of her bagel, Helen gazed at her. After a beat, she said: "You don't seem very happy about this."

Amanda shrugged. "It was unexpected."

"So what brought this about? Something bad?"

"Well, definitely not something good."

"Give me the number," Helen said, because this was their way of talking about Amanda's job without actually talking about Amanda's job. "One to ten."

This morning, Diane Vogel would have woken up in an empty bed. Her husband's clothes in his closet, his toothbrush by the sink: the trip wires were infinite. Yesterday had made the guilt concrete. Amanda hated the idea of putting a number on his death. She hated that she knew exactly what that number was. "Like a seven."

"Bad, then."

"Yeah. Bad." She sighed. "Although it's not just this one thing. It's part of something bigger. Normally I don't mind a challenge. But this one. I'm kind of worried about it."

Helen was a good listener. She wasn't the type to fill a silence, especially when she sensed a theme was being worked out. Amanda was always the one to change the subject, to pivot from the things they weren't allowed to discuss. Her mind whirred through options like a deck of cards. She could ask her mother about her book club; about Sidney's new board appointment; about the kids, Amanda's half siblings, Vanessa and Caleb.

But she had to do this. She spoke quickly, before she lost her nerve. "Can I ask you something? It's about Dad. It's about what happened in Helsinki."

Helen arched an eyebrow. "You mean the affair."

"Yes. Well, sort of. Did you know anything about the other woman?"

"Not much. She was British. Her name was Mary. I only saw her the one time. You were there, too, actually."

"I was?"

"It was outside our apartment. You were tiny, you wouldn't remember. In the moment, I didn't realize it was *her*. I had suspected something like it for a long time. But I didn't actually put it together for several months."

"You suspected? And you didn't say anything to Dad?"

"It was just a hunch. I didn't have any evidence. And I thought, if I ask him about it, he'll just say no. Your father was a good liar. That was his job. And then I would be wondering if he was lying or telling the truth, and that sounded exhausting. It was already so hard. He worked all the time. I was trying to keep you and me afloat. So I just . . . lived with it. It's okay, sweetheart. It was a long time ago. A *long* time ago."

Amanda's face contorted in discomfort. The smell of cream cheese was making her queasy. There was, she realized, a good reason she had never asked about the affair. Probably there were things a child wasn't meant to know about her parents. But what choice did she have? She said: "How long had you suspected him?"

"The first time or the second time?"

"There were *two* affairs?"

"No, no. It was the same woman. Both times I confronted him around your birthday. When you turned four, in 1987. But he apologized, and I agreed to give him another chance. And then when you turned six, in 1989. That's when I decided to leave. I don't know why it always happened on your birthday." She shook her head. "No, that's not true. I know why. It's because when I looked at you, at this beautiful child, I knew that I couldn't keep doing this to you. I couldn't let you grow up with my resentment. Your birthday had a way of reminding me of that."

"My birthday," Amanda echoed. "And we moved to New York right after that?"

"In May. It took me a few weeks to get everything together."

"And Dad left Helsinki about . . . let's see . . . nine months later?"

"Oh." Helen furrowed her brow, puzzled by this new line of inquiry. "Well, right. Nine months. We left in May. He got his transfer in February."

"Did you believe it?"

"Believe what?"

"The story about him requesting a transfer."

Amanda had heard rumors about her father's departure from Helsinki in 1990. Charlie had always claimed that he had requested the transfer; that he was burned out by the Clandestine Service; that he was ready to come home for good. But the transfer, inevitably, carried the suggestion of disgrace. Amanda had always suspected there was more to the story. "It just doesn't seem likely," she added. "That he would actually *want* that."

"I remember it so well," Helen said. "I was making dinner. The phone rang, and it was your father, saying he was coming back. He said our leaving had been a wake-up call. I guess I *did* believe him. He *did* sound different. But that phone call . . . It was also when I realized I wasn't in love with him anymore. I thought, if Charlie is telling the truth, if he really has changed, then he is going to make some woman very happy. *God*, that was a sad phone call. But part of me also knew it had to happen. It was the only way for us to both be okay."

The kitchen was quiet and calm. Across the table, Helen was unruffled by the old memories. Amanda believed in the sincerity of her mother's belief. But it hadn't actually answered her question. Those nine months. Helen leaves Charlie in May 1989. Charlie leaves Helsinki in February 1990. If it was really as simple as that, if Helen's departure was the wake-up call, then why did he wait those nine months to change his life?

The gap didn't make sense. Those nine months. Something had happened in those nine months.

• • •

In 1984, Maurice left Helsinki for a new teaching position in Paris. Helen wouldn't go so far as to *blame* the changes in their marriage on Maurice's departure. On the other hand, it seemed like more than a coincidence that, soon after Maurice left, her and Charlie's disagreements went from run-of-the-mill to—well— fundamental.

She had gotten pregnant soon after arriving in Finland. Helen gave birth to Amanda Margaret Cole, named for two of their grand-mothers, on April 18, 1983. That first year wasn't so bad. There was constant fatigue, but it was a shared fatigue. Charlie, a workhorse at heart, was happiest when he had something to keep him busy. Keeping a newborn alive was the most relentless kind of busyness. The nature of his work sometimes kept him away, but when he was there, he was *there*.

And in that first year, Maurice was good company to all of them. He doted on the baby. He spoke to her in Russian, saying she was the smartest child he'd ever met. He gave her a beautiful set of wooden blocks for her first birthday. Helen had been scared by the thought of raising their child abroad, of being so far from grandparents and cousins, of missing holidays and birthday parties and summers at the Old Lyme beach house. But when Amanda arrived, Helen re-alized that it was okay. She was going to grow up with something different. Not better, not worse; just different.

And then, in the summer of 1984, Maurice told her that he was taking the job in Paris. He would be leaving in a few weeks. "No!"

she cried. "Oh, God. I'm sorry. I don't mean that. Oh, Maurice. I'm happy for you. I am! I just can't imagine you not being here."

The two of them were sitting in the living room, watching Amanda traverse the Berber rug, bought years ago in Algiers. She had taken her first tentative steps, but she still preferred the speed and reassurance of crawling. "It's a short flight," Maurice said. "I'll come back often. Every other month, at least."

"Still. Oh, Maurice. We're going to miss you so much."

But Helen told herself—and believed, she really did believe—that things would be okay. Gradually, she was adjusting to life in Helsinki. She'd met a handful of other moms through the local playgroup. With Amanda, her days gained a structure they had been lacking. And suddenly, out of nowhere, the toddler was acquiring preferences, opinions, habits. Her daughter was becoming so *specific*, and Helen found this enchanting. She would miss Maurice, but he had to do what was right for him, and she would adapt. She always did.

What she hadn't banked on was Charlie's reaction. At first he was sulky and quiet, refusing to talk about it, unwilling to admit to his feelings. If anything, Charlie seemed strangely resentful, like he was taking the departure personally. And then, a few weeks later, he came home with a grim look on his face. "I have to go to Washington," he said.

"Why?" Helen said, while attempting to spoon applesauce into Amanda's mouth.

"I have to brief the director about something."

It was a short trip, just a few days. But then, almost as soon as he was back, he was off again. This cadence was new. In the past, he'd never had to travel this much. Nor had he had this number of weekend and overnight shifts. When Helen asked where he was going, Charlie only gave bare-bones answers. Par for the course when married to a spy, but in the past, Charlie had always been semi-apologetic about this withholding. Now he almost seemed to *enjoy* it. "I don't get it," Helen said, after yet another spur-of-the-moment trip. "It was never like this before. Did something change?" Then, unable to conceal her prickliness, she added: "They do realize you have a toddler, right?"

"It's my *job*, Helen," he snapped. "It's not like I have an *option* here."

And because she'd had a long day with their teething, tearful, fussy daughter, she stayed silent, deciding not to wade into that eternal, godawful, breadwinner-versus-homemaker fight. They'd had it too many times already.

In December of that year, the embassy hosted its annual holiday party. Helen found herself talking to a man named Jack. The men who worked with Charlie always had names like Jack and Bill and Bob. Partway through the conversation, she realized she was meant to know who Jack was. Jack was important. Charlie had told her about him. But in addition to the teething, Amanda was going through a new phase of sleep regression, and Helen's mind felt like mush. Jack finally saved her when he said:

"I have to admit, it's a big job. But I count myself lucky. Great people here in Helsinki. Outstanding people. They make it easy for me to look good." He chuckled, and Helen's memory snapped into place. Of course! Jack was the new station chief. Or newish. He'd started in the summer, right around the time of Maurice's departure.

"Charlie's been especially great," he continued. "Always happy to go the extra mile. Always volunteering to step up. Real team player. I know it can't be easy with a little one at home. But it never stops him from raising his hand. I just want you to know." He rested his hand on her shoulder. "I see the sacrifice, and I appreciate it. I mean the sacrifice *you're* making."

"Oh," Helen said. "That's . . . well, that's nice to hear."

When she excused herself to get another drink, she noticed

Charlie across the room, head tipped back in laughter. Chipper old Charlie Cole, hail-fellow-well-met. He was so likeable, but he also *liked* being likeable, and this was the problem. He would never let his colleagues see his frustration, or fatigue, or anxiety. Which meant that he kept it to himself until he got home, at which point Helen, and Helen alone, was forced to bear the brunt of his mood.

As the night went on, her sense of aggravation mounted. So there wasn't some dramatic new operation afoot. There wasn't some save-the-world ploy. This was simply Charlie doing what came naturally. Helen understood that this trait was hardwired into him, that he would never *really* change. But she also believed it was her spousal right to call him out on it.

"You should have checked with me." They were back at the apartment, had just paid the babysitter. She spoke quietly, not wanting to wake Amanda. "All of this travel, Charlie? The overnight shifts? Jack told me you keep volunteering for them. It's kind of shitty to hear that."

He shook his head. "You don't get it."

"Well, then, explain it to me. I'm listening."

"It shouldn't be like this." Charlie sounded morose. He'd had a few more drinks than usual. "I'm thirty-three. I've got nothing to show for myself."

"What are you talking about?"

"I can tell what you're thinking, Helen. But this isn't a *vanity* thing. It's not just about getting Jack to like me. Christ almighty. I'm shallow, but I'm not *that* shallow."

She was a little taken aback by the accuracy of his perception. "Charlie," she said gently. "You've got plenty to show for yourself."

"Not where it counts. Almost three years in Helsinki. Three years in a city packed with spies, and I haven't managed to recruit a single agent. I'm fucking this up. This should be my big moment, and I'm fucking it up. I'm just so goddamn *mediocre*."

She blinked. What the fuck was happening? Charlie had

experienced bouts of insecurity in the past, but nothing like this. She was confused, but she was also angry, because this was self-pity in the extreme. She wished that Maurice was there. Maurice would tell him to snap out of it, and Charlie would actually listen to him. Charlie respected Maurice, because he was a part of his world, but because Maurice didn't actually have any power, it kept Charlie's people-pleasing complex in abeyance.

And this was when she realized: *Oh. He doesn't just miss him. He needs him.*

They were standing in the kitchen. Charlie had moved to the refrigerator to get a beer. His back was turned, his shoulders hunched forward. Helen's heart swelled with tenderness. "Oh, honey," she said. And she was about to say that she thought she understood, but then Amanda began to cry.

Charlie looked up, but Helen said, "It's okay. I'll get it."

After changing Amanda, she carried her into the kitchen, bouncing her lightly against her shoulder, trying to guide her back to sleep. Charlie sat at the kitchen table, his head in his hands. Amanda was babbling and gurgling, but he didn't hear her. "I'm sorry," he said. "I'm so sorry, Helen. I know this hasn't been fair to you."

"I'm only asking that we talk about it. You have to do what you have to do. But this is our *life*, Charlie. Let's just talk about these things before you decide."

"I'm going to try to be better," he said. "I promise."

But he didn't try. Not really. And though it took several more years to play out, if Helen had to put a date on it, that was probably the beginning of the end.

CHAPTER SIX

Kathleen Frost was better known as Kath, but she was best known as the only person at the agency who intimidated Director Gasko. Like Charlie Cole and Osmond Brown, she came from the last generation of the Cold Warriors, but unlike them, she never feared becoming a victim of the director's purges. And even if such an absurd possibility were suggested to Kath, she would retort, in her gravelly voice: "That young man? Please. I *wish* he had the guts to fire me. God knows I'm sick and tired of this place. But every time I tell him I'm quitting, he just sticks his fingers in his ears and pretends not to hear me."

That morning in late August, back in Rome station, Amanda was sitting in her office, waiting nervously for Kath to arrive. It had taken Gasko a while to track her down, but now Kath was allegedly en route, and allegedly planning to arrive that day. The rumors had circulated through the Clandestine Service for years. Kath Frost had understood the KGB better than the KGB itself did. Kath Frost had sniffed out more double agents than anyone in agency history. Kath Frost had accurately predicted exactly what Mikhail Gorbachev would say to every Western leader he ever met. And Kath had accomplished all these things while also being a woman.

Working in the Clandestine Service wasn't easy for anyone, but it especially wasn't easy for a woman. They didn't teach you this during training. Amanda had learned it the hard way, in a variety of stations and safe houses and windowless offices. Her first lesson came in Mexico City, at age twenty-six, while arguing with a senior officer over the fate of an agent. "It's wrong," Amanda had said. "You made her a promise, and as soon it gets tough, you want to break that promise." The senior officer rolled his eyes and said life wasn't fair, hadn't she heard? "Yeah," she said. "But this isn't about fairness. This is about you being lazy."

The next day the station chief summoned Amanda to his office. "He told me you were getting emotional," he said. "You can't let yourself get emotional."

"But I wasn't. He *is* lazy. It's an objective fact. Also, sir. Respectfully. How much do you trust the judgment of a man who can't even fight his own battles? I mean, really. Why does he have to involve you in this?"

"See, there you go again."

"There I what again?"

"These ad hominem attacks. Look, Amanda. I run a certain kind of operation here. I need a certain kind of team player. I'm sorry, but I don't think this is going to work out."

It had surprised her, honestly, that two grown men could be so offended by a few words uttered by a twenty-six-year-old woman. How was it possible to endure a life, especially this life, with such delicate sensibilities as theirs? Back at Langley, awaiting her next assignment, nursing her pride, she wondered if she should have done things differently. The thing was, she didn't doubt her conviction. (She'd managed to slip a warning message to the agent before leaving Mexico City.) Without her conviction, she had nothing. But the color, the tenor, the *intensity* of that conviction: apparently this would have to be modulated. She would have to finesse her way to her end goals. So she learned to show them only what they needed to see, and kept the rest of herself private.

But the *them* had only ever been men, and now she wondered if the same approach would work with Kath Frost. For someone who had recently been promoted to station chief, Amanda was feeling painfully insecure. In the past month, she'd made only the barest progress on the Vogel case. The main thing she'd done was to establish the protocol for Semonov, now back in Moscow, to contact the agency. When he was ready to set a meeting, he called a number, asked for Vladimir, said he needed to get his car serviced. CIA officers in Moscow would handle the meetings and dead drops. It was too risky for Amanda herself to travel to Russia, and too obvious a red flag for Semonov to travel to Italy more than once a year.

She'd also taken a start at constructing a timeline of Senator Vogel's final months. Each piece of paper in that manila folder was marked with a date. There were flight manifests that indicated where Vogel had been: Davos in January, Courchevel in February, Maastricht in March for the European Fine Arts Fair, Emilia-Romagna in April for a Formula 1 race. Taken together, the itinerary formed a portrait of the European social calendar for the zero point zero one percent.

Frustratingly, there was one date she couldn't pin down. The final date, May 30. There were no records of Vogel having flown anywhere. Possibly his source had traveled to him, and the meeting had taken place in New York or Washington, but that didn't seem likely. Amanda was certain another explanation was at play, but she couldn't see what. Unlike human intelligence, this wasn't her strength. Put her in the room with another person and an hour later she would emerge with their trust. But when it came to sorting through dry documents like this? She was average at best, and right now they needed better than average.

"Oh, sure." Kath was standing in the doorway, surveying the office. "Charming. Love what you've done with the place."

Kath plunked herself in the visitor's chair. She looked like she had wandered onto the set of the wrong movie. She wore a linen dress belted at the waist, a chunky turquoise necklace, a pair of red cowboy boots. Her gray hair hung long and loose over her shoulders. She craned her neck. "Not even a plant? A plant would go a long way."

Amanda glanced down at her own navy suit and white button-down. She'd never thought much about her clothes, but now that she actually looked at them, they struck her as both basic and hideous. "I, um, haven't had time to redecorate," she lied.

"Well, here I am," Kath said. "I came straight from the airport. Actually, no, I stopped for breakfast. They ran out of vegetarian meals by the time they made it to the back of the plane. The back of the plane! The CIA couldn't even spring for economy plus. So I made it from Anchorage to Rome on one package of peanuts, if you can believe that."

"Well." Amanda extended her hand across the desk. "It's great to finally meet you."

"So," she said, as they shook hands. "You're Charlie's kid."

Amanda startled. Not *that* many people at the agency knew both Charlie and Amanda. Even fewer knew that Charlie was her father. Although Amanda supposed she ought not to be surprised that the legendary Kath Frost was one of them.

"We overlapped in Geneva, way back in the day. He was a nice guy. Most of them are assholes, so you remember the nice guys." She sighed. "You know I was in Alaska when John called? Every year I take August off, every year I try to find a place where they can't find me, but these people we work for, my God, they are *relentless*. There I was, in a little log cabin in the middle of Denali, totally anonymous, happy as can be, and then one morning this ranger shows up and hands me a satellite phone and says, 'Ma'am, it's for you.' Jesus Christ. I haven't had a real vacation since Nixon was in the White House. And you know what kills me? They spend a small fortune to track me down, and then they make this seventy-three-year-old woman fly the middle seat in the back of the plane from Alaska to goddamn *Rome*."

Amanda was experiencing a kind of synaptic overload. "You call him John?"

"Oh, believe me, he's asked me to stop." She cocked an eyebrow. "He said it undermines his authority. It sends the wrong message. And I said, 'Well, *John*, that's the point, isn't it?' Anyway. The middle seat is bad enough, but when you're half-starved and there's a crying baby next to you, it means you're not going to get the slightest bit of sleep, so you might as well get started. I spent the plane ride going through everything. Listen, Amanda, if I thought you cared about these things, I'd act deferential and ask you to tell me the whole story, get me up to speed, etcetera, but I don't think you care about these things. Am I wrong?"

"Uh, no. No, that's fine." She shook her head. "Wow. Sorry. It's just . . ."

"It's just that I'm not like most of the Langley folks you've met?" Amanda smiled. "Not really."

Kath laughed, a pleasantly guttural sound. "You'll get used to it. Everyone does."

. . .

Back in July, before flying back to Rome, Amanda had told Director Gasko about the papers. She kept the precise origins a secret. A trusted source, close to the senator: that was all she said.

Walking into his office that day, she thought she'd made her decision. No way, no *way* she was going to cover for her father and risk jeopardizing the investigation. The last seventeen years of her life had been shaped by allegiance to the agency. She was proud of the work she'd done. This was her integrity. This was her *identity*. And now her father was asking her to . . . what? Just let it dissolve in a warm bath of sentiment?

Gasko read the papers in silence. He reached the end of the folder. She had to come clean about Charlie's strange request; had to tell the director that her father was clearly hiding something. It was now or never. *Come on*, she thought. *Start talking. Right now.*

Right now! But there, in the thick silence, it suddenly occurred to her. The obvious outcome of telling Gasko: the agency needed to investigate the Vogel story, *and* the Charlie story, *and* the way they were linked. The conflict of interest was glaring. She, as his daughter, would instantly lose the assignment.

But she badly wanted to see this through. The Russians assassinating an American politician was uncharted territory. Plus, Amanda was the person Semonov trusted. What if, by removing herself, she destroyed any chance at progress? Despite her diligent rehearsals over the last few days, despite her intellectual certitude that coming clean was the right thing to do, she found herself abandoning that carefully written script. Instantly, instinctively, a new plan had formed. Stay quiet. Pursue the intelligence. Get the answers, and *then* tell Gasko. He would ask her why she had lied. She would tell him the truth: that she didn't see any other way. He would be furious, of course, but she would cross that bridge later.

"So," Gasko had said. "Let me see if I'm getting this right. They're figuring out a way to hold these companies hostage. They drive the stock price up through some . . . Actually, I don't understand that part. *Meme* stocks? Anyway. They drive the stock price up, which creates leverage, because no one wants the price to go down. And then they call up the CEO in question, they tell him or her what to do. And, voilà, the CEO falls in line."

"It's clever, right?" Osmond's phrase came to mind: "It's the soft underbelly."

It was a mark of the plan's elegance that, the first time Amanda read the Vogel papers, she found herself wondering why this hadn't been done before. Gruzdev had figured out a way to tilt the global playing field in his favor, not by manipulating the leaders of other countries—his rivals were on alert for that, and besides, it rarely worked—but by manipulating levers of power where they *actually* existed. Which was to say, inside American corporations.

The average American was basically indifferent to the problems of the rest of the world. The average American didn't have an opinion about, say, how the Chinese government treated their ethnic minorities. Sometimes a sense of outrage grew hot enough to spur the country to action, but most of the time, Americans didn't bother to expend much energy on dealing with the problems of the rest of the world.

Except that the rest of the world still existed. The average American might be indifferent to Uyghur detention camps in western China, but what about the American companies that had dealings in China? There was no way around it. They *had* to take a position on these things. These corporations had built out entire teams to craft their policy portfolios. It had become a well-trod career path, from the State Department to places like Disney, or Coca-Cola, or Google. Even Georgia Markopolous, who worked for the national security advisor and was currently grappling with the spread of Islamic terrorism in western Africa, had lately been the recipient of overtures from a Fortune 500 company that, of all things, specialized in making board games.

Positions on Uyghur detention camps, on border disputes in Kashmir, on human rights in Saudi Arabia: at first glance this had nothing to do with selling movie tickets and soda, except that the Chinese went to the movies, too. Saudis drank Coca-Cola, too. World-shaping geopolitical decisions increasingly lay in the hands of these businesses. And Gruzdev had figured out a way to manipulate these businesses to his ends. *Finger on scale of algorithm. Plant idea, create virality, stock goes up. Leverage.* This was an easy, efficient route to compliance. *Greed usually sufficient. Don't want music to stop.*

"But the actual mechanism of it," Gasko had said. "The finger on the scale. Whose finger are we talking about? Who is actually making this leverage happen? The papers don't tell us anything about that, right? So how do we figure that out?"

Amanda had known, of course, that this would be Gasko's next question. But before she could say anything, he interjected: "Actually, I know *exactly* who you need."

. . .

That August day in her office, Amanda said: "So what jumps out at you?"

"You mean you don't want to waste the next hour telling me *your* interpretation of the situation?" Kath smiled. "I'll give him this, John did say I would like you. How about we take a walk? I've been stuck in a tin can for the last nineteen hours."

They left the embassy and set off toward the Villa Borghese. Kath explained that she did her best thinking while walking. "Gets the blood flowing," she said. "The ideas, too. God, I love this city. Don't you love this city? Have you ever seen such a perfect day?"

It was the swan song of the Roman summer. In the park they followed a white gravel pathway lined with tall stone pines. Trunks as long and graceful as a giraffe's neck, crowns of foliage shaped like broccoli. "Here's what strikes me," Kath said. "How beautifully it blends the blunt and the subtle. In the end, essentially, the leverage is a kind of thuggery. Mob tactics. They have these companies in a chokehold. But the way in which they *arrive* at the leverage, that's the innovation. It's sophisticated. Were you familiar with this phenomenon?"

"Meme stocks?" Amanda said. "Sure. Of course."

Kath turned, squinted at her.

"Well, actually, no. Not really. But I've been getting up to speed. I think I understand the basic mechanism of it."

"This way." Kath touched her arm, steered her to the left. She set a quick pace, the kind Amanda rarely encountered beyond the island of Manhattan. "So. Tell me how it works."

"These investors—amateurs, right? Day traders, regular people at home—they decide that some stock is the cool new thing. So they start buying it, talking it up on social media, it creates this frenzy, the price shoots up. And eventually, usually, the stock price comes back down to earth, but sometimes it stays up. And I'm assuming that when the prices stay up, when these companies get rich and manage to *stay* rich, that those are the ones we want to pay attention to?"

Kath nodded. "Essentially. But this is one of the clever things. There *is* a pattern among those whose prices stay elevated, but it's not universally true. There's plenty of noise to hide the signal."

"What do you mean?"

"On the one hand, you have plenty of American companies that do business with Russia and take favorable stances. But a lot of them have pretty steady market caps. On the other hand, you have plenty of companies whose market caps have skyrocketed thanks to this new trend. But a lot of these meme stocks haven't caused any substantive corporate changes of note. We are looking for a very slender Venn diagram. But I don't think that part will be hard. What's going to be hard is figuring out how these frenzies actually start."

"On those message boards, right? And then the word spreads, and then it's on Twitter, and it's all over the place, and then—"

"How much time have you spent on those message boards? People are tossing out hundreds, *thousands* of ideas a day. But when you log on, only a few make it to the home screen. Only a few get clicked on, and only a few start to spread. That's where it begins."

It suddenly clicked. "The algorithm. The finger on the scale."

"Exactly. And this, for my money, is the cleverest part. They don't have to create the entire frenzy. They only need to nudge it in the right direction. Get the ball rolling. Do enough to stoke the enthusiasm, suppress the naysayers. The algorithm determines which ideas spread. And they found a way to get inside."

• • •

Without asking permission, Kath commandeered Rome station's sole conference room. For security reasons, she insisted that the ten-digit combination to the conference room change every day.

One day in September, when Amanda finally remembered the day's code and got the door open, she found Kath sitting in front of the paper-covered wall. Kath was slouching down, her arms crossed, her legs stretched out. Rachmaninoff played on the speakers. "Anything?" Amanda asked, raising her voice to be heard over the music.

Kath shook her head.

In just a matter of days, Kath had given form to the formless: the machinery of conspiracy had been mapped and labeled with clinical precision. The wall was beautiful to behold, covered with evidence, graphs showing wild growth in a company's stock price, articles describing internal changes at said company. The changes, Kath had discerned, tended to happen nine or twelve or eighteen months after the initial frenzy, long enough that no one bothered to link the two. The media company that fired their steel-spined general counsel, replacing her with someone much more lukewarm on the First Amendment. The investment bank reopening their Moscow offices after a long absence. The oil company that decided to shift their focus to drilling in the Russian Arctic. Public records, hiding in plain sight.

Kath, it was obvious, had a knack for it. Although the rest of the station didn't see her genius. To them, Kath just looked like a kooky old woman holed up in the conference room. And she *was* kind of kooky. One night, when Amanda suggested they break for dinner, Kath declared that she didn't believe in dinner. It ruined your sleep, she explained, and was bad for your digestion. In addition to not believing in dinner, she also thought Tchaikovsky was a sentimental jingoistic sellout of a composer. She also slept for precisely six hours and fifteen minutes every night and never took naps. She also doodled mountain ranges in the margins of whatever paper was before her. Stalin had drawn wolves, she told Amanda, when he was stuck in a meeting. She saw the wisdom in this (same idea as the walks: the mind was sharper when the body was occupied), but wolves were tricky to draw, so she'd picked mountain ranges.

Amanda found herself spending a lot of time in the conference room, more than was strictly necessary, letting her other station chief duties fall by the wayside. At the end of that first week, she looked at Kath and thought: *She's becoming a friend.* It had been a while, because life in the DO wasn't exactly conducive to making new friends. But Kath had a way of putting her at ease.

That day, Amanda walked over to the speaker and turned down the Rachmaninoff. On one area of the wall were pictures of half a dozen men. Kath murmured: "The leak. Vogel's source. It has to be one of them."

"And they were all at Davos," Amanda said. "And they all over-lapped with Vogel."

"Correct."

"And there's no way to narrow it down."

"There's *some* way to narrow it down. I just don't know what it is yet."

It had been Kath's hunch that the source, the person whose confessions were recorded in the senator's spidery scrawl, was a Russian oligarch. The Kremlin itself wouldn't carry out the algorithm-manipulation scheme. They would rely on an interme-diary, a person whose allegiance was assured, but who could also move easily among the global elite. A person who wouldn't be out of place in Courchevel or Cannes; a person with multiple fluencies, smart enough to supervise a team of hackers, connected enough to have his calls taken by, say, the CEO of a media company whose market cap had recently tripled.

Amanda asked: "Which of them had the motive? Which of them really hated Gruzdev?"

"They're not doing Gruzdev's bidding because they *like* him," Kath said, with an edge of irritation. "It's because they're terrified of him. And with good reason."

Amanda cocked her head. The half dozen men even *looked* the same. Kath finally turned around. "Stop hovering," she snipped. "Are you going to sit or not?"

"Well, you're in a bad mood."

"And you're about as useful as a chocolate teapot."

Amanda laughed. "A what?"

"I mean it. Make up your mind. Stay or go."

"I'll stay," she said, but she took a seat at the other end of the room, where her presence wouldn't disturb Kath's concentration.

· · ·

A few days later in Moscow, Konstantin Nikolaievich Semonov picked up the phone, dialed a memorized number, and said: "I would like to make an appointment with Vladimir to have my car serviced."

After a brief pause, the voice at the other end replied: "Vladimir is on vacation right now. But Adrian can fix your car instead. Please bring it tomorrow at nine a.m."

The next day, Semonov took the Metro to VDNKh. He checked his watch as he emerged from the station. He'd left plenty of time, just to be safe. Feigning leisure he didn't feel, Semonov walked slowly through the park, down the wide plaza, toward the monumental stone arch at the entrance that commemorated the triumph of Soviet-era agriculture. He had always been conflicted about this arch. It was a garish thing, topped with golden statues of a strapping Soviet tractor driver, his Soviet farmer-wife, and an abundant sheaf of golden Soviet wheat. The message was patently absurd, given how many millions had starved to death in the Soviet Union. And yet, he thought, if they tore down these falsehoods, what would remain? History was hard to come by in Moscow. The Soviets had ruthlessly destroyed the old buildings, old monuments, old memories. Sometimes it seemed better to leave these monstrosities intact, no matter how awful, because if they didn't—then what would they be left with?

Semonov checked his watch again. He walked to the west side of the park, where buses were discharging the first tourists of the day. The area was busy and hectic, the cars blatantly ignoring the traffic signs. He stood on the corner, waiting. Finally, right at 9 a.m., the silver Lada pulled up to the curb. Semonov opened the door on the passenger side, ducked his head into the car, and said: "Hello, Adrian. The car is running well?"

The driver, Adrian or whatever his name was, nodded. "It needed a new battery."

Semonov climbed into the passenger seat. As they began driving, he asked nervously: "Are we going somewhere?"

"Not really. We're just going to drive for a while."

They headed south on Prospekt Mira, toward the Third Ring Road. After several minutes of silence, Adrian glanced over at his passenger. Fidgety hands, roving gaze: about the normal level of nerves. Adrian had been doing this job long enough to know that, in certain cases, chitchat was pointless, even counterproductive. The best cure for anxiety was, simply, to endure the anxiety. Give it a few minutes. Semonov would acclimate. And sure enough, several minutes later, the Russian cleared his throat and said: "You work with Amanda Clarkson?"

Adrian nodded. On paper, and in the eyes of the wider world, he and Amanda were both employees of the State Department. In reality, they had been in the same training cohort on the Farm many years ago, during which she had impressed Adrian, and everybody else, with her freakish talent. "She's an old friend," he said.

"A nice woman," Semonov said.

"Yes. She is."

"Is she married?"

"Uh . . . no. She isn't."

"She must be very picky."

Adrian stifled his smile. Rolling meetings like these were designed to be efficient. It was simply a chance for Semonov to give

Adrian whatever he needed to give him. But (and it never ceased to amuse him) in even just a few minutes, you could get the strangest window into another person's brain. Eventually, Semonov sighed and pulled out a USB drive. "I don't know how useful this will actually be," he said. "But I hope it will help."

• • •

Over the following days, the USB drive traveled a careful course. Back to the embassy in Adrian's pocket, then from Moscow to Rome via diplomatic pouch, where it underwent a thorough inspection to ensure it didn't conceal any Trojan horse malware. Finally, a junior officer knocked on Amanda's door and said: "Package for you."

She opened the envelope and took out the drive. It was just a bit of metal and plastic, and maybe it wouldn't prove to be anything, but still: this moment always filled her with reverence. The unknown possibilities. Until she removed the lid from the box, the cat was alive. Amanda placed the drive on her desk and gazed at it for a solid minute. It was one of her private superstitions, the hope that patience might prove something to the Fates, might help her odds.

She plugged it in, and hundreds of documents popped up on her computer screen. A little over a month had passed since Semonov's return to Moscow. It was unlikely that he would have come across actionable intelligence in that short span of time. And yet, you never knew.

She clicked through emails, memos, other bureaucratic flotsam and jetsam. He was thorough; understandably so. Though Semonov was aware of the Vogel assassination, he wasn't aware of the bigger picture surrounding that assassination. Without knowing what he was looking for, he erred on the side of giving them everything. Amanda clicked and clicked.

Nothing, nothing, nothing. Two hours later, her eyes were gritty and her stomach was rumbling. But just as she considered taking a break for lunch, something caught her attention.

She sat up straight. Took the elastic from her wrist, pulled her hair back. Okay. Here was something: a memo from earlier in the summer, outlining a request for passports and visas for two men traveling to Egypt on July 20. The request, fulfilled by Semonov, that had ultimately resulted in Vogel's death. The two men listed on this memo were designated not by names but by numerical codes, which meant she now knew the codes for Tweedledee and Tweedledum, these two members of Unit 29155.

Unit 29155 was the violent dark heart of the GRU, the people who carried out assassinations, ambushes, and poisonings. Rarely did Semonov work with them. He spent ninety-nine percent of his time creating documents and paper trails to backstop the more ordinary GRU officers, the ones who traveled the world under diplomatic cover. She felt an extra jolt of energy, now that she knew what she was looking for.

She kept clicking and clicking, and at last, her eye caught again on the familiar numbers: the codes for the men in Unit 29155. The memo specified that they were going to travel to Iceland. Semonov, again, would be tasked with fabricating the necessary papers. Her adrenaline spiked for a second (*Actionable intelligence! Iceland is where they're going next!*), but then she noticed that their travel dates were specified, too. August 24. The trip had already happened.

·   ·   ·

"Iceland," Amanda said, bursting into the conference room. "Did something happen in Iceland?"

Kath spun around. "Iceland?"

"Tweedledee and Tweedledum. They were there last month."

Kath stared at Amanda for a beat. Then she broke into a grin. "Of course. *Of course.*" She walked over to the wall and tore down five of the six pictures. Most of the oligarchs flew private, but occasionally they appeared on commercial flight manifests, and Kath had been mapping their travel as best she could. She pointed at the remaining oligarch, who gazed out at them from under a pair of thick eyebrows. "Ivan Komarovsky. He was in Iceland in August, too."

"I thought Komarovsky was the least likely of the bunch."

"That's the genius of it!" Kath exclaimed. "The oligarchs tend to toe the line. Not Komarovsky. He's been critical, *scathingly* critical, of Gruzdev. Not just once, not just twice, but over and over. God! Yes, see, he fit our criteria in a technical sense. His hedge fund, his financial sophistication, and so on. But I just didn't believe he would be willing to carry the Kremlin's water. But you see it, don't you? You see the brilliance of this?"

"Um," Amanda said.

"It's part of the plan. He's only critical of Gruzdev *with Gruzdev's permission*. Same reason Gruzdev allows other political parties to hold seats in the Duma. The veneer of opposition lends legitimacy. Also"—she pointed at another piece of paper—"Komarovsky and Vogel were neighbors, back in the day. Vogel's hedge fund had an office in London. He kept a mansion in Mayfair, right next door to Komarovsky."

Amanda stepped toward the wall. She peered at the oligarch's features. "So this is it? You think we found our source?"

Kath laughed. "Oh, honey. I *know* we found our source."

CHAPTER SEVEN

The next morning, Kath appeared in Amanda's doorway with a frown. "Well," she said. "Unfortunately, it seems like it worked."

"What worked?"

Kath closed the door. "Tweedledee and Tweedledum. Their job is to kill, or to intimidate, and Komarovsky isn't dead, which means they went to Iceland to send a message. And it seems like the message worked."

She kept explaining. Ivan Komarovsky arrived in Iceland on August 24 to attend an investing conference in Grindavík. Fresh air, hiking, horseback riding, backroom deals among the super-elite. Very wholesome. It was a four-day conference, but Komarovsky left abruptly after just two, returning to London on August 26. The very next day, someone with the username GalaxyBongo posted an item to Reddit with the headline: "MACH undervalued . . . good feeling about this one." Within a few hours, the post had been upvoted, shared, screenshotted, tweeted, and eventually climbed to the top position on the main page. That was Sunday night. When the market opened on Monday morning, the share price for Aeromach, which traded under MACH, climbed from $26.77 to north of $30, then $35, then $45.

"Aeromach," Amanda said. "The defense contractor?"

"And listen to this. Komarovsky's hedge fund, Pavel Partners, they already own a good slice of Aeromach. It's another layer of cover. Because when Aeromach gets taken for this wildly lucrative ride, Komarovsky calls up the CEO and says he wants to have a conversation. Well, sure. No problem. The CEO has to keep his shareholders happy. That poor sucker will have no . . . What is it? Why are you shaking your head like that?"

"I was just thinking. Iceland. Tweedledee and Tweedledum. The GRU killed Bob Vogel. Why not kill Komarovsky, too?"

"Because Bob Vogel was disposable. Komarovsky isn't. He wouldn't be easy to replace. Tipping the algorithm without anyone noticing? Not easy. Not easy at all."

"Careful, now. You almost sound impressed."

"Of course I'm impressed. It's impressive."

"I was joking," Amanda said, which was only half-true. "Anyway. Okay. So he's back to doing the Kremlin's bidding. Let's get London to start tailing him."

This part, she knew, wasn't going to be easy. Amanda couldn't just walk up to Komarovsky and ask him to please consider turning back to their side. Between Egypt and Iceland, the GRU had evidently terrified him into compliance. Amanda would need a card to play, a piece of leverage, to persuade the oligarch back in cooperating with the Americans.

•　•　•

A few days later, while walking toward the Spanish Steps in search of pizza bianca for lunch, Amanda described to Kath the surveillance they'd put in place in London. They needed that surveillance to yield an opening, a weak point, something to give her an advantage over the oligarch. "I just hope it works," she said with a sigh. Then she noticed Kath's expression. "What? What's that look for?"

"Would you consider yourself a romantic, Amanda?"

"What?"

"An idealist? An optimist? No. Of course not. You would consider yourself a realist. How many times have I heard it, from your kind? *We know how the world really works.* That's what they always say. *Leave the idealism to the rest of them. We're too hardened for all that.* And yet I have never, *never* witnessed anything like the blind faith of a field officer."

Amanda bristled at this. "I didn't say it *will* work. I said I hope it does."

"But in your heart of hearts, of course you think it will work. Otherwise you wouldn't do it at all."

"So, what are you saying? It's better to do nothing?"

"Of course not. I'm just saying that I find it amusing."

She rolled her eyes. "Did anyone ever tell you that you can be kind of annoying?"

Kath kept smiling. "Maybe once or twice."

They walked in silence for a while. As her irritation subsided, Amanda began to suspect the provocation had been purposeful. Kath had wanted to rattle her cage, remind her not to get carried away. She glanced over. Kath, ever the mind reader, said: "Consider it a compliment. Not everyone can take it."

"You know, I've been meaning to ask. Are the rumors true? Did you really turn down the chance to be Moscow station chief?"

"That path was never particularly interesting to me."

"So you *did* turn it down?"

"You know there wasn't a female station chief until 1978? And they made *that* poor woman cool her heels for thirty-six years before they woke up and saw how smart she was. I thought, no way am I putting up with that. So I told them, let me tackle the agency's archives, they're a mess. *Someone* needs to make sense of these memos and cables. Of course, they loved that. Me knowing my place, me knowing the difference between men's work and women's work. Stick her in the archives! We'll never hear from her again."

"That doesn't quite answer the question."

"Fieldwork was never my thing. You learn more about the enemy from reading history than from following around some sad-sack KGB agent who drinks too much and hits his wife. The truth is that fieldwork is often overrated. The problem with human sources is that people develop emotional attachments to those sources. It makes it impossible to think clearly."

"So you're *not* a romantic, then."

"Actually, I am. That's why I stick to the dry stuff. I fall in love too easily."

Kath was laughing. Amanda had no idea whether or not she was kidding.

• • •

Later that same week, a thousand miles away, Ivan Komarovsky said to his wife: "I have a meeting with Vitsin tonight, so I won't be home for dinner."

"Vitsin?" Anya Komarovsky raised a perfectly groomed eyebrow. It wasn't even 8 a.m. in London, but already she was impeccable: the dress and heels, her hair in a sleek chignon, her lipstick just so. She woke up early every morning, giving herself at least an hour to ready her appearance, and another hour to pray in their private chapel. It wasn't vanity, not exactly. It was that Anya treated her position as the third Mrs. Ivan Komarovsky as a full-time job, and she worked hard to fulfill the obligations of that job. "You have forgiven him, then?"

Vitsin, their art dealer, had recently sold a Francis Bacon out from under their noses. At least this was what Komarovsky had told his wife. He kissed her goodbye and said: "There will be others. I'll see you tonight, Annushka."

That evening, the hostess at the Chiltern Firehouse greeted him by name. As Komarovsky was whisked past the hordes enduring the long wait, he felt, once again, the irony of his position. *You can have mine!* he thought. *I don't even want to be here!* But, of course, he wasn't here because he *wanted* to be here. He hated this restaurant for the very reasons Vitsin thought it suited to their regular meetings. Vitsin was an art dealer with a fancy address in Soho, and this was precisely the kind of place—so loud you couldn't think, so fashionable it verged on hysterical—an art dealer would frequent. Komarovsky followed the hostess toward their usual table. His driver-turned-bodyguard, Osipov, followed at a discreet distance and took a seat at the bar.

Vitsin was waiting, lounging against the leather banquette, his collar open, his Rolex peeking from his suit sleeve. They had been working together for over five years, during which time Komarovsky had watched his handler's performance become increasingly refined. Vitsin chose a 2001 Barolo from the wine list. When the sommelier delivered the bottle, he engaged in the pantomime: the nod, the pour, the sip. Vitsin grimaced. He told the sommelier to bring something else. Beneath the table, the oligarch jiggled his knee. In the past weeks, since returning from Iceland, Komarovsky had been gripped by a roller coaster of panic, anger, shame, fear, regret. But right now he simply felt annoyed. Vitsin was drawing this out on purpose.

When the wine had been corrected, and they were finally left alone, Komarovsky hissed: "Vitsin! What is the meaning of this? Are you such a coward that you must send a pair of thugs to Iceland to do your bidding?"

"Have some wine." Vitsin nudged a glass toward him.

"Worse than a coward. It was idiotic!"

Vitsin smiled, silky smooth. "I'm afraid I have no idea what you're talking about."

"They stuck out like sore thumbs. Their tracksuits and trainers and thick necks. Hammering on my door in the middle of the night, waking up half the hotel! Do you realize, Vitsin, who might have seen them? Do you realize who sponsors that conference?"

"A large American investment bank," Vitsin replied. "With whom you are very friendly. But calm yourself, Vanya. I have no idea what you're talking about. What happened in Iceland?"

He was playing dumb. Vitsin had probably assumed that Komarovsky would be suitably chastened by the episode, would never want to revisit it. But Komarovsky couldn't let Vitsin think he was so easily manipulated and intimidated. No! Even if Vitsin no longer believed the original explanation, even if he knew full well about Komarovsky's meetings with Vogel, Komarovsky wasn't going to let him know that *he* knew that. He would maintain his innocence to the very end. So he recounted for Vitsin what had happened:

On August 24, he landed at Reykjavik Airport. Osipov, who had flown with him like always, drove him to the luxury resort in Grindavík, where the conference was taking place. On the second night of the conference, he was woken by a knock. Okay, this was an exaggeration—it was Osipov, not the thick-necked thugs, who knocked on the door—but Osipov was loath to let strangers near his boss, so whatever they had done to gain his cooperation, it was surely bad. The two thugs ordered Osipov to remain outside. One of the thugs stood at the door, arms crossed. The other told Komarovsky to sit.

"You have not done what is asked of you," the thug said. "This is a problem."

Komarovsky explained, as he had already explained to Vitsin many times before, that he was waiting on the Aeromach approach because of wider economic conditions. The market wasn't favorable. It wasn't likely to respond well. They only had one shot, and if they blew it, that was it. They ought to trust him. It would be better to wait until conditions improved, which might be a few days, or a few weeks, and then—

"Enough!" The man slammed his fist against the dresser. "This is not a conversation. This is an order. There are consequences for disobeying an order. Are you so stupid that you need me to spell them out?"

That was when he realized it wasn't a bluff. That was when he realized that, somehow, they knew about his meetings with Vogel. Part of him had been bracing for this, ever since Bob Vogel collapsed under the hot Cairo sun. And, strangely, that part of him was relieved. Violence had a way of clarifying things. *Consequences.* Komarovsky shook his head and said, quickly, that he understood. Of course he understood.

He lay awake the rest of the night, staring at the ceiling, counting down the hours until he could get the first flight back to London. It was bad luck of timing that he'd been forced to fly commercial; their jet was undergoing repairs. As soon as he was home, he got a message to the programmers, the cogs at the heart of his finely tuned machine. Within a few hours they had assembled at East Ferry Road, and the user GalaxyBongo was posting about the underrated aspects of a certain American defense contractor. With the programmers' help, the post went viral, the stock price climbed, and the virtuous circle took hold. It was working. He was fulfilling his end of the bargain. He was safe.

Only after a few weeks, when the fact of his still being alive had calmed him down, did Komarovsky take offense at the stupidity of Vitsin's plan. By sending those thugs to Iceland in such public fashion, Vitsin had basically pointed a giant neon arrow at Komarovsky for the benefit of every person at the conference. CORRUPT RUS-SIAN OLIGARCH, it said. TRUST HIM AT YOUR PERIL.

When he had finish explaining, Komarovsky scowled. "So I hope you're happy," he said. "And I hope you're ready to take the blame if this whole thing falls apart."

"But truly, Ivan Ivanovich. I'm as confused as you are. I have no idea what they meant." Vitsin was, it seemed, committed to this act. At the end of dinner, when they said goodbye, he said soberly: "This must have been a miscommunication. I will get to the bottom of it."

Komarovsky, having asserted himself, felt better about the whole thing. Vitsin had clearly realized the idiocy of his mistake. Now he had to come up with a face-saving measure, a scapegoat on whom he could shunt responsibility.

The next week, Komarovsky received a call from the Vitsin Gallery. The Basquiat they had been discussing was ready for viewing. He was asked to stop by at 3 p.m. that day.

The Vitsin Gallery was in a prime location in Soho. The Russian billionaires buying mansions in Belgravia and Knightsbridge and Mayfair needed to decorate those mansions. The snooty English gallerists were willing to take Russian money—everyone in England, at the end of the day, was willing to take Russian money—but it always came with a certain unpleasant flinch, a subtle sneer at those Slavic manners. Vitsin had stepped into this breach, knowing that Russians preferred to deal with their own kind, selling them the Freuds and Hirsts and Koonses they coveted without a trace of judgment. Despite knowing nothing about art, Vitsin had become wildly successful. What the gallery lacked in pedigree it made up for in volume.

Vitsin's assistant showed Komarovsky to the office in the back. She offered to fetch him a cup of tea—black, very sweet, like always?—but he shook his head and said, "No, not today."

After she closed the door, Vitsin said: "No one has heard of these men."

Komarovsky snorted. "You dragged me here just to keep lying to me?"

"Whoever those men were, we didn't send them."

"I don't believe you."

"But why would I lie about this? Why would I want to look this foolish? Like I have no control over my own agent's situation?"

This was a good point. If Komarovsky knew anything about his handler, it was that he abhorred any appearance of weakness. And yet . . . and yet it just didn't make sense. If Vitsin didn't send those thugs, then who did? Vitsin looked at him mournfully, as if inviting Komarovsky to peer into the depths of his soul. Think of everything they had shared. Why would he lie to him?

Aha! Komarovsky thought. *So now he's appealing to my sympa-*

thy. Fat chance of that. Komarovsky reminded himself that Vitsin was a professional liar. That was his job. And Komarovsky's job? It was staying alive. If they were going to play these mind games, then fine. *Fine*. He had learned his lesson. He would play along.

· · ·

On some level, Komarovsky had been expecting this. He had always known there was a not-insignificant chance his betrayal would become known to Moscow. Hadn't he warned Bob of that very thing?

It had been a risk, trusting his old friend. But he and Bob Vogel ran in the same circles, and despite everything, they had so much in common. It had been easy. That was the surprising part. The betrayal had been so *easy*. His resentment had been building for years, like a slow and scentless gas, but he might have just lived with it forever. Until his old friend finally sensed it, and then offered to solve it.

The last time he'd seen Bob was in late May, in Mykonos. Bob and Diane were staying in a villa down the street from Ivan and Anya. They ate at the same restaurants, swam at the same beaches, sailed on the same yachts, played tennis on the same courts. Bob had walloped him in straight sets. He was tough and wiry and tanned, fitter than ever. He grinned and teased Komarovsky: "You're letting yourself get fat, Ivan."

Maybe that was the problem. They laughed, and teased, and admired pictures of each other's grandchildren. They lowered their guards. They forgot to be afraid. Whereas, in the beginning, Komarovsky had been appropriately frightened. "You can't tell anyone," he'd insisted. "No one. *No one*. If word of this gets back to Moscow—"

"It won't. I promise you, it won't."

"Especially no one in the CIA. Moscow has a mole. Ever since the Cold War. The mole tells them everything."

Bob raised an eyebrow. "I heard something about that, but isn't it just an old rumor? A story to scare the children?"

"More than a rumor," Komarovsky said. "I was even told his name."

•   •   •

A typical day in London went like this. In the morning, a black Rolls-Royce fetched the oligarch from his mansion in Mayfair. He was driven to Pavel Partners in the city. After a few hours at the office, he might have lunch with his older daughter at Annabel's. Then they might go to Harrods, where his daughter might help him choose a cashmere sweater or a silk scarf for Anya. Then a few more hours at the office, then back home, and then he and Anya would be driven to that evening's social destination: a charity ball at Grosvenor House, a dinner party in Kensington, a show in the West End.

After a few weeks, Amanda knew his routine by heart. But the driver seemed to double as a bodyguard, never letting Komarovsky out of his sight, and even if she *could* get close to him, she didn't have any leverage. The paranoia of a Russian oligarch was a thing unto itself, and that was before he'd been threatened by a pair of thugs. What lay before her would be difficult. Not impossible—but difficult, exceptionally difficult.

The waiting game was making her squirrelly. There was incremental progress in the conference room, Kath gradually clarifying their picture of the scheme, but the awe with which Amanda regarded Kath's *Beautiful Mind*–esque methods had lately morphed into frustration that she, Amanda, was so bad at these things. "Let me help," she said one day. "How can I help?"

"You can get them to buy a decent espresso machine for the kitchen. The time I spend walking to the café across the street is time I could spend working."

"I'm serious."

"So am I. I appreciate the offer, Amanda, but this kind of thing is easier to do alone."

Two things could be true at once. A given operation could be your number one, all-consuming, life-or-death priority. At the same time, days and weeks might pass without you actively *doing* anything about it. To not be driven crazy by this, you had to be able to compartmentalize. You also needed to step outside the operational bubble, every now and then, and reestablish contact with reality.

For this, Amanda mostly relied on her constant text exchanges with Georgia. She was fully immersed in the drama of her best friend's life, the workplace gossip, the romantic disappointments, the feuds with her neighbors. Georgia, who had wanted to be an actress before realizing that, at five feet eleven inches, she would tower above many of the men, had a penchant for taking things personally, and a gift for turning these slights into a story. Amanda followed the ongoing saga of Georgia's life the way her mother followed MSNBC, or her father followed baseball: for entertainment, and also escape.

Her mother and father, too, were her portals to the real world. Her father in particular. They spoke every week without fail; if she missed their usual Sunday phone call, he worried. It didn't necessarily make sense, given their shared-but-not-shared careers, but when Amanda talked to Charlie, it had a way of shifting the rest of her life—which was to say, her career—to a more distant perspective.

The last few times they'd spoken, though, it had been awkward. That the source of this awkwardness was so obvious didn't make it any less so. "How's life in Rome?" Charlie asked, and a question that once would have been innocuous now felt barbed. *What rocks are you turning over? What are you learning about me?* "Fine," Amanda replied. Then there was a floundering beat of silence. She ought to be better at hiding her discomfort. She ought to be able to pretend! But her mental discipline was failing her.

She had rules for herself. One glass of wine on weeknights. Hard liquor only on special occasions. Beer never, because beer brought back memories of that last beachside bender in Thailand that she would rather forget. *But desperate times*, she thought, as she stopped by the wine stall in the market for the third night that week. She was up to two or three glasses a night, because she needed the help falling asleep. A worthwhile compromise, right? Because if she couldn't sleep, then she *really* couldn't do her job. Amanda always held herself to high standards—you didn't get to be station chief by age forty without high standards—but the pressure she felt on this one was different. She had lied to Gasko out of the belief that she alone was equipped to run this operation. If the lie was going to be redeemed, incremental progress wasn't enough. She needed a breakthrough. She needed to knock this out of the fucking park.

• • •

And so, in October, as they were walking up the steep incline of the Janiculum Hill, Amanda announced: "I'm going to Russia."

Kath, several feet ahead on Via Garibaldi, shot a skeptical look over her shoulder.

"Semonov won't be back in Italy until next summer," Amanda explained, breathless from climbing the hill. If it were up to her, they would have done the sensible thing and taken a taxi to the cocktail party. "That's too long to wait."

"Hmmph," Kath grunted.

"He's pushing me," Amanda said. "Gasko. He wants to see progress."

"The director is driven by politics. You're closer to the situation than him. You need to make these calls."

"I *am* making these calls. And my call is that we need leverage on Komarovsky. And the current situation isn't yielding anything, and I need to act."

"Well, if that's the case, why invoke the director at all?"

The comment annoyed her. Maybe it had been a bad idea to bring Kath. They were headed to a cocktail party at the American Academy in Rome, where the ambassador was greeting that year's class of Academy fellows. Back in the summer, when Osmond Brown had returned to Rome to pack up his apartment and show Amanda the ropes, he took her to lunch, a pricey place near the Pantheon, one last meal on the agency's dime. "A piece of advice," he said, while cutting into his vitello tonnato. "Our ambassador has the cognition of a small child. If he can't see you, he doesn't believe you exist. The man loves a party. You need to go to these parties. They are completely useless and yet stupidly important."

It was, actually, one of Osmond's better pieces of advice. Parties were a gold mine of information. Parties were a whetstone to the knife of a liar's skill. Usually it was better to go alone—it was easier to only have to account for yourself—but, also, sometimes it was nice to mix it up. So, that afternoon, she stopped by the conference room and asked Kath: "Do you have plans tonight?"

The party was in full swing when they arrived. The ambassador was holding court near the marble-topped bar, where bartenders poured prosecco and mixed negronis, where the brass chandelier cast a flattering golden glow on the crowd. Amanda ordered a glass of Chianti, and Kath ordered a Pellegrino. As they filtered through the high-ceilinged reception rooms and into the courtyard, mingling with the artists and scholars who would reside at the Academy for the next year, Kath played up the country bumpkin bit. "Oh, sweetheart, I'm from *Idaho*," she said to a novelist, who was describing his moral opposition to adverbs. "I don't know about those kinds of things."

Kath seemed to be enjoying herself, but as they parted ways with the novelist, her smile faded. She balled up her napkin and said to Amanda: "I'll say it again. It's a bad idea. Going to Russia. It's too risky."

Amanda sighed. "I told you. I need to turn up the pressure on Semonov."

"I disagree. He's been making regular drops. He's doing what you asked him to do. But, even if you do want to turn up the pressure, you have people on the ground in Moscow for that. *You* don't need to be the one to do it."

"But I'm—"

"It's a huge risk, Amanda. It's crazy. They know who you are. They know you're with the agency. The minute your plane lands, they'll be all over you."

"There's this thing called tradecraft," she snapped. "Ever heard of it?"

Kath arched an eyebrow, and Amanda felt a pang of regret. "I'm sorry," she said. "That was rude. I didn't mean that."

"Oh, come on. Of course you meant it."

"I didn't—"

"It's fine, Amanda," Kath interrupted. "I disagree with you, but you can do whatever you want. I'm not your *mother*. You don't need my permission."

•   •   •

And so Amanda went.

A week later, she drummed her fingers against the armrest and stared out the window at the Baltic Sea. The flight attendants were passing through the cabin, asking for seats and tray tables to be returned to the upright position. They would be landing in St. Petersburg in twenty minutes.

What came next was a well-worn routine, one she had done dozens of times: sliding her passport across the counter, giving a noncommittal smile as the border official tried to decide whether she really was Amanda Clarkson, State Department employee, here on government business. Not that the Russians ever bought it. Anyone who worked for the American government was, ipso facto, a spy for the American government. But the diplomatic passport was like gold, a literal get-out-of-jail-free card, and so the whole charade had long since ceased to make her nervous.

This time, though, felt different. As the plane descended through Russian airspace, Kath's voice echoed in her head. *A huge risk.* If things went awry, Amanda would be protected from the worst, but what about Semonov? What if, in meeting with him, she led them directly to him? Was it fair, what she was going to ask him to do? Probably not. But she had also meant what she said: their window was closing.

There were several reasons for the urgency. In the past month, Aeromach's stock price had continued to rise. It was approaching the point at which Kath estimated the enthusiasm would max out, which meant that Komarovsky would commence his approach. If they wanted to stop the squeeze, they had to get going. A second reason was the potentially eroding strength of Komarovsky's conscience. Whatever sense of moral obligation the oligarch once felt—whatever spark of courage Vogel had summoned—with the Aeromach squeeze well underway, it was obviously fading.

And a third reason. How much longer could she keep this up? Not the running of the operation. That was hard, but a familiar kind of hard; the kind of hard she had trained for. What was unfamiliar, what was borderline unbearable, was the play she suddenly found herself trapped in. The only other person who knew about the Charlie situation was Jenny Navarro, and Amanda couldn't exactly call Jenny up for a little heart-to-heart. Eventually she would have to talk to someone about this tangled knot of loyalty, if only to preserve her own sanity.

Focus, though. One step at a time. Komarovsky came first. In addition to his routine, she had memorized his biography. He was an oligarch in the classic sense. After the USSR collapsed, and the Russian government came up with a privatization scheme to speed the country into capitalism, he and his ilk took the chance to seize control of entire industries for pennies on the dollar. It didn't matter that he was a mathematician by training, that he lacked any experience as a businessman. Ivan Komarovsky was smart, scrappy, and driven. In the early 1990s, he acquired a shipping business that was worth over $20 billion for the cost of $3 million in privatization vouchers.

That was his first fortune. Then he sold the shipping business, moved to London, and with the proceeds of the sale started a hedge fund. He staffed the fund exclusively with fellow mathematicians, and the result was his second fortune. Pavel Partners had offices in London, New York, and Hong Kong and, notably, not in Moscow. His money, too, was kept outside the country. Komarovsky had once said, in an interview with the *Financial Times*, that he didn't invest in Russia (though there were *numerous* attractive opportunities, he added patriotically) because he didn't want sentiment to cloud his judgment. "Though I live in London, Russia is forever my home," he declared. "But my love for my motherland, my *rodina*, means that I cannot see her clearly. She is the favorite child whom I can never deny. And so, if there is a profitable opportunity in Russia? Alas, I must resist, because I will not think rationally, I will lose my head, and I will fall short of my obligations to our investors."

To the wider world, Ivan Komarovsky had little to do with Russia, let alone the Russian government. Though he kept a mansion in Rublyovka, the well-heeled suburb of Moscow, and a dacha on the Black Sea, not far from Gruzdev's secretive mega-palace, it was more a gesture than anything else. He was a British citizen. He was respected in global financial circles. He gave generously to cancer research institutes in the UK and America. He was publicly critical of the Kremlin. Ivan Komarovsky moved among the Western elite as though he was one of them, because, in many ways, he *was* one of them.

Kath later claimed that she'd always had her doubts. She'd heard rumors that Komarovsky had attended Gruzdev's seventieth birthday party and had delivered the most obsequious toast of the night, which, when you considered the other attendees, was saying something. The oligarch had two faces: the clear-eyed capitalist versus the patriotic loyalist. A central question plagued this operation. Which part was real, and which part the act?

The plane juddered and rattled as it made contact with the runway. With thickly accented English, the flight attendant said: "It was a pleasure to have you aboard. Welcome to St. Petersburg."

PART III

CONSPIRACIES INSIDE CONSPIRACIES

CHAPTER EIGHT

"Is everything okay?" Grace asked. "You seem distracted."

Charlie, who had been glancing over his shoulder to see whether that was in fact his agency colleague at a nearby table (it wasn't), startled at the question. For sweet, shy, soft-spoken Grace to have gotten up the nerve to ask this question meant that he was doing a truly terrible job of concealing his anxiety.

"Oh, fine," he said heartily. "Just thought I recognized someone. Anyway! What did you think of that last movement?"

On this Saturday evening in October, after a performance of the National Symphony Orchestra at the Kennedy Center, they were having a late dinner at an Italian restaurant on Pennsylvania Avenue. Unfortunately, the finer qualities of both the music and the meal were lost on Charlie. He *was* distracted. Sometimes the anxiety was manageable, and sometimes it was impossible, and tonight was one of the impossible nights. Earlier that day, Amanda had texted to say she wouldn't be able to keep their phone date because she was getting on a plane the next day. In normal times he would think nothing of this. But now, that tiny seed gave rise to a terrifying bloom of questions. *A plane to where? For what? What is she working on?*

And this whole complicated mess, this insane and unconsidered plan, it was a problem entirely of his own making! Truly, he was the stupidest man who had ever lived.

His half of dessert remained untouched, which, given his sweet tooth, was a sign of just how bad things were. Grace took a bite of tiramisu, unperturbed. It seemed like she might have believed

Charlie's earlier denial. She had a remarkable capacity for trust. Obsession wasn't her style, nor was conflict. It was what made her so wonderful to be with, so deserving of her name.

Watching this lovely woman take another bite of dessert, Charlie had a painful vision of the months to come. Amanda's work would keep torturing Charlie. Charlie would keep lying to Grace. Grace would keep tolerating his evasions. That last part was the kicker. It wasn't fair to Grace. She hadn't signed up for this mess.

After the waiter cleared the half-eaten tiramisu, Charlie said: "You were right, before. I *am* distracted. It's been a strange time at work."

"Strange in what way?"

"I can't really . . . I can't explain. But there's something, it's sort of complicated, it's going to be taking up quite a lot of my time."

"Oh," she said. "Okay."

"A *lot* of my time. I won't have much of a life beyond the office."

"Oh," she repeated. "How long do you think it will last?"

"That's the thing. It could be a while." Charlie looked down at the tablecloth, unable to meet her gaze. "A long while."

After several beats of silence, Grace said: "You'll be too busy, then."

He nodded at the tablecloth, his cheeks on fire.

"Well," she said slowly. "Okay. I see."

He finally looked up. "I'm so sorry, Grace. I'm really sorry."

They said goodbye outside the restaurant. As he watched Grace walk away, her ash-blond bob, her sensible low heels, her navy blue dress, he found his eyes filling with tears. He really liked her. He maybe even (a word he hadn't let himself use since Helen) loved her. Her presence in his life had been a reprieve, but she was too good for him. This, he knew, was the restoration of the natural order.

· · ·

A Sunday in Helsinki. November 1985, about a year after that holiday party at the embassy. A supermarket in the Ullanlinna neighborhood, a few blocks away from Charlie and Helen's apartment. It began as these things always begin. The simplest contact: one hand brushing against another.

"Oh dear," she said, stepping back. "I'm so sorry. Please. You take them."

One bunch of bananas remained on the shelf. They had both reached for it at the same time. "Of course not." Charlie stepped back, too. "They're all yours."

The woman smiled. The symmetry of her oval face was marred only by a small scar on her chin. This tiny irregularity brought her prettiness into focus. "I couldn't possibly. You might starve to death."

He smiled, too. "How do you figure that?"

"Perhaps you were only here for the bananas." She nodded at his empty cart. "If I deprive you of these, what else will you eat?"

"Your accent. You're British?"

"And you're American, I take it."

"Always nice to meet another expat." He extended his hand. "I'm Charlie."

She blushed. "I'm Mary." She was even prettier when she blushed.

He encountered her again the following week. Same time, same place. This time, she was perusing the citrus. "How were those bananas?" he said.

"Oh! Not very good. I'm afraid, Charlie, that my guilt kept me from enjoying them."

"You poor Brits. That's the difference between us. We Americans don't get hung up on these things. To the victor the spoils, right?"

It happened again the following week, and the week after that. "We have to stop meeting like this," Charlie laughed. Apparently he and Mary were on the same schedule. Sunday evenings were his time to grocery shop, when Helen gave him the list of what she needed for the week ahead. It was one of his rare domestic contributions. He liked the feeling of returning to the apartment, arms laden with groceries for his wife and child. It was a small but concrete sense of accomplishment on the home front.

Where, unfortunately, it wasn't going well. Things were improving at work, but there appeared to be a directly inverse relationship between the health of his career and the health of his marriage. Jack, the new station chief, liked him. Then again, Jack liked everyone, so how much did it really count for? Charlie's attack of insecurity had subsided, but it hadn't quite disappeared. Now it was like he was on a perpetual treadmill, every breakthrough yielding more questions to answer, every achievement creating the need for the next achievement. After work took its share, little remained by the end of the day. When he got home late and slipped into bed, Helen was obviously awake—she was a light sleeper—and yet she never murmured a hello, never asked where he had been. Whenever Charlie apologized for how busy things were, she shook her head and said: "That's not the issue."

"It's not?" He blinked. "Then what *is* the issue?"

Charlie was still dazzled by the fact of being married to Helen. Her gifts, quietly alluring when she was twenty, now shone strong and bright as the sun. She was beautiful and smart and opinionated; she was good with strangers; she was a fantastic cook; she was an even better mother. But as the years went on, she didn't seem to *need* much from him. She was self-sufficient, almost to a fault. Charlie would have liked more tasks like the Sunday evening grocery shopping, but when he asked for these assignments, she always said, with a slight edge of aggrievement: "It's fine, Charlie. I know how busy you are."

So Charlie began to look forward to Sunday evenings for reasons that had nothing to do with husbandly hunting-and-gathering.

After a few months, he and Mary had reached an unspoken agreement. They lingered in the produce section, waiting for the other person. From there they would wend slowly through the aisles, stopping along the way, stretching the shopping to an hour or longer. Talking to her was easy. They clicked. He told himself he wasn't doing anything wrong. She was new to Helsinki; she needed a friend. Charlie was just being a nice guy. It was just a little friendly conversation in the dairy aisle.

Mary admitted to being lonely in this new city. Not all the time. It was okay when she was at work, when she was distracted, but when she was alone in her attic apartment, she felt invisible. *No one in this city knows who I am.* Standing by the bakery case, blinking back tears. *If I died in my sleep, no one would even notice.* Her upper lip trembling with emotion. It was just a little sympathy. Just a little honesty between a man and a woman. *I'm so glad I met you. I can actually* talk *to you, Charlie.* But it wasn't like he was taking her to bed.

Until, in February 1986, he took her to bed.

It just . . . happened. There was no external catalyst. No argument with Helen, no screaming baby, no overpowering surge of lust. Mary had mentioned where she lived. On the evening in question, on his way back from a meeting with a source, Charlie was walking near the harbor. He looked up and realized he was outside her building. She had described her attic apartment so vividly, the gabled windows and slanted ceilings, the hot plate, the futon, the clawfoot tub. Impulsively, he pressed the buzzer. Upstairs, when she opened the door, she broke into a radiant smile. (The purity of it! The unabashed joy, the total lack of disharmony!) He felt his heart skip. "I'm so happy to see you," she said.

They had sex on the futon, the kind of fast, hard, clothes-ripping sex he hadn't had in years. After, Mary started crying. "I didn't mean it," she said. Her lip trembling, her body fetal-curled in guilt. "You have a wife. You have a child. I'm so sorry. I didn't want this to happen." And Charlie held her, stroking her hair, murmuring that it was okay; it was only this one time. "We made a mistake," he said. "People make mistakes."

He saw her again the next week at the supermarket. At first it was a little tentative, a little awkward, but then it wasn't. They walked the aisles, they talked and laughed. Their old routine and nothing more. Time went by, and the pleasing glow of virtue returned. Charlie was proving something to himself. No more sex. No more mistakes. Obviously he had screwed up. The memory of that episode would forever fill him with guilt. But it really *was* just that one time. He had escaped this thing by the skin of his teeth.

· · ·

And then, a couple of months later, in April, he had a hard day. For the past ten months, Charlie had been cultivating a visiting physics professor at the University of Helsinki, a highly regarded Soviet scientist. The professor was loath to return to the Soviet Union at the end of the term, which was where Charlie came in. The defection would be a career-making prize. But that April day, the professor told Charlie that he had changed his mind. He couldn't do it, after all. His wife and children were homesick. For the sake of his family, they were going back to Russia.

Ten months of work for nothing. Charlie felt like shit. He was a shitty officer. Then he would go home and Helen would look at him and he would remember he was a shitty husband and a shitty father, too. Why couldn't anything be *easy*? He was walking home, but the thought of home was suddenly unbearable. So he turned around. He pointed himself toward the harbor, toward the consolations he knew would greet him in that attic apartment. As he pressed Mary's buzzer, he was no longer kidding himself. He knew that a second time would mean a third time, and a fourth and a fifth. But he told himself he needed this. Whatever resolve he once possessed was gone.

• • •

Mary had moved to Finland for work. She was a secretary at a British telecom firm in London. When there was an opening in their Helsinki office, she had put in for a transfer. It was her first time abroad. She showed Charlie her passport, blank but for the single stamp admitting her to Finland. "Someday I'd like to travel," she mused, flipping through the empty pages. "See the world. Like you, Charlie. You've been everywhere."

Even more than the sex, this was the best part of being with Mary. The glamour of his career had long since worn off. The cinematic moments, the dead drops and brush passes, paled in comparison to the endless demands of bureaucracy. The cables, the contact reports, the memos from their cousins in MI6. At the CIA, everything had to be recorded on paper. Charlie spent most of his time typing. It wasn't helped by the fact that he was a lousy typist, hunting and pecking his way through those interminable reports. He had been doing this job for over a decade now, but at the end of the day, he was basically a glorified paper pusher.

But Mary saw him in a different light. Even if he was, to her, just an ordinary diplomat named Charlie Franklin, that cover story was enough to dazzle her. Charlie shared the sanitized version of his stories, descriptions of life in Algeria and Switzerland and Germany, the parties he'd been to, the powerful people he'd wined and dined. After they had sex, she rested her head on his chest and said: "Tell me more about that funny man in Algiers." In her eyes, he was finally the kind of person he had always wanted to be: brave, and interesting, and admired.

One night in the attic apartment, while Mary was making toast and boiling an egg for a postcoital supper, she said: "You know, darling, how my boss is determined to set me up? She knows this man at the British embassy, and she told me the most *interesting* thing. Apparently he actually works as a spy. I'm not supposed to tell anyone. She showed me his picture. Not terribly attractive, but I'm tempted to say yes, just for the thrill of it. Can you imagine? To say that I've been on a date with a spy?"

A wiser man would have seen this for what it was. But as Charlie lay there, watching Mary tap a spoon against the egg, he thought with annoyance: *But I'm meant to be the most interesting person in her life.* So this other guy had upped the ante? He would respond in kind.

It started small. Telling her his stories, he let slip the sort of minor details that caused her eyebrow to arch with curiosity. Then he would pause, almost as if he regretted it.

"What?" she would urge. "Darling, *what*? Tell me!" It was a delicious high, this seizure of her interest. He feigned a kind of noble reluctance, a fig leaf of propriety, making *her* ask the questions, making her work for it. But the high was addictive, too. Once he started, he found he couldn't stop. It was stupid, obviously. But, then again, who was Mary going to tell?

CHAPTER NINE

Amanda Clarkson, the economic attaché, was in St. Petersburg to attend a conference on multilateral trade. During her time at the State Department, Ms. Clarkson had coauthored several white papers on agricultural tariffs. It was the top result when you googled her name.

Amanda Clarkson would surely have found the conference fascinating. Amanda Cole was bored out of her mind. But she went through the motions—nodding along to the keynote talk, raising her hand to ask a question, conference badge on a lanyard around her neck—for the benefit of the FSB agents stationed throughout the Four Seasons. Though the FSB was entirely separate from the GRU, where Semonov worked (as she'd learned in her training, the GRU dated back to the Russian Revolution, whereas the FSB had emerged from the post-Soviet wreckage of the KGB), that didn't make the agents any less dangerous.

The hotel was a grand old palace that had once housed the Ministry of War. Her room had a view of St. Isaac's Cathedral. That first night, as she settled into the deep soaking tub, her limbs buoyant in the warm water, she remembered her first trip to Russia, back in 2004. Funny to think how her relationship with this country, this backbone of her career, this pillar of her identity, had begun with such a lark.

It was easy, as a solo twentysomething traveling the world, to make friends. Those years were one long experience of letting herself get caught up in the slipstream of other people's plans. When she befriended a group of sunburned Australian backpackers in a dollar-a-night hostel in Berlin, and they said they were headed to Finland to see the northern lights, she thought: Why not? And when they decided to continue onward to Russia: What else did she have to do? She still had some of the money from her stint teaching yoga in Morocco, enough to keep her going for at least a few months.

Closing her eyes in the bathtub, the memories of that trip felt as immediate as the warm water on her skin. From the very first moment, Russia had been different. When the plane had landed in St. Petersburg, the border officers pulled her aside and grilled her for hours, certain that this American woman was lying to them about the true nature of her travels. Later, after they released her, she reunited with the Aussies at a divey spot on Nevsky Prospekt. Together they laughed at her misadventure, and there was reassurance in that laughter, in the pierogis with dill and sour cream, in the cold glasses of vodka. And yet she woke up the next morning with a residue of caution. An awakened sense of alertness. A week later, her antipodean friends decided to heed their homing instinct and head south for the winter. But she decided to stay on, to see more of what this place had to offer. Why not?

The overnight train to Moscow, third class. The flyer in the coffee shop, ENGLISH TUTOR NEEDED. The money was enough to pay for the room she rented from the Belarussian widow. In the apartment next door to the widow lived a young man named Jakob. He, like the border officers, was puzzled by Amanda's decision. Frowning, he said: "You are brave to travel alone. Brave and stupid." But she stayed, and she stayed. There were October snowfalls. Poetry readings in clandestine bars. Jakob and his friends adopted her, lent her warmer clothing for the winter, called her their stray American puppy. On New Year's Eve there was a party, fireworks over the Moskva, Jakob kissing his boyfriend Ilia at midnight, a rare semi-public display of their verboten affection. She remembered looking around that party, the sleeves of the borrowed wool sweater dangling long over her hands, and feeling so peaceful. This place, strangely, was beginning to feel like a home. She wondered if she might find herself ringing in the next year, and the next, and the next, here in Moscow.

She shook her head. The splashing sounds echoed against the bathroom tile. She concentrated on the warmth of the water, the floral scent of the soap. It always happened like this. Crossing the border into Russia was a trip wire, reactivating the most potent parts of her memory. She had to actively remind herself that nineteen years had passed since then. Now wasn't the time to lose herself in the past. Things in the present demanded her focus.

The next morning, when she came downstairs for breakfast, Ambassador Romanoff was already waiting for her, seated at a table in the back corner of the glass-ceilinged Tea Lounge. "Am I late?" Amanda asked, glancing at her watch.

"Alas, no. I got a wake-up call at four thirty a.m., though I'm certain I asked for the call at six thirty. I couldn't get back to sleep. So I gave up." Romanoff gestured at the silver French press. "Already on my second pot."

"It's smart. You have to admit. Earlier wake-up calls mean they sell more coffee."

"You always did have an active imagination," he said, smiling. "So. Ms. Clarkson. How are you finding the conference?"

"Interesting, so far. I'm especially looking forward to today's agenda."

"Ah, yes. I'm sure you are."

When the waitress came to take their order, she was predictably hostile. Abe Romanoff, the American ambassador to Russia, possessed several qualities that served him well in this job. He was fluent in the language; he had a lifetime of diplomatic experience; he had a long record of integrity. But most useful was his high tolerance for pain. Men followed the ambassador everywhere he went. The harassment ranged from scary to absurd. They broke into his house, slashed the tires on his car, planted slanderous stories in the media, requested unwanted wake-up calls, ordered waitresses to treat him badly. But this, Romanoff knew, was simply the price of doing business.

They gossiped their way through breakfast. Romanoff had been at the State Department for almost forty years, and he knew where the skeletons were buried. He had the diplomat's gift for remembering those intricate webs of human connection, the rivalries and affections and relationships. As the waitress cleared their plates, he said: "I've been meaning to ask. How's your father doing?"

"He's still driving," Amanda said. She had made her father's fictional counterpart into a long-haul trucker, because, well, because she had to pick *something*. ("A trucker, huh?" he'd said, when he got wind of her legend. Strangely, he seemed delighted. "I might actually like that. As long as I could bring Lucy.")

"Must take a lot of stamina," Romanoff said. "Is he ever going to retire?"

"The end of this year, apparently." She paused. "I think he's dreading it."

"He's worried he won't know what to do with himself."

"Something like that."

"Well." Romanoff reached across the table, patted her hand. "He'll figure it out."

The gesture looked genuine. With his bushy beard and kind eyes, Romanoff was just the type to offer such avuncular reassurance. And he meant it, probably, but even as he did, a slip of paper passed from his fingers to hers. When he stood up, Amanda moved her hands into her lap.

"Thank you for breakfast," she said. "It's always nice to catch up."

"Good luck today," he said pleasantly.

· · ·

Partway through the panel, Amanda stood up and squeezed past her neighbors. "Bathroom," she whispered apologetically. "Sorry. Pardon me."

A woman was at the sink, washing her hands. Amanda went into a stall and waited for her to finish. After she heard the door open and close, she stepped out. Just as the note had indicated, the backpack was waiting behind the potted palm in the corner. Several minutes later, Amanda emerged from the bathroom wearing glasses, curly brown hair, jeans, sneakers, and a windbreaker, bearing no resemblance to the suit-wearing diplomat who'd entered.

The backpack also held a glossy brochure and a ticket for the 10 a.m. hydrofoil to Peterhof. She had thirty-two minutes to make the short walk from the hotel to the ferry embankment on the Neva River. She took the side exit from the hotel, toward the golden dome of St. Isaac's. She turned left and then left again. Her leisure was purposeful: stopping at a coffee shop to order a pastry, circling the block, meandering through the park that faced the hotel, snapping pictures of the sculpture of Nikolai Gogol. She arrived at the embankment a few minutes before the hydrofoil left, certain that she hadn't been followed.

Though it was a gray and gloomy day, the boat was nearly full. The last passenger to board was a man in a brown leather jacket. The engine roared at a deafening pitch as the boat accelerated into the open water of the Baltic Sea. The cabin was damp and chilly. From her seat in the back, Amanda pretended to examine her brochure for Peterhof, the lavishly restored summer estate of the tsars, but her gaze kept flicking up, toward the man in the leather jacket. If she arrived at Peterhof and suspected she'd been followed, she would take the red scarf from her backpack and wrap it around her neck. That would be her signal to Semonov that she had been spotted, and the meeting was off.

She stared at the man. This was nothing like their meetings in Rome. Here in Russia, if things went wrong, they would go seriously wrong. When was the last time she had actually felt the trailing breath of danger? Life in Rome was too safe. Danger kept you sharp. It occurred to her, belatedly, that this might be yet another reason she wanted to take this trip, her desire to skirt that edge. Maybe her ego was clouding her judgment. (In her head, she could hear Kath laughing. *No shit, Sherlock.*)

After about forty-five minutes, the roar of the engine subsided. In the quiet, the waves sloshed against the hull. The passengers shuffled down the gangplank, onto the pier, in single file. Amanda, sitting in the back, was the last to disembark. It had started raining. The wind, stronger here than in the city, blew the rain sideways. She shoved her hands into the pockets of her windbreaker and walked slowly down the pier. The man in the brown leather jacket was moving toward the entrance to the park, without so much as a backward glance. By the time she made her way through the ticket queue, he was far ahead, disappearing into the crowds.

She exhaled. Thirty minutes until she was due at the Pyramid Fountain. Now it was up to Semonov. If all was well, he would walk past the fountain bareheaded. But if he had detected surveillance, he would be wearing an orange knit hat. And then Semonov would return to Moscow, and Amanda would return to Rome, and that would be that, all their careful preparations for naught.

She arrived at the Pyramid Fountain a few minutes early, scanning back and forth. It wouldn't be difficult to spot him amid the crowds of tourists. Semonov was tall, and he would be alone, and God willing, he would be bareheaded despite the foul weather.

Right on time, he appeared. No hat. Another exhale. Amanda waited for him to notice her. He glanced around, clutching a rain-soaked brochure, visibly nervous. Finally he spotted her, across the fountain. She held his gaze for two seconds, three seconds, four seconds. Longer than was necessary, strictly speaking, but she wanted to communicate that it was okay. They were safe. Everything would be all right. He needed that reassurance, and honestly, so did she.

Amanda walked east, away from the central axis of the palace. As she traveled deeper into the sprawling grounds, the crowds of tourists thinned. Jakob, her friend from Moscow, had once told her the story. The estate was the lavish result of Peter the Great's jealousy. The tsar had visited Versailles in the early 1700s, and when he returned from his French sojourn, he scrapped the existing plans for his summer retreat outside St. Petersburg. He would build something even bigger, even better than Versailles. Peterhof was a good metaphor for the country writ large. Just like Russia herself, it was warped by its size. The park was far too big to see in a single visit, so the tourists stuck to the heart of it, to the palace and the fountains and the formal gardens. The rest of the park—which was to say most of it—was virtually empty.

But Amanda always thought the edges were the most beautiful part. The dirt roads, the old trees, the out-of-time solitude. When she reached the easternmost edge, she stopped in front of a glass booth. The guard inside was snoozing in his chair. A wall separated Peterhof from the adjacent Alexandria Park, and a separate ticket was required to enter. She rapped on the glass and handed over three hundred rubles. In this gloomy weather, she and Semonov might be the only visitors the guard saw all day. She didn't love this—she would have preferred the concealment that came with a crowd—but they were making do with what they had.

Alexandria Park was opposite in spirit to the manicured gardens and golden fountains. Tsar Nicholas I created it a century after Peter the Great's death, wanting his own summer retreat, an untamed rural idyll to escape the public eye. The Romanovs had built a private chapel on the land. The Communists had let the chapel decay, but it had been restored in the last few decades, and was now gleaming white, a bright jewel nestled in the dark forest.

The chapel was enclosed by a fence. Amanda stood outside the locked gate. Another security guard appeared from around the corner. "The chapel is closed today," he said.

"That's too bad," Amanda said. "My mother told me not to miss it."

"The organ is undergoing repairs," he replied.

"Hopefully it will be fixed in time for her birthday," she said.

The guard looked at her warily. Then he took a key from his pocket and unlocked the gate. As she followed him into the chapel, she muttered: "Thank you."

The guard was the brother of a bellhop at the Metropol in Moscow. When they were scrambling for a secure location for their meeting in St. Petersburg, Amanda remembered the bellhop's brother, and decided to call in the favor. With his sullen expression, he clearly didn't like what he was being asked to do. Though the guard didn't know their names, or the reason for the meeting, his involvement still came with a risk—but, she reminded herself, *everything* came with a risk.

Semonov was waiting by the altar. Amanda touched his arm. "Everything okay?"

"I think so," he said.

The guard could only guarantee them thirty minutes of privacy. They had to get right to it. "Those two men from Unit 29155," she began. "Do you see them often?"

"Not often," Semonov said. "But from time to time, yes."

"They work in a different building? They don't mix with the rest of the GRU?"

He nodded. "I'm not even meant to know who they are. But they seem to like me. Or, I should say, they are *amused* by me."

"What do you mean?"

"They like to tease me, to pass the time. They get bored, they come see me."

"And what kinds of things do they talk to you about?"

"Ah. Well." He looked away, cheeks reddening. "That's the thing."

"Something happened," she said. "It's okay. You can tell me."

He shook his head at the floor. "Just teasing. That's all."

"Kostya," she said. "It's best if you tell me *exactly* what happened."

· · ·

It happened back in the summer, not long after he returned from Rome, and the goons from Unit 29155 returned from Cairo. The two men appeared in his doorway. "Semonov," Tweedledee said. "I have a question for you. Where did I get this sunburn?"

Semonov frowned. Was it a trick question? "You were in Egypt."

"Wrong. You don't know where I was. You have *no idea*. Do you understand what I am saying?"

Semonov blinked once, twice. Then he understood what Tweedledee was saying. Belatedly, the men had recognized how stupid it was to brag about killing Vogel. If their superiors found out, they would be furious, or worse. But Semonov was also, unfortunately, a stickler for detail, and there was a flaw in the reasoning. "Yeeees," he said slowly. "But you see, I have the memo right here. Look. Papers needed for two men arriving in Cairo on July twenty-first. I don't know *why* you were in Cairo." He arched a meaningful eyebrow. "But it would be illogical for me to say I didn't know you were even *going* to Cairo."

Tweedledee stepped forward and planted his fists on Semonov's desk. "You are a very stupid man," he said. He noticed the framed photograph on the shelf. "This is your wife, yes? Why did this woman marry such a stupid man?"

Tweedledum sneered, "She must be a stupid woman."

His wife! It was one thing to insult him, quite another to insult Chiara. His heart thumping, he spun around, snatched the picture from the shelf, covered it with his hand. "Please leave my office," he said tightly.

"Ha!" Tweedledee barked. "You wouldn't want her to see you like this, would you? Cowering like a dog? Then get this into your thick head. You don't know who we are. You don't even know that we exist. Understand us *now*, you idiot? Or do we need to pay you and your wife a visit in that pathetic apartment in Tagansky that you call home?"

Even months later, in the cool quiet of the chapel, Semonov blushed in the retelling. The memory of humiliation was just as bad as the humiliation itself. "After that, I thought I would never see them again," he said. "But every so often, they appear in my office."

"As a threat?" Amanda asked. "They want to make sure you're being obedient?"

Semonov shook his head. "I doubt they consider me capable of disobedience. To them I am like an animal, easily trained. Whip a dog once, he learns his lesson. No, no. It's as I said before. They get bored, they like the distraction. And also, I should say, these men are very insecure."

She cocked her head.

"You can see it in the way they talk," he explained. "How they act, how they behave. They kill for a living, but they are insecure. They like to spend time with sad little Semonov to make themselves feel more powerful."

"Huh," she said, the gears starting to turn.

"But as harmless as sad little Semonov might be, they *do* realize how foolish they were. Sometimes they brag, but never about specifics. I'm certain they'll never mention anything like Vogel again. I don't expect for—what is the phrase? For lightning to strike twice."

True enough, she thought. Unless you attached a tall metal rod to the roof of your house.

The wind was picking up, spattering rain against the windows. The guard outside would be checking his watch. Amanda drew a deep breath. This was reckless, she knew. But they needed results. "Kostya," she said. "We found out why they killed Senator Vogel. Would you like to know the reason?"

He raised his eyebrows. "Would I like . . . ?"

"After the risks you've taken for us," she barreled forward, "I think you deserve the truth. Senator Vogel was in the middle of uncovering a corrupt scheme being carried out by the Russian government. That's why the GRU killed him. Because he was going to expose this awful, illegal, *dangerous* corruption. And we also found out how Vogel discovered the scheme. He was working with a man named Ivan Komarovsky. Do you know who Ivan Komarovsky is?"

"The businessman?" he said. "The one who owns the football team?"

"That's right. Komarovsky was ordered by Gruzdev to carry out this scheme. At first he went along with it. You understand what it's like. You are told to do something, and you must do it. But eventually Komarovsky became so disgusted, so *appalled*, that he decided to speak out. His conscience couldn't stand it. So he was working with Vogel to expose the truth."

His eyes widened.

"Now, as for the scheme itself. I *want* to tell you about it, but it's risky. You only need to look at Senator Vogel to see that. The less you know, the better off you'll be. Unless—"

"No!" Semonov interrupted. "No! You don't need to tell me."

"You're sure?"

"It's fine! I believe you!"

"Well, if you change your mind . . ."

He shook his head vehemently. "I won't."

"Good. Okay. So, Kostya. Here's what I need from you. We need to talk to Komarovsky. But before we do, we need to know what they said to him in Iceland."

Semonov gave her a blank look.

"You remember Iceland. Back in August, you were asked to make those papers? Those two men from Unit 29155 were there to see Komarovsky. To deliver a message."

"Oh," he said.

"And we need to know what that message was."

"But I can't . . ." Semonov started sliding the zipper on his jacket up and down, trying to calm the trembling in his hand. "But they'll know. They'll know!"

"Of course they won't," she said soothingly. "Kostya, listen to me. These men are idiots. You're a thousand times smarter than them. You'll make it seem like the most natural thing in the world. They'll have no idea what you're doing. They might act like thugs, but listen to me. They're not in charge. *You're* in charge."

The zipper slid up and down, up and down.

"I promise you," she said. "I wouldn't ask if it weren't important."

·   ·   ·

She made it back to the hotel in time for the last event of the day. After stopping in the bathroom to change back into her suit, she found a seat in the back, just as the speaker began expounding on the fascinating subject of (she checked the program) "International Cooperation on Intellectual Property Law." She spent the rest of the evening in a daze of relief. Had Semonov resisted, she would have had to resort to coercion, which was much more unpleasant. But Semonov, in the end, had acceded to her request with a stoic nod. *Thank God*, she thought. *He's one of the good ones.*

The next morning, as she was checking out, Amanda asked if she could leave her bags at the hotel for a few hours. Her flight back to Rome wasn't until the afternoon. Outside she began walking toward the Winter Palace, merging with a stream of tourists. That morning was clear but cold for October, the brilliant blue sky highlighting the fading reds and oranges of autumn. She jammed her hands in her pockets, having failed to pack gloves.

The Palace Square was packed with visitors, mostly Chinese tour groups. Not many Americans chose to travel to Russia these days. They pictured the country as a dark, forbidding, unhospitable place. But here in St. Petersburg, on this bright blue morning, the picture looked different. The Winter Palace gleamed in the sunshine. The ticket queue stretched across the plaza. Plenty of well-to-do travelers were happy to spend their money in Russia, to buy museum tickets and restaurant meals and hotel rooms; they just weren't American. Tourism was a big business, a lifeblood. How strange to realize that America was utterly irrelevant to this lifeblood.

Inside the Winter Palace, she climbed the staircase and wove through the crowds, eventually reaching the Rembrandt Room on the second floor. Ambassador Romanoff waited in front of a gilt-framed painting, hands clasped behind his back. Amanda stopped beside him. "So what's the big deal with this Rembrandt guy?" she murmured.

He turned to her, eyes twinkling. "You're in a good mood."

"I'm not even being sarcastic. I don't know anything about art."

"This one is called *Sacrifice of Isaac*. Do you know the story?"

She shook her head.

"So," he said. "Abraham had a son named Isaac, whom he loved very much. God told Abraham to sacrifice his son. Abraham brought Isaac to the top of a mountain. He had the knife in his hand, he was about to plunge it into Isaac, and then—as you can see—an angel appeared to stop Abraham. He had passed the test, the angel declared. His son could live. Abraham didn't have to actually *do* the unthinkable. He only had to show God that he was *willing* to do it."

"Wow." Amanda tilted her head. "Still, if I were Isaac, I'd be pissed."

"That's one interpretation of the story," Romanoff said. "But there's another. I actually like the other one better. This one says that, actually, the test was the other way around. Abraham was testing *God*. Even as he raised the knife, even as he was about to plunge it into Isaac's heart, he knew that God would put a stop to it, because the God he believed in was good and moral. The God he believed in would never permit such suffering. And when the angel intervened, Abraham's belief was proven true. Powerful, isn't it? That extreme, *extreme* form of trust."

Amanda felt her face flush. When she'd first glanced at the painting, it seemed . . . well, frankly, it seemed like every painting in the room. Which was to say, not her cup of tea. But Romanoff's story had caused her to see something in the dynamic between Isaac and Abraham, between Abraham and God. She felt uncomfortable for reasons she didn't understand. Or, rather, for reasons she preferred not to understand.

Romanoff touched her arm. "Over here," he said. "This one is very popular."

The Return of the Prodigal Son hung on a nearby wall. Several tour groups jockeyed for space in front of the painting. As Amanda and Romanoff edged closer, they were bumped and jostled by the crowd. Amid this chaos, Romanoff's minders wouldn't be able to hear what they were saying. "Did you get what you needed?" he asked quietly.

"Yes," she said. "Thank you. I know it wasn't easy to pull everything together on such short notice. I owe you one."

Romanoff dipped his head. He had been told the agency needed to arrange a crash meeting with a high-value source. That was it. The rest was strictly need-to-know. Plenty of other ambassadors would have resented this, believing that intelligence ought to be the tool of diplomacy, not the other way around. But Romanoff seemed content with the separation. Side by side, he and Amanda gazed at the painting. Sometimes she envied people like him. His way of living was cleaner. Kinder.

"So," he said. "You're heading back today?"

"I wish I could stay longer. I've missed this place."

"I'm sure you have." After a beat, he added: "You know, I always find it funny, Amanda. Where the line gets drawn."

"What line?"

"Well, if your vice is booze, or sex, or gambling, then that's it. The agency will never let you past the first interview. But they still hire junkies. It's just junkies who are addicted to other things. The action. The adrenaline. The never-ending drama."

She bristled. "You can't actually compare those things."

"I've seen just as many people ruined by that kind of addiction as by the others."

"It's not some *lark*." She was suddenly remembering how annoying Romanoff could be. "I had a good reason for coming to Russia."

He squinted at the painting, leaned a little closer. "I worry about history repeating itself," he said. "Do you know why the Cold War lasted as long as it did?"

"Because they wanted to kill us and we wanted to kill them."

He smiled, bemused by her tone. He was, at least, *aware* of how annoying he could be. "That was part of it, of course. But, also, it's because certain people were enjoying themselves too much to stop. Not *most* people. Most people aren't that cruel. But a few powerful people, on their side and on ours: They loved the game. They loved having an enemy, having a crusade. My God, you look back on those years and they seem almost baroque. Double agents. Triple agents. Mole hunts. Conspiracies inside conspiracies." He turned to her, no longer smiling. "You're a smart person, Amanda. I know you had a good reason for coming. I'm saying you ought not to get confused about what that reason is."

• • •

Amanda flew back to Rome with his words circling in her head. No, she thought. Romanoff didn't get it. Conspiracies inside conspiracies: that wasn't her. He thought she *liked* this kind of thing? He thought she was *choosing* this kind of thing?

In the last few weeks, she'd started to realize she needed to tell

Kath the truth about the situation. And this, finally, this intense desire to prove the know-it-all ambassador wrong, gave her the push
she needed. The next day, back in the station, Amanda told Kath
about the meeting with Semonov, and then she said: "And I have to
tell you something else. It's kind of . . . it's hard to explain."

"Oh, don't worry. It can't *possibly* be worse than trying to un-
tangle these stop-loss orders." Kath smiled, then noticed Amanda's
stricken look. "What? Amanda. I'm joking!"

"You're going to think I'm a terrible person."

"No such thing as a terrible person. Only terrible actions."

"It's just . . . I don't know how to . . ."

"It's okay," Kath said. "Just start at the beginning."

So Amanda's mouth began forming the words, the story of her
father meeting Jenny Navarro, of her father burning that piece of
paper, of her father asking her to lie for him. It felt surreal, and
slightly idiotic, this crossing of a bridge she couldn't uncross. But
every time she thought about scurrying back to the solitary safety
of the secret, she thought of Romanoff, that arrogant jerk. So she
kept talking. Kath remained remarkably calm, which made it easier.
Finally she said: "But he showed you the paper."

"He said he wanted it to be my decision, not his."

"Well, that's just about the most cowardly thing I've ever heard."

"Cowardly?"

"*Your* decision. Sure. Okay."

"I don't know." Amanda felt defensive. "Maybe he was trying to
be honest."

"Although I guess, in a way, it makes everything much simpler.
Look at it this way. If Charlie really wanted to keep this a secret,
whatever this is, he wouldn't have told you about it. Simple as that.
He gave you that breadcrumb because he *wants* you to find out. So
you're really just doing what he wants. Right?"

"I don't think it was like that."

"What year did you say he left the DO? The early nineties? I wonder if—"

"Kath. Please stop."

"A strange time, of course. So many loose ends. The thing is—"

"Please!" Amanda shouted. "Stop it!"

"Stop what?"

"Stop doing your voodoo Sherlock Holmes thing! This is *my* problem. Okay? And don't pretend like this is going to be some easy decision to make. The idea that he actually *wants* me to find out? Jesus! Isn't *that* a convenient way to look at it."

"I'm not saying that the desire was entirely *conscious.*"

"Just shut up! Just stop!"

Amanda dropped her head into her hands, pressed her palms into her eyes. After a minute, when the adrenaline passed, she realized she was acting like an asshole. Kath was just being Kath; she was only trying to help. Come to think of it, *Kath* was the one who ought to be upset. Hadn't Amanda just done to Kath what Charlie himself had done to her? Burdening her with this awful secret? *Hey, so I've been lying to you this whole time! And now you're stuck with it, too! Fun, right?*

But Kath touched her on the arm. "I'm sorry," she said. "It can be hard for me to switch off agency mode. I'm aware of this."

"I made a huge mistake," Amanda mumbled.

"In what way?"

"I should have told Gasko."

"Absolutely not. You did the right thing."

Amanda lifted her head, surprised at this. "It's a conflict of interest."

"It's a motivation. You just need to harness it." Kath shook her head. "I'm glad you told me. I was beginning to wonder."

"You could tell I was lying?"

"Going to Russia. Pestering me for updates every five seconds.

You've been like a woman possessed! Has anyone ever told you, Amanda, that you're an exceptionally annoying boss? Well, clearly there was a reason for this madness. I couldn't see it, but now I can. You need to get in the room with Komarovsky. He's the one who gave Vogel your father's name. He's the one who can connect those dots. So you'll stop at nothing to get there."

Despite herself, Amanda smiled. "You thought I was crazy."

"Sweetheart. You *are* crazy."

CHAPTER TEN

One evening in late October, an email landed in Charlie's inbox.

Guys, it began. *I feel like a jackass, but if I didn't send this email, Marjorie said she was going to do it for me. See below. There's a dinner next month at which I'll be making some remarks. The food will be terrible, you'll need a tux, my speech will put you to sleep. Yeah, so, don't all say yes at once.*

Steve Raines was one of Charlie's oldest friends. He was being honored by Mount Sinai with a career-capping award for distinguished service as their chief cardiac surgeon: dinner at the Plaza in New York City, black-tie dress, big-name donors. Charlie saw right through the false modesty of the email. Raines was proud, rightfully so. For this reason, despite his lack of appetite for tuxedos and a chicken-or-steak banquet, Charlie knew he had to say yes.

On that November day, driving up I-95, he tried to remember the last time he was in New York. Last year? The year before that? When Amanda was little, he did this drive all the time. Friday evenings on the sidewalk outside Helen's apartment, their daughter running toward Charlie with an enormous grin, her backpack flapping against her shoulders. And then, on Sunday afternoons, the reverse, Amanda running back to her mother's arms. At the time, those handoffs had been acutely painful reminders of what he no longer had. But the years had softened the memories, and now they filled him with nostalgia.

When Amanda grew up, he and Helen had less reason to

interact. They spoke on the phone once in a while, but that was it. Driving through the Lincoln Tunnel, he was struck with a sudden desire to see her. Probably she was too busy. Probably she would make up an excuse, even if she wasn't. But what did he have to lose? After he checked into his hotel in Midtown, and hung his tuxedo in the bathroom, running the shower to help loosen the wrinkles, he dialed her number. She picked up on the second ring.

"Are you kidding?" she said. "Of *course* I want to see you, Charlie. How's tomorrow afternoon? You can come over for coffee."

And so there he was, knocking on her door, holding a bouquet of dahlias. When Helen opened the door, he thought: *She's exactly the same.* Her green eyes, her crooked smile, her unchanged Helenness. She was as beautiful as ever, and yet the beauty registered in a different way. It used to make him feel possessive. Now he merely thought: *How strange that I shared a life with this woman, once upon a time.*

"Want the tour?" she said, ushering him inside. The apartment was bright and airy, with high ceilings and built-in bookshelves. Helen and Sidney were students when they got married—she at Hunter's School of Education, he at Columbia Business School— but those shoestring days were a distant memory. Sidney did some kind of work in finance (Charlie was never sure exactly what), and Helen, after many years as a public school teacher, was now the head of an education nonprofit. Charlie took it all in. "This is nice," he said. "I mean it. A lot of places around here are kind of . . ."

"Stuffy? Chintzy? Toile curtains and mallard ducks?"

He smiled. "You always did hate my mother's taste."

"It's all relative." She gestured at the Eames chair in the corner. "Like that chair. I love it. Some would call it hideous. And they wouldn't be wrong! It took me a while to learn that lesson. Let's go to the kitchen. I'll put these in water. They're lovely, Charlie. You really didn't have to."

There was coffee in the coffeepot, a plate of cookies on the table, still warm, smelling of cinnamon. Helen opened a cabinet and stood on her tiptoes, straining to reach a vase. Charlie hesitated for a moment—was it weird?—and then stepped forward. "Here," he said, plucking it from the top shelf, handing it to her.

No, it wasn't weird. None of it was weird. Helen seemed to feel the same way. "I'm really glad you called," she said. "This is nice. We should have done this a long time ago. You know, whenever I ask how you're doing, Amanda just says 'He's good.' She never goes into detail."

"If it's any consolation," he said, "she does the exact same to me."

"She still calls you at four o'clock on the dot?"

"On the dot. And you at five o'clock?"

"Isn't it kind of amazing?" Helen said. "She was such a head-in-the-clouds kid. Lost in her own little world. And look at her now. So diligent. So punctual!"

"I guess she knows that, by now, we'd worry if she didn't call." He shook his head, recognizing his mistake. "I shouldn't say 'we.' I'm just speaking for myself."

"No, you're not. I agree entirely." She smiled. "She's a good girl, Charlie."

"She's the best."

Helen lifted the coffeepot. He nodded in response, and she re-filled his cup. "You saw her over the summer? When she was back?"

"Briefly. We had dinner. I think it was just before she came up to see you."

"Right." A wrinkle appeared between her eyebrows. "About that."

Charlie had just picked up another cookie, but now he set it back down. "Did something happen?"

"I was debating whether to say anything. When I saw her in July, it seemed like she was under a lot of pressure. Stressed. More than usual. And then she was . . ." She paused, squinting at him. "She was asking me some questions. About Helsinki."

The Afghan, man of the world that he was, was unsurprised by Charlie's appearance. They began to review the particulars; the first order of business was establishing how they would next get in touch. An hour later, promises made, the Afghan was driving back to his hotel in Helsinki. Watching his taillights disappear into the dark forest, Charlie sighed with relief. It was the rare recruitment that had gone right.

Maurice turned to Charlie. "What's going on with you?"

"What? I thought that went well."

"I mean last night. What on earth was that about?"

"I don't know what you're talking about."

"That ridiculous coughing fit," Maurice said. "What was that?"

Whenever Maurice was in town visiting, Helen made a point of cooking an especially elaborate dinner. The night before, she had pulled out all the stops: beef Wellington, mashed potatoes, treacle tart. "I don't know why," she'd said. "But I just have this *thing* for England. My Irish ancestors would be so ashamed."

Maurice sipped his port, then said, "Ashamed or not, that was sublime, Helen."

"I love beef Wellington. It's not exactly au courant, is it? But it's so elegant. And yet also comforting. Good *lord*, Grandma Dennehey must be rolling in her grave."

"Maybe you need a trip to England."

"That's a good idea, actually. Why not?" Helen turned to Charlie, smiled. "Fancy a holiday, darling?"

Her mock accent wasn't very good, but it was enough to ring a bell in his guilty subconscious. Charlie thought of Mary, and he started to cough. It escalated, getting so bad that he had to excuse himself. "Sorry," he croaked, hurrying away. "Down the wrong pipe." When he returned to the table, he avoided Helen's eye. She didn't seem to make anything of it, but apparently Maurice had.

"I was just coughing," he insisted. "That was it."

"You cough when you're scared."

"It wasn't—"

"What are you doing, Charlie? You're lying about something. So I'll ask you again, and I will also ask that you show me this modicum of respect. We've always trusted each other. If we don't trust each other, what good is this?"

Lying? He wasn't lying. He didn't like that word. Months into the affair, and Charlie had become expert at the cognitive dissonance. It was the same as any other operational cover. When he was with Mary, that was just one version of himself. Anyway, he was going to end it soon. And until he did, it was kinder to keep Helen in the dark. There were barriers between Charlie's many selves. The firmest barrier was that which separated the husband of Helen from the lover of Mary. "I don't know what you're getting at," Charlie said.

Maurice stared at him. He said: "There's another woman."

"Of course there isn't," he said automatically.

Then, silence. And in the silence, Charlie felt the clarifying possibilities of confession. *There's another woman*. It was the world's most predictable error. Charlie had fucked up, but look: so had millions of other people. And their lives went on. Maybe telling the truth would be a relief. So he swallowed, and said: "I mean. Yes. There is."

"How long?" Maurice asked.

"April. Well, February. Technically."

"What's her name?"

"Mary. She's English."

"Ah," he said. "And how did you meet?"

"At the grocery store. We always did our shopping at the same time."

The expression on Maurice's face suddenly changed.

"Really?" Charlie said. "It's that shocking that I actually do the grocery shopping?"

"How much does she know about you?"

"Nothing. She thinks I'm a diplomat at the embassy."

"Bullshit."

"She's just a secretary, Maurice."

"Bullshit," he repeated. "Have the favors started yet?"

"The favors?"

"A phone number. A name. Something that seems perfectly innocuous, but enough to—"

"Come on. I know how it works."

"Apparently you don't. A pretty young woman just *happens* to run into you in the grocery store, and you aren't even skeptical?"

Charlie felt his heart thumping. "You're being paranoid."

"I'm being rational."

"But how do you—"

"Listen to me, Charlie. You have to come clean. Beg Helen for another chance. Beg the agency for another chance. That's the only way through this."

"But I haven't—"

"Eliminate any chance of blackmail. That's the only way."

Maurice was overreacting. He was definitely overreacting. Mary? A *spy*? It rewound through Charlie like a reel of film. Her ailing mother in England. The postmarks on the envelope. Brixton, London, SW9. Her addiction to PG Tips, her suitcase stuffed full of tea after her most recent trip home. Proof, all of it. The plane ticket from that same trip, LHR to HEL, sitting on her kitchen counter. Her fixation on Princess Diana, her ever-replenished supply of tabloid gossip. She was English, through and through.

Wasn't she?

His mouth opened and closed in silence. His neurons drowning in panic. His pulse racing, his skin sheened with sweat. This kind of visceral reaction wouldn't be happening if Charlie didn't know, on some level, with just as much certainty as Maurice himself, that Mary had been playing him all along.

Maurice could see what was happening. With utter calm, like a doctor issuing a prescription, he told him precisely what to do.

Write down a record of everything he and Mary had discussed. Tell Jack and take whatever punishment he issued. Tell Helen and do the same. It wouldn't be pleasant, but he would be okay. Charlie nodded. He felt twisted with shame, but if anyone was going to catch him in the lie, he was glad it was Maurice.

Because they had to stagger their departures, Charlie stayed in the safe house for a while after Maurice left. It was so obvious, now. Incredible, actually, that he hadn't figured it out on his own. At least Helen didn't have to know of his humiliating idiocy. Nor did Jack. He would tell them that he had pieced it together himself, the truth about Mary. Charlie tidied up the house, straightening the pillows on the couch, washing the dishes in the kitchen. It was as he started to turn off the lights that he thought of the switch in the closet.

The switch that controlled the microphone, hidden in the wall, which connected to the tape recorder. The agency liked to have records of conversations like the recruitment of the Afghan businessman. The switch had been turned on. Of course it had; Maurice wouldn't have forgotten. It had remained on this whole time.

He imagined Jack listening to that tape, hearing for himself the extent of Charlie's stupidity, the depths of his denial. If the misadventure with Mary didn't kill his career, *that* sure would.

But what if there was no tape? If you wanted real privacy in the safe house, you turned off the recorder. You weren't *supposed* to, but sometimes people did it. In the closet, Charlie turned off the switch. He rewound the tape, found the moment when the Afghan left, paused it. His finger hovered over the Erase button.

He would come clean. Wasn't that what mattered?

Charlie pressed Erase.

At first, driving away from the safe house, he felt relieved. Thank God he'd remembered about the microphone. The roads were icy, and the darkness was dense. Snowflakes caught in the beams of his headlights. He drove carefully. On the road ahead, a shape emerged from the forest. Charlie pressed the brake and the car eased to a stop. The animal stepped forward, into the light. It was a reindeer. They never came this far south, this close to the city, and yet there it was. The fur glazed with white snow. The antlers like curls of calligraphy. The whole thing like magic.

I wish Helen could see this, he thought.

Helen. Her green eyes flecked with gold; her wryly crooked smile. The mother of his child. How could he have done this to her? She was too good for him. He knew that; she knew that; the whole world knew that. But this would make it too stark to ignore. If he told her, she would leave him. Simple as that.

Well, of course. An unbidden voice. A voice that belonged to his cruelest self. *That's why you erased the tape.*

The reindeer had disappeared, swallowed again by the black winter forest. The snow was falling faster.

You lied to Maurice, the voice said. *And he believed it. Take a bow, Charlie. You must be better at this than you think.*

.   .   .

There had to be another way out. What had he given her, anyway? A little bit of gossip. Some name-dropping here and there. Nothing. It was nothing.

So the next day, in his gentlest tone, he told her it was over. Mary sat on the futon, blinking at him. "You can't do this," she said.

"I'm sorry, baby. But I have a wife. A child. I have to do the right thing."

She blinked again. Then she said: "Well, I suppose I should congratulate you."

This gave him a bad feeling. Was she being sarcastic?

"On finally figuring it out, I mean. I'll be honest, darling. I was beginning to wonder."

"I have no idea what you're talking about," he blustered.

"Charlie, sweetheart. It's okay. This needn't be so dramatic.

You're only seeing it now, but it's been true all along. Nothing has to change between us."

She smiled. She was playing with him. She was *enjoying* this. He felt a surge of anger. "Fuck you."

"Well, yes." She laughed. "That's exactly what I'm saying."

"You don't have anything on me!" he shouted. "Just leave me the fuck alone." Then he stormed out and slammed the door.

The anger felt good in the moment, but the hangover wasn't worth it. That raw outburst had only revealed to her just how scared he really was. It was only a matter of time until Mary took advantage of that fear to get her way.

It happened a few days later. Coming home from work, he spotted them outside their building. Helen, holding Amanda's hand. Amanda, gazing up at the strange woman. And Mary, gazing back at her. Helen was the first of the trio to spot Charlie. "Good timing," she called out. "There's someone I want you to meet."

She had been putting up these flyers, Helen explained. They had gotten to talking.

"I've been working as an au pair," Mary said, with a saccharine smile. "But my family is leaving, so I'm looking for a new position. And I'd heard there were some lovely American families in this area. And lovely American girls with lovely names like Amanda."

"Mommy," Amanda whispered. "She sounds like Mary Poppins."

"I wish we could help you out," Helen said, ignoring Amanda's tugging hand. "But I'm home with her all day. I don't work." She shot Charlie a look. "Most of the embassy wives don't. You might have better luck in a different building."

"Well, if you ever need a babysitter, or that sort of thing, then I—"

"We're fine," Charlie interrupted. "We already have a sitter."

Helen said to Mary: "Yes. Of course. We'll take your number. It's always good to have another option." Several minutes later, when they were back inside the apartment, she said caustically: "It wouldn't have killed you to be polite. Isn't that part of your job? Being good with strangers? *Hello?* Charlie. Are you even listening to me?"

But he couldn't hear anything Helen was saying. Coming after his wife? Coming after his *daughter*? This anger had a different quality from his panicked shouts. This anger burned steadier, stronger. He would go see Mary that night. He would make it crystal fucking clear. She was going to blackmail him into cooperating? Make him dance like some demented puppet? Fine. *Fine.* But over his dead body would she touch Helen and Amanda.

• • •

Maurice opened the front door, surprised to see him. "Charlie!" he said. "I didn't even know you were in New York."

"It was last-minute. A thing for a friend. And then I was in the neighborhood—seeing Helen, actually—and thought I'd stop by. Hope that's okay."

They sat in the living room, where Mozart was playing and a fire was burning in the fireplace. Surely Maurice could tell something was wrong. Surely the anxiety radiated from Charlie like a strong odor. And yet, so much time had passed. They weren't as close as they had once been. No longer could they immediately say to the other: *You're acting strange.* The clock ticked on the mantel. With a slightly stiff politeness, Maurice said: "So. How is Helen?"

Charlie shifted in his seat, feeling guilty for what he was about to do. Maurice had lived in this apartment, the parlor level of an old town house on East Seventy-First Street, for three decades. The décor never changed. The brocade sofa, the oriental rugs, the silver samovar, the perpetual smell of woodsmoke. This current incarnation of Maurice Adler was also the longest-lasting: in this life he was a philosophy professor at Hunter College, the genteel dinner party guest, the charming older gentleman. But Charlie was about to blow up Maurice's quiet afternoon and shove that incarnation aside. What he needed right now was the younger man, the man with sharper edges, with harder clarity.

"Well." Charlie coughed. "It's not Helen I came to talk to you about. It's Amanda."

Maurice lifted an eyebrow. "Is she okay?"

"I'm guessing you heard about her promotion, right? Helen probably told you. Station chief at age forty." Despite everything, he still felt a glow of pride. "That's sort of how this whole thing began. I mean, as far as I can tell."

Charlie explained. How Amanda's promotion came directly on the heels of Senator Vogel's death; how Jenny Navarro found the papers in Vogel's office and gave those papers to Charlie; how Charlie had given those papers to Amanda in turn, requesting to be left out of it; and how Amanda was now asking exactly the questions he feared her asking. "About Helsinki," he said. "About what really happened."

Maurice furrowed his brow. "You can't be particularly surprised by this development."

"But she's—"

"Your daughter is one of the youngest station chiefs in history. A person doesn't get there without a sizable degree of ambition."

"But she wouldn't—"

"Wouldn't what?" Maurice sounded impatient. Irritated, even. "Wouldn't disobey you? Wouldn't prioritize the investigation over your wishes? Charlie, you had to *know* this was a possibility. More than a possibility. A likelihood."

His cheeks flushed. "I just . . . I thought I'd have more time. To figure out what to say."

"Well, you don't."

"I need help, Maurice. *Please.* I need a plan. You're the only person I can talk to about these things."

"Amanda is my goddaughter."

"I know that."

"I take that very seriously."

"I know you do."

"And what do you even want? In an ideal world, how do you see this ending?"

"I guess . . . I don't know. I haven't thought about it."

Maurice frowned. "Well, Charlie. Think about it. I'm going to make some tea."

He retreated into the kitchen, from which Charlie heard the water splashing, gas stove clicking, dishes clattering. The sounds had a Pavlovian effect, plunging him into a deep chamber of memory. In 1989, right after Helen left for good, Maurice came to stay for a while. He was on summer break from his teaching job in Paris. They were roommates in Helsinki for the next few months. Maurice cooked for Charlie; he cleaned for Charlie; he helped him come up with a plan while making endless cups of tea. He had stuck with him, even in the shit. He had been a good friend. Charlie had trusted him with his life.

Maurice returned with a tray of tea and cookies. Charlie took a deep breath. "Okay," he said. "Here's what I think. Amanda is going to find out about Särrkä eventually. That's fine. I was desperate, and deceitful, but there could have been *lots* of reasons for that. Right?"

Maurice's gaze slipped into the middle distance. Eyes narrowed into darts. This was his thinking face.

"I mean." Charlie sat up, growing more confident. "Who else knows? Me and you, and Jack and Mary. And Jack died in 2005. And Mary died on Särrkä." He drank his tea to suppress the tickle in his throat. "If I don't tell Amanda, and you don't tell her . . ."

"But Mary could have told others *before* she died. She told at least one person. *Somebody* gave your name to Bob Vogel." Maurice squinted at him. "And you have nothing to do with this scheme Vogel uncovered?"

"Nothing. I swear, Maurice, nothing."

"So the first question is who gave Vogel your name. I wonder . . ." He shook his head. "But no. That's probably too neat."

"What is?"

"We can deduce that Amanda got a tip about Vogel. Yes? But was the person who tipped her *also* the person who warned Vogel about you? But, you see, this would assume they went to Amanda because they know Amanda is your daughter. Which assumes that they *wanted* this to happen. Which means this whole thing is designed for the express purpose of trapping you, and trapping Amanda, in this nasty situation." He paused. "Which isn't *impossible.*" Another pause. "But is it *likely*? Would that really be their objective?"

Maurice descended into silent thought. The clock kept ticking. Finally, he sighed and said: "Well, I suppose that's the only place to start. How, specifically, did Amanda find out about the Vogel assassination? How much did she know? You know Osmond Brown, don't you? I think you should ask him to a friendly lunch."

"On what pretext?"

Maurice gave a terse laugh. "Isn't this what you once did for a living, Charlie?" he said. "I think it's time for you to resurrect those skills."

CHAPTER ELEVEN

For a while, after Semonov returned from St. Petersburg, there was no sign of the agents from Unit 29155. Weeks went by. Were they avoiding him on purpose? Did they *know*?

Then, finally, in mid-November, they appeared.

"Maybe you thought we'd forgotten about you," Tweedledee said, leaning against the doorjamb. "But we never forget about our friends, do we?"

Tweedledum sank into the spare chair. "Is he our friend?"

"I'm feeling charitable today."

It was curious. Anticipating this moment, Semonov had expected to feel nervous. Paralyzed, even. Instead, he found that instinct took over. With an air of wounded casualness, he said: "I suppose you've been busy lately."

"*Very* busy. But we know how you are, Semonov." Tweedledee pointed a finger at him. "You do your best work when we're here to keep you in line. Isn't that right?"

"Does the unit have a new request? Is there an upcoming trip?"

"Always so *professional*. No, no, not today."

"Ah." Semonov slumped, feigning disappointment.

Tweedledum laughed. "You've missed us!"

He shrugged, fiddling with the papers on his desk. "I like to know that the work makes a difference. That, in a small way, I'm helping to keep our enemies in line, like you do. That's what you do, isn't it? When you travel to places like Iceland and the rest?"

Tweedledee smiled. "You aren't so ignorant after all. Yes, we keep the enemy in line. If they require a . . . lesson. Yes, a lesson. Then we give them that lesson."

"I suppose it needs doing," Semonov said. "People in other countries want to attack Russia because she is strong. People in Iceland and the rest."

Tweedledum said, "Well, Iceland was different. That was a particular kind of enemy."

"What kind of enemy?"

"The worst kind. The Russian who forgets his allegiance to Russia."

Bingo.

Semonov shook his head. "What kind of man forgets such a thing?"

"He's *not* a man." Tweedledee's voice dripped with scorn. "He lives like a pampered prince, with his mansions and yachts and airplanes. He's weak, and rotten to the core."

"I've heard of such things happening," Semonov said. "The Russians who move to the West, to places like New York or Paris or London."

"Dogs, all of them. And they ought to be shot like dogs. Though we aren't without mercy. We always give them a chance to fix their mistakes."

"And what if they don't listen?" Semonov lowered his voice. "These people you describe, have you ever had to . . ."

"Kill them?"

Both men laughed. By now they were radiating lethal contentment, like two lions napping in the sun after a kill. This was it, Semonov thought. This was the time to strike. "So the man in Iceland. Did he fix his mistake?"

"Oh, yes. He was terrified."

Semonov sighed. "Still. It saddens me."

"Poor little Semonov! You pity the man? Is that it?"

"No, no. It saddens me to think of a Russian betraying his

country. I have even heard rumors." He glanced at the open door, speaking in a whisper: "Rumors of these rich men working with the Americans. Is that . . . Have you ever heard such things?"

Tweedledee smiled. "You think we were born yesterday?"

They were relaxed enough, by now, to alleviate any possibility of suspicion. The problem, now, was that they were *too* relaxed, parrying his questions, not taking the bait. How to reawaken their insecurity? What would sting them back into bragging? They were simple men. They wore their prejudice like a badge of honor. They were better than the West. They were better than America. What else? They were better than Semonov. They were better than— *Aha*, he thought. *Yes. This should do the trick.*

"Well," Semonov said. "I heard these rumors from my friend at the FSB. He seemed to know a lot about these things. He's told me many stories." The two men frowned. Semonov continued: "*Many* stories. Many times has he had to defend Russia from America. Once he even received a commendation from President Gruzdev."

Voice dripping with scorn, Tweedledum said: "The FSB. The *FSB*. Why would you listen to those idiots?"

Most of the time, to be honest, Semonov forgot the rivalry even existed. There was a long-standing tension between the GRU and the FSB. Ostensibly the two Russian intelligence services shared the same goals, but what really mattered to each of them was that *they*, and not their rival, be the one to achieve those goals. This pointless Cain-and-Abel psychodrama was mostly perpetuated by those who had nothing better to think about it, which was to say those in the uppermost echelons, and those, like Tweedledee and Tweedledum, who only knew how to define themselves by hatred.

Semonov's words were like a red flag to a bull. Tweedledee sneered: "The FSB understands nothing about the world. It's thanks to your *friends* at the FSB that we had to go to Iceland in the first place."

"They can't even handle their own agents!" Tweedledum added.

"And then we have to go and clean up their mess! And will they ever thank us for it?"

"Hah! Thank us! How can they, when they don't even realize what is wrong?"

Semonov could sense himself losing control of the conversation, but he had his orders. He took a deep breath and hoped, desperately, that their tempers were hot enough to mask the obviousness of his next question. "The man in Iceland," he said. "The one you went to see. Is he one of those people? Was he working with the Americans?"

"Don't let those fools fill your head with their stupid ideas."

"So he wasn't? But then—"

"Pathetic," Tweedledee spat. "The FSB doesn't even realize they have a traitor on their hands. A corrupt, cowardly traitor. But he takes one look at us, and *blam*." He smacked his fist into his palm. "*Blam*. He runs right back to London and does what he is told."

• • •

Shortly after, the contact report landed on Amanda's desk in Rome.

She read it once. She read it a second time, to be sure. Then she sat back in her chair, tilted her head to the ceiling, and let out a laugh of relief, the knots in her shoulders beginning to dissolve. *Thank you*, she thought, unsure who she was addressing. *Thank you. THANK YOU.*

The outset of the report wasn't promising. Describing the encounter to Adrian, Semonov was convinced he had failed. Despite his provocation, he had learned nothing of what the GRU had said to Komarovsky in Iceland. He hadn't realized that the *nature* of his provocation was, in fact, a stroke of genius.

In the conference room, Amanda found Kath humming along to Rachmaninoff and working through a tall stack of documents. "What are those?" Amanda asked, cocking her head to get a better angle.

"S-1 filings."

"How thrilling."

"You'd be surprised." Kath glanced up. "Well, *you* certainly look pleased."

"Semonov got them to talk about Komarovsky. And listen to what they said."

After Amanda finished telling the story, she said: "You see what this means? Vitsin. The gallery owner in London. We always assumed Vitsin was GRU. And that, therefore, he was the one controlling the goons from Unit 29155. But what if—"

"What if he's FSB," Kath interrupted. "Yes. Of course. That makes perfect sense."

Several beats of silence, during which both women thought the same thing. Russia had multiple security services, each with its own specialty. A scheme like this, one involving elite oligarchs and market manipulation and corporate string-pulling, was exactly in the FSB's wheelhouse. Because the assassins were GRU, they had also assumed Komarovsky's handler was GRU, but had they ever had any solid proof? Why hadn't they thought to question this sooner?

"So," Amanda said, scraping her hair back into a ponytail. "Let's run through this. Vitsin is FSB."

"Vitsin is FSB," Kath repeated. "Vitsin relays instructions from the Kremlin. The targets. The list of demands. Komarovsky follows those instructions."

"And when he doesn't? There was that stretch of time when he stopped cooperating, after he and Vogel started talking. Why didn't the FSB catch on sooner?"

"Because," Kath said, "Komarovsky has the upper hand. This is his turf. His sense of when to strike, of when the market has an appetite for the idea. Vitsin will never understand any of that. And it doesn't translate to Kremlin-speak. So when Komarovsky tells them he needs to cool his heels, suspend trading because conditions aren't right, or there's a bug in the algorithm, or whatever the excuse, they believe him. They don't question him. They don't even know what questions they should be asking."

"Right. So earlier this year, when he paused the scheme, that by itself didn't raise any red flags. He gave them a reason, they swallowed it. *Vogel* must have been the tip-off. Someone realized they were meeting. But someone at the GRU, *not* the FSB. So the GRU suspects that Komarovsky is betraying the Kremlin. More than suspects. Even they wouldn't kill Bob Vogel without being certain."

"So the GRU kills Bob Vogel," Kath said. "They bully Komarovsky into submission. And, meanwhile, do they tell the FSB what they've discovered? Or do they keep them in the dark about this agent's traitorous behavior?"

Amanda was quiet for a minute. "No," she finally said. "It's too juicy. It could be useful. A bird in the hand beats two in the bush."

"Good, Amanda. You're starting to think like them."

Their leverage. This was it.

• • •

Officially, the Russian government had only a modest cadre of diplomats at their embassy in London. The precise number fluctuated based on the temperature of the relationship between the Kremlin and 10 Downing Street. At the present moment, 10 Downing Street wasn't particularly pleased that these oligarchs—who were, after all, tax-paying citizens of the United Kingdom—kept turning up dead throughout London. Mysterious heart attacks and strokes, muggings and burglaries gone wrong: Funny, wasn't it, how this bad luck tended to afflict Russians in particular?

Whenever the problem became too glaring to ignore, the prime minister handed a list of names to the Russian ambassador. The diplomats on that list boarded a plane back to Moscow, and for a time, a handful of desks and chairs at the Russian embassy sat empty, gathering dust. But once the public's thirst for justice had been slaked—which never took as long as one thought it might—the prime minister would quietly permit the numbers to rise again.

The two sides were expert at the kabuki, knowing, of course, that these official diplomats were mere props. The people to *actually* worry about had no apparent connection to the Russian government. Hundreds of FSB agents thickened the streets of Mayfair and Knightsbridge, enmeshing themselves in stylish nightclubs and art galleries, behaving like card-carrying members of the global elite. They lived under deep cover, beyond the reach of the public tit-for-tat. It was, in a sense, better this way. Simpler. It spared the British government from engaging in real antagonism. The Russian wealth flooding into the country had, after all, improved the lives of so many barristers and bankers and peers. Unfortunately for the wealthy Russians, it also meant that the laws and protections of the British government didn't necessarily apply to them.

But back in 2002, when he moved to England, Ivan Komarovsky had no idea that any of this would come to pass. Back in 2002, Komarovsky thought he was freeing himself from the whims of Moscow. At that point, Nikolai Gruzdev was just two years into his open-ended tenure as Russian president, but already any smart person could see that he was nothing like the most recent batch of Russian leaders. Not a reformist, like Gorbachev. Not a drunk, like Yeltsin. No, Gruzdev was a throwback to the autocrats of yore; a tsar for the twenty-first century. A man who wanted to control everything for himself.

Before he left Russia, Komarovsky extricated himself from the state-owned shipping business he had purchased in 1993 and walked away with a respectable profit. His friends laughed at him, because the value of the shipping company was only going up, and only an idiot would leave that fortune on the table. But Komarovsky used his profit to start a hedge fund in London, and while the fund's returns would never approach the might of a Gazprom or Rosneft, the fund was *his*. Komarovsky believed that, unlike those who had chosen to stay in Russia, he was truly free.

The illusion lasted less than a year. One day in April 2003, he and his family trooped down to the Old Marylebone Town Hall for their citizenship ceremony. (The normal process having been sped along by—what else—money.) They swore their allegiance to Her Majesty the Queen and celebrated with lunch at the Ritz. A fine spring afternoon, cottony clouds and blooming daffodils, citizenship papers in hand, gratitude in his heart. He didn't realize it until later, until it was ripped away from him, but in that glorious twenty-four-hour stretch, Komarovsky had felt truly British. He had succumbed to the softening civilities that made the country such a pleasant place to live.

But the very next morning, when a strange man stopped him outside his house in Mayfair, the downside of that softening became apparent.

The bright blue sky. The black Bentley idling by the curb. The stranger in a well-tailored suit, leaning against the lamppost, calling Komarovsky's name. They spoke for some minutes. There was, in truth, nothing particularly alarming about that conversation. It was a mark of Komarovsky's newfound naivete that he considered it a funny coincidence, nothing more, that this stranger happened to show up on his first morning as a British citizen.

But now, decades later, recalling it made him feel ill. *That was your chance*, he thought, so many years later. *Your only chance to say no.* Because once you let this kind of guest into your house, you could never ask him to leave.

·   ·   ·

Komarovsky had had a number of handlers since then. By the time Alexander Vitsin arrived on the scene, he had long since resigned himself to participating in this charade of loyalty. Vitsin had been with him for about five years. And Vitsin, to his credit, was good. Beneath the Savile Row costume, he had a core of Siberian steel.

During their first meeting, Vitsin explained that Komarovsky's help was required. The Kremlin had identified a new opportunity. He was a man of valuable talents, and this was a unique chance to help his country. And he loved his country, didn't he? He wanted Russia to be strong and successful, didn't he? For the next five years, Komarovsky did what was asked of him. He saw no other choice in the matter. He had gotten rich by understanding the free market, by harnessing the dynamics that drove prices up and down. Now he was being ordered to distort the forces he had respected so much.

There had been that wonderfully delusional stretch of time when he thought he could resist this fate; when he had confessed to Bob Vogel and set the racket aside. But really: How did he ever think he was going to get away with it? Didn't he know how the world worked? Didn't he know that virtue couldn't last? The middle-of-the-night episode in Iceland had been a cold dose of reality.

And now here he was, picking up the phone, resuming his role as the Kremlin's favorite lackey. It was a November morning in the Pavel Partners office in London. The Aeromach share price had been climbing steadily for the last two months. They had reached the point of maximum leverage, and it was time for Komarovsky to make the call.

After a bit of small talk, he said: "David, listen. I have a proposition for you. Much better to explain it in person. Can you come to London?"

David Hopkins, the CEO of Aeromach, didn't usually respond to requests like this. But for the sake of a major shareholder like Ivan Komarovsky, he was willing to rearrange his schedule and jet across the Atlantic. The next day, Hopkins arrived looking especially jovial. And why shouldn't he? His company's value had more than doubled since September. He smiled as they shook hands. "So coy, Ivan," he said. "Making me fly all this way just to cop a feel."

"I guess I should congratulate you. What's it at today? Eighty-seven a share?"

"Eighty-eight. Well, and, Ivan, congratulations to *you*. Your slice is worth a pretty penny these days."

Komarovsky indicated for Hopkins to sit. "You think it can last?"

"I absolutely do. The market is finally realizing what we've always known. How many times did we say the stock was underpriced?"

"So it's not just a fluke."

"Tell me, Ivan. You've always been bullish on Aeromach. Do *you* think it's a fluke?"

"Ah, well." Komarovsky took a sip of tea. "I actually have something specific I'd like to discuss with you."

"You know, I was waiting for you to call."

"You were?"

"Sure. This gives us the chance to maneuver a little bit. Spend more on R and D. Expand our reach. I know that's always been what you've wanted."

"I like you, David. But I don't think you have the slightest idea what I want."

Hopkins's smile faded. As a former military man, this was the part he struggled with. He didn't know what to do when faced with unhappy board members or shareholders. The instinct for hierarchical deference remained too strong within him.

"What I want," Komarovsky continued, "is for you to halt the development of those new missiles. The ones you've been promising to sell to Poland."

Hopkins blinked. "That's a six-billion-dollar contract."

"Correct."

"But why would we—"

"David," he said soothingly. "David, David, *David*. Let me finish. Of course, you don't *have* to do this. You can do whatever you'd like. But I should warn you that if those missiles proceed as planned, the Aeromach stock price is going to plummet. It will go even lower than where it was over the summer. You know, you were right. It *wasn't* just a fluke. There's a specific reason the stock began to climb. You just don't understand what that reason is."

Hopkins blinked again. "I don't understand."

"Yes, well. As I said."

"But I don't . . . Ivan, what is this? Some kind of blackmail?"

"Yes."

After a beat, Hopkins laughed bluffly. "I'm sorry, Ivan. This isn't going to work. You don't own *nearly* enough of the company to go around making these demands. So, what? If I don't play ball, you'll issue a statement, announce you're selling your shares? And you think that's enough to cause the price to plummet?"

"Oh no, no, no. David! Don't be absurd. I don't pretend that my words carry such weight. But you're familiar with how this whole thing started. Someone posted about Aeromach, the post went viral, the world responded accordingly. But *why* did the post go viral? Who do you think caused that to happen?"

Again, that uncomprehending blink. This part always took longer than expected. It was frankly shocking, the degree to which these CEOs thought they *deserved* this newly profitable position. They were innocent in the way Komarovsky himself had once been innocent. They thought this was the market at work! But the market was just people, and they failed to understand how easily people could be manipulated. Hopkins was proving especially difficult. Maybe it was simplemindedness, or maybe it was a military stubbornness, or maybe Komarovsky himself was rusty at this. Even once he had grasped the mechanism, Hopkins remained fixated on the question of *why*. Why was Komarovsky so against the idea of Poland possessing these missiles? "Do you really need me to tell you that?" Komarovsky said. "David. Think about it. Do you really *want* to know?"

But the poor dumb man did want to know, and so Komarovsky explained. "And, yes, David, I see what you're thinking. You could call the authorities in your country and expose this whole scheme.

But will they really believe you? And if they did, won't it make you look terribly stupid? We're friends, after all. I've been a shareholder in Aeromach for *years*. Just this spring you were a guest on my yacht."

Hopkins was turning ashen, the color draining from his face.

"I'll tell you what," Komarovsky continued. "No need to take my word. I'll *show* you. That ought to make things easy. Your daughter, the older one. She's a producer at that Hollywood studio, isn't she? Well, keep an eye on that. Tomorrow someone will say something about the studio. And it will spread like wildfire, and their price will start to climb, and *then* you will believe me, won't you? Okay, David. I'll await your call."

·　　·　　·

That same night, after returning from yet another black-tie gala, Komarovsky stopped in the foyer and kissed his wife on the cheek. "I'm sorry, Annushka," he said. "I'll see you in the morning."

She nodded. Though she was young, she wasn't naive, and she understood there was work she couldn't know about. Wearily he dragged himself back out into the cold, where Osipov had kept the car idling. Komarovsky climbed into the back seat and said: "East Ferry Road."

Four years ago he had rented a storefront near Canary Wharf, an old hair salon whose back room now housed his team of programmers. It was a forgettable corner of the city, a squat building with beige brick walls and metal shutters over the doors, harsh fluorescent streetlamps and garbage bags piled outside every night. Komarovsky unlocked the door and stepped inside. This part still looked like a salon: vinyl chairs with ripped padding, bumpy linoleum flooring, cracked mirrors along the walls. He would have liked to rip those mirrors down—he hated catching his reflection in the shadowy darkness—but that would have required hiring a contractor, and it was unwise to expand the circle of awareness beyond what was absolutely necessary.

In the back of the salon was a steel door with an electronic keypad. The old storage room was now the nerve center of the operation, crammed with desks, computer monitors, and a blinking stack of servers. A generator sat in the corner in case of a sudden power cut. The air was warm, thick with the scent of stale coffee and takeout curry. Cooler currents drifted from the air conditioner in the corner, installed to keep the server from overheating.

He had summoned the five programmers earlier that day, after his meeting with Hopkins. They didn't so much as glance up when Komarovsky entered. He stood behind Yulia and asked: "Everything is good?"

Without looking at him, she nodded. Her eyes were locked on the screen, her fingers flying across the keyboard. It was, he thought, not unlike watching Lang Lang perform a piano concerto, or Jackson Pollock fling paint across a canvas. Anything, when done at the highest level, could fill a person with awe. As he sat down, he envied Yulia this purity of purpose. He was the one with the mansions, the cars, the planes—but who, really, was happier?

"Why are you shaking your head?" Yulia asked, still glued to her screen.

"Never mind," Komarovsky said. "Show me the new code."

"This is a bad time to interrupt."

"Indulge me."

Technically they worked for him, technically he paid their salary, but they weren't motivated by money. What they cared about was the challenge of cracking this supposedly uncrackable algorithm. The programmers had countless opportunities to profit from this manufactured momentum, and they never did. Komarovsky had them followed and monitored their bank accounts—just as a precaution—but it only confirmed what he already knew. He trusted them precisely because of their fuck-off attitudes. Komarovsky didn't need to chaperone them, didn't need to spend so much time in this cloistered room. But he did because, well, because he *liked* it here. He liked the blinkered focus, the underdog camaraderie, the sense of uncompromising rigor.

Wearing an annoyed frown, Yulia walked him through the new code. When she finished, she sighed loudly and reached for her noise-canceling headphones. Komarovsky walked across the room and switched on the electric kettle to make tea. It was funny, he thought. An hour ago he was longing to climb into bed. Now that he was here, he felt wide awake.

Around 5:30 a.m., Yulia stood up, put on her jacket, and left. Soon the others followed. A user by the name of HotDogQueenzzz had posted about the Hollywood studio in question, and already the algorithm was churning the post to the top of the feed. Komarovsky checked his watch: he had just enough time to get home and take a short nap before showering, changing, and heading to the offices of Pavel Partners. Where, in a matter of hours, after the markets had opened and the shares began to skyrocket, he would receive a conciliatory phone call from Aeromach CEO David Hopkins.

But instead of hurrying, he lingered before the whiteboard. The programmers had spent a good part of the night arguing, scribbling out code, pointing out the mistakes, erasing, writing again. His heart swelled with fondness. This was the part he found hard to explain. "What you're doing is wrong, Ivan," Bob Vogel had said to him. He remembered that exchange so well: sitting before a crackling fire in an elegant canal house in Amsterdam, a bottle of Barolo decanting on the sideboard. The righteous intensity of his friend's gaze. "You're taking these companies, *honest* companies, and you're ripping them to shreds on behalf of a man you hate. You can't feel good about that."

Of course he didn't. But the work itself felt separate from the corruption it served. He was like a scientist, prodding the fabric of the universe, observing cause and effect. It was hard to make Vogel understand. Americans were *never* able to understand. How many times had it been asked of him? *Wasn't life in the Soviet Union miserable? Weren't you cold, and hungry, and tired?* Yes. Of course. Every day. *Then why the nostalgia? Why do you claim to miss it?*

Because, despite the hardship, they had the dignity of playing on their own field. Because, even if the socialist experiment was failing them, at least it was *their* experiment.

Komarovsky switched off the lights. Tested the door to make sure it had locked, retraced his steps through the salon. Outside, he rolled down the metal shutter, locked the padlock, and began walking. He always asked Osipov to park a few streets away. He didn't like to draw attention to the storefront, even though East Ferry Road was usually deserted at this hour.

Strange, though. As he began down the sidewalk, a woman appeared from around the corner. She wore a long puffy jacket, shapeless as a sleeping bag. She was short; the hem nearly touched the ground. Hood pulled up, hands shoved in pockets. Komarovsky pitied her. She would only be walking in this area, at this particular hour of the day, if she was a tired old beggar, or something of the sort.

But as she got closer, she lifted her head. The hood fell back. The streetlights illuminated just enough of her face for Komarovsky to freeze. She was young, with apple-round cheeks and a freckled nose—and she was looking right at him.

PART IV

EAST FERRY ROAD

CHAPTER TWELVE

They walked down East Ferry Road toward the Thames, where the river rippled in the gray dawn light. As they sat on an empty bench on the promenade along the water, Komarovsky's expression remained studiedly blank. She had suggested they find somewhere quiet to talk. She took the fact that he hadn't immediately told her to go fuck herself as a good sign.

"My name is Amanda Clarkson," she began. "I work with the State Department. Again, let me offer my condolences. I know you and Bob Vogel were close."

"Miss Clarkson," he said. "This charade isn't necessary. Why don't you get straight to the point, so I can give you my answer and we can say goodbye."

She cocked her head. "You don't seem surprised to see me."

"I try not to let anything surprise me."

"Even in Iceland? Even that didn't surprise you?"

Irritation flickered across his face. "Those men were merely—"

"Were merely Vitsin's messengers? But what did Vitsin say, when you told him about it? Did he claim to know nothing about them? I bet you thought he was lying. But here's the thing, Mr. Komarovsky. Vitsin really *didn't* send them. Those men don't work for the FSB." She paused. Leaned forward. "Would you like to know who they were?"

"I know what you're doing, Miss Clarkson. Miss Clarkson from the State Department. Well, you can tell the *State Department*"— he practically spat those words—"that I have no interest in becoming their lackey."

"You'd prefer to leave yourself to the mercy of those thugs?"

"It's none of your business."

"We can protect you from them."

"Protect me?" He laughed bitterly. "Oh, yes. You'll protect me like you protected Bob?"

"We didn't know he was in danger. But we know that you are."

He lifted his shoulders in indifference. He was in danger? Of course he was. He was the linchpin of a deeply corrupt, Kremlin-backed scheme. He was the sword meant to pierce the profitable shield of America's capitalist system. Amanda wasn't telling Komarovsky anything he didn't already know. So she plunged forth:

"Here's the situation, Mr. Komarovsky. The two men who came to see you in Iceland, they were the ones who killed Senator Vogel. And they've let you live for now, but how long does that tolerance last? What happens when they're done with you? Surely you've heard the stories about Unit 29155."

At this, he glanced over.

"You're working for the FSB," she continued. "But those men aren't FSB. They're GRU. You're a smart man. You know how deep that rivalry runs. Think about it, Mr. Komarovsky. You've gotten yourself caught between two very dangerous, very demanding masters." Another pause. "I want to show you something."

She drew the photograph from her pocket. A frame from the security footage in Cairo Airport. The date and time stamped in the corner: the day before Bob Vogel was murdered. "You recognize these men," she prompted. "Don't you?"

Komarovsky took the photograph, gazing at it with unreadable stillness. But there, in his left hand, the tiniest movement. Running his index finger over the edge of his thumb, back and forth, back and forth. He had a good poker face, but that subtle tic: he was scared. At the very least, he was thinking.

"Bob Vogel was a good person," she said. "He was trying to do the right thing. And you, too, Mr. Komarovsky. You're *also* a good person. That's why you confided in him. Why not finish what you and Senator Vogel started?"

"Because Bob was my friend. And you, Miss Clarkson, are a stranger."

He tried to pass the photograph back to her. "Keep it," she said. "It's yours."

"I don't want it." He brandished it at her, but she kept her hands folded in her lap.

"It's been hard on Diane," Amanda said. "They were the real thing, you know? They had their sixtieth anniversary this year. *Sixty* years. Incredible. I don't know how she's going to cope. It's just so hard. Bob, you know, *Bob* had signed up for this. He got involved with you with his eyes wide open. But Diane got the short end of the stick. I saw her, back in July, right after he was murdered. She told me they used to argue about it. They both wanted to be the person to die first. When you love each other like that, being the person left behind—it's just too painful."

(Diane hadn't actually said any of this, but it seemed like something she *could* say.)

"There's always risk, right?" she continued. "No matter what. You were smart. You moved to London because you knew better than to trust Russia with your safety. With your *family's* safety. But Gruzdev is persistent. He doesn't let go that easy. So you agreed to work with the FSB, and obviously that was a risk, too, but you had to do what you had to do. And so here you are, tangled up with the GRU *and* the FSB, again trusting Russia with your safety. You decided to play ball. Okay, fine. That was your decision to make, and you made it. But what about Anya?"

He whipped around. "What *about* Anya?"

"Did *she* sign up for this? Did she agree to these risks? It's not just about you, Mr. Komarovsky. What do you think Anya would want? Would she really trust the Russian government to keep her safe? Would she want to live at the mercy of these men?"

He blinked at her, then turned back to the river. Amanda knew, from their surveillance, that Komarovsky was loyal to Anya. *Unusually* loyal, for an oligarch like him. He cared about her more than anything in the world.

For a while, he was silent. "You see how it is, right?" she said softly. "The GRU will always know what you did with Bob Vogel. That will always hang above your head. How can you ever be sure that you're safe with them? Look, Mr. Komarovsky. There are no perfect solutions. There are only imperfect options. Obviously you don't owe us any kind of allegiance. But you're a smart man, and I think you understand that we're your—and Anya's—best chance at safety."

⁂

They kept talking. She could tell, from his slumping posture, that he was going to acquiesce even before he said the words. The rising sun turned the sky periwinkle blue. Across the river, the domes and columns of Greenwich Hospital clarified in the transparent morning light. They established how Amanda would next get in touch. Komarovsky checked his watch and said: "Osipov will be wondering where I am."

"Your driver," Amanda said. They stood up, started walking away from the river. "How long has he been with you?"

"Twelve years."

"Quite a long time."

"He's the best in London. I have to keep raising his salary to stop him from being poached."

As they walked, Komarovsky's shoulders began to straighten. Each step was taking him back to the daylight world, back to his life as a confident, in-control businessman. He said: "How well did you know Bob?"

"Not very," she said. "But I grew up in New York, and he was our senator. I remember writing letters to him for civics class. One time I asked him to please send me a copy of the new Goosebumps book. And he actually wrote back. He suggested, very nicely, that I try the library instead. I guess I thought a senator was something like Santa Claus."

He smiled. "We were neighbors, a long time ago, when he and Diane kept a home in London. His daughters used to babysit my daughters. They were good girls. Not spoiled, like mine. I spoil my girls terribly. I want to give them everything."

"Well, sure. You love them. That's only natural."

After a beat, he said: "How old are you, Miss Clarkson?"

"Oh," she replied. "Uh. I'm forty years old."

"You seem younger." He gave her an appraising look. "This probably works to your advantage. But I won't make that mistake. Clearly you are not to be underestimated."

"Well, thanks. I guess."

He shook his head. "Oh no, no. I don't mean that as a compliment."

. . .

They needed a secure location for their meetings, and luckily, there were plenty of vacancies on that sad stretch of East Ferry Road. The landlord wasn't inclined to ask questions, especially when one of the black bag guys from London station offered to pay six months' rent up front, in cash. An extra layer of concealment was provided by the back alley, which ran the length of the block. A week later, the first time Komarovsky traversed the trash-strewn alley from the old hair salon to the old kebab shop, he arrived with nose wrinkled and brow furrowed.

"Not quite the Riviera," Amanda offered.

Komarovsky sighed. "Beggars can't be choosers."

After installing the hidden cameras and listening devices, the black bag guys had restored the kebab shop to its previous neglect. Wires dangled from the drop ceilings, soda cans lay crumpled in the corner. Amanda didn't need to draw attention to the fact that the CIA had worked it over, even if Komarovsky assumed as much. The first day, Komarovsky walked up to the windows, which were lined with faded copies of *The Sun* and the *Daily Mirror*. "I find it odd," he said, touching a fingertip to a sun-bleached photograph of Kevin De Bruyne, midfielder for Manchester City, "how many times I've walked past this shop without ever noticing it."

Amanda checked her watch. "While we're waiting for Kath, I thought we could—"

Komarovsky looked up, alarmed. "Kath? Who is Kath?"

"Kath Freeman," Amanda said, using her alias. Then she proceeded to explain, with only minimal exaggeration, how Kath had singlehandedly unraveled the truth of the scheme. She was hoping to shake him up a little, knock his confidence loose, but that didn't quite work.

"*Really?*" he said eagerly. "She did this by herself?"

An hour later, Kath arrived straight from Heathrow, wheeling a suitcase behind her. As she struggled to lift her suitcase to the table, evidently heavy with the many files she'd brought from Rome, Komarovsky sprang to his feet and said grandly, "Allow me."

"Well." She arched an eyebrow. "Aren't you just the gentleman."

As she began removing her papers, he hovered behind her, practically quivering with anticipation. "Tell me, please. How did you do it? What gave it away?"

"Sit down," she said. To Amanda: "Is he always like this?"

Lightly, Amanda said: "Maybe someone has a crush."

"Oh, no. He doesn't like women born in the twentieth century."

He looked hurt. "That's not true. Anya was born in 1993."

Laughing, Kath took her time, squaring the files into neat stacks across the table. When she was done, she slid aside the empty suitcase and sat down across from Komarovsky. Her long silver hair was loose over her shoulders. She wore red lipstick and a black cashmere turtleneck. She rested her chin in her hand, gazing at him philosophically. "You know," she said, "I don't *have* to tell you anything."

"True," he replied. "But are you really that heartless?"

A coy smile. "What if I am?"

"Then, I would say, you should be working for our side, not yours."

(Were they *flirting*? Amanda wondered.)

"Well," Kath said, reaching for one of her manila folders. "I'm only telling you this because it's such an amateur mistake. The tail numbers, Ivan."

He frowned. "Pardon me?"

"You've been clever. Very clever. I'm okay with admitting that. Part of me admires what you've pulled off. So. Let's see if I've understood this correctly."

As Kath talked, Komarovsky's mouth settled into a thin line. His eager curiosity, Amanda realized, had really just been a desire to point out the flaws in Kath's understanding, to catch her in a mistake. But Kath wasn't making any mistakes. The manufacturing of the algorithmic enthusiasm. The fact that Komarovsky was a legitimate shareholder in the targeted companies, which meant the CEOs would always take his calls. How they were loath to let their share price dip back to previous levels, and the changes they were willing to implement, and how this aligned with Gruzdev's agenda. There was a pattern, but it was hiding in plain sight, because these meme stocks were a genuine phenomenon, and plenty of times the enthusiasm *wasn't* manufactured. Komarovsky had done an excellent job of covering his bases. Of making sure no one could connect him to it. She paused. "Just checking. Am I getting all this right?"

Komarovsky swallowed. "Explain what I missed," he said hoarsely. "Please."

"Actually, you were the one who gave me the idea," Kath said.

"When we heard about Iceland, I thought, 'Aha. This must be our man.' But I wanted to be sure, so I looked into your travel. I wanted to see where you and Vogel overlapped. Puzzling, though. Your name wasn't on any flight manifests. And then I realized: Of course. This man doesn't fly *commercial*. Iceland was the rare exception. I don't know why, maybe your Gulfstream had a flat. Now, they're called private jets for a reason. You block your tail number so your movements aren't visible to the hoi polloi. But we have ways of getting past that block. Obviously."

She grinned, clearly enjoying herself.

"From there, it was easy. Davos, Courchevel, Cannes. You and Vogel always overlapped for at least a day. You even answered the question that had been bugging us for such a long time. Where was that last meeting? The one on May thirtieth? There was no record of Vogel flying anywhere around May thirtieth. I hadn't thought to unblock the tail numbers, but then I did, and there it was: on May twenty-ninth, a plane belonging to one of Vogel's friends flew from New York to Mykonos.

"And this made sense. Because, by then, Vogel knew enough to know that he had to be careful. He couldn't leave those blatant breadcrumbs behind, linking the two of you. So he asked to borrow a friend's plane. That was enough for me to connect you with him. But it was also enough for me to learn what's coming next. Aeromach. Wow. That's a big one, Ivan."

Komarovsky's face had turned sallow and gray, like an over-cooked piece of meat.

"Patterns everywhere," Kath continued. "You just have to know what you're looking for. So I started checking the tail numbers for the jets associated with the targeted companies, and sure enough, the jets would fly to London just days before announcing these changes. So when a defense contractor like Aeromach starts sky-rocketing, back in September, I'm thinking: hello! And I start watching the tail numbers. And then, just last week, the day before

Amanda talks to you—delicious timing, isn't it?—their jet lands in Heathrow, and our team spots David Hopkins entering the office of Pavel Partners. So what's it going to be, Ivan? You're Gruzdev's favorite errand boy. What's on his shopping list this time?"

·   ·   ·

At the end of that first day Komarovsky left the kebab shop in a mood of utter defeat. Amanda wondered if Kath had been too hard on him, but Kath said it was necessary. Komarovsky was good at deluding himself. If another person were to point out his obvious guilt, he would just dismiss them as stupid, simpleminded, blind to the bigger picture—which he, in his intellectual brilliance, could see. But occasionally someone came along who, even he had to admit, was just as smart as him. Possibly smarter. This was why Bob Vogel had eventually gotten through. This was why Kath had to be certain that Komarovsky found her just as intellectually intimidating, if not more, as he had found Vogel.

It worked. The next morning, Komarovsky was ready to pledge his allegiance to Kath. "I brought you something," he said, taking a slim paperback from the pocket of his coat. "This book is very special to me. I don't like to part with it. But you, Miss Freeman, *you* will understand the significance of the story. Being the connoisseur that you are."

"I'll give it a shot." She tossed the book aside. "Amanda, how's that coffee coming?"

Komarovsky placed a hand over his heart. "And I must apologize, Miss Freeman. I realized that I never thanked you."

"For what?"

"For finally making me see the terrible irony of the situation," he explained. "Sometimes humiliation is necessary to remember what we have forgotten. Materialism is the sin of our human condition. Money, houses, cars, *possessions*, they tie a man too closely to the earth. He fails to remember that his *soul* is what matters.

But when we are alive on this earth, alas, money is necessary. The only way to survive the condition is to remain clear-eyed about the compromise. But there are moments in my life when I have forgotten."

"*Moments*, Ivan? Remind me how much Pavel Partners has under management? Five billion? Six?"

He shook his head. "Many moments. But you see, Miss Freeman, your method of discovery reminds me of how sordid this work really is. Private jets." He grimaced. "Private jets. *This* is what my world has become."

• • •

Over the next few weeks, in that old kebab shop on East Ferry Road, they settled into their roles: Kath in charge, and Komarovsky trying desperately to impress her. Amanda stayed in the background, making coffee, observing the verbal ping-pong. At first she liked this dynamic. It was nice, after the last few months of constant effort, to cede leadership and hang out at the edge. Kath was methodically working her way through Vogel's notes, pinning down every nitty-gritty detail, understanding exactly how Komarovsky had achieved his end. It wasn't enough for them just to stop the oligarch. He had spotted a weakness, which meant it was only a matter of time until other people spotted it, too. They had to understand exactly how these future antagonists would try to exploit the system.

Amanda made coffee. She watched them talk. But there with her, hovering in the corner of the room, was another presence: the unasked question, the last page, now destroyed, from Vogel's folder. Apparently Kath could feel this presence, too. She turned to her and said, with a casual air: "Amanda, just checking. Is this tracking with the papers we found in the senator's study?"

"Oh. Uh, yeah. It's all tracking."

"We should double-check. Make sure."

"Yeah, I'll do that. You two keep going."

Kath gave her a meaningful look. Amanda could feel the silent judgment, but the truth was, this wasn't Kath's forte. Human beings weren't fixed entities, like numbers and letters on a piece of paper. Amanda was allowed to change her mind, if she wanted.

Maybe she *shouldn't* try to learn the truth about her father. Her increasing sense of nausea, her mounting dread: maybe this was her body's way of telling her to reverse course. She began to consider this possibility. *What if I changed my mind?*

They had brought in a whiteboard to help sketch out the scheme, to lay out the interlocking of so many complex gears. Komarovsky was clearly enjoying himself, his sleeves rolled up, bantering with Kath as they worked, occasionally calling out for another cup of coffee. At first Amanda had found him sort of funny. Charming, in a way. But as time went by, and her nauseating dread increased, she began to resent him. More specifically, to resent the fact that he knew why her father's name was on that paper.

What if I decided that I didn't want to know? There could be reasons—tactical, logical—to change her mind. Amanda was a good liar. She wouldn't have to tell Kath the truth, which was that the idea of confronting Komarovsky, of asking him to explain the presence of her father's name on that piece of paper, that this idea was beginning to scare her shitless.

·   ·   ·

She was now in the habit of a few glasses of wine each night to help her sleep. She told herself that her consumption had remained steady—it wasn't like it was suddenly skyrocketing—and gave herself permission to venture further afield.

It was amazing, in retrospect, how quickly the spiral happened. One night Amanda opened a bottle of wine and, instead of saving the second half, decided to finish the whole thing. It was wonderful. She slept better than ever. The next night she did it again. Then she thought it might be nice to switch things up. The fact of being in London, away from her normal life, also gave her permission to break her usual rules. Bless England and her pubs on every corner. Bless the fact that no one looked askance when she ordered a pint of lager with lunch. Bless the bracing bitterness of a gin and tonic, bless the salty rinse of a dirty martini, bless the throaty smoke of bourbon. Good *lord*, she loved drinking. By now she was waking up cotton-mouthed at 3 a.m., headaches in the morning, but she didn't care. She loved it. She fucking loved it.

There had been occasional lapses over the last seventeen years (a bad breakup, a botched operation in Lebanon, Georgia's thirty-fifth birthday party), but for the most part, Amanda kept it under control. Not since her round-the-world trip had she drank like this. What no one warned you about backpacking was that, in order to endure the marathon of sketchy hostels and mildewed travel towels and peanut butter sandwiches, you developed certain coping mechanisms. Every city in the world had at least one cheap bar with cheap booze. Social lubricant, liquid blanket, liquid courage: booze was the solo traveler's best friend.

It was funny, though. When she got to Russia, she mostly stopped. She spent that winter in Moscow with Jakob and his friends and, despite being surrounded by rivers of vodka, she found that the desire to drink had simply . . . vanished. The ease with which she stopped surprised her. It was *after* what happened in Russia that it got really bad. She went on an epic bender in Thailand. Six blurry weeks, as far from Moscow as she could get, back among her fellow five-dollar-a-day travelers. Amanda told herself it was a reward after enduring such a brutal loss. But it felt less like a reward and more like an annihilation, and eventually it terrified her into quitting.

But this wasn't like that. This was fine! Other than the headaches, she was completely functional. Yes, there was the matter of her un-asked question. Yes, there was Kath's judgment radiating from across the room. But they were holding Komarovsky to task, and that was her job, wasn't it? She was doing her job. She was doing a *good* job.

After three weeks in London, though, Kath finally confronted her.

It happened over a Friday night dinner at a hole-in-the-wall Burmese restaurant, one of Kath's favorite places in London. Annoyingly, it didn't have a liquor license. Kath said: "Look. Amanda. The elephant in the room. I know what you're going through."

"I doubt that," Amanda said acidly.

"It's a difficult situation."

"Oh, you mean the fact that my father has some shameful secret buried in his past? And I'm the one who has to dig it up?" She grimaced, rearranging her plate of uneaten garlic noodles. "Thanks for the sympathy. But, actually, you *don't* know what I'm going through. Wasn't your father literally a Sunday school teacher?"

"I'm not talking about that."

"Really? What else is there to talk about?"

Kath sighed. "You idiot. I'm talking about your drinking."

Amanda looked up, heart thumping. "I drink a normal amount."

"You think I don't see it? Amanda. I've been sober thirty years. Thirty years, three months, sixteen days. It was my best friend until it wasn't. I don't talk about it much because, honestly, it's tricky to talk about. Now, look. I'm not trying to be dramatic. Not saying you need to get yourself to a meeting or anything like that. This is just me being practical. Right now you need to be on the top, the *top* of your game. This is the biggest operation of your career and you're giving it, at most, fifty percent. And I've been working my ass off, and now you're going to risk blowing the whole thing?"

"I'm not—"

"Komarovsky is *smart*, Amanda. He's been around the block. You need to be better than him. Got it? You don't want him making the connection between you and Charlie Cole. If he does, then, *poof*. It's all for nothing. He'll never trust us again."

The thumping of her heart now felt less like fear and more like fury. "You think I don't know that?"

"You aren't acting like you know it."

"Oh, yeah. Sure. And you're the expert on how I'm supposed to act."

With a level stare, Kath said: "I know a coward when I see one."

. . .

Amanda stormed out of the Burmese hole-in-the-wall, planning to find the nearest bar and drown herself in gin. But after two blocks, she stopped in her tracks. She'd stuck Kath with the check. So she was a drunk—yes, she was a drunk, why not admit it, who gave a flying fuck—but even if she was a drunk, she wanted to be fair.

By the time she got back to the restaurant, Kath was standing up and buttoning her coat. Amanda watched her through the window. The waiter handed her something: Amanda's abandoned noodles, which Kath had boxed up. She knew that Amanda would need to eat something. And suddenly Amanda was remembering the last three weeks in their East Ferry Road headquarters: Kath always putting food in front of her. Scones, muffins, sandwiches, soups, trying to help her soak up whatever was in her stomach, trying to take care of her. She had known. She had known this whole time.

When Kath emerged into the gloomy December drizzle, Amanda was blinking back tears. "I'm sorry," she said. "You're right. I'm so sorry. I've just been so stressed about this thing with my dad."

Kath pulled her into a hug. Then she stepped back and said: "It's okay. I know what we have to do."

Monday, Kath decreed, was D-Day. The longer they waited, the more suspicious Komarovsky would find this silence. They had covered everything else in the dossier; why not the piece of paper that mentioned Charlie Cole? They had the weekend to get Amanda back into fighting shape. Kath, unsurprisingly, had very specific instructions, and Amanda was willing to follow those instructions exactly. No coffee, no sugar. A diet of spicy broth and red meat. Hot baths after dinner, bitter herbal teas before bed. They spent Saturday and Sunday taking vigorous walks across Hampstead Heath while role-playing the conversation. After they had huffed their way to the top of Parliament Hill, they paused to take in the view. "You know what's playing in my head right now?" Amanda said. "The theme music from *Rocky*."

Kath shrugged. "Never saw it."

"*What?*"

"So sue me. I was a little busy in the seventies."

When she woke up on Monday morning, Amanda felt more clearheaded than she had in weeks. She looked at the pantsuits hanging in her hotel closet, and realized she hated all of them. They were frumpy, ill-fitting, unflattering. How had she ever worn these? Why had she never listened to Georgia? The only other option was her ratty jeans, which were splattered with mud from the heath. She hated them slightly less, and figured they would be fine.

That morning, Komarovsky arrived bearing a white box with a festive ribbon. Christmas was just a few days away. "For you," he said, handing the box to Kath. Then, a beat later, he added: "For *both* of you."

"Bribery, Ivan?" Kath said.

"Daylesford makes the best Christmas cake in the city. At least this is what I'm told. Unfortunately, Anya has ordered me to lose ten pounds by January."

The tag, dangling from the green-and-gold ribbon, said: FROM PETER, JEMIMA, ROBBIE, AND ALL YOUR FRIENDS AT BARCLAYS. "Ah," Kath said. "Well. How thoughtful of you."

Kath carried the regifted cake to the table in the corner where Amanda was, as usual, tending to the coffee. "Cheap bastard," she muttered. "You're good, right?"

Amanda nodded. "I'm good."

Komarovsky stood by the whiteboard, rolling up his sleeves, ready to begin. "You see this, Miss Freeman?" he called out. He lifted his hand toward the whiteboard with a proprietary air, like a painter admiring his own canvas. A hot blade of aggravation cut through the last of Amanda's lingering nerves. "I wanted to show you how—"

"Sit down," Amanda interrupted. "We have to talk about something."

Komarovsky was amused by her tone. "You're energetic this morning."

"Sit. Now."

He looked at Kath, but she just shook her head, so he walked to the table and lowered himself to his chair. Amanda took a deep breath. D-Day. Now or never. "Senator Vogel's notes," she said. "There was a piece of paper with a name written on it. There was a star next to the name."

"Ah, yes. I was wondering when you'd finally get around to this. Although I see why you've put it off. It's close to home, isn't it?"

Her breath caught in her throat. "Excuse me?"

"Let's be honest about this, Miss Clarkson. Charlie Cole is your colleague. You don't work for the State Department. You work, like he does, for the CIA."

Okay, she thought. *It's okay. He doesn't know.* "You gave his name to Vogel. Why? This isn't his area. He has nothing to do with this."

"Well, yes. And I wanted to keep it that way."

"What does that mean?"

"The CIA has a mole. An agent recruited during the Cold War. I heard about it a few years ago, from a woman at a party. A woman, I should say, who is in a position to know. Haven't you ever wondered why it's so difficult for you to recruit Russian government assets? It's because they know about the mole, and they're terrified."

Sweat prickled along her hairline. "That's why you didn't want Vogel telling anyone at the CIA. Because Charlie Cole is a double agent."

"He's working for Moscow. He has a direct line to the Kremlin."

"Charlie Cole," she repeated. "Charlie Cole is a double agent."

He looked at her quizzically. "Are you okay, Miss Clarkson? You seem quite—"

"Jesus Christ!" Kath shouted. "Of course she's not okay! You just suggested that the CIA has a goddamn *mole*, Ivan. Nothing about this is okay!"

"Yes, but it's—"

"You can't just toss out a name like that! This is a *serious* accusation you're making. We're going to need specifics. What happened? How did they turn him?"

"I don't have any specifics."

"Then what the fuck do you have? A rumor isn't good enough."

"It was good enough for Bob."

"Bob was an amateur," Kath barked. Then added: "May he rest in peace. Amanda? What do you think, are you buying this?"

Kath wasn't going to let her back down. And her performance of outrage was invigorating; it was contagious. Amanda crossed her arms and chimed in: "Color me skeptical."

Komarovsky glanced back and forth between the two women. "You don't believe me?"

"I believe that you believe it," Amanda said.

"What does that mean?"

"It means this woman might have given you bad intelligence on purpose. You're a Russian oligarch who lives in London. You know a lot of powerful Americans. It means she might have started a rumor for exactly this reason. So that you would think twice about ever cooperating with those powerful Americans."

He blinked at Amanda. "You think she was lying to me."

"I think it's possible."

And, yes, this was true. It was possible that her father's name was part of a misinformation campaign. The Russians were known to do this, to start rumors and sow doubt, including about employees in public-facing roles, whose real identities were known, just like Charlie-the-PR-flak's was. It was possible they found his name on the internet and picked him, randomly, as a scapegoat. It was possible—but was it likely? *Occam's razor,* she thought. His murky exit from Helsinki. His request that she leave him out of it. He was hiding *something.* What were the odds that, out of every name they could have picked, the Russians just happened to pick his?

"No." Komarovsky shook his head vigorously. "*No.* She wasn't lying."

"You can't know that," Amanda said, though she didn't really believe herself.

"Yes, I can. You're forgetting the entire reason I'm here. Bob is dead. The GRU found out about us. *Somebody* told them what was going on."

CHAPTER THIRTEEN

The assignments started small. The first one came in March 1987. Charlie Cole and Benjamin Hacker, a newly minted junior case officer, were conducting surveillance on a government delegation visiting Helsinki from Moscow. They parked across the street from the restaurant and watched the group of dark-coated Russians emerge. "Ten bucks says they're headed to the club on Ratakatu," Hacker said.

Charlie said: "Too easy. I'm not taking the other side of that."

Hacker leaned forward, peering through the windshield of their Opel Astra. Some officers read magazines; others listened to the radio. Hacker, a freckled farm boy from Iowa, and the newest addition to Helsinki station, had decided gambling was the best way to pass the time during these tedious surveillance shifts. There was a tattered $10 bill that he and Charlie were constantly passing back and forth. Despite the age gap, the two men had an easy rapport, a comfortable shtick. Hacker the bachelor, Charlie the family man, Hacker the shit-disturber, Charlie the peacekeeper.

At the end of the night, when the Russian delegation was safely ensconced in their hotel and they'd handed over duties to the next shift, Hacker said, "Feel like getting breakfast?"

Charlie shook his head. "I'm headed back to the station."

"Aren't you off this weekend?"

"Just need to get a few things done. Behind on some contact reports."

It wasn't exactly a lie: he *was* behind on some contact reports.

His comically slow hunt-and-peck typing skills were a well-known fact throughout the station. So much concealment, he was realizing, could be found within the existing contours of his life. Some excuses were so explicable, so natural, that they were practically true.

On this Saturday morning, the station was deserted. Sitting at his desk, Charlie paused his typing. He stood up, looked over the walls of his cubicle, surveyed the empty desks. "Hello?" he said softly. Then, more loudly: *"Hello?"*

Silence. Silence so perfect that it felt like a taunt.

He sat back down, took his key from his pocket, and unlocked his file cabinet. He pulled out the list and set it on his desk. It was a thin sheet of paper, marred with coffee rings and grease stains. An utterly ordinary document, a carbon copy, one of many: a list of KGB officers in Helsinki whose names and faces were known to the CIA. Charlie considered it. Of course, he could see why she wanted it. It was useful for the KGB to know which of their officers had been made. But was he actually endangering anyone by giving this to her? Was it really *that* bad?

Yes, you fucking idiot. Of course it's that bad.

Okay. Bad, then. But was it worse than what might happen to Helen and Amanda if he decided not to cooperate?

(In the months that followed, he would realize that this internal exchange, this evaluation of relative badness, was now the sole calculation that defined his life.)

He folded the list into a neat square. He took off his shoe, slipped the square into his sock, put his shoe back on. The folded corner of the paper poked against his ankle, but soon he got used to it. The station remained empty for the rest of the day, but had anyone been there, that would have been okay, too, because Charlie, typing away, looked like a perfectly ordinary CIA officer on a perfectly ordinary Saturday morning.

·   ·   ·

Many decades later, on a day in late January, Charlie Cole was standing outside an Ethiopian restaurant in a Fairfax strip mall, reminding himself of how it felt to inhabit a lie-that-also-wasn't-a-lie. He and Osmond Brown were finally having their lunch date. Charlie, as he'd explained to Osmond, was fast approaching retirement, and was seeking advice on how to handle the transition. "Happy to help!" Osmond had replied, with surprising chipperness.

See, it was funny, Osmond said. He'd expected to hate it. All of it. He'd been one of those people who saw retirement as a punishment. A lifetime of hard work, and *this* was what he got? His identity snatched away in one fell swoop? Not to mention the pill boxes, the AARP magazines, the senior citizen discounts, the crossword puzzles, the orthotic shoes, the transition lenses, the failures of his body, the thinning hair, the slackening skin, the weakening bones, the patronizing language, the early bird specials, the march of indignities that paved the road from here until the end. Not to mention the end! The big one, the End with a capital *E*. Why would *anyone* want that?

Therefore he was shocked, pleasantly so, to discover that he had been entirely wrong.

"I just got back from Jupiter," he said, as they sat down at the table. "My niece was the one who convinced me. I said I didn't want to be such a cliché, the snowbird down in Florida. She said it's only a cliché because it's an objectively good idea. And you know what? I loved it. Made an offer on a condo last week. Have you ever been to Jupiter?"

Charlie shook his head. "Not Jupiter specifically, but I had an aunt in—"

"She was right! My niece, this twenty-five-year-old kid, she was right. It's paradise. Turns out I actually *like* being a cliché. I like blending in. I'm just another boring old man. No one notices me. No one cares! Spent my whole career trying to be anonymous and only now do I finally have it. Let me tell you. It's liberating."

Advice about retirement? Charlie had worried about the flimsiness of this pretext. But Osmond, absorbed as he was in his energetic stream of commentary, didn't seem to question it.

"It's funny how much you can get wrong about yourself," he continued. "Take this restaurant. I thought I hated Ethiopian food. Had one too many bad experiences in Addis Ababa. Then one day I'm walking through West Palm Beach, and I pass this Ethiopian place, and I think, 'Well, why not? If I was wrong about retirement, what else was I wrong about?' You ever had Ethiopian before? No? I'll order for us." When the waitress arrived, Osmond enunciated the names of the dishes with the relish of a college student embarking on a semester abroad.

The restaurant, wedged between an Edible Arrangements and a Pet Depot, was surprisingly busy during this Monday lunchtime. Several customers waited by the front door. They were turning tables quickly. Charlie would need to hurry if he wanted his questions answered. But the food arrived, and immediately Osmond started instructing Charlie on his technique. "You do it like this," he said, tearing off a piece of injera. "And then like this, and like this." As Osmond waxed poetic about the visceral pleasure of eating with one's hands, about how the West had really gotten this wrong, Charlie couldn't get a word in edgewise.

After a while, Osmond sat back, taking a breath to digest. Charlie decided to seize his opening.

"Your niece sounds great," he said. "It's nice to know the next generation has things under control. Makes it a little easier to let go, right? Although, to be honest, it's hard to accept that Amanda is old enough to be a station chief. I still think of her as a little girl."

"She's a good one." Osmond nodded. "She was always very diligent. Thorough."

Charlie smiled. He did love talking about his daughter. The lie that also wasn't a lie. "She got that from her mother. Funny, though. It took a while for it to surface. She was a distractible kid. Head in the clouds. I was surprised when she decided to go down this path. But maybe she knew this job would give her what she needed."

"Discipline, you mean."

"And the stakes of it, too. She went through a phase where she thought everything was bullshit. 'No one's gonna *die* if I flunk history.' That kind of thing. But then she took this job, and the stakes actually *are* life-and-death, and it—it changed her."

"Heh." Osmond's tone grew quieter. "Yeah. I remember what that felt like."

The waitress brought Charlie a second can of Diet Coke. While cracking it open, he continued nonchalantly: "It seems like you two got along. She spoke highly of you."

A slight lift to Osmond's brow. "Really?"

"Sure. She said you were a good boss."

"Well, I guess that's nice."

"I don't know if it matters at this point." Charlie gazed at his soda, as if pouring it into his glass required immense concentration. "But I think she feels some guilt over her role in your . . . Well, that is, if she caused any changes to your, uh . . . timeline."

His eyebrows arched higher. "How kind of her." Osmond couldn't quite keep the snark out of his voice. "Nothing like the pity of the young, is there?"

The waitress came over to ask if they were finished. "Obviously not," Osmond snapped. After she turned away, he continued bitterly: "You know, I've had time to think. I've had nothing *but* time to think. And I have to say, Charlie. Your daughter didn't waver an inch. She was relentless about it. Borderline disrespectful. Honestly, if things had gone differently, if she had been wrong, I probably would have tried to get her transferred to a different station."

He paused, grimaced. "Yeah, I know. I sound like a rotten old bastard. Anyway, doesn't matter. She was right. I was wrong. No two ways about it. After it happened, I felt humiliated. Miserable.

But the thing is, I didn't feel *angry*. How can you be angry at some-one who was objectively right? Doesn't matter that she's younger, that she's less experienced. Actually, you know." He tilted his head. His tone softened again. "I wonder if Amanda is the reason I wound up listening to my niece."

The waitress came by. Apologizing for his earlier outburst, Os-mond asked for the check.

Fuck, Charlie thought. *Fuck, fuck.* "Listen, Osmond," he said. "Thanks so much for the advice. I admire how you've navigated the retirement thing with composure. So little is within our control, isn't it? But you've made the most of it."

"Yeah." Something clouded Osmond's gaze. "I guess."

Charlie lowered his voice. "I just don't want Amanda taking the wrong lesson from this. Sure, recruiting an agent takes skill, but whether the agent turns out to be productive . . . That's sheer dumb luck, isn't it?"

Osmond, now lost in thought, said: "She has her convictions. Maybe I never did."

The waitress took Charlie's credit card. They had two minutes, three tops. "Did you ever meet the guy?" This was risky, but what other option did he have? "Amanda's source, I mean. The one who warned her about the assassination. Sounds like he was a real char-acter."

Osmond snapped back to attention. "She told you about him?"

"I know, she probably shouldn't have, but we're family. We bounce things off each other. Anyway, sounds like he was an inter-esting guy. A bit . . . quirky?"

"Quirky." He snorted. "Now *there's* an understatement."

"So you did get to meet him?"

"He just didn't look right." Osmond grimaced. "I walk past the conference room and there's some weird, sweaty guy, pacing back and forth. And then Amanda comes into my office and says that this Semonov guy, the guy in the conference room, that he's the walk-in. The brave and mighty hero. *This* guy? You can't be serious."

"Semonov," Charlie repeated. "Right. Yeah. I couldn't remember his name."

"It didn't make any sense. It was so *random*. He's the guy who makes the passports at the GRU, and he overhears these other guys talking about Bob Vogel? And then he's on vacation in Italy, and while he's there, la-di-da, he decides to stroll over to the American embassy and raise the alarm? But I have to give her credit. She just *knew*, somehow. That girl, she's something. She's like a human lie detector."

. . .

"Well, obviously, it isn't the same source. This fellow—Semonov, you said?—this fellow who walked into the embassy wouldn't have been the one talking to Senator Vogel. He would never have access to that kind of detailed information."

It was a few weeks later, a cold morning in New York. Maurice stood by the fireplace, tending to the flames. Charlie said: "So what does it mean? What do we do with this?"

"I'm not sure there's anything to be *done*. But take heart, Charlie. Apparently Semonov knew nothing about you. He clearly didn't give them your name that day in the embassy. If Osmond had any reason to be suspicious of you, he never would have agreed to meet you for lunch. And he certainly wouldn't have spoken so openly about Semonov."

"So, in other words, until the moment I gave Amanda those papers, she didn't suspect me of anything."

"Well, yes. But you had a good reason. Those papers were a critical source of information, and you said it yourself. You didn't want to impede the investigation."

"It was a stupid thing to do."

"It was the *right* thing to do. You know that, Charlie."

They were silent for a while. Charlie stared at the embers in the fireplace: they were alive, shimmering, almost bejeweled. In the last several months, he had experienced the entire spectrum of terror. Sweat-drenching, sheet-twisting nightmares. Paranoid glances at the car down the block. Half-baked plans of escape to Morocco, Samoa, anywhere without an extradition treaty. But the worst were the moments of total paralysis, the moments when his frantic mind simply gave up. When he realized there was nothing to do but lie down and let the train flatten him. He'd come to New York hoping that Maurice would have an idea, but here he was: another dead end. "It's not going to work, is it?" he said.

Maurice stood at the fireplace, coaxing the flames. "What isn't?"

"What we talked about, back in the fall. That maybe Amanda would find out about Särkkä, and, okay, that's fine, but I don't want her to find out about . . ." Charlie trailed off.

"She's very good at her job."

"Yeah." And he thought, but didn't say, *unfortunately for me.*

"Sooner or later, she'll come to you with her questions. Like Osmond said. She can tell when a person is lying. You'll have to tell her about Mary. There's no other choice."

He sighed. "I'm fucked."

"Charlie," Maurice said. Then, more sternly, "*Charlie.* Look at me."

Reluctantly, Charlie obeyed.

"Amanda will ask you for the truth, and you'll tell her the truth, and it's going to be okay. Do you understand? You're not the person you were thirty-five years ago. You've changed. You made those terrible mistakes. But it's in the past. What you had with Mary died with Mary. She's gone, Charlie. It's time for you to accept that. You need to let yourself move on."

She's gone, Charlie.

But what was he supposed to say to that? So he returned his gaze to those narcotic, mind-emptying flames.

CHAPTER FOURTEEN

"That was great," Kath said, after Komarovsky had left. "Good idea to plant that seed of skepticism. The rumor-as-disinformation thing."

Amanda collapsed into her chair. She felt shapeless and limp, like a deflated balloon. Kath tidied up, rinsing their coffee mugs, humming to herself. *He's working for Moscow*, Komarovsky had said. *He has a direct line to the Kremlin.* Amanda wasn't quite sure what this feeling was—fatigue, sadness, fear—but it was awful. In her mind she saw tsunamis crashing into placid shores. How could a thing so heavy arrive so quickly?

He'll never forgive me, she thought. When she was twenty-two, and newly returned from her world travels, chastened by what happened in Thailand, haunted by what happened in Russia, she sought her godfather's advice about what she was planning to do next. Maurice said that her instinct was correct, that it was a good idea, that she would make a good spy. This pleased her—it was rare for the elliptical Maurice to give such direct advice—but still, she took it with a grain of salt. "I guess you can't really *know*, though," she'd said. "I think I could be good at it, but he probably thought the same thing."

"Your father, you mean? I think he had very different reasons for joining the agency. It was mostly because his own father before him had done this. And he wanted to impress him."

She remembered thinking, even at the time, even at the age of twenty-two, that impressing one's father didn't seem like a wise rubric for making decisions. But right now, in this situation, the wisdom or non-wisdom of it didn't matter. Because if Charlie believed in this rubric (and wasn't the very nature of his request to her evidence of that belief?), that was enough to guarantee this whole thing would end badly. There were two doors. Behind one was a treasonous daughter; behind the other was a treasonous spy. She lifted her head. "It's a game," she said. "It's rigged. Either way I lose."

Drying her hands on a tea towel, Kath shrugged. "We'll see."

"No, seriously. I just had an epiphany. *I'm fucked.* Either way I'm fucked."

"Is that really how you feel?"

"How else could I feel?"

Kath shrugged again. "Okay. So you're fucked. So now what?"

"It's like, it doesn't matter what I do."

"Right. And I repeat. Now what?"

"I don't know." After a pause: "You got one of those old cyanide pills handy?"

Kath smiled. Then she began to laugh. Amanda, to her surprise, began to laugh, too.

• • •

They paused their work with Komarovsky over the holidays. He and his family were spending Christmas in Gstaad. Kath was headed to an undisclosed tropical location. Amanda was planning on a quiet stretch of catch-up in Rome before they reconvened in January.

She unlocked the door to her apartment. In the weeks of her absence, it had acquired an alien air. The bare walls and lone bowl on the draining board sparked the same question as did those frumpy pantsuits inside her carry-on: Who was the person who thought *this* was a good idea?

It occurred to her that she could do something about this. Then it occurred to her that maybe she *should*.

On Christmas, she FaceTimed with Georgia. After being passed around to say hello to every single member of the sprawling Markopolous clan, Amanda said: "Okay, so. I need your help."

After describing what she needed, she said apologetically, "I know it's a lot," but Georgia replied: "Amanda Margaret Cole, you just shut the fuck up. This is *literally* my dream come true." Within days, the boxes began to arrive. Amanda had wanted to surrender the decisions entirely to Georgia, but Georgia said: "Nope. We're gonna teach a woman to fish." Express shipping was expensive, but it was Amanda's credit card, so who cared? Georgia picked out a few things to start, shirts and sweaters and shoes and dresses. Once she tried them on, and once she decided what *she* liked—she meaning, crucially, Amanda—they would go from there.

On New Year's Day, Amanda woke up early. Other than the watery warble of the pigeons outside the church, the Roman streets were silent. She arrived at the station and found it empty, too. She was finally putting a dent in the backlog of work, and it felt good. The awareness of her situation remained, but when she was reviewing the rote paperwork, the pain of it diminished. It became more like the throb of a toothache, omnipresent but dull. She'd never much enjoyed this part of the job, but now she felt a strange gratitude for it, this paper-sorting, this soothing work of entropy reversal. *Maybe Kath is onto something*, she thought.

And then—the timing was uncanny—a voice called out: "Anyone home?"

Kath appeared in her doorway. "Let me tell you something," she said, plunking herself down with a sigh. "Key West is hell on earth. They should put Jimmy Buffett in jail."

"You were in *Florida*?" Amanda raised her eyebrows. "I can't picture it."

"Turns out, neither can I."

"I thought you weren't getting back till the fifth."

"Maybe I missed this miserable place. I like the sweater, by the way." Kath cocked her head. "That's a good color on you."

• • •

At dinner that night, Kath observed that Amanda seemed a bit better. Amanda agreed with this. "I don't want to say it's been easy," she said. "It hasn't. Not at all. But it's kind of . . . *simple*, you know? It's just, like, get through the day. Wake up and do it again. And it sucks, but what else are you going to do?"

Kath nodded. Amanda was talking about the Charlie thing, but also the drinking thing, and Kath seemed to understand this. "It's funny," she continued. "It felt so *dramatic* when Komarovsky told us about the rumor. But a little time goes by, and it becomes just another piece of the puzzle. And it's a big puzzle. And there are a lot of pieces."

"And you have to take them one at a time."

"Exactly." After a pause, Amanda said: "Actually, I've been wanting to thank you."

"For what?"

"Well, you've been so cool about everything. I know I've been kind of . . . messy. And you always give good advice."

"Oh, stop. I'm bossy, that's all." Kath shook her head, but Amanda saw a trace of color rise in her cheeks. And then Kath changed the subject. Funny, Amanda thought. Kath, so comfortable in her own skin, so genuinely *herself*, seemed the type who would accept compliments with graceful ease. But wasn't this the most essential lesson of her work? The alpha and omega of human intelligence: everyone wound up surprising you.

• • •

One piece at a time. This approach carried them back to London, through January and February, through their meetings with Komarovsky. Amanda was careful to invoke the Charlie Cole rumor every so often, reassuring the oligarch that they were keeping the operation airtight, extremely need-to-know, in case the rumor had any merit: concerned, but not *too* concerned.

Luckily, Komarovsky was too absorbed with his own problems to scrutinize her performance. David Hopkins, the CEO of Aeromach, was proving stubborn. In the months after their initial conversation, Hopkins had gotten it into his head that maybe *he* had leverage in this situation, too. So Komarovsky wanted him to cancel that $6 billion contract for those Polish missiles. Okay, fine. But this was already an uphill battle for Hopkins—don't forget he had to contend with his board of directors—and if Aeromach announced this change, and the market freaked out, and the stock price went down, it would be his head on a spike, and certainly it would be *better* for Komarovsky if Hopkins was still around, right? So here's what he wanted. On the day they announced the change, Komarovsky had to make sure the market *liked* the change. Understood?

As Komarovsky grumbled about the thickheaded entitlement of Americans, Amanda's mind was whirring. "No," she said. "Wait. Hang on a second. This is *good*. We can use this."

And so, on a fast-approaching day in early March, Ivan Komarovsky would walk into the gallery in Soho. He and Vitsin would, as usual, retreat to the office in the back. While Komarovsky described Hopkins's demand to Vitsin, and asked what the Kremlin wanted him to do, Amanda and her team would be listening in a nearby van.

When she told Komarovsky he was going to have to wear a wire, he balked. "What if Vitsin searches me?"

"He's never searched you before."

"But what if—"

"He's *not* going to search you. But if he does, you give us the signal and we get you out of there. We'll be through that door in thirty seconds flat."

They needed hard proof to link the Kremlin to these manipulations. Without the recording, they only had Komarovsky's word.

And of course Amanda trusted him, of course Kath trusted him, but if they were going to bring this all the way to the White House, they needed more than trust.

This, she knew, would be their only shot. Komarovsky's performance might work once. It wouldn't work twice. He and Vitsin didn't usually talk about these things. Vitsin didn't know the first thing about taming the egos of brash American CEOs. Such a stark deviation from the usual pattern would catch his handler's attention. The operation had more contingencies than Amanda would have liked, but there was no such thing as a perfect plan. Sooner or later, they had to take the plunge.

The team performed multiple dry runs. The first time, the signal from the transmitter concealed in Komarovsky's cuff link failed to reach them. The nature of Berwick Street meant that a white panel van idling by the curb would be too conspicuous, so they'd parked around the corner on Livonia Street, but apparently even twenty yards was asking too much of the transmitter. In a mild panic, Amanda wondered if they were going to have to scrap it and start over. But then Bram, one of the guys from the agency's Office of Technical Service, said: "The lamppost. The one outside the gallery. There's a utility box at the bottom. We can install a repeater inside the box. It'll give us another hundred yards, easy."

On the second dry run, sitting in the van on Livonia Street, Amanda donned her headphones. There, crystal clear, she could hear Komarovsky flirting and laughing with the gallery assistant. Oh, yes, there was the boss. Right this way. Seats creaking. Door closing. "It's Anya's birthday next month," Komarovsky said to Vitsin. "And you know how desperate she is for that Peter Doig. Can you work your magic, my friend?"

Amanda gave a thumbs-up to Bram. The repeater worked perfectly.

· · ·

On the day before the operation, they ran through it one last time.

"And while you're talking, if you suspect that he's onto you?" Amanda asked.

Komarovsky recited: "I say, 'David is on his yacht in Miami.'"

"And if you're in *imminent* danger?"

"I say, 'Please, Sasha, don't you remember that night at Novikov?'"

If that happened, the team was prepared to enter the gallery, retrieve Komarovsky, and hustle him to the American embassy. The British authorities wouldn't be *thrilled* about the storming of Vitsin Gallery, but it was also possible they would never hear about it. Deep cover officers, like Vitsin, didn't enjoy drawing any attention to themselves.

"And if there's no problem, and everything goes smoothly?"

"Osipov will drive me here."

Amanda nodded. "Good. But if you have even the *slightest* sense that something is wrong, don't come here. You'll only lead the FSB directly to us. Got it? Just get in the car and have Osipov take you home."

.   .   .

"He's on the move," said a staticky voice on the radio. "Getting in the car now."

Amanda took a deep breath. "Copy that," she said.

It was the next afternoon. She and Kath were in the back of the van on Livonia Street, with Bram in the driver's seat. The second operative from OTS, the one who had just radioed in, was following the black Rolls-Royce as it departed Pavel Partners. The third operative from OTS was sitting outside a café on Berwick Street, with a direct sightline of the gallery. Bram turned around. The breast pocket of his blue work suit was embroidered with the logo of a fake plumbing company, which also decorated the outside of the panel van. "You good?" he said.

"Good," Amanda answered for both of them, because Kath was engrossed in a pile of documents. "You?"

Bram nodded. "Gonna get a little shut-eye. Wake me up when he's close." He settled into his seat, pulled his baseball cap over his eyes, and, within seconds, started to snore.

Time was moving in strange ways. The last weeks had flown by—there had been so much to do, preparing for this moment— but now they were here, and the afternoon was passing in a slow drip. She checked her watch, but somehow it had only been four minutes since Komarovsky left the office.

The radio crackled with periodic updates on his progress through the London traffic. Amanda kept checking her watch. Kath kept turning pages, muttering to herself. On the day of a big operation, some people wore lucky socks, or drank their coffee out of a special mug. Kath liked to surround herself with the evidence, to *literally* surround herself with it, to arrange the papers in a kind of magic circle, like an on-the-fly version of the conference room back in Rome station. She claimed that it helped steel her nerves. ("Like reciting the catechism," Amanda suggested. Kath gave her an odd look. Amanda shrugged and said: "Sunday school.")

Shrieks and laughter from the sidewalk outside the van. School had just let out for the day. Eventually, the staticky voice on the radio said: "Turning onto Mortimer Street." Amanda leaned forward and shook Bram's shoulder.

And then it was happening. The Rolls pulled up along the curb on Berwick Street. Komarovsky emerged, wearing a navy blue suit and sunglasses. He ducked his head into the open door of the car and said: "I'll call you when I'm done."

"Sure thing, boss," Osipov replied. The voices came through loud and clear, now that the transmitter in his cuff link was within distance of the signal repeater.

Bram caught Amanda's eye in the rearview mirror. She nodded. "All right," she whispered to herself. "Here we go."

The second operative, the one at the café, said: "Target approaching gallery now." The third operative said: "Taking up position in the alley." As part of their prep work, OTS obtained blueprints for the building on Berwick Street and had discovered a back door. They would have eyes on both entrances.

For a brief moment, standing outside the gallery, Komarovsky paused. Across the street, the operative at the café removed his baseball cap and set it on the table. Komarovsky removed his sunglasses and placed them in his breast pocket. Confirmation that the audio was working. Confirmation received. He turned around, opened the door, and disappeared from sight.

"Ivan!" a bright voice said. The audio remained crystal clear. The cheerful click of high heels across the floor. "How nice to see you. I didn't realize we were expecting you."

"Oh, you weren't. I just happened to be in the neighborhood. Is Alexander around?"

"He is, but let me just . . ." Heels clacking back across the floor, her voice growing fainter. "I'm terribly sorry, Ivan, it looks like he's still on the phone. Do you mind very much waiting a few minutes?"

"Of course not."

"It shouldn't be long. Can I get you any tea?"

"Tea would be lovely."

Deep breathing, creaking floorboards. Amanda didn't need eyes on Komarovsky to know what he must look like: shifting his weight, glancing at the doors, hands in his pockets to hide the fidgeting. A minute later, as the heels clacked back across the floor, he said: "Wonderful. Thank you."

"It's funny, you know. Alexander was just talking about you this morning."

"Really?" He cleared his throat. "Why . . . why is that?"

"Oh, no. I don't want to spoil the surprise."

"My dear, you must tell me. This weary old heart isn't up for surprises these days. You don't want me to keel over and die of a heart attack, do you?"

She laughed. "Well, then, do you promise to act surprised?"

recorder. When I got home and checked the audio, it was completely fuzzed up. You couldn't hear a thing. Only white noise. If Vitsin takes that precaution for a conversation that *isn't* incriminating, of course he'll do the same for one that *is*."

"But this never happened during our test runs."

"Because Komarovsky never said anything meaningful during our test runs. And Vitsin trusts him, at this point, so he doesn't bother jamming *every* conversation they have. But when his agent starts yammering about David Hopkins?" Kath gestured toward Berwick Street. "Vitsin flips the switch. He'd be an idiot *not* to. And we know he's not an idiot."

Amanda stared at Kath. "Are you certain about this?"

"Of course not. I'm not certain about anything."

"Bram?" she said. "What do you think?"

He shook his head. "You're in charge, Cole."

"Well, what are our options? Other than sitting here and doing nothing?"

"We still have our extraction plan."

"Right." Kath rolled her eyes. "Great idea. Storm the gallery and blow his cover sky-high. If we go in there, Amanda, that's it. We lose any hope of a second chance."

"You seriously think we're going to get a second chance?"

"I'd rather keep the option open than not."

Amanda closed her eyes. Bram and the other operatives were former Navy SEALs. If she asked them to extract Komarovsky, they would succeed. Without question, they would succeed. And his cover would be blown, but he would be safe. Anya and his children would see him again.

But where would that leave her? And where would it leave Bob Vogel? And Diane Vogel? And Konstantin Semonov?

See, people usually got this wrong. The hardest part of the job wasn't the action. It was the moments of passivity; the moments when there was nothing to do but sit there, letting things unfold, white-knuckling your way through it. Amanda took a deep breath. "Fine," she said. "We wait. But as soon as he walks through that door, we find a way to intercept him. Got it? I need to know what the fuck we're dealing with."

CHAPTER FIFTEEN

During that spring of 1987, Charlie learned to cover his tracks. The Friday overnight shift, for instance. It was useful. If an officer worked surveillance on Friday night and had to return the car to the station on Saturday morning, it was entirely under-standable that he might go upstairs, take advantage of the peace and quiet, and catch up on work for a few hours.

Sometimes these excuses were actually true. That day—Saturday, April 18, to be precise—happened to be a truthful day. He wasn't at the station on any treasonous errand for Mary. But he was wired from the coffee he'd drunk during his overnight shift, and he was behind on paperwork, and, spurred by the constant awareness of his betrayal, he felt like he ought to be giving the agency one hun-dred and ten percent. The irony was rich. In his effort to offset the bad with the good, Charlie was doing better work than he'd done in years.

Later in the evening, the coffee wearing off, his eyes gritty from lack of sleep, he finally called it quits. Stepping outside into the fresh spring air, his hunger awakened. He wondered what Helen had planned for dinner. Lasagna, he hoped. She was on an Italian kick lately, and she made an excellent lasagna. But as he started home, Charlie had the nagging sense that he was, somehow, meant to help with dinner. There had been a plan. Right? Wasn't he meant to pick something up? But now he was nearly home, so maybe he would just have to go inside and ask her. He rounded the corner to their street and looked up at their building, and for some reason, the light coming from their living room window suddenly caused him to remember:

April 18, 1987. His daughter's fourth birthday.

Oh God. He checked his watch: just past 6 p.m. *Oh God.* The birthday party had begun at noon. He was meant to pick up the cake from the bakery in the morning, on his way home from his shift. Chocolate cake, vanilla frosting, decorated with a drawing of Elmo. Helen had stopped him as he'd walked out the door on Friday, saying, "You won't forget the cake? It's already paid for. Just give them my name." And Charlie nodded, even while feeling offended by the question, because what kind of father forgets his own daughter's birthday?

He climbed the stairs like he was ascending to the guillotine. He opened the door to find the living room scattered with detritus: a red balloon bobbing against the ceiling, frosting-smeared plates, crumpled paper napkins. A string of colorful handmade rainbow letters tacked to the wall spelled out: HAPPY BIRTHDAY AMANDA.

Helen and Maurice were sitting at the far end of the living room. Maurice looked up, but Helen kept her gaze fixed on Maurice, saying: "No, keep going. You were telling me about that student of yours."

Maurice cleared his throat, uncertain. "Right. . . . This student, he was saying, well, uh . . ."

"I'm so sorry," Charlie said. "Helen, I'm so sorry."

"Yes, well. Thankfully Maurice was able to pick up the cake."

"Helen." His voice was fraying. "I can't believe I forgot, it just—"

"Maybe save the explanation for your daughter. It was *her* birthday, after all."

"Is Amanda . . . ?"

"I put her to bed. She was exhausted. Maurice? Can I get you more coffee?"

All the while, she refused to look at him.

Maurice stood up. "No, no. I've stayed too long as it is."

Helen accompanied him to the door, brushing past Charlie. She said goodbye, closed the door, and turned to Charlie. He thought it would be a relief, this moment when she finally looked at him, but he was wrong. This was even worse. Helen stared at him with uncomprehending disgust. "I always wondered," she said, "why you were so rude to that woman. But it makes perfect sense. She's your mistress."

"I—What?"

"Don't play dumb, Charlie. It just makes you look worse."

"But I'm not—"

"I saw you. I was dropping Amanda off for a playdate. You came out of the building, and a minute later, she came out, too. Don't you *dare* lie to me. Don't pretend this is some bullshit with your job. This is twisted. I mean, this is really sick. This woman comes up to me and Amanda and pretends to be a babysitter and meanwhile she's *sleeping* with you? What kind of a person does that?"

He opened his mouth, but she snapped: "No! Shut up! You don't get to talk."

"Helen. *Helen.* Please let me explain."

"I knew something was wrong," she said. "I knew it *months* ago. Your clothes smell like perfume. You come home with a bruise on your neck. But somehow I explain it all away. I don't let myself see it. Until it becomes too fucking obvious to ignore." Her voice broke. "In broad daylight. On the same street as Amanda's best friend. What the fuck, Charlie. It's like you *wanted* me to find out."

He dropped to his knees. "It was nothing. Helen. It meant nothing."

"It's *not* nothing. You don't get to say that."

He shuffled forward, wrapped his arms around her legs. She was nearly knocked off-kilter ("No, no, Charlie—stop it! Just stop it!"), but he held her tighter, and pressed his cheek against her dress. "I love you," he said. "I don't deserve to love you, but I love you. Helen. Helen. I love you more than anything in this world."

This time, she didn't manage to stifle her sob. "And I waited for you," she said. "That's the worst part, Charlie. I thought you would come clean. I thought you must have a scrap of conscience left. I was naive. I was an idiot. You were *never* going to tell me."

. . .

He stood up and held her while she cried, her head cradled against his chest. He offered to explain everything, but she didn't want to hear it. Had he slept with this woman? Yes or no? That was enough. She didn't want more than that. Eventually Helen pushed him away, her face blotchy and swollen, and said: "You're such a fucking asshole, Charlie."

He spent the night on the couch. The ambient glow of the streetlights cast a dim gray rectangle across the ceiling. Charlie felt nauseous. *I was naive. I was an idiot.* It had always been Helen's greatest gift, her ability to believe that any person, even the most despicable, would eventually do the right thing. She had believed this about him. And Charlie, in the worst way possible, had proved this tenet wrong. He had broken her heart, broken their vows, but what filled him with the most shame was the idea that he might have broken her capacity for trust.

He must have slept at some point, because around dawn, as the sky was lightening, he woke to the soft pad of footsteps across the carpet. Amanda stood at the end of the couch, dressed in her flannel nightgown. Her thumb was in her mouth, and in her other hand she carried a plush Elmo. She took out her thumb and whispered: "Daddy!"

It was the first Charlie had seen of her. She climbed into his lap. He stroked her hair, silky and warm, tangled from sleep. Swallowing the lump in his throat, he said: "Did you have a good birthday, sweetheart?"

"We played Pin the Tail on the Donkey. Linna had never played it before."

"Linna," he said. Linna Kivi. Amanda's best friend from preschool, the one whose family lived near the harbor, on the same street as Mary. He had known this, he had *known* this, and yet it had never factored into his behavior.

"And, Daddy, Daddy! Guess who won!"

"Let me guess." He squeezed her tighter. "Was it a little girl named Amanda Cole?"

She wriggled with pleasure. As she continued whispering about the party (somehow knowing she was meant to whisper: the dawn light, her father on the couch, her mother in the next room), Charlie felt another wave of shame. The anchoring heft of her body, the powdery smell of sleep. His daughter. He had done this to her, too.

Later that morning, Helen came into the living room to find Amanda nestled alongside Charlie. Amanda was asleep again, her thumb in her mouth. Charlie had remained rigid, not wanting to wake her with his movement. Flatly, Helen said: "You're still here."

"Of course I'm still here."

"Of course. Sure. Well, since you're still here, you can take care of our daughter. I'm going out."

He craned his neck, watching her walk toward the door. "Where are you going?" he whispered, but she either didn't hear him, or, more likely, knew that she was under no obligation to answer his questions.

When Amanda woke up for good, Charlie attempted to make them pancakes. Amanda sat at the table, Elmo clutched in her lap, watching as the pancakes smoked and blackened in the skillet. "You're doing it wrong," she said gravely. "Mommy doesn't do them like that." So Charlie agreed to let her put ice cream on her pancakes to make up for the burn, and it was as he was scooping out the ice cream that Helen walked through the front door.

Of course she was going to come back. Helen might walk out on Charlie, but she would never, *never* walk out on Amanda. But still. To actually see her, standing there in the kitchen, gave Charlie the smallest thread of hope. Their eyes met for a long second. Two seconds, three seconds. Amanda tugged impatiently at his sleeve. "Daddy," she said. "The *ice cream*."

·   ·   ·

After the confrontation, Helen slept like a rock. The wondering, the worrying, the infinite loops of speculation, they had driven her crazy over the last few months. So he was having an affair. So now she knew. She passed out as the exhaustion reached its climax.

But the next morning, as soon as she opened her eyes, she was struck by the inevitable question. *Now* what was she meant to do? Her first year at Conn College, Helen had gotten a bad flu. The illness made her horribly homesick. Her mother, who could hear it in Helen's voice, immediately got in the car. Mrs. Dennehey spent the next several nights sleeping on the dorm room floor, feeding Helen soup, laying cool cloths against her brow. This felt just like that, but a thousand times worse. She was a thirty-three-year-old woman with a four-year-old daughter, but as she curled into the fetal position, her eyes filling with helpless tears, all she could think was: *I want my mom.*

Theoretically she could call her parents, but it was still the middle of the night on the East Coast. The phone ringing at 1 a.m. was a terrifying thing, and she didn't want to scare them. She would have to wait another five, six, seven hours to talk to them. She imagined her mother's unreachable voice and cried for a while longer. What would she say? What advice would she give? What do you do when you find out your husband is cheating on you? Helen didn't know. They didn't teach you that at Conn College. But her mother would know; she would say any number of wise things. Things like, *Eat something. Take a hot shower. Take a walk. Go to church. Pray.* Pray? Yes, that was absolutely something her mother would tell her to do.

She took a hot shower. She ate something. She saw Charlie on the couch, Amanda asleep beside him, and told him she was going out.

Her walk took her past the neighborhood park. It was the first real day of spring, the breeze turning mild, the snow finally melting. It wasn't until she arrived at the church, and saw the lilies on the steps outside, that she remembered what day it was. It wasn't just Sunday; it was Easter. *Well*, she thought mordantly. *Maybe that makes us even.* Charlie had forgotten about the birth of their daughter, but Helen had forgotten about the resurrection of Christ.

Mass had already begun. Helen slipped into a pew in the back. It had been—She didn't want to think how long it had been. The service was in Finnish, but the rhythm was familiar enough that she was able to follow along. As Catholic churches went, this one was modest. Tattered red carpet, simple white walls. And yet: the scent of incense, beeswax, and lily. The sound of voices joining in hymn. The warmth of a stranger's hand during the passing of the peace. The rituals brought her a measure of calm, of comfort.

And was that it? Was the reassurance simply a physical thing? Chicken broth for an aching throat, damp cloth for a fevered brow. Or did it mean more than that, even after so many years away? She walked up the aisle, dipped the wafer in the wine. She felt lucky, having come back on this Sunday of all Sundays. The Easter pageantry cranked up to eleven. If anything could manage to distract Helen from herself, it was this.

At first the timing felt like a cruel twist of fate: that she had found out about the affair on their daughter's birthday, that the two things would forever be paired. Four years later (she and Amanda living in New York, regularly attending Mass again), the timing felt like a gift, that the day she walked back into the church happened to be the holiest day of the year. And many years after that (the Helsinki chapter of her life now vague and distant) the timing didn't seem to mean anything. It wouldn't have mattered if it had been an ordinary Sunday. The resurrection happened every week, not just on Easter.

And was that it? The question followed her back to her pew, the wafer and wine dissolving slowly on her tongue. She was thirty-three years old. For the past twelve of those years, to the wider world, she had been Mrs. Charles Cole. (He hadn't *insisted* she change her name, not exactly, but the expectation was clear enough.) They could be married for another twelve, and another twelve and twelve after that, but it would never change what had always been true in her heart. She was always going to be Helen Martha Dennehey, the studious bookworm, the scrappy middle sister, the girl who needed her mother to get her through the hard times.

Of course this meant something to her. How could it not?

At the end of Mass, she shook the priest's hand and thanked him in clumsy Finnish. She began walking away, and then she turned around, looking back at the church. She didn't feel at peace, not by a long shot, but for the first time in weeks, she felt the *possibility* of peace. A twinge so fleeting that she couldn't even be sure. The weathered red bricks, the bell tower and steeple. *Home*, she thought. *This is a home.*

And the sight of Amanda, smiling gleefully at the container of ice cream. *Home.*

And the sight of Charlie, gamely scooping out that ice cream. *Home.*

Was he her home?

Maybe. Maybe not. She didn't know yet. But maybe, for now, for the sake of that smiling little girl, she would be willing to try.

CHAPTER SIXTEEN

An hour later, Komarovsky sat across the table, hand trembling as he reached for the coffee mug, into which Amanda had just poured two inches of whiskey.

"Calm down," Kath said. "You're getting carried away."

He gulped the liquor and held out the mug. Amanda obliged with another two inches. "He knows," he said hoarsely. "He definitely knows."

"This is based on what?"

"He was angry. Very, very angry."

"Because David Hopkins is threatening to fuck things up and Gruzdev won't be happy about that. Of course he's angry."

"Kath," Amanda cautioned.

"What? I'm not going to *baby* him, Amanda. He's a grown man. So it didn't go like we planned. There's no need to go crazy like this. Honestly, Ivan. You're *fine*."

There had been a moment, right after Komarovsky emerged from the gallery. When he caught sight of Amanda, sitting at the café across the street, the little color that remained in his face suddenly drained away, and she thought: *He's going to bolt. He'll take his chances with the GRU and FSB rather than keep working with us.* Quickly, she'd stood up, crossed the street, brushed past him, and slipped a scrap of paper into his hand. He'd obeyed the instructions for now, but he could change his mind at any moment. So Amanda spoke softly, patting his hand. "It's okay," she said. "Take your time."

He gave her a weak look of gratitude. Kath rolled her eyes.

A minute later, she inquired gently: "Can you tell us what happened in there?"

"He didn't believe it. He insisted Hopkins was bluffing. 'He won't pull out. Of course he won't pull out.' He thought I was an idiot for thinking that he might."

"So what does he want you to do?"

"He wants me to get Hopkins to shut up and do his job. He doesn't care how it happens. These Polish missiles, Vitsin made clear, they are *very important* to Moscow. So if I don't fix this, Moscow will be very disappointed."

Komarovsky grimaced and stared down at the table. The three of them were silent for a moment. Then he looked up. "But wait. Why are you asking? You know this already."

"Well," Amanda said. "Actually. About that."

When she told him about the jammed signal, Komarovsky jumped to his feet and yelped. "It's okay!" Amanda said. "I *promise* you, Ivan. It's okay. I understand how scary this sounds. And I'm not going to stop you from leaving. You're not our prisoner. But you should let Kath explain. I think you'll find it reassuring."

Kath nodded. "Vitsin is a professional. This isn't any cause for alarm."

Komarovsky was breathing hard, overtaken by animal panic. "If you'll just sit down," Amanda said, steering him back to the table. "There. There. There you go."

Kath explained. The explanation was good. Even Amanda, despite knowing it was just guesswork, found herself convinced. Kath didn't try to soothe his panic like Amanda did. Instead she cut through it, summoned his more rational self. A reserve of trust had accumulated between them over the past three months; now was the time to cash that in. Gradually, she managed to calm him down.

"But none of this solves my problem," Komarovsky said. "Which is that, if I don't get Hopkins in line, it's my head on a platter. So what do we do?"

The truth was that Amanda didn't know. She didn't yet have a plan. Komarovsky gazed at her like a frightened dog, as if she were his owner considering euthanasia, as if she held his life in her hands. *Which I kind of do*, she realized. It might be that they had reached the end of this operation. That pushing it any further was too risky. "Miss Clarkson," he pressed. "Please. You must have an idea. We've come this far. I want to see it through. I owe it to Bob."

She squinted at him. *I owe it to Bob*? Those words left her slightly unsettled. Suddenly there was a question she wanted to answer. She didn't know why she hadn't thought of it before.

Afternoon was turning to evening. The room was growing dimmer. They kept the lights off in the kebab shop to avoid drawing notice. She turned toward the newspaper-covered window. And then, at that moment, the windows brightened slightly. The streetlights on East Ferry Road had just switched on.

A satisfying *click* of an idea.

She turned back to Komarovsky. Stared at him for a beat. Then said: "You go ahead and do it. Give Hopkins what he needs. Get him to cancel the missiles. Keep your cover intact."

He blinked at her. "Go ahead?"

"Yes."

"But . . . but this . . . Are you sure?"

She cocked her head. "You're not relieved? I thought you'd be relieved."

"But I don't understand."

"You just do what you have to do," Amanda said. "And I'll worry about the rest."

. . .

After Komarovsky left, Kath said: "So what is it?"

Amanda started clearing their coffee mugs from the table, throwing the empty whiskey bottle into the trash. "What is what?"

"The plan. 'Give Hopkins what he needs'? You're not *really* going to let him commit another round of securities fraud, are you?"

"I'm going to let him try," she said. "He won't actually be able to pull it off. But that's assuming my hunch is right. I need to get to Washington."

"Washington?"

"I have to check something. I'm going to try to get a flight tonight. I'll call you in the next few days."

• • •

When Jenny Navarro took the job on K Street, she could imagine the scowl on Senator Vogel's face. He detested lobbyists as a rule. *That's nice*, she sometimes thought, when her old boss bragged about never taking a dime from special interests. *But, you know, not everyone on Capitol Hill is as rich as you.* At some point during his ascent from the lower class to the global elite, the altitude change had caused Bob Vogel to forget that, in modern-day America, integrity didn't come cheap.

But Jenny had student loans to repay. Her parents had just refinanced their house for the third time. The brakes on her sixteen-year-old Civic were worn out. The lobbying firms waited a few days, out of respect, but the week after Vogel's funeral she had several offers from the biggest shops on K Street. They paid six times what she'd been making as his chief of staff. She said yes to the most ethical-seeming option.

Now, several months into the gig, Jenny had concluded that this wasn't a bad life. The work wasn't particularly interesting, but it was a new language to learn, and she'd always liked a challenge. And she liked her colleagues. A lot of them were in similar situations, trying to save a little money before going back into government service, enough to pay off their debt or pull together a down payment. They cashed their paychecks with their eyes wide open.

Of course, some grew addicted to the comforts. A new car, an upgraded wardrobe, a bigger mortgage. Jenny made a private sport of it, trying to predict which of her coworkers would succumb to the glow-up, and the expensive maintenance thereof. (Inevitably, the person in question would also stop calling themselves a lobbyist, preferring the easier-to-swallow "public affairs consultant" instead.) Not that she went around saying these things. Her boss had no idea of her true feelings about the job. "You've got a knack," he observed. "You'll make partner in record time."

Jenny didn't bother correcting his assumption. The truth was that she knew she would work there for a few years, and then she would leave. It wasn't her job to explain herself to him. It *was* her job to, for instance, persuade the junior senator from South Carolina of the benefits of offshore wind farms.

On a Thursday in March, Jenny and the junior senator had just finished lunch at Charlie Palmer. He'd ordered the oysters and the Wagyu striploin and a dry martini. Jenny had stuck to her usual seared scallops and club soda with lemon. On this early spring afternoon, the sunlight was changeable and watery, clouds scudding rapidly overhead. Blink and they'd be back in the oppression of D.C. summer, soupy heat and soaked blouses. Out on the sidewalk, she extended her hand and said: "I'll send over the draft when I'm back at my desk. I think you'll find it interesting. And if you don't, I'm sure we can find a way to *make* it interesting."

The senator laughed as he shook her hand. "Always a pleasure, Ms. Navarro."

As she watched the senator walk away, across Louisiana Avenue toward the Capitol, a voice behind her said: "You're good."

Jenny startled. When she turned around, there she was: Amanda Cole. That horrible woman! That sower of paranoia, that causer of nightmares, that figure of deceptive innocence. "I'm sorry," she said, smiling politely. "I didn't mean to sneak up on you."

"Yes." Jenny took a step back, her heart thumping. "You definitely did."

"Can I walk you to your office?"

Jenny took another step back.

"Or I could come to your apartment tonight? What would be convenient?"

"What would be convenient is for you to leave me alone."

"Look, Jenny. I know I made you a promise. And I hate breaking my promises."

"I'm serious. Leave me alone."

"I can't. I'm sorry. This is really important."

Diane was right, Jenny thought. *This was exactly what she warned me about.*

•   •   •

Months earlier, on the July morning after the funeral, Diane Vogel asked Jenny Navarro to come over. In the penthouse kitchen, Diane was surrounded by platters of food. "When my father died," Diane said, unwrapping a tray of Danish and muffins, "my mother said, 'Well, Diane, maybe now you'll finally lose that baby weight. Grief is a natural appetite suppressant.' It was just about the stupidest thing I've ever heard. Are you hungry? I'm starving."

The windows were open to the warm summer morning. Sounds of traffic drifted up from Park Avenue. Diane reached for a blueberry muffin, separated the domed top from the cakey bottom, stared at each piece for a moment. Then she stood up, threw out the bottom half, sat back down, and took a big bite of the top. "Bob had this thing about wasting food," she said, through a mouthful of muffin. "But I don't like the bottom half. I'm old and I don't care. So I guess that's one perk to being a widow. Okay." She brushed the crumbs from her fingertips. "Jenny. About yesterday. That woman who pulled you aside."

"Oh," Jenny said. "I didn't realize you saw."

"I'm assuming she told you the same thing that she and Director Gasko told me? Right. So you know, too. Honestly, when they did, I was relieved. I *knew* it couldn't be a stroke. Bob was healthier than ever. They didn't tell me much. Only that they—how did they put it?—they possessed intelligence suggesting that the Russians were involved in the assassination."

She nodded. "That's pretty much what she told me, too."

"Which means that my suspicions were correct. And his, too, I guess. In a different way."

Jenny frowned, puzzled.

"So Bob didn't tell you about it either? No. Of course he didn't. You know, Jenny, that you were like a daughter to him. He would have wanted to protect you from it, too. That's what he always said. He was just trying to protect me. Protect me." Diane grimaced. Then she said: "And here I thought he was being paranoid."

Diane slipped into a silent fugue, staring down at her mug. Jenny noticed that the coffeepot in the middle of the table was empty. She jumped to her feet, eager to combat the moment with some useful action. A few minutes later, when the coffee was ready, Diane was still lost in her thoughts, her hands wrapped around her mug. "More coffee?" Jenny said. No response. But she refilled it anyway, and the revived warmth of the mug snapped Diane back to attention. "Oh, bless you," she said.

"Some people compartmentalize," she resumed. "Not him. You saw how he was. His work was his family was his life. Everything mixed up with everything else. We were each other's sounding boards. But whatever he was up to with Ivan Komarovsky, he decided it was too dangerous to share with me. And I told him that if this thing, whatever it was, if it really *was* that dangerous, he *had* to tell me. He had to think clearly."

"Komarovsky," Jenny repeated. "I don't know that name."

"He was our neighbor in London, years ago. He and Bob hadn't spoken in a decade, maybe more. Until January. Bob ran into Ivan at Davos. And then again in February, at Courchevel. Our paths kept crossing. It took me a while to realize it wasn't accidental.

Bob wouldn't tell me what they were working on. 'It's important,' he said. And I said, 'Why are you getting into bed with this man? This Russian oligarch. Why do you trust him?' And he said, 'Because I have to. Because I'm the only person *he* can trust.' And now he's dead. So you see what I mean? I was right about Komarovsky. Bob was right to be paranoid. It's like a twisted O. Henry story."

Jenny swallowed. "Did the, um . . . Did the people from the . . ."

"From the CIA."

"The people from the CIA. Did they know about this? About Komarovsky?"

"No."

"But did you . . ."

"Did I tell them about my suspicions? No. I didn't. Would that have been useful to them? Probably. But do I want to get dragged into it, the way my husband got dragged into it?" There was a long silence. "I have children. I have grandchildren. I'm sure you can understand that."

In that moment, Jenny had been wrestling with what to say about the papers in Senator Vogel's office. Telling Diane, not telling Diane: both avenues felt like a betrayal of some kind. But Diane had just said it herself: she didn't want to get dragged into it. So that settled it.

"The reason I'm telling you all this," Diane said. "If it comes to it, Jenny. I think you should do the same. Stay away from it. I was dismayed to see that woman talking to you. She shouldn't have done that. If she ever tries to talk to you again—"

"She won't," Jenny interrupted, thinking of the promise Amanda made, the evening before, on the bench in Central Park. "She promised she won't."

"Well, good. But if she does—or if anyone else from the CIA does, for that matter—for your own safety, I think it would be best to steer clear."

• • •

Amanda stepped forward and touched Jenny's arm. Jenny's first instinct was to slap her hand away and tell her to fuck off. But they were standing here in broad daylight, in this sea of D.C. power lunchers, and Amanda's fingertips were barely grazing the fabric of Jenny's jacket. Jenny didn't want to be the asshole here.

"It's about Senator Vogel," Amanda said quietly. "We're close to cracking it. But we're not there yet, and you're one of the only people who can answer this question. He gave his life for this, Jenny. And now I'd be really grateful if you would talk to me. Just for a few minutes." Amanda seemed to take her silence as assent. She gestured down the sidewalk. "Do you want to walk for a while?"

And so they walked for a while, through a wide canyon of grand government buildings and glassy law firms. Amanda craned her neck, peering up at the clouds. "I wish I was in town longer. I always manage to miss the cherry blossoms."

The small talk was meant to calm her down. Jenny resented this. She also resented the fact that it was working. A few blocks later, her pulse was almost back to normal. Amanda, seeming to sense this, said: "So. We've made a lot of progress, continuing the work Senator Vogel was doing. We're very close to getting the evidence we need."

"Good for you," Jenny said tartly. Then: "Sorry. I didn't mean it like that."

"Sure you did. And I get it. You think we're on different sides here."

"No, I don't. It's just that . . ."

"That someone warned you to stay away from us." Amanda gave her a sideways glance. "Was it Diane Vogel?"

"How did you know?"

"An educated guess. The point is, we now know what Senator Vogel was trying to expose. And we know who his source was. But what we *don't* know is how much the senator trusted this source. So. Did he ever talk to you about a man named Ivan Komarovsky?"

Jenny thought for a moment. She thought carefully. "No."

"You're sure?"

"Yes."

"Oh. Well. Okay."

Amanda was visibly disappointed. Jenny felt bad about this, even though, strictly speaking, her answer was honest. Bob *hadn't* ever talked about Ivan Komarovsky to her. Literalism was the fastest exit ramp from this stressful conversation. But the literalism didn't feel *great*. Jenny knew a lawyer who once managed to defend his client from a class action lawsuit because a comma changed the meaning of the word *dismemberment. Jesus, Jenny*, she thought. *When did you become one of those people?*

"But Diane did," Jenny blurted out, before she could think twice. "Talk to me about Ivan Komarovsky, I mean. The day after Bob's funeral. That's when she told me. She assumed that Bob was working with him on—well, on whatever it was."

Amanda lit up. "That's great. That's *great*, Jenny. And what did Diane say about Komarovsky? Did she say whether Bob trusted him?"

Jenny shrugged. "She implied as much. And, for my part, I don't think Bob would have taken that risk if he *didn't* trust him. And he obviously knew he was taking a risk. That's why he kept it such a secret from us."

"Us?"

"Me and Diane," she clarified. "He didn't usually conceal things from me. He basically *never* concealed things from Diane. So I think she felt weirdly vindicated. She thought Bob should have listened to her, asked for her opinion. If he had, she would have told him to stay away from Komarovsky. And then he would still be alive."

Amanda raised her eyebrows. "Stay away from Komarovsky?"

"Yeah. Bob trusted him, but *she* didn't trust him. She didn't say why. But Diane clearly assumes that Komarovsky is the reason her husband wound up dead."

They were stopped at the corner of Fourth and E, waiting for the light to change. Jenny squinted at Amanda. "But why aren't you just talking to Diane directly?"

"Diane made it very clear that she didn't want to get involved."

"So did I."

"Yes, but I could tell you didn't mean it." After a beat, Amanda added: "That's a compliment, by the way."

The light changed, and they crossed the street. They were silent during the rest of the walk back to K Street. Amanda was clearly preoccupied, thinking through whatever came next. Jenny supposed she ought to feel annoyed by this, at being used and discarded like an empty soda can. But she didn't, and this surprised her. If anything, she felt envious. Jenny would return to her meetings and conference calls, and Amanda would return to her—well, what *did* her life look like? Jenny had only the vaguest notion. Surely it was more interesting than the life of a corporate lobbyist. (An admittedly low bar.)

Jenny extended her hand. "Good luck," she said. "I hope you get to finish what he started." And she was surprised, again, to find that she meant it.

•   •   •

First thing the next morning, Amanda had an appointment to see Director Gasko. He was a notorious early bird, but she had arrived even earlier, and she clocked his approving glance when he spotted her outside his office. Inside he gestured for her to sit. Without preamble, she said: "I think Komarovsky is playing us."

Gasko, who had been hanging his suit jacket on the back of his chair, paused. He cocked his head, pressed his hands into the top edge of his chair. "Explain."

"Earlier this week, when we tried to record his conversation with Vitsin, a frequency jammer blocked us. Kath said this was standard operating procedure for the FSB. No cause for alarm. At first, I thought she might be right. But afterward, while we were debriefing Komarovsky, something felt off."

"How so?"

"Komarovsky was expecting us to tell him to cancel the Aeromach push. It was almost like he *wanted* me to tell him to cancel. Like he was suddenly actually concerned about the fate of this company. It felt *fake*. Like, you know, the lady doth protest too much."

"And that's it?" Gasko lowered himself into his chair. "A hunch, in other words?"

"No. There's also our source inside the GRU. He talks regularly to the goons from Unit 29155, and every once in a while, he asks about the 'bad guy from Iceland.' The last time our source brought him up, they were hesitant to say anything negative. Which is highly out of character."

At this, she felt a stab of guilt. She should have listened to Semonov. Should have known that, if he was picking up on something weird, there *was* something weird. But when she'd read the contact report from Moscow, back in January, she'd decided there could be lots of reasons for Tweedledee and Tweedledum suddenly clamming up about Komarovsky. Maybe they realized it was stupid for them to tell tales out of school. But Semonov had thought enough of this change to report it to his handler, and Amanda should have taken it seriously. She'd had weeks—months!—to take it seriously, and she hadn't.

"And there's one more thing," she continued. "Yesterday I went to see Jenny Navarro. You remember her? Senator Vogel's chief of staff. I wanted to know if Vogel had ever talked to her about Komarovsky. If she had any sense of how much Vogel did or didn't trust him."

"So she knows the truth about how he died?"

"Yes."

Gasko frowned. "A little over your skis there, Cole."

"I know. I'm sorry about that."

"No, you're not."

"Anyway." She forged ahead. "Vogel never talked to Jenny about Komarovsky. But, after the funeral, *Diane* talked to her about him. Diane knew that her husband and Komarovsky were up to something suspicious. For some reason Diane didn't want to share that information with us, even though knowing it was Komarovsky would have saved us a *whole* bunch of time—but anyway. Fine. Okay. Spilled milk. My point is that Diane Vogel never trusted Komarovsky. She's a smart woman. I'd take her judgment seriously. The Vogels and the Komarovskys spent a lot of time together last year."

"So she thinks, what? That Komarovsky ratted him out? But why?"

Amanda shook her head. "I'm not necessarily sure Komarovsky was the one who betrayed Vogel. Any number of things could have tipped the Russians off. Vogel and Komarovsky weren't airtight. But all these bits and pieces got me thinking. Step back for a minute. If we know anything about Komarovsky, we know that his loyalty is fungible. He'll do whatever he needs to do to survive. That's why he agreed to work with us in the first place. He likes to keep the doors open."

Amanda paused. She was aware of how much of this was pure guesswork. But she was inclined to believe the theory, and more urgently, she needed Gasko to believe it, too. She continued: "So what's one more door, when it comes down to it? I think Komarovsky has shifted allegiances yet again. I think he's working with the GRU. I think he came clean to them about his relationship with us, and I think *he* was the one jamming the signal, not Vitsin, with the GRU's help."

(There was, of course, another obvious alternative: that Komarovsky had nothing to do with the blown operation. The CIA very possibly had a mole, and the mole had very possibly warned the Kremlin. Though the circle of the London operation was small, it was still penetrable. This could have been the moment to come clean and tell Gasko about her father. But then what? She wanted to see this through. She *had* to see this through.)

"Huh," Gasko said. A long pause. "I guess I could see it. I'm not saying I buy it. I'm saying it's *possible*. Either way, we have to figure out what to do about Aeromach. And how we're going to get the proof we need." Gasko squinted at her. "But I'm getting the sense that you already have something in mind."

"I do," she said. "Although it's sort of . . . blunt."

"Nothing wrong with blunt," he said. "Tell me what you need."

CHAPTER SEVENTEEN

In that first year of working for Mary, Charlie let himself imagine a different version of the story. One in which the documents were mere chicken feed, a way to establish his bona fides without giving anything away. *A KGB officer tried to seduce me. I let her think I'd fallen for it. But the whole time, I was the one recruiting her.* It wasn't beyond the pale. If Charlie managed to turn Mary to *their* side? Then every betrayal would look like tactical brilliance. The months went by, the betrayals mounted, and he clung to this idea. Redemption. Lemons into lemonade.

Until a slow Tuesday in January 1988, when those lemons became unredeemably sour.

At the end of the workday, Hacker stood up and asked if he was coming. Charlie explained that he was picking Amanda up from a playdate, and it was right on the way home, so he was going to keep working until then. "Glamorous life of a spy, right?" he said, and Hacker laughed. As the station gradually emptied, Charlie remained at his desk, diligently typing up a contact report.

Last summer, a memo had circulated through CIA stations in Europe about the Stinger missiles that America was supplying to the insurgents in Afghanistan. The missiles were lightweight and highly portable: a mujahideen fighter could pick it up, prop it on his shoulder, point it at the sky, and take down a Soviet helicopter in one shot. Some people questioned the wisdom of arming the mujahideen with these weapons, but these voices were drowned out by those in Washington who were eager to seize the moment. The

Soviets were in retreat, losing the war. These weapons would help bleed them dry. The memo took pains to demonstrate that every penny of Operation Cyclone was worth it.

Mary knew about this memo. She wanted a copy of it.

•　•　•

For security reasons, the station didn't have a Xerox machine, but the embassy did. It was in a small room on the second floor, near where the ambassador's secretary sat. Several months earlier, back in the summer, Charlie had stopped by the secretary's desk and said sheepishly: "Glynda, do you think you can find it in your heart to help an old man get out of the doghouse?"

She peered over the edge of her glasses. "What do you think I do here all day?"

The thing was, he explained, his daughter was in a summer camp, and he was supposed to help her with an arts-and-crafts project—a collage of her family—and it was due tomorrow, and he'd promised to help with it, but he had completely forgotten about it until that morning. "I brought these in"—he was carrying their old photo albums from Algiers and Bern and Berlin—"and thought I could make copies of them. But I have no idea how to use that machine. Will you show me?"

Softened by sympathy, Glynda showed Charlie which buttons to press. For the next several minutes they stood there, watching the images of Charlie and Helen's younger, smiling selves emerging from the machine.

Months had passed, and Charlie had become well-acquainted with that machine. Now, on that January evening, when the last person had left the station and he was finally alone, Charlie walked over to the station's metal safe and entered the combination. He slipped the Stinger memo inside the photo album, which he'd kept at the office as a handy excuse. He carried the album under his arm and, humming nonchalantly, opened the door to the embassy proper.

The rest of the building was deserted, too. As he stood at the Xerox machine, Charlie paused. The distant hum of a vacuum cleaner. *Almost* deserted, then. Well, that would have to be good enough.

An hour later, he stood in Mary's apartment. She read the memo with what struck him as an unusual degree of attention. "This is very helpful," she murmured. "Thank you. You're getting to be quite good at this, Charlie."

As he walked home, he told himself, as usual, that it hadn't been a big deal. (Right?) After all, Washington couldn't stop crowing about this weapon. When you thought about it, the information in the memo wasn't that much more revealing than what you could read about in the *New York Times* or the *Washington Post*. Chicken feed. (Right?) Just chicken feed.

Then again, for chicken feed, Mary seemed awfully interested.

• • •

Her requests were becoming more specific, acquiring an edge that had previously been lacking. In March 1988, it was the schematics of the Stinger missile. In June, it was the location coordinates of an important tribal chieftain in the Panjshir Valley. In September, it was the names of the top officials in the Soviet-allied Afghan government who had taken cash payments from the Americans.

Her shopping list included other items, too: information related to the Star Wars program, or the Contras in Nicaragua, or the AIDS epidemic. Maybe the requests were legitimate, or maybe they were designed to throw him off the scent. But Afghanistan—Charlie felt increasingly certain of this—was the meat-and-potatoes of her work, her central preoccupation.

The timing might have seemed odd. Gorbachev had long planned the withdrawal of Soviet troops from Afghanistan, and by now the drawdown was almost halfway over. But wars like these neither began nor ended neatly. The KGB were in Afghanistan well before the first soldier arrived. They would remain in Afghanistan well after the final soldier departed. The world would soon stop paying attention, but Mary and the KGB would remain.

Charlie had to turn this around. But the problem was, the longer this went on, the bigger the payoff would have to be. The hole he'd dug himself was growing deep. By late 1988, he was dealing in much more than chicken feed. The information he was handing over to Mary and the KGB: allies might well die as a result. He had to find her weak point.

But what was it? He snooped through Mary's apartment while she was in the bathroom—and found nothing incriminating. He parked himself in the café across the street from the telecom firm—but she diligently adhered to her cover, arriving at 8 a.m. and leaving at 6 p.m. Sometimes he followed her at night, but that was harder to swing, because he and Hacker often had surveillance shifts, and when he didn't, he felt that he ought to at least put an appearance in on the home front.

Fall turned to winter. He was detaching from his own life. Charlie had the bizarre sense that he was watching himself in a movie. The little pine table in the kitchen, the sounds and smells of dinner cooking, the people he loved most in the world, his wife, his child: Didn't this man know how good he had it? He wondered, sometimes, if it wasn't too late to come clean. His cowardice was destroying everything he had.

Amanda, at least, was a blessed source of distraction. Perched on her booster seat, she told long, complicated stories about school. "I learned a song today!" she said. "It's about a, about a, about a *witch* who puts the bad children in the ocean." Often she wore her cowgirl costume, left over from Halloween, to the table. It was like she had been crafted in a laboratory for the very purpose of easing the tension between Helen and Charlie. After dinner the three of them would do the whole routine, bath time and pajamas and *The Polar Express*, which was the only book she ever wanted to read, despite Helen's efforts otherwise.

But when they closed her door and the distraction ceased, the mood in the apartment changed. Charlie washing the dishes, Helen drying. Any more wine for you? No, thank you, I'm okay. Theirs was the heartbreaking politeness of strangers. How was your day? Oh, it was fine. The usual. How was yours? They would read for a little while in the living room, Helen absorbed in a novel, Charlie staring passively at his imported copy of *Newsweek* or *Sports Illustrated*.

He didn't register the words. Mostly his mind drifted back in time, slipping into reveries. Their younger, smiling selves. Helen, standing beside Lake Geneva, squinting across the clear blue water and saying: "It's almost *too* nice. Honestly. The Swiss are a bunch of show-offs." Helen, walking through the whitewashed alleys of the Casbah in Algiers, pointing at a gray kitten in the doorway. "What do you think?" she whispered. "Should we take him home?"

And further back, to summers in the musty old Dennehey beach house, sand in the sheets, the smell of Coppertone. To nights in her narrow dorm room bed, Neil Young blasting down the hallway, batik-shaded lamps tinting their skin red. To the first time he brought her home to Greenwich, the eerie hush of the foyer, Helen shifting nervously in her wooden clogs. "Dennehey," Mr. Cole said, shaking Helen's hand. "Your people must be Irish." His mother, at least, was a little more polite. They talked about what Helen was studying, and at one point during dinner, she turned to Charlie and said: "You've certainly found yourself a smart young woman."

Later that night, Charlie said: "That wasn't too bad, right? My mother clearly loves you."

"*Loves* me?" Helen laughed. "I don't think so."

"She kept going on about how smart you are."

"It wasn't meant as a compliment."

He frowned. "How could she not mean that as a compliment?"

"Charlie." She brushed the hair from his forehead. "I think you're wonderful, but I'm not sure you really understand how women work."

Sitting at the kitchen table, he remembered Helen's long-ago observation. He also remembered something Hacker recently said. "I have this theory," he'd said. "Women are harder to recruit. They just don't *think* like us. They're more subtle, somehow. Is that sexist? If I mean it in a nice way?"

It occurred to him that he, Charlie, had never actually recruited a female agent. Not a single one, in all these years. He had tried, but none of the targets had worked out.

How had he never seen this pattern before? And why on earth did he imagine that he was going to suddenly break this streak of failure with *Mary*, of all people? She would never let him get a glimpse of her real self. Her insecurities, her hungers, her weaknesses.

She understood him. But he understood nothing about her in return.

He didn't stand a chance.

This was the moment Charlie started giving up.

• • •

Helen didn't know about the silent decision Charlie had made. But she, like everyone, could see the external manifestations of it: his hunched shoulders, his paunchy belly. He'd stopped running. He ate too much. Food was one of the few things that could distract him. That inner voice of shame only seemed to shut up when he was eating his third donut or tearing open another bag of potato chips. Or, strangely, when he was reading about the Yankees. They were having another disappointing season, but he found that he actually liked reading about a bunch of losers.

Helen was more patient than he deserved. It began to baffle him, her decision to stick with this depressing head case of a husband. He could sense the end coming, and yet he felt powerless to stop it.

It finally happened in May 1989, on a Saturday morning a few weeks after Amanda's sixth birthday. Helen said to Amanda, "Go

She shook her head. "Charlie, I'm going to talk for a while. I don't want you to say anything. Okay." Just let us talk."

He did as she asked and kept his mouth shut. It was strange. It was like one version of him was there in the room, blowing up to explain, and another version was already looking back on this from some future point. The pain of loss was always twinned with the pain of remembering. "You never understood how much I was

PART V

THE GODFATHER

CHAPTER EIGHTEEN

After a little less than forty-eight hours in Washington, Amanda boarded a red-eye back to Heathrow. The plane touched down on Saturday morning. On Monday, Aeromach would announce their changes, and Komarovsky would juice the stock price. They would have to move fast.

A few hours later, they gathered in a secure room in London station. Kath was carrying a plastic bag from Pret a Manger. She caught Amanda's look. "What?" she said. "I'm starving. I brought extra. Amanda? Bram?"

Amanda shook her head. Bram shrugged. "I could eat."

Kath slid a sandwich across the table. "Turkey and cheddar. Amanda, are you sure? You should eat something. You look upset. Or was Gasko that intolerable?"

"He was fine. Listen, Kath, you remember the time we lost power in the kebab shop? And I went outside to see what was happening, and that construction crew was working down the road, and it turns out the crew has permission to shut down power on stretches of East Ferry Road when the project requires."

"I remember."

"And we left, and went out the back alley, and we walked past Komarovsky's spot. There's that bathroom window in the back. I remember thinking it was weird that the bathroom light was still on. Because the whole block had lost power."

"Yeah," Bram said. "Because they have a generator."

"Exactly!" Amanda exclaimed. Then she turned to Bram. "Wait. You already knew?"

He shrugged again. "I may have gotten up to some extracurricular activities."

Kath arched an eyebrow. "What does *that* mean?"

"It means that after the frequency jammer, or whatever that was, I wanted to do a little extra digging on Komarovsky. Their security was a joke, by the way."

"And *when* were you going to tell us about this?"

"Chill out, Frost," he mumbled, through a mouthful of sandwich. "It's not a big deal. See, she's happy I did it. Aren't you, Cole?"

Truthfully, she was overjoyed. Amanda felt like kissing Bram. Maybe it wasn't a *great* idea for the OTS guys to be running rogue, breaking-and-entering on their own initiative, but still: Bram had just saved them a whole lot of time. Trying for sternness, Amanda said: "Kath is right. You should have told us." Then: "But this is great, Bram. What did you find?"

"Honestly, not much. That's why I didn't mention it. But yeah, like you were saying. They have a generator. Not surprising. They can't risk losing power in the middle of the work."

"How big is this generator?"

"Two hundred kilowatts. Like what you'd park outside a football stadium. It has a diesel tank, holds enough fuel for twenty-four hours." He shook his head. "Those really aren't supposed to go inside, you know. The fumes are bad for your lungs."

"Is there a way to drain the tank without them realizing it's been drained?"

"Sure. No sweat."

"Great," Amanda said. "*Great*. Next question. How hard would it be for someone to turn off the power for East Ferry Road? For, say, thirty minutes on Monday night?"

"Normally impossible." Bram balled up the sandwich wrapper. "But I've talked to some of the guys on the construction crew. The foreman is paying them under the table. I bet he'd be happy to take a bribe. And, if not, we can always threaten to report him to the tax authorities."

• • •

Around 5 p.m. on Monday, Komarovsky stood across East Ferry Road, watching Yulia enter the hair salon. The other programmers appeared soon after.

He glanced to his left, to his right. The street was quiet. He walked past the old kebab shop, slowed his stride to peer through the gaps in the yellowed newspaper. The room was empty. Amanda had told him to go ahead and give the Kremlin what they wanted. There was no other way to keep his cover intact. This was what she had said. Yes, he told himself nervously. Yes, it was okay, because this made sense. He was important to the Americans.

Komarovsky keyed in the combination. When he entered the back room, Yulia and the others didn't even glance up. He found himself envying the code monkeys their tunnel vision. The nauseating uncertainties of the bigger picture didn't affect them. They only had to worry about the algorithm, which always worked exactly as designed.

Yulia pulled up a page on her computer screen and sighed. Komarovsky jumped to attention. "What? What is it?"

"Shell closed above sixty-five today."

"What? Why? What does that mean?"

She frowned at him. "Why are you acting so strange?"

Heat climbed through his face. "Answer me!"

"It's bad for me," she said, leaning forward, unzipping her backpack, retrieving a twenty-pound note. "But it's good for Sergei. I just lost a bet. Do you understand what a bet is? Or do I need to explain this, too?"

Time crept past. His uncooperative stomach twisted and roiled. He went into the bathroom, hunched over the toilet, dry heaved, but nothing came out. He told himself it must have been something he ate. Probably the salmon he'd had for lunch. It hadn't looked right.

Komarovsky kept a close eye on the market. There were only slight fluctuations in MACH's price, nothing out of the ordinary, but every spike and dip caused his chest to tighten. At 9:15 p.m., after close of the market in New York, Aeromach would announce they were canceling their $6 billion contract with the Polish government. Immediately after, a user by the name of Porno_Bacon_God would declare that this was a genius move. *MACH to the moon*, followed by a string of emojis. At the same time, Yulia and the other programmers would breach the digital wall and make the necessary changes to the algorithm, which would send that post to the top of the feed. It wouldn't take much. Just a little gasoline, here and there, to get the fire started. MACH was now trading at $312 a share on the NYSE. But after Porno_Bacon_God's post went viral, it would climb even higher in aftermarket trading, and David Hopkins could rest easy, knowing the market had just given him the cover he needed to carry out this move.

Almost there, he told himself. Soon enough, the whole thing would be over. He just had to get through the next hour.

At 9:07 p.m., he became aware of pressure in his bladder, having drunk six cups of tea in the past two hours. He stood at the toilet, and for several wonderful seconds, as he stared out the chicken-wired window to the back alley, the satisfaction of relieving himself quieted the mania in his head. He zipped up his pants, washed his hands, caught his reflection in the mirror. He looked terrible. He looked so *old*. He blamed this on the harsh light above the sink. A rusty pull chain dangled from the bulb. He began to reach for the chain, but before he even touched it, the light went out.

In the darkness, he blinked. A coincidence?

And then he heard a shout from outside the bathroom door.

•　•　•

The entire back room was in darkness. Yulia was using the flashlight on her phone to illuminate the fuel gauge on the generator. "It's empty," she shouted.

He hurried over. "That's impossible. I checked it yesterday. It was full. Sergei!" he barked at one of the other programmers. "Go see what happened. It must be that construction crew. Tell them to turn it back on!"

"It's nine ten," Yulia said, as Sergei ran out the door. "We have less than five minutes."

"Let me see that." Grabbing her phone, he saw that Yulia was right: the black needle on the fuel gauge rested at empty. He opened the tank, used the flashlight to peer inside. Empty. He banged his hand against the machine. "Where's Sergei?" he barked. "What's taking so long?"

Sergei returned, breathless from running. "Power is off for the whole street," he said. "It won't be back on for at least thirty minutes."

"Tell them that isn't acceptable! Go! Tell them!"

Sergei shifted uncomfortably. He was skinny, pasty, and completely unintimidating. He didn't need to tell Komarovsky how unlikely that was to work. Their computer screens were black. The room, normally filled with the dense mechanical hum of the servers, was dark and silent. Yulia looked at her phone. "Two minutes."

"The petrol station, then! Sergei! Buy as much diesel as you can carry!"

"The gauge is probably broken," Yulia said calmly. "It gave you a false reading."

"No! I checked the tank, too. It was full. Someone emptied it!"

The programmers stared at him. They had never seen him lose his cool like this.

"Shit!" he shouted. "Shit, shit, shit!"

Yulia checked her phone again. "It's nine fifteen."

He was in the grips of a wildness. His heart pounding like a drum, his brain filled with a screeching wail. He had known something was wrong. *He had known.* But he had plowed ahead, stupid, stubborn, because he didn't want to think through the logic of what something-being-wrong would mean. And now!

And now Aeromach was making their announcement. And now the stock price was plummeting. He stared at his phone, watching this unfold. And now that phone was ringing, and he wanted to ignore it, he wanted to run away and disappear forever, but he couldn't. Because right now, if he didn't try to save himself, no one else would.

Komarovsky pressed the button. Before he could even say hello, David Hopkins's voice hissed through the speaker: "You rat-fucking bastard. *What the fuck is going on?*"

·   ·   ·

Across town at London station, Amanda and Kath listened to the call unfold in real time.

"Out!" Komarovsky barked at the programmers. "Get out!"

"We had a deal, Ivan. So, what? You think I'll keep playing along? You think I'm just going to sit here and fucking *swallow* this? You motherfucker."

"David. David! Let me explain. We lost power. And our generator failed. Just give us a little time! We can fix this. I know how this looks, but I swear to you—"

"Your generator failed? Are you kidding me? Isn't that convenient. I *knew* it, Ivan. I knew it from the moment I walked into your office, and you told me about this little plan of yours. Fucking *Gruzdev.* Sit! Stay! Lie down! Cancel the missiles! I'm not your *puppy*, Ivan. I'm not just going to run around doing whatever you and Gruzdev—"

(Although this wasn't the point, Amanda found herself borderline impressed by Hopkins's lunatic, foul-mouthed rage. Too many years of military deference, she supposed, and eventually you were bound to snap.)

"David. *David*. We can't do this on the phone."

"—want me to do. So you thought you could have your cake and eat it, too, huh? String me up like a puppet *and* embarrass me while you're at it. I'm done, Ivan. It's over. I'm calling the Feds. I'm telling them exactly what you're up to. And by the way. The missiles? Forget it. We're keeping the contract. We're walking it back. My people are putting together a new announcement right now."

"It was just a hiccup. Give me a few minutes. I promise you, the market will *love* this."

"Why the fuck would I ever trust you again, Ivan? Your *generator* failed? You're playing me, and I'm done."

A beat of silence. Komarovsky had one last card to play. Dropping his voice to a whisper, he said: "David. Please. I need your help."

"I don't care."

"I'm begging for mercy. My life is in danger."

"You should have thought of that earlier."

"I didn't want to do it! Any of it! But they had a gun to my head. They're going to kill me, David. Please. *Please*. I'm begging you."

"Don't put that on me, you asshole."

"I have a wife. I have children!"

"And *I* have a wife! And *I* have children! And who the fuck knows what you were planning for them! This isn't my problem. I'm going to hang up and I'm going to call the FBI and if Gruzdev doesn't kill you first, we are going to fucking *bury* you. Goodbye, Ivan. Enjoy burning in hell."

• • •

When the call ended, Kath opened her mouth to speak, but Amanda held up a finger. Her laptop gave her a readout of the activity on David Hopkins's phone. Back in D.C., she'd persuaded Gasko to call his friends at the FBI and issue the tap. Hopkins losing his temper in such incriminating fashion was exactly what they hoped would happen.

"He was bluffing," Kath interjected. "Obviously he's not calling the Feds."

"I know," Amanda murmured. "But I want to see . . ."

To see if he was having an attack of conscience? To see if he was at least googling the protections afforded to whistleblowers? But, no: Hopkins was fighting for his own survival. He was approving the new press release; he was checking the market reaction; he was entirely engaged in crisis management. Several minutes passed. Nothing. Of course not. It had been too much to hope that he might turn himself in.

She sighed. "Yeah. Okay. Let's see what happens now."

Komarovsky, like any self-respecting billionaire, was deeply paranoid about his digital security. They had never been able to tap his phone, but on Sunday night, when Bram was draining the generator, it occurred to her that he could plant a bug in that back room on East Ferry Road. Normally the interference from the servers would make it impossible to get a clear signal, but maybe, during the blackout on Monday night, the signal would work. Maybe they would catch something useful. So Bram stuck a coin-sized microphone to the underside of one of the desks, and stashed a signal repeater behind a dumpster in the alley, and now, across town in London station, the audio was crystal clear.

Komarovsky breathing heavily, muttering to himself. "He doesn't know where to go," Kath observed. "He doesn't know where it's safe."

His phone rang again. He took a deep breath. "Vitsin, hello," he said calmly. "Yes. Yes, I know. We had a power outage. It's just a hiccup. Yes, I saw that. I just spoke to him. It's okay. We have a plan. It's all going to be fine. You will tell them that? Yes. Good."

He hung up. Several more minutes passed. Amanda's own phone vibrated. She picked it up and saw a text from Bram, who was stationed outside the Komarovsky mansion in Mayfair. *Visitor incoming*, he reported. *Mystery man. Older, sixties or seventies. Gray hair. Dark suit.*

Older. Not Vitsin, then. And not the thugs from Unit 29155, either. Someone they didn't know. *Anya just answered the door*, Bram texted. *Didn't seem to recognize him.*

A moment later, Komarovsky's phone rang yet again. "Oh fuck," he whispered to himself. "Oh, no. No. No."

He took a deep breath and answered: "Annushka?" Pause. "Who?" Pause. "And what is his name?" Pause. "Yes, darling, let him in. Right away. Offer him a drink. Make sure he is comfortable." Pause. "I'll have Osipov drive me home. No, darling. Nothing to worry about. I was . . . expecting him. I had just forgotten. That's all. I'll see you soon. Okay? Very soon."

· · ·

Osipov was parked a few blocks from East Ferry Road. Another OTS officer was waiting, ready to tail the black Rolls-Royce. Komarovsky ran toward the car. He slammed the door and the Rolls peeled out with a screech. It wove through traffic, blew through yellow lights and stop signs, making it back to the mansion in Mayfair in record time.

The CIA had no way of knowing what was happening inside the Komarovsky home that night, but Amanda felt certain, agonizingly certain, that this was it. This was the conversation that would reveal the truth. Who was he working for? Where did his true allegiances lie? Had the whole thing been for show? Was he, after all, the one who had turned on Vogel? She texted Bram: *Tell me THE SECOND there's any movement.*

An hour later, Bram reported: *Mystery man leaving the house.*

The gray-haired, dark-suited man walked to his Volkswagen and drove away. The other OTS officer now switched to tailing him, radioing the movements to Kath and Amanda.

The Volkswagen drove slowly through Belgravia, through Westminster. Almost *strangely* slow. He crossed the Vauxhall Bridge. Amanda felt a mounting sense of dread. "Turning on Lambeth Road," the officer said. "Turning on Parry Street. Oh, shit," he said. "Shit. We're—"

"You're outside the embassy," Amanda said.

"I didn't think—"

"He saw you tailing him." She sighed. "It's fine. It was too much to hope for."

So that was it: the gray-haired mystery man was Komarovsky's GRU handler. A handler would have known, of course, to expect the surveillance. He made a U-turn outside the embassy and, winkingly, flashed his lights at the OTS officer on his way past.

· · ·

In the conference room, they waited for updates from Bram. Right now it was Komarovsky's move. Until he made that move—until Amanda had a sense of his plan—she could only sit here, waiting, doing nothing.

Finally, as dawn approached and the sky faded from black to gray, Bram texted: *Leaving the house. Both of them. Suitcases.*

Suitcases. *Do they look scared? Worried?*

Too far to tell. Then: *I'm following.* And then: *They're taking the M4. Probably headed to Heathrow.*

Kath leaned over to look at Amanda's screen. "Heathrow?" She stood up. "We should go. We can stop him before he gets on the plane."

But Amanda stayed seated, staring at her phone. Heathrow meant one thing: Komarovsky was headed back to Russia. She shook her head. "No."

THE HELSINKI AFFAIR • 263

Kath looked at Amanda like she was having a stroke. "Are you crazy? So we know he was working with the GRU. So let's use this. Let's *squeeze* him. We can get so much more juice out of this!"

Kath wasn't wrong. This was the ultimate leverage. Komarovsky was scared of Gruzdev; scared of the FSB; scared of the GRU. The Americans were his only chance at safety. And think of what he knew! About the inner workings of the Kremlin, about Gruzdev, about what might be coming next. Now, finally, he would *have* to tell them the truth. And Kath was making these points, but Amanda wasn't really listening. She was thinking, instead, of that afternoon in the Winter Palace. The dim chill of the Baltic sky outside the Rembrandt Room. *Double agents. Triple agents. Mole hunts. Conspiracies inside conspiracies.* If you loved the game, why would you ever want it to stop?

"No," Amanda repeated. "We can't believe anything he tells us."

"But we don't—You're not—you're not *seriously* considering letting him go."

"He was working for the GRU this whole time. We can't trust him."

There was genuine pain on Kath's face. Her rapport with the oligarch hadn't been an act, then. "They'll kill him," she said faintly. "You know they'll kill him, eventually."

"Maybe. But that isn't our problem."

Kath sank back into her seat. "Brutal," she said.

After a beat, she added: "Remind me to never get on your bad side."

CHAPTER NINETEEN

Four days after Helen left, Maurice arrived in Helsinki. Jack, the station chief, had summoned him from Paris to make sure Charlie didn't do anything drastic in his despair, like commit suicide or defect to the Soviet Union. Standing in the doorway, surveying the depressing living room tableau that surrounded Charlie—curtains drawn, bathrobe covered in crumbs—Maurice said: "I can see you would prefer to wallow in your misery. But this is no longer an option. I'm going to unpack, and you're going to clean this place up."

He was too numb to argue. Of course Maurice could see what was happening. As Charlie trudged across the room, filling the trash bag with crumpled beer cans and empty potato chip bags, he realized that things couldn't get any worse. What was the point in fighting back? What would he be fighting *for*? Helen and Amanda were gone. He was ashamed that Maurice was seeing him at this pathetic rock bottom, but he also felt the smallest glimmer of relief. He was finally ready to take Maurice's original advice, given years earlier in the safe house in Fastholma, and come clean about everything.

Maurice handed him a cup of coffee. "I didn't do it," Charlie said mournfully. "I didn't listen to you."

"Start at the beginning," Maurice instructed. "Leave nothing out. Understood?"

Charlie stared down at his slippers. *Do it*, he thought. *Rip the fucking Band-Aid off, you chump.* It was difficult to form the words.

They came heavy and sluggish, nearly choking him on the way out. The first part was the hardest to admit. See, at the beginning, it was black and white: you were either a traitor, or you weren't.

But he forced himself to keep talking, and gradually it became easier, because once you crossed that line, what was another betrayal? And another, and another? The humiliations were burned into his mind with precise clarity: every classified memo, every code name, every geographic coordinate. Head hanging mournfully, he concluded: "And I know what you're going to say. I have to come clean. I know."

There was a long pause.

"Actually," Maurice said, "I'm not sure that's a good idea."

Charlie looked up in surprise.

"This is a disaster, Charlie. You've done too much damage. So now you have to make this be *worth* something. Mary believes you work for her. That she has you under her thumb. Well: turn that around. Use that to your advantage."

"I tried that already. She's bulletproof."

"You didn't try hard enough."

"I tried as hard as I could."

"You think this is about you?" Maurice snapped. "You think this is about what you feel like doing? You've put people in danger, Charlie. *Real* danger. You owe it to them to fix this."

• • •

Those ten days were the longest stretch of time they'd ever spent together. Charlie was grateful for the companionship, even if Maurice was a very particular roommate, a neatnik with even higher standards than Helen. Maurice also felt no compunction about emptying Charlie's beer down the sink, even though it didn't seem unreasonable for a man whose wife had just left him to want a beer.

They made an odd couple. Though Maurice was only a few years older, he acted like he was born in a different century. They sometimes talked tactics, but more often Maurice took a philo-sophical approach. Though many of his observations struck Char-lie as uselessly vague, no better than fortune cookie wisdom from a mustached Yoda in a tweed jacket, in certain moments they cut through his mind like the clean ring of a bell.

"I've seen how you are with Helen," Maurice observed, one night over dinner. "And I believe your intentions are good. You try to pro-tect her. You don't want to hurt her. But don't you see, Charlie, how this strength is also a weakness? It's a universal truth. A person's greatest strength is always, *always*, also their greatest weakness."

That night, lying awake in bed, Charlie kept thinking about it. When it came to Mary's weaknesses, he was stumped. So, then: What was her greatest strength? She was disciplined, obviously. An excellent actress, too. And she was canny. She could see what lurked beneath another person's exterior. Years ago, that evening in the grocery store, she had sensed the loneliness behind Charlie's smile. She had mirrored that loneliness back to him. She had given him exactly what he craved: a person he could rescue. A problem he could fix.

On Sunday night, with a mixture of benevolence and sternness, Maurice told Charlie that a week of moping was enough. It was time to get back to work. Charlie's sense of dread on Monday morning proved correct: most of his colleagues mumbled awkward hellos and backed away as if Charlie carried a contagious disease. Hacker, at least, was unruffled. "Sorry to hear about Helen. That sucks. You know my parents got divorced."

"Oh. I didn't know that."

"My mom moved to Chicago when I was in middle school. My dad was angry for a while, and then he was sad, and then he got back to normal. And you know what? The whole thing was a relief. By the end, they were so unhappy. Maybe it sounds like bullshit, but honestly, it was the best thing for me and my brothers."

"Huh." Charlie swallowed. "And your father got back to normal?"

Hacker shrugged. "People get used to things."

That afternoon, Charlie knocked on Jack's door. He volunteered to take on extra surveillance shifts to make up for his absence. He needed to stay busy, even if it was supremely boring work. Tailing the same people day after day, week after week, rarely yielded anything. People were predictable. Charlie thought about this during one of his shifts, trailing the Soviet cultural attaché as he left the embassy at the end of the day. Most of the KGB officers in Helsinki were known to the agency. But Mary, somehow, had always managed to fly under the radar.

After those ten days, Maurice had to return to Paris and finish his teaching duties for the semester, but the question he'd planted in Charlie's mind kept buzzing. Mary's strength—Mary's weakness? Charlie didn't have the answer, but he wasn't going to stop until he did.

. . .

In early July, in Helsinki, another knock on the door. This time Maurice was carrying a bigger suitcase. He said: "I'm going to spend the summer here. I think you need my help."

Charlie didn't bother contradicting him. He hadn't made an ounce of progress. It was like trying to scale an icy mountain without a pickax: there was nothing to hold on to. As he passed his intelligence to Mary—almost all of which, at this point, concerned Afghanistan—he found himself staring at her. Where was she from? Did she have a family? Did she suffer from any human affliction whatsoever? A mystery, all of it.

Charlie kept volunteering himself for surveillance shifts. "Good man," Jack remarked. "You're a real team player, Cole." Charlie would be lying if he said he didn't derive some pleasure from this newfound reputation. But the pleasure had its limits. One week in August, he realized that he had offered to take a colleague's Sunday overnight shift. That was Sunday evening in New York, his ironclad time for calling Helen and Amanda, which was the highlight of his week. In the past, the choice would have been difficult. Now he didn't even hesitate. Ignoring the ghost of his old people-pleasing self, Charlie told his colleague he was sorry, but something had come up, and he couldn't take the shift after all.

A few days later, walking home from work, Charlie thought again about that moment. He was proud of his choice, but undoubtedly Mary would say it was foolish. You never knew when the breakthrough would come. Success required constancy, and constancy required discipline, and without discipline, you would never win. To make the choice Charlie had made was tantamount to admitting defeat. Her pride would never allow such a thing.

Defeat. Something about that word snagged at his consciousness.

Defeat. He thought again of Mary's preoccupation with Afghanistan. By now the withdrawal of Soviet troops was over. The Soviets had been careful not to use this word, *defeat*, though defeat it inarguably was. To ordinary Russians, the humiliation didn't matter. Too many sons and brothers and husbands and fathers had been sacrificed to this bloody war. But would the prideful men and women of the KGB agree with this calculation? Would Mary?

No, he thought. *Of course not.*

At the same time, rumors were circulating through the CIA. The KGB was increasingly unhappy with Gorbachev's conciliatory leadership. There were reports of KGB officers taking their own initiative, ignoring the Kremlin's diktat, confident that they, not the sellout Gorbachev, knew what the country really needed. And what about Mary? The war had ended months ago, but her interest hadn't waned one iota. Could it be that Mary's Afghanistan fixation was more than a fixation? Could it be that she and her colleagues were preparing to *do* something about this humiliating defeat?

A lightning bolt of possibility ripped through his brain.

He was jogging, then he was running. He burst into the apartment, sweaty and breathless, and found Maurice in the kitchen, chopping vegetables. "I have an idea," Charlie gasped. Once he'd caught his breath, he explained. Maurice nodded along: he'd heard those rumors, too. It struck him as entirely plausible that a faction of the KGB might, despite the Kremlin's orders, decide to take matters into their own hands.

"She's too proud to let something like this just happen," Charlie said. "She would fight back. Of *course* she would fight back."

·   ·   ·

He had to find the patterns within the pattern. He forced himself to slow down and study the documents he passed to Mary. Details. Places and names. The name of one particular mujahideen commander in the Panjshir Valley kept appearing: Ahmad Baraath.

Baraath was a legendary fighter, a guerrilla in the mode of Che and Ho Chi Minh. Even the Americans spoke his name with reverence. *Stone cold*, they said. *One tough motherfucker.* He featured regularly in her requests. Baraath had orchestrated dozens of ambushes on Soviet troops; he was responsible for the death of hundreds, if not thousands, of her countrymen.

In early August, Charlie sat at his desk, reading a report from Islamabad station. The Soviets were gone, but the Afghan Communist Army kept fighting, trying to preserve the increasingly fragile regime against the encroachment of the mujahideen. The report described a recent meeting between Baraath and a top Communist commander. They were seeking to negotiate a cease-fire in one particularly bloodied corner of the country.

But did the KGB really want a cease-fire? Or did they want to inflict as much harm as possible on the enemy mujahideen? The negotiations would undoubtedly take a long time, but Baraath had the respect of his countrymen. He would eventually succeed; it was just a question of when.

That night, over dinner, Charlie said: "They're fixated on Baraath. They want him dead. That has to be it."

"It would be a coup," Maurice agreed. "Both substantive and symbolic."

"But they can't get to him. He's too careful. Anyway, this isn't exactly earth-shattering news, is it? I mean, *of course* the KGB wants Baraath dead."

"No, it isn't. But think of it this way. You could already make an educated guess about Mary's objectives. What you're doing now, bit by bit, is turning those educated guesses into measurable probabilities."

• • •

It was hard not to want to *do* something with this. He could stride into Jack's office and announce that Mary was a KGB officer, and that the KGB was going after Baraath. But was this enough to make up for his transgressions? No. Definitely not. He needed, somehow, to convert this grasp into real leverage.

Patience was never his strong suit. Years ago, Helen had told him about something called the marshmallow test, an experiment concocted by some headshrinker out at Stanford. Charlie had said: "You should eat the first marshmallow. Obviously. They could be lying to you about the other marshmallow." He was joking, but also not.

His vigorous sense of momentum was beginning to flag. Pickax in hand, he was inching his way up that icy mountain, but the work was tiring, and frustrating, and it rested entirely on him. Maurice's company had provided the illusion of shared effort, but as he prepared to return to Paris in early September, that illusion was shattered. During their last dinner together, Maurice said: "It'll be okay, you know. There's always the telephone."

"We can't talk about this on the phone. It isn't secure."

"Not this, but we can talk about other things."

Charlie sawed into his pork chop. He'd been in a bad mood for days. "Yeah. Sure. Like what?"

"Like anything. Life goes on. You can call me and tell me how the weather is. Or what you ate for dinner. Or whatever might be on your mind." Maurice paused. "I know what it feels like, you know."

"What what feels like?"

"Being alone." Pause. "Being lonely."

"I'm not *lonely*. I'm just being *practical*. I need a sounding board for this stuff. That's all."

Maurice glanced down; he seemed hurt. Charlie felt a sharp spasm of guilt, but he didn't know what to say, so he stayed quiet. He drove Maurice to the airport early the next morning. For some reason, as Charlie watched him disappear through the revolving door, he had a lump in his throat. Driving away, he wondered if this was what Maurice had been talking about. This uncertain, hard-to-swallow feeling. Loneliness? He shook his head. No. Charlie was humbled, he was remorseful, he was determined—but he wasn't *lonely*.

His drive home took him through the harborside district. It was a crisp morning, the water glittering in the sunlight, the trees along the promenade holding the last of their summer green. A handful of joggers, a mother pushing a stroller, a boy riding a bicycle. Up ahead, the stoplight turned yellow. Charlie pressed the brakes. While he was stopped, he looked out over the harbor. There was a couple walking north along the promenade. The woman looked familiar. Charlie leaned forward and squinted. If it weren't for her red hair and heavy black glasses—

The light turned green. His heart was thumping. He accelerated, then a block later turned onto a side street. He parked the car and hurried back the way he came. The couple was still walking on the promenade, now a dozen yards ahead of him. Charlie quickened his pace. The woman was wearing a shapeless coat. His gaze traveled down to her shoes. Low black pumps, with scuff marks on the heel. They looked familiar.

The couple stopped and turned to face each other. She spoke; he nodded. The woman crossed the road; the man watched her disappear. Then the man turned around. He began walking south on the promenade, right toward Charlie.

In the split second before Charlie averted his gaze, he got a clear view of the man's face. He recognized him. This man was a prominent politician. A leader of the Finnish Rural Party. A party well-known, among other things, for its anti-Soviet views.

•　•　•

He couldn't believe his luck. But wasn't this the trick to a successful recruitment? Recognizing when luck had befallen you, and then making the most of it.

Charlie spent the next month tailing the politician-turned-KGB-asset across Helsinki. His office in parliament, his well-kept home in Eira, gourmet restaurants, shops in the Design District. Matti Sorsa had expensive taste, the kind of taste that far exceeded the income of a party leader, especially the leader of the populist, anti-elite Finnish Rural Party.

One night in October, Charlie waited across the street from one of those gourmet restaurants. When the group emerged, he followed at a discreet distance. The other men gradually peeled off, one by one. Sorsa kept walking. Soon he was outside his house, standing on his doorstep, digging in his pocket for his keys. It was late. The street was deserted. "Excuse me," Charlie said, stepping forward. "Sir? I think you dropped this."

Sorsa turned around. Charlie was holding up a wallet. Sorsa patted his breast pocket and shook his head. "Ah, thank you, but no. I have mine here."

"But I saw you drop it." Charlie extended it toward him. "Just back there. I saw it with my own eyes. I didn't imagine it, I swear."

Sorsa looked at him warily.

"I'm sure I'm not mistaken," Charlie insisted.

"No, no, I don't think—"

"Because I recognized you." Charlie stepped forward again, keeping a tight distance between them. "Mr. Sorsa, isn't it? Matti Sorsa? Well, it's only fair that I introduce myself, too. I'm Charlie Franklin. I'm a diplomat at the American embassy."

Sorsa blinked.

"We at the embassy think highly of you, Mr. Sorsa. We admire what your party stands for. We especially admire how you stand up to the Soviets. I really think the two of us ought to find the time to sit down and talk."

"Well." He coughed. "Yes. Certainly. But you see, my schedule, I'm afraid, very complicated."

"How about this weekend? Sunday morning? Oh no, wait." Charlie slapped his forehead. "I forgot. Sunday mornings are no good. That's when you meet your lovely redheaded friend. No, that's not a good idea. You definitely shouldn't cancel on *her*. Am I right?" He laughed.

"Ha," Sorsa echoed, with a strange rictus grin.

"You've put yourself in a tricky situation, Mr. Sorsa. I know you didn't mean it to be like this. It started small, right? Just a favor, here and there, for a pretty woman. And then one day you wake up and, despite the fact that you're the leader of the country's most prominent anti-Soviet party, you find yourself working for the KGB. I bet it's scary. I bet you think there's no way out."

Sorsa was now wide-eyed, back pressed up against the door, nowhere else to go. Charlie almost felt bad. Almost.

"But there *is* a way out," he continued. "And we want to help. So. Mr. Sorsa. Let's take another look at that schedule of yours."

CHAPTER TWENTY

In April, David Hopkins sat beneath the blue whale in the American Museum of Natural History in New York City, itching and fidgeting in his tuxedo. He never knew what to do with himself at these charity galas. His wife tried to explain to him the fluid nature of power in this room—some years it belonged to the tech founders, other years to the hedge funders—but he, with his West Point ways, never entirely grasped how quickly the rise and fall could happen.

He found it especially difficult to pay attention to the honoree that night, a well-preserved heiress in a sequined gown. Beneath the edge of the table, he checked his email. He hadn't heard from Komarovsky in almost four weeks. After the disaster of that *we-were-just-kidding* Polish missile walk-back, he'd been busy trying to convince the Aeromach board members that he wasn't totally nuts. The stock price had collapsed, but at least it had finally stabilized. And, by this point, Komarovsky was probably dead. Hopkins was beginning to think that maybe, *maybe*, he had escaped this misadventure with his freedom intact.

Hopkins looked up from his phone, aware that the honoree had stopped speaking. She squinted into the light, peering toward the back of the room. "What's going on?" she murmured. "Is this . . . ?"

Table by table, the attendees turned to look over their shoulders, toward the entrance to the hall. Dozens of men in blue windbreakers were descending the staircase. Hopkins's stomach lurched. *No*, he thought. *No, no.* Desperately, he wondered if they were there for someone else. At a gala like this, there were easily half a dozen white-collar crooks in attendance.

But they stopped at his table. By now the room was pin-drop silent. The agent gestured for him to stand up and expose his wrists. "David Hopkins," he boomed, his voice echoing through the hall. "You are under arrest for conspiring to commit securities fraud on behalf of Nikolai Gruzdev and the Russian government."

• • •

Tipped off ahead of time, the press was already gathered outside the museum. Flanked by a pair of windbreakered agents, blinded by a sea of camera flashes, Hopkins was marched down the steps to Central Park West and shoved into the back of a van. The footage would run on a loop on cable news for the next twenty-four hours.

Kath Frost had assembled a list of the CEOs who had worked with Ivan Komarovsky. Several of these men (they were invariably men) were also in attendance at that night's gala, and the remainder were guaranteed to see the news coverage. While the FBI didn't have smoking-gun proof against the rest of them—not like with Hopkins, with that phone call—they knew that the sight of Hopkins hauled out in handcuffs would prove terrifying, and motivating.

For good measure, the Feds let certain other tidbits leak out. The morning after the arrest, a cable news anchor said gravely: "We're hearing rumors of more arrests to come. David Hopkins is just the tip of the iceberg."

In the days that followed, knocking on doors from Greenwich to the Upper East Side to Tribeca, the FBI met with each person on Kath's list. For most, a little dose of Game Theory 101 was enough to get them to talk. *Right now*, they said, *you have the chance to cooperate. Tell us what you know and we'll reduce the charges to something manageable.*

Some saw through this bluff. They knew the FBI didn't *really* have anything on them. Otherwise they'd be in handcuffs, just like

Hopkins. When this happened, the agents simply shrugged and played the next card. *Your decision*, they said. *But if you don't want our protection . . . Well, then, I'd suggest you get your affairs in order. Nikolai Gruzdev doesn't like loose ends. You saw what he did to Bob Vogel.*

It took a little while—stops and starts, lawyers gumming up the works—but in time, the FBI obtained confessions from every person on Kath's list. Not one of them chose to stay quiet and protect Komarovsky. Even though they'd known the guy for years. Even though they'd liked him, and had maybe even enjoyed that slight frisson of transgression that came from working with him. Even though they were aware that every confession would add to Gruzdev's fury; aware that every confession was another nail in Komarovsky's coffin. Because, at the end of the day, there had been nothing sentimental about those arrangements. *Better him than me*, they thought, without exception.

· · ·

Around this time in April, after the successful conclusion to the East Ferry Road operation, Amanda flew to D.C. for the debriefing. Director Gasko asked her to join the White House meeting; President McAllister wanted to congratulate her personally. She nodded along as the president described the sanctions they would be imposing on Russia, and how they were rallying the rest of the U.N. Security Council to do the same. The precision of their discovery, the fact that they knew *exactly* how Gruzdev had staged his attack, this had scared the other global powers into thinking he might do the same to them. The operation was deemed hugely successful, and McAllister was palpably grateful: an election loomed in November, and with his poll numbers, he needed any win he could get. *Remember this*, she told herself, as she stood in the Oval Office, shaking the president's hand. It ought to have been a career highlight.

But she'd done a poor job of concealing her distraction. "You were kind of checked out, back there," Gasko said, as they returned to Langley. "Everything okay?"

"Oh. Yeah, I'm fine. Just tired."

"Fair enough. I'd say you've earned your vacation."

Kath had suggested much the same thing. A few weeks earlier, as they were packing up the old kebab shop on East Ferry Road, she'd said: "You should take some time, Amanda. Get some fresh air. Go sit on a beach. Clear your mind. That's what I would do."

But Amanda shook her head. "I need to get this over with."

Amanda erased the whiteboard, though the marks didn't disappear entirely; it would always carry a palimpsest of the last few months. She could sense Kath looking at her. Those unspoken questions: Was she really up to it? Or would she, when confronted with the stark truth, seek the same solace as a few months ago, and descend into the same boozy spiral? Why should she be any braver this time around? With Kath's silent concern radiating from across the room, Amanda felt a flicker of doubt. Kath's instincts were almost always correct.

But some things she had to decide for herself.

• • •

Decades later, Amanda remembered nothing of the baptism itself. She had only a vague recollection of the celebration that had followed, the Dennehey clan squeezed into the back room of an Italian restaurant, the kid cousins hopped up on Sprite and cake, her white dress stained with tomato sauce. This was in 1991. Despite the fact that they'd been regularly attending Sunday Mass since moving to New York, Helen had waited to baptize Amanda, telling her daughter that she had wanted her to make up her own mind.

Eight-year-old Amanda immediately said yes. She was going through a phase of intense attachment, thanks mostly to Helen's new relationship with a man named Sidney Wilson, and she would do anything to keep her mother on her side. Amanda was also aware, thanks to the sophistication of Manhattan second graders, that baptisms often came with presents.

By 1991, Maurice had moved to New York, too. Helen asked Maurice to be Amanda's godfather. Despite Amanda's entirely lackluster embrace of faith, it was Maurice who got her through the rocky years that followed: her adjustment to Sidney as a stepfather, her disinterest in school, her mouthiness to her teachers, which Helen, who herself was working as a teacher, found particularly hurtful. Maurice never scolded or talked down to her; he treated Amanda like an adult, even when she had the temper tantrums of a child.

That morning in April, the day after the White House meeting, she'd taken the train from D.C. to New York. She stood outside the town house on East Seventy-First Street and buzzed the doorbell labeled ADLER. At the last second, she remembered to turn off her phone and slip it inside the heavy black nylon pouch at the bottom of her bag. She trusted Maurice with her life—that was why she was here—but that didn't mean it wasn't wise to take precautions.

Maurice opened the door, beaming at her. As they hugged, Amanda registered that the gap in their height was closing. She'd always been shorter than him, but he had lost at least an inch since she'd last seen him. Like Helen, he was shrinking with age. Inside, the apartment looked the same as ever (the carriage clock, the silver samovar, the butterflies mounted behind glass), but that day, suddenly, it struck her as the apartment of an old man.

"You don't seem surprised," she said, as she settled onto the sofa and Maurice took the chair. "So I take it he told you about the situation?"

"He did. And I confess, my dear, I've been wondering when you would come see me."

"I know. I've been dreading it. I think I kept hoping that if I waited long enough, that it would just . . . that the problem would take care of itself."

"It's okay to be angry with him. He put you in a difficult situation."

"I just don't understand," she said. "Helsinki. It's so obvious that something went wrong. This whole story about him being burned out, wanting to leave the Clandestine Service for personal reasons. How did anyone buy that?"

Maurice nodded. "I never thought the cover story would last this long. But this is something I've often underestimated. People have a remarkable ability to see what they want to see."

"So you know the truth." A beat. "You've always known the truth."

Delicately, he cleared his throat. "Yes."

"And you never turned him in? You never said anything?"

"Well," he said. "It's a little more complicated than that. How about I make us some tea, and then I'll tell you the whole story."

.   .   .

Decades earlier, in Helsinki. As expected, thanks to Sorsa's expensive taste, it had been relatively easy to flip him: without batting an eye, the CIA could triple what the KGB was paying him. On the most basic level, Sorsa didn't care about the Russians, nor the Americans, nor the Finns. He cared about gourmet food, fine suits, French wine. His mercenary indifference was the most useful thing about him. Assets like this, those who were utterly sanguine about their betrayals, often made the best spies.

Jack, the station chief, was thoroughly pleased. They would play Sorsa back in as a double agent, use him as a window into the enemy's operations. "This is fantastic, Cole," he said. "*Fantastic*. Like I always say. Hard work pays off." Not realizing, of course, that Sorsa was just the way station to the bigger prize.

As fall progressed, Sorsa and Charlie met once a week. This was faster than the typical cadence, but Charlie didn't have time for a slow-and-steady seduction. He needed a way to neutralize Mary, and he needed it *now*. "She wants us to tone down our rhetoric,"

Sorsa explained, at one of their early meetings. "She feels that the Rural Party is aggravating the divide between the Soviet Union and Finland. She gives me talking points."

"What else?" Charlie pressed.

"There are some documents." Sorsa shrugged. "Minutes from our meetings. Committee reports. Drafts of legislation."

"What committees do you serve on?"

"The Environment Committee and the Audit Committee." Sorsa glanced around the safe house. "Do you have anything to eat? I'm missing dinner right now."

Charlie scrounged together some rye bread with butter and tinned herring. For good measure, he opened a bottle of wine, too. Sorsa was pleased by this. "I must say," he said, "it's nice not to be treated like the enemy for a change. My new opinions haven't made me very popular with my colleagues. I told her it was a risk, and I was right."

"What do you mean?"

Sorsa held out his glass, and Charlie poured him more wine. "The rest of the party is determined to isolate me," he said. "They stripped me of my position on the Foreign Affairs Committee. It used to be easy enough. But now that they've frozen me out, I have to sneak around late at night, stealing things from other peoples' desks."

"Foreign Affairs," Charlie echoed. Something was beginning to click. "Within that committee, is there anything *particular* she seems interested in?"

"Well, yes. In fact, she's obsessed with Afghanistan."

Bingo. Soon after, at Charlie's request, Sorsa began bringing along copies of the documents he passed to Mary. Charlie scanned quickly through the papers, looking for the familiar name, for the pattern within the pattern. With deliberate casualness, careful not to spook his prey, he said: "Matti, can I ask. Does the name Ahmad Baraath mean anything to you?"

Sorsa frowned. "No. Who is that?"

"So she's never mentioned that name?"

"Not that I can recall."

But it was only a matter of time. Charlie was confident: Sorsa had been sent to him for the purpose of his salvation. He just had to be patient, and wait for the sign.

• • •

And sure enough, the next week Sorsa said: "I have good news. Well, I don't know if it's *good* news. But it will certainly interest you. The Finnish government is proposing to hold peace talks in January. Negotiations between the mujahideen and the Afghan Communists." He handed Charlie a document. "Look at the list."

The name jumped out at him. Attempting to keep his voice steady, Charlie said: "And when you say the Finnish government is proposing?"

Sorsa gave a mock bow. "I imagine she has *something* planned, but she said this idea would be a way of . . . how did she put it? Getting me back into the party's good graces. Peace talks to help burnish our antiwar image. Well, she was right. The party loved the idea. Already there's been talk of moving me back to the Foreign Affairs Committee."

"So the men on this list. They'll be here. All of them. Here in Helsinki."

"I'm absolutely dreading it." Sorsa took it upon himself to open the wine. "You're familiar with these multilateral negotiations? Next week the Afghans arrive for the negotiations *before* the negotiations. Do we use a round table or a rectangular table. What time do we start. How long are the breaks. Do we serve coffee or tea. And so it will be my job to prevent them from murdering one another over the seating arrangements."

"The negotiations next week," Charlie said. "Will Ahmad Baraath be here for those?"

"I gather he's too important for this kind of thing. No, the mujahideen will be sending along their more junior commanders. Baraath won't be here until January. You were right, though." Sorsa arched an eyebrow. "She seems *very* interested in him."

. . .

The next day, practically vibrating with excitement, Charlie said to Jack: "This is her chance to take out the mujahideen leadership in one fell swoop. Dead in a back alley, made to look like a mugging gone wrong. Or something like that. Easier to get to them in Helsinki than in the Panjshir Valley."

Jack nodded. "We should warn them not to come."

"Well, but I was thinking. That would obviously tip her off. And Sorsa's been a good asset. We should keep him in play."

"Charlie, this is *Ahmad Baraath* we're talking about. Losing him could change the whole course of the war. I'm inclined to let Baraath know he's walking into a trap."

Charlie had anticipated this. But if they merely foiled this plan—sure, Mary would be annoyed, but she would still be a free woman. Which meant she would still pose a threat to him. *Make this be* worth *something*, Maurice had said. Now Charlie was setting the bar a notch higher. He wanted his freedom, too.

"It's bigger than that," Charlie said. "It's not just Baraath. There's a rift between the Kremlin and the KGB, right? If we catch them in the act—going rogue, running their own assassination program—it could give Gorbachev the excuse he needs to kneecap the KGB once and for all. We'd be giving him political cover. Think about how big that would be."

Jack frowned. "That's a pretty big if."

"Then what if we de-risk it? Split the baby. Baraath's lieutenants are coming to Helsinki next week. Let me meet with them. Not to *warn* them, exactly. But to, you know, suggest they take sensible precautions. Remind them that we care. Because, if this plan works, we don't want them thinking that we were, you know. Using them as bait."

After a beat, Jack nodded. Fine. Charlie could meet with the Afghans next week when they came to town for the negotiations before the negotiations. It wasn't until Charlie got home that he remembered: next week was also Thanksgiving, when he was supposed to fly to New York.

He'd put in the request months ago. Charlie hadn't seen his daughter since she and Helen left, back in May. His eagerness to see Amanda was the biggest part of it—the sound of her voice on their phone calls, the aching awareness that she was growing taller, growing older, and that he was missing it—but there was also his eagerness to prove to Helen, and to himself, that he was a different kind of person. The separation, he had come to see, was a chance for him to try again. The Atlantic Ocean was a blank slate of possibility. Over the last few months, he had been making progress. When he called, it was evening in New York, and Helen was often making dinner. With the comforting sounds of chopping and stirring in the background, he asked her how her night classes were going, what she was reading, how her sisters were. Gradually, her responses were becoming more generous, like in the old days: the details and wry observations, the very Helen-like way of telling a story. It was a long road back toward her trust, but he felt that he was walking it.

And so, that night, Charlie picked up the phone with a pit of dread in his stomach. After he broke the news, Helen was silent. Then, in a fierce whisper, she said: "You *know* how much she's been looking forward to this. She's been crossing the days off on the calendar. It's all she can talk about."

"I'm really sorry, Helen. I didn't have a choice."

"Bull*shit*, Charlie. Of course you have a choice."

The intensity of Helen's anger caught him off guard. It made him angry, too. "You have no idea what I'm dealing with here," he retorted.

"Think about what you're doing right now. Really *think* about it, Charlie. This is your daughter. This is your *family*."

"I have to go."

"Fine. Go. Go live your life."

"Don't be such a brat, Helen."

"Oh, go *fuck* yourself, Charlie."

She slammed down the phone. He stood there, heart pounding, blood roaring in his ears. What the fuck was wrong with him? His plan had been to grovel, to apologize. He was in the wrong here. He knew that. He *knew* that. He was tempted to call her back and retract the words he'd just spoken—but what would that accomplish? The issue, in the end, wasn't actually what he said. It was what he did, or, rather, what he failed to do. Short of changing his plans and getting on that plane to New York, what else could repair this breach?

A flicker of doubt. What if this Sorsa situation was too good to be true? There was only one person with whom he could talk about this. So he picked up the phone and called Maurice, and asked him if he could come to Helsinki.

The next day, Charlie opened the door. "You're a good friend," he said. "I'm sorry to make you do this. Come on in. I'll explain over dinner."

Maurice agreed to come along to their meeting at the safe house the next night. There, Charlie introduced him to Sorsa. "My colleague is an expert in Afghanistan," he lied. "He'd like to ask you a few questions."

The questions were meaningless, a mere excuse for Maurice to conduct his invisible measurements. Sorsa was his usual breezy self, which seemed like a good thing, but he couldn't be sure. After Sorsa left—Charlie kept in suspense all night by Maurice's poker face—Charlie finally turned to him and said: "So?"

"Well," Maurice replied. "He gives us no *reason* to doubt him. He's not pretending to be something he isn't. Now, this isn't the same as saying that I definitely *believe* him, mind you. But I don't see anything amiss."

The flickering doubt was gone. Charlie drove them home with a regained sense of calm.

• • •

The next week. Charlie sat in the hotel lobby, checking his watch. Almost 7 p.m. The Afghans would be on time. Baraath was known to run a tight ship. In the chair next to him, Hacker was jiggling his knee nervously. This was by far the biggest operation either of them had worked on. "There they are," Charlie said. It was 6:59 p.m. "Let's go."

Two men emerged from the elevator, one older, one younger. By prior arrangement, the Afghans crossed the lobby, entered the hotel restaurant, and walked through the swinging doors that led to the kitchen. Charlie and Hacker followed at a distance.

In the kitchen's walk-in refrigerator, surrounded by cartons of eggs and crates of apples, the four men shook hands. Khalil, the older of the two Afghans, had a thick beard and a ramrod bearing. Awad had patchy facial hair and a skinny build. Their breath was visible in the frosty air.

"Please give my best to General Baraath," Charlie said. "We're looking forward to seeing him in January."

Khalil nodded briskly. "He as well."

"I'll get to the point. We both know that the Russians haven't really left Afghanistan. They remain involved in the fight, no matter what Moscow might say. But they're losing that fight, thanks to you."

Another brisk nod from Khalil.

"And, as you know, there are plenty of Russians here in Helsinki," Charlie continued. "We want to be sure that General Baraath will be taking precautions while he's in town. We have no knowledge of any direct threats. But we only have so much influence in this city, and the general is an important man. If certain people try to get too close to him, under some kind of pretext . . . You understand what I'm saying?"

Another nod. They were professionals; they knew their Virgil. Beware Greeks bearing gifts.

*   *   *

Awad, the skinny younger man, hadn't spoken a single word during the meeting. He struck Charlie as little more than a glorified errand boy, a scrub brought along to carry the bags, to hold the door and fetch the coffee. But the next day, Awad sent a message to Charlie, asking for a meeting. Same place, same time, just the two of them. When Charlie walked into the refrigerator, Awad blurted out: "What you were saying yesterday. I think it's a setup."

"The peace talks?" Charlie furrowed his brow. Whatever happened, he did *not* want Baraath's lieutenants calling off the trip.

"No." Awad shook his head. "The people offering to sell us weapons."

"Weapons?"

"Nerve agents. Sarin. Mustard gas. It doesn't make sense. Why these people would be selling to our side. We're the enemy. But I say this and they tell me I am naive!" Awad was babbling, clearly terrified. "They tell me we do whatever we need to do to win this war. Yes. I know. But they are the *enemy*!"

"Hang on," Charlie said. "Wait. What people are you talking about?"

"The Russians."

"The *Russians* are selling weapons to the mujahideen? That doesn't make any sense."

"This is what I say, too!" Awad said, bouncing up and down on his toes. "But this is the whole reason for the trip in January! We bring the money and they bring the weapons and then we go home and we use those weapons to kill Communists. But *they* are Communists. So why would they want more dead Communists?"

"Good question," Charlie said, gears turning. "So, wait. You're not really here, right now, to set terms for the peace conference. The conference is just the pretext. You're here, right now, to set terms for the exchange."

Awad nodded.

"And have you met with the Russians on this trip?"

"We met her last night, after we left you."

"Your contact is a woman?"

"Yes."

·　·　·

Awad described the terms of the exchange, which Khalil and Mary had finalized the night before. It would take place on Särkkä, the small island in the harbor, half a kilometer offshore. The Russians and Afghans would travel to the island separately, by boat, on the night of January 12. Both sides would come with guns ready, with backup at hand—Baraath was no fool, he was sure to take precautions—but Helsinki was her turf. Charlie could see it, clear and vivid: red splatter on white snow, the bloodbath, the betrayal. This was it. This was how she would strike. The intel was an enormous breakthrough. Which was exactly why Jack was so skeptical.

"So you're telling me that this guy," he said. "This Awad. He suddenly had an attack of conscience and decided to tell you, an American, about the mujahideen's top secret weapons exchange with the Russians? I don't know. It smells fishy."

"Because it *is* fishy," Charlie insisted. "The Russians selling chemical weapons to the mujahideen is ludicrous. Awad sees that. He didn't *want* to tell me. I'm his last resort. He tried talking about this with Khalil. Khalil just told him to shut up."

"Well, then, it's still the case that Khalil trusts the Russians. Why?"

"He trusts *her*. I met this woman before. Remember, I told you about that? She tried to recruit me." Charlie swallowed, suppressing the tickle in his throat. "I saw through it, but still. She can be extremely persuasive."

"Persuasive enough to hoodwink a top mujahideen commander?"

"Absolutely."

"But not persuasive enough to hoodwink a CIA officer?"

Charlie blinked. "Do you . . ." He swallowed again. "Do you mean . . ."

Jack broke into a grin. "The look on your face! I'm razzing you, Cole. Of *course* you're smarter than Khalil. You think I'm going to trust some random guy from some muddy village more than I trust *you*? But look. We have to be *absolutely* sure about this. We show up on January twelfth and it turns out it's a setup for *us*? That we're the ones being played? We need more than just Awad. I want you to find a way to verify this, okay?"

Charlie would have laughed if he hadn't felt so much like crying. Leaving Jack's office, he thought mordantly: *Yeah, sure. You want to verify it. And I want a pony.* Mary was a professional. She ran a tight operation. Charlie had gotten lucky with Sorsa, luckier with Awad, but the odds that it would happen a third time—no way. Lightning didn't strike like that. What was he supposed to do? Ask the loquacious, wine-loving Sorsa if he knew anything about this top secret weapons exchange? And when Sorsa looked at him blankly, he'd have to report that failure to Jack, and that would be that?

Mary, caught red-handed on Särkkä. Hauled back to Moscow in humiliation. Locked in the basement of Lubyanka for her disloyalty to the Kremlin. Executed, even.

And Charlie, a free man.

Was he really going to let this slip away?

• • •

"We're good to go," Charlie said, the following week. "My source, the politician, he verified the story."

Jack raised his eyebrows. "He did?"

"She put him in charge of the bribes. Pay off the customs inspectors at the port. Pay off the police. Get them to turn a blind eye. She's got him in a position where he's actively helping to facilitate an assassination. It's kompromat. It's enough to keep him under her thumb forever."

The words rolled easily from his tongue. Because even if they weren't true, they *could* be true. So Awad's intelligence hadn't been enough for Jack. But Jack simply wasn't close enough to the situation. Jack didn't see how perfectly this aligned with Mary's agenda. Jack couldn't *understand* it the way Charlie understood it.

It wasn't really a lie. It was merely an act of translation.

PART VI

BLOOD ON SNOW

CHAPTER TWENTY-ONE

Maurice had just finished telling her about Särkkä. And Särkkä, Amanda knew, was the crux of the story. Särkkä was what cast the longest shadow. But she was hung up on an earlier part.

"This woman comes up to him in the grocery store," she said. "I saw it right away. You saw it right away. How did *he* not see it, too?"

"It's the same issue, my dear. People see what they want to see."

"But that's so selfish."

"I don't disagree."

"It's so fucking *selfish*."

Maurice was quiet. On a rational level, Amanda had long since realized there was a nefarious explanation for her father's name on that paper. She had long since deduced that Charlie had done bad things. And she'd always known that he'd had an affair. But perhaps some other part of her, that flesh-and-blood animal part, had clung to the impossible notion that the affair was just an affair, smoke without fire: a mistake that went no further than that.

"I should have turned him in," she said bitterly. "From the very beginning."

(Somewhere in her mind, Kath's knowing snort: *Ya think?*)

A plate of ginger biscuits sat on the coffee table. Amanda had ignored them for the duration of the story, but now she reached for one, and it made a loud crunching noise as she chomped. She reached for another. *Chomp, chomp, chomp.* The aggression of the action was oddly soothing. *Fucking hell*, she thought to herself. *My father is a Russian spy!* In this ongoing war between Russia and America—a war in everything but name, a war that had never really ended—she and her father were on opposite sides. How the fuck was she supposed to keep living her life with that knowledge?

As if reading her mind, Maurice said: "But I think it ended on Särkkä."

She looked up. "You don't think he's still working for them?"

"Your father has changed, Amanda. I've been witness to it over the years. He's a different kind of person."

"But you don't know that for sure."

"Correct. Unfortunately there is only one person who *does* know that for sure." He added: "It could be a good thing, my dear, for you to hear what he has to say. And it could be useful for him to see you in this capacity. As a person with a full-fledged career of her own."

"Then I guess I should go get myself a new bulletproof vest." Noticing the shadow cross his face, she said: "I'm just joking!"

"Actually," he said quietly. "On that note. Before you speak to him. You may want to take certain . . . precautions."

"Precautions how?"

"He knows about your source in the GRU."

"Wait. *What?*"

"That fellow named Semonov. Now, I have no reason to think Semonov is in danger, but perhaps you should—"

Amanda jumped to her feet. "What the fuck!"

"—consider moving your agent to safety before speaking to your father."

"Why," she said, grabbing her coat and bag, rushing toward the door. "*Why* are you only now telling me this?"

• • •

But she didn't stick around to hear his answer. She ran to Helen's apartment to get her suitcase, then went straight to the airport for the first flight to Rome. Intellectually she understood the nature of

Maurice's dual loyalties, that his love for both Amanda and Charlie required a fine balance. But emotionally, she was furious. A man's life was at stake. Yes, Semonov had agreed to play a risky game. But he hadn't agreed to *this* particular game.

The next day, back in Rome station, she yanked open the safe and looked for the most recent cables from Moscow, the ones coded with Semonov's alias. She scanned through the papers, looking to see if Adrian, on the ground in Moscow, had reported anything amiss. An extraction was a last resort. They were a messy business, now more than ever. If something went sideways, and they wound up in Russian custody . . . She shook her head. Their diplomatic relations with Russia were (to put it mildly) strained, and they would only get worse with the sanctions coming down the pike.

But the cable, sent last week, made it clear what had to happen: *Asset had no new information to share. Reports that he hasn't seen Tweedledee and Tweedledum in three weeks, but doesn't think this absence is cause for alarm. Suspects they are away on assignment.*

· · ·

Särkkä, the site of the exchange, was part of the string of small islands that comprised the old Suomenlinna Fortress. Suomenlinna dated from the eighteenth century, from when Finland was part of Sweden, and Sweden wanted to guard the harbor from the wider waters of the Baltic Sea, especially from nearby Russia.

"I wonder if that's why the Russians picked it," Hacker said, as they trudged through the knee-deep snow. It was a January evening, and he and Charlie were doing their final round of reconnaissance on the island. "The irony of it. Must feel good, right? Like a *screw you* to their old enemy." He crouched down, examining an opening in the stone wall. "The muskets would have gone there. Cool, right?"

Charlie shivered. "Let's keep moving," he said. "It's freezing out here."

Särkkä was less than a thousand feet wide at its widest point.

There was a wooden dock on the western edge of the island where, in the summer months, the ferry picked up and dropped off tourists. The dock was where, according to Awad, the Russians would be waiting for the Afghans on the night of the exchange. From there, the Afghans would follow the Russians up the path, through an arch in the stone wall, and into the enclosure of the fortress, where they would be shielded from the sight of any passing boats. Then the Russians would produce a chest containing the nerve agents. If everything was in order, the Afghans would produce several suitcases of cash. The Russians would then lead the way out of the fortress and back to the dock. The Russians would depart the island first, followed by the Afghans. This choreography had probably been one of Baraath's requirements: at no point during the exchange would the general be forced to have his back to the Russians.

As the exchange was happening, the KGB would believe they had total privacy. Charlie had suggested that they plant listening devices inside the fortress walls. Seppanen, the Helsinki police captain, and the rest of his men would be concealed throughout Särkkä, ready to make their arrests. Charlie's opinion was that they ought not intervene until the last possible second. The goal, he reminded Jack, wasn't just to make the arrests, but to provide the Kremlin with solid proof of the KGB's treasonous dealings.

As the date approached, he had occasional moments of doubt (could he really trust Awad? And weren't the Helsinki police known to leak like a sieve?), but for the most part, Charlie felt calm. He was certain, absolutely certain, that he had this right.

Sometimes to a degree that was apparent to others. On Monday evening, a few days before the Afghan delegations were scheduled to arrive, Sorsa was expressing optimism that the peace talks might *actually* accomplish something. They might *actually* manage to negotiate a treaty between the mujahideen and the Afghan Communist Army. Charlie, knowing the truth of the matter, couldn't manage to conceal his derision.

"Oh, I see," Sorsa said. "You can't imagine that I would actually desire such an outcome. You think I'm a purely selfish actor. Well, I am both selfish and unselfish at the same time."

"The talks weren't even your idea," Charlie pointed out.

"It doesn't matter. Peace is a good thing." Sorsa tsked. "You're being very cynical. Just because it's her idea doesn't make it a *bad* idea."

• • •

In Rome, Amanda immediately sent a cable to Adrian. She had strong reason to believe their asset was in danger. They would activate the extraction.

Things moved quickly. They had formulated the plan months ago. She made the necessary calls. Adrian delivered the message to Semonov. Five days later, Amanda and Bram were on a plane to Helsinki.

There, she and Bram arranged to rent a boat for the week. They were on their honeymoon, Amanda explained to the proprietor with a smile, planning to camp along the islands and inlets outside the city. The proprietor was a typical Finn, which meant he was practical-minded, and as such highly concerned with the young couple's preparedness. Did they understand how cold the nights were? Did they have adequate food and water? Did they know to leave a wide berth from Russian waters? Because the Russian navy was very *particular*, and didn't take kindly to wayward tourists.

It was the first week of May. At this northern latitude, the nights were short. Their destination was five hours by boat from Helsinki, and one night's worth of darkness wasn't enough for the round trip. As dusk descended, they loaded up the boat with their tent and sleeping bags, with their first aid kit and butane stove, with enough food for at least a week. If anyone stopped and questioned them, the last thing they needed was for their meager stores to puncture their cover story.

Bram piloted them slowly away from the dock and out of the harbor, careful not to leave a wake or draw attention. When they were finally in open water, he called to Amanda, "Ready?"

She glanced over her shoulder. The lights behind her were like jewels in black velvet. Among them was the island of Särkkä. She shivered at the nearness of it. "Ready," she replied, with a confidence she didn't quite feel.

• • •

On Friday morning, Charlie was sitting in the hotel lobby, paging through a newspaper, when a group of men emerged from the elevator. Despite their near-identical dress, the green jackets and khaki pants and *pakol* hats made of soft wool, it was clear which one was the leader. General Baraath walked with a loose stride, a rolling gait that favored his left leg, which had once taken a bullet during a battle in Takhar Province. As they crossed the lobby, Baraath spoke to Khalil. The general's eyebrows slanted playfully upward, like a gabled roof. He looked like he might begin laughing at any moment.

The general was unlikely to face danger while moving around the city, surrounded as he would be by a contingent of armed foot soldiers. Särkkä was the weak point. On Särkkä he would only be accompanied by Khalil and Awad. The rest of his foot soldiers would stay behind.

Several hours later, just before midnight, the Americans and Finns were assembled inside the fortress. Twenty-odd officers from the Helsinki police force, plus Hacker and Charlie. Seppanen would release his men when, and only when, Charlie had given the go-ahead. "My men are on the line," he grumbled, for the umpteenth time that night. "And you, the American, you are the one who makes the decisions. Tell me how this is fair."

"Because if it weren't for us, you'd have a mass execution on your hands," Charlie said. "A whole bunch of murders to investigate, and a whole lot of international uproar."

Still grumbling, Seppanen went over to the window, peering through the blackout curtain at the courtyard. Hacker said: "Maybe cut him some slack, boss. He's nervous, that's all."

Charlie checked his watch again. T-minus five minutes until the Russians arrived, T-minus ten minutes until the Afghans arrived. The bulk of his bulletproof vest was unfamiliar. It had been, what, sixteen years since he'd worn one of these? Not since his initial training in 1974. He'd taken refresher courses in weapons handling, but those only helped so much. A flicker of last-minute apprehension. He looked at Hacker with envy. Hacker was so much younger, and by virtue of being younger, so much closer to the wellspring of stupid bravery that convinced you this job was a good idea.

The radio crackled. "Greeks on the move," the voice said.

"Copy that," Charlie said. Their headquarters were in the closed-for-the-season restaurant inside the fortress. Chairs stacked by the walls, dustcloths on the tables, an array of weapons and A/V equipment. Earlier that night, when the Americans and Finns had landed on the eastern side of the island, they'd approached the fortress from the other direction to avoid leaving telltale footprints. The Russians and Afghans, landing on the western side, would have no idea that anyone else was there.

A few minutes later, a different voice, speaking from the dock. "Greeks have landed."

Then the first voice again, from the mainland. "Trojans on the move."

("So the Russians are the Greeks, and the Afghans are the Trojans, and I guess that makes me, what, Cassandra?" Charlie said, when Jack told them the code names. Jack said: "You're forgetting a crucial difference. The Trojans didn't actually listen to Cassandra.")

Then the second voice again. "Trojans have landed."

"How many?" Charlie asked.

"Six Greeks, three Trojans," the reply came. "Walking up the path now."

Charlie went to the window. He heard them before he saw them, the microphones catching their footsteps as they crunched through the glazed snow in the courtyard.

• • •

Amanda and Bram piloted the boat east, deeper into the reaches of the Gulf of Finland, into Russian waters. After several hours, they approached a sparsely populated area called Primorsk. This forested coastline had traded hands many times, from Russia to Finland and back again. Off the coast of Primorsk was a densely wooded island with rocky beaches, where they would make camp for the night.

Bram cut the outboard motor and raised it from the water. The waves nudged the boat toward the shore. When they were close enough, they jumped down, landed in knee-high water, and grabbed the bowline. They dragged the boat ashore, draping it in camouflage netting, gathering pine boughs to weave into the netting.

Bram pointed at the tree line. Silently, Amanda nodded. They shouldered their backpacks and began to walk. Within the forest, the darkness was absolute. Untouched by human hands, it was a formidable obstacle: undergrowth snagging their footsteps, branches barring their progress. As they went deeper and their eyes adjusted to the darkness, the density of the trees became a good thing, protecting them from the rest of the world. They reached a small clearing. Bram stopped and said: "How about this?"

They pitched their tent and unrolled their sleeping bags. Bram offered to take the first shift, but Amanda shook her head. "I won't be able to sleep," she said. "I might as well stay up." She promised to wake him in four hours. Within minutes, she could hear him snoring. She opened her backpack and took out bread and peanut butter. After she ate, she performed another inventory of their supplies. She checked that the guns were cleaned and loaded.

The sky was beginning to lighten; the forest began to fill with birdsong.

• • •

Fifteen miles away along the coastline, in a small Russian village called Zelenaya Roshcha, Konstantin Semonov was greeted by a similar chorus. Chiara was asleep, oblivious to the dawn, but he had been awake for at least an hour. It occurred to him that this would be the last morning of his life in which he woke up in Russia; the last morning of his life in which he heard his native birdsong.

A few days earlier, back in Moscow, he was leaving for work when he noticed the woman across the street. She was sitting on a bench, wearing a yellow rain jacket, with a small white dog on a leash. Right away, he knew what this meant. And it was funny. For the last eight months he had prayed to see this woman, her yellow jacket, her white dog, because those would be the signs of his imminent freedom—but when the moment arrived, he felt conflicted. The work he was doing, he suddenly understood, was important. Fighting back, righting his wrongs: it gave him purpose. He realized, suddenly, how much he was about to lose.

That night, back in the apartment, with the TV at maximum volume, he whispered the truth to Chiara. She was surprised, but only briefly. (Perhaps, he thought, she had known all along.) She squeezed his hand and whispered: "Tell me what we have to do."

They packed their smallest suitcases, just enough for a short weekend trip. The next morning, they took the train from Moscow to St. Petersburg. From there they rented a car and drove west. A few hours later they were in the village of Zelenaya Roshcha. There was a shabby Soviet-era resort on the water, a collection of wooden cabins tucked amid the tall pines. The bedding smelled of mildew, the hot water didn't work, and the meals, which were served in a larger central cabin, were forgettable at best. At dinner that Friday night was only one other family: a mother, a father, two young boys. It appeared the rest of the cabins were unoccupied. Inwardly, Semonov breathed a sigh of relief.

On that Saturday morning, as the birds greeted the new day, he lay in bed and tried to savor the moment. Years ago, he had dreamed of living abroad. Not since he was a much younger man had he felt this sense of possibility; this defiant faith in what the world had to offer.

·   ·   ·

"Do you believe in karma?" Amanda asked, finally interrupting the silence. Bram, who turned out to be an avid consumer of presidential biographies, had spent most of the day reading. Amanda had spent most of the day staring into the forest. She kept trying, and failing, to think of something to say. Now dusk was falling, and they were dismantling camp.

Bram gave her an odd look. "Didn't clock you as the hippie type."

"I just . . ." she said, but she trailed off. There was no way to explain what she meant without explaining the larger story. Anyway, *karma* wasn't exactly the word for it. It was more like a sense of time folding in upon itself, an eeriness that had been with her ever since they passed through the Helsinki harbor. Decades ago, on a different island in the Gulf of Finland, her father had bet everything on one operation, just as she was about to do. The outcome? "A disaster," Maurice had said. "A bloodbath." She wasn't stupid enough to think that Charlie had *wanted* that outcome. Every person believes himself to be the hero of the story. Charlie had been trying, genuinely trying, to make things better. He had been listening to his instinct. But he was a human, in possession of human weaknesses.

And what about me? she thought. While folding the tarp she froze, suddenly beset by panic. *Seriously, Amanda. What the fuck! You're an alcoholic! You think you don't make mistakes, too?*

"Yo," Bram said. "What's going on in there?"

"I think I'm freaking out," she muttered.

"Do you want to skip? You can hang back and we'll meet you here."

"What? No. I can't do that."

"Sure you can. I've done a shitload of extractions, and this one is pretty straightforward. No offense."

"But it won't work. The asset doesn't know you."

"So what? It's not like he was expecting to see *you*. That wasn't in the plan. You were the one who insisted on doing this herself. You can still sit it out."

There was a brief time in her childhood, that year after she was baptized, when Amanda believed she had a hotline to God. She would ask for signs, and He would give them to her. The fact that her questions were so stupid (should she go to the school dance with Max? What should she name her pet gerbil?) didn't affect the clarity of His answers. She wondered, now, if this was another sign. Was she meant to take Bram's offer? Was she meant to sit this one out? Would her involvement only lead to more disaster, more bloodshed, a repetition of the same mistakes?

"Fuck," she exhaled. "I don't fucking know."

"Well, then, I'm going to decide for you. Okay? Get your shit together, Cole. Let's go."

•　•　•

That night on Särkkä, the Russians entered the courtyard first. Six of them total, five men plus Mary. Two of the men carried a large metal chest, a handle on each end, hoisted aloft above the deep snow. Mary pointed at an area across the courtyard. The sky was clear. It had been a full moon the night before, and the snow amplified the moonlight. Then the Afghans came into view. Baraath led the way, followed by Khalil and Awad.

Awad kept glancing over his shoulder, back in the direction of the dock. He was smart enough to intuit that *something* would happen as a result of his conversation with Charlie, some kind of interference from the Americans.

The Afghans stopped, their backs to the covered windows from which the Americans and Finns were watching. Mary extended her hand. "General Baraath," she said.

Baraath took her hand, calm and bemused. "I pride myself on having a good imagination, but I never imagined a moment quite like this."

"Nonetheless," she said, "I'm glad we've had this chance to meet."

(Her fake English accent remained intact, but her voice sounded different. Lower, smoother. More *real*, somehow. Charlie felt a twinge of apprehension. He leaned forward, but as he did, he noticed his breath fogging up the glass. He quickly rubbed the glass clean.)

"Shall we?" Baraath asked, and Mary gestured for him to go ahead. He lifted the lid of the metal chest. Awad stepped forward, holding an instrument over the contents. "A spectrometer," Baraath explained. "You understand the need."

Mary dipped her head.

A few moments later, the spectrometer made a chirping noise.

Inside, Seppanen hissed at Charlie. "What is this? You promised it wasn't going to be real. You said the chest was going to be empty."

"I never promised anything."

"If my men are exposed to these nerve agents—"

"It's fine. It's a *tactic*, that's all. She's lulling them into a sense of safety."

Outside, Baraath nodded at Khalil and Awad, each of whom was holding a duffel bag. The Afghans stepped forward and handed them to their counterparts. Mary unzipped the bags, briefly glanced inside, then zipped them back up.

"You won't even count the money?" Baraath asked playfully.

"I know that you're a man of your word."

"How rude of me not to show the same courtesy."

She gave a slight smile. "Well, the risk you're taking is bigger than ours."

That taunting tone to her voice. She was playing with her prey before the kill. This was it! Any moment now, she would strike. "Hacker," Charlie whispered. "*Hacker*. You hearing this?"

Hacker was standing at the next window, his camera trained through a sliver in the curtain. The spectrometer, the cash. Between the cameras and the microphones, they had more than enough proof of the KGB's treason. More than enough for the Americans to take to Gorbachev and show him what was happening. Seppanen, realizing this, was quite literally breathing down Charlie's neck. "It's time," he hissed. "You have what you need."

"*Hacker*," Charlie whispered again. It was within Charlie's power to unleash the police, to carry out the arrests, to bring this night to an end. But something was bothering him. Something was off. His partner could sense it, too. "Hacker, what is it?"

Hacker kept staring out the window. He was prickled and alert, like a dog before a storm. "We were wrong," he said. "She's not going to kill him."

•   •   •

On Saturday night at the shabby waterside resort, Semonov and Chiara ate their dinner in the central cabin. Semonov kept glancing at the other family. It was crazy, he knew, to imagine GRU counterintelligence would follow him all the way to this remote village. Crazier still to imagine them staging this fake family as a way of concealing their agent. That wasn't their style. If they were watching Semonov, they would want him to *know* they were watching. Chiara could sense his nerves. She reached across the table and gave his hand a steadying pat.

After dinner, they returned to their cabin. Semonov had requested the one closest to the water, at the edge of the property. From their front porch they could hear the waves lapping. In a few hours, a boat would arrive to carry them away. Was it really going to be this easy? In the quiet darkness, he and Chiara would walk out of that cabin, leaving everything behind. Their wallets, their phones, their passports, their suitcases: anything that might risk identifying them as Russian.

They passed the time playing cards. Mostly they were silent. Semonov kept checking his watch. A few minutes before 11 p.m., he nodded at Chiara. They stood up and put on their boots and jackets and hats. They had been told to dress warmly for the boat ride.

They walked down to the beach and along the shoreline. About a half kilometer west of the property was a small cove. A thin cuticle of sandy beach separated the pine trees from the water. They stood with their backs to the forest, waiting, waiting. Sweat coated his palms. His chest felt tight, his throat squeezed thin as a straw. He glanced over at Chiara. She had her eyes closed. "My love," he whispered. "What are you doing?"

Eyes closed, she smiled. "I'm thinking about waking up in New York City."

And then he heard the throaty growl of the engine. The boat, when it came into view, was surprisingly small. An aluminum boat with an outboard motor, which didn't look capable of traveling such a far distance. Two people were on board, one tall, the other short. He squinted. Could it be . . . ? "Miss Clarkson!" he shout-whispered, waving at her. "It's you!"

She waved back. Then she hopped over the edge of the boat and waded ashore, looking like a child in her oversized poncho. Semonov felt tenderness for this strange little woman. They hugged. Then, in silence, she gestured for them to follow her to the boat.

.   .   .

As they hugged, Amanda could smell the spiky sweat of fear radiating from Semonov's skin. It was good that she had come. She had done the right thing. In this moment, of all moments, Semonov had needed the reassurance of a familiar face.

With this realization, her nerves began to lessen. They were okay. They were almost there. *I'm not like my father*, she thought, ushering Semonov and Chiara toward the boat. *My story has a different ending.*

CHAPTER TWENTY-TWO

Hacker, staring out the window at the snowy courtyard. "She's not going to kill him."

"*What?*" Charlie said.

"Look at them."

Across the courtyard, the Russians had hoisted the duffel bags over their shoulders. They were walking back toward the stone arch. Charlie blinked. *No*, he thought. No! Mary wanted to kill Ahmad Baraath. He knew this. He *knew* this. This was the foundation upon which he had built his redemption.

But the three Afghans were standing in the courtyard, unharmed, watching the Russians retreat.

"No, see, look," Hacker whispered. "She actually *respects* him. You can just tell."

(Respect. This was why Mary had sounded so different.)

And then Baraath, his breath visible in the frosty night, turned to Khalil. The microphones picked up their exchange in Dari. Khalil grew animated, evidently trying to dissuade Baraath from something. But just before the Russians reached the arch, Baraath said: "Wait, please! I have a question."

Seppanen was practically foaming at the mouth. Hacker glanced over at him. "He's right, boss. We should be moving by now. We don't want to wait any longer."

But Charlie held up a hand. The moment the police swarmed the courtyard, that would be it. The truth about Mary's intent would escape his grasp. He needed to know whether he had been right.

Outside, Mary turned around. With a placid smile, she said: "You're wondering why we've agreed to this."

"We've been your enemy for a long time," Baraath said. "You could have sold these weapons to Najibullah and his men instead. My people have told me—what is the phrase? Not to look the gift horse in the mouth. That there is probably a simple explanation. That, probably, we are willing to pay more than Najibullah is willing to pay. But I don't believe that this is the *real* explanation." His eyes twinkled. "I suspect that you are playing both sides. Is that so?"

Mary's smile faded. The other Russians behind her, the muscle, the non-English speakers, exchanged confused glances.

"In fact, we have a source inside the Communist Army," he continued. "He has heard rumors that Najibullah recently procured these very same nerve agents."

"Perhaps they were stolen."

"Perhaps. But, again, I don't believe this."

"Well, General Baraath. The truth is that this is your war now. Not ours. This was merely a business transaction."

Baraath laughed. "A business transaction! Oh, no. I think you're interested in much more than our money. I have a theory. Would you like to hear it?" His tone remained tauntingly light. "You're doing this to sow chaos. To make the fight bloodier than ever. Let the two sides slaughter each other. You want us weak. A weak Afghanistan is a useful Afghanistan."

Mary took a tiny step backward. One of the Russians moved his hand to his waist. The dark metal of a gun glinted in the moonlight.

Baraath held up his hands. "No, no. I'm a man of my word, as you said. We agreed to this *business transaction*." He chuckled. "I was curious about your motive, that's all. I don't particularly *care* about your motive."

In a tight voice, she said: "You are free to believe whatever you want."

"You aren't frightened, are you? We have no intention of hurting you."

Then, a flash in her eyes. A hardening.

In a split second, Charlie foresaw what was going to happen. "Shit." He whipped around. "Shit, shit. Seppanen. Let's go. Let's move. *Now.*"

"Perhaps you've forgotten how to count," Mary said, with suddenly furious pride. "Excuse me, General Baraath, but *you* hurt *us*? And how would this happen? Do you not see that you're outnumbered?"

The radio crackled and screeched as Seppanen started issuing orders to his troops.

Mary glanced over her shoulder. On her cue, the Russians drew their weapons.

But Baraath, hands still in the air, kept smiling. "Only if you don't count the Americans," he said. "And, given that they're here for you, I think you ought to count them."

•   •   •

Chiara and Semonov had climbed aboard the boat. Amanda was next. She was wading into the water when she heard the shout behind her.

She locked eyes with Bram. She was familiar with moments like this, when it felt like the terror might take over, when you were tempted by paralysis. But if you had trained hard enough, if you had the discipline to endure that fleeting moment—the muscle memory would kick in. She and Bram stared at each other in silence. They both knew exactly what to do.

Her back to the forest, Amanda raised her hands high. In the boat, Bram did the same. They waited one second, two seconds, three seconds. And then, in perfect unison, they moved.

Bram shoved Chiara and Semonov into the bottom of the boat.

Amanda pulled out her gun and spun around. The man on the beach had his gun raised, pointed right at her, but Amanda was faster. She squeezed the trigger and clipped him in the shoulder.

As he stumbled backward, she sprinted forward and tackled him at the legs. She kneeled on his back, shoving his face into the sand. Bram was right behind her, gun aimed at the tree line. He'd seen movement in the forest. He shouted in Russian: "If you run, I'll shoot!"

The crack of another shot, then a strangled yell. Higher-pitched, feminine. The man beneath her began to thrash. He was tall and strong. Amanda's weight wasn't enough to keep him pinned down. "Bram!" she shouted. *"Bram!"*

But Bram was in the forest, wrangling the other person. *You have a gun*, she thought, struggling to keep the wounded man down. *Use it, you idiot!* One shot to the head, it would be over. This, too, was part of the training. But the wounded man was yelling in Russian, and Amanda spoke Russian, and she understood what he was saying. "Don't touch her!" he was yelling. "Don't touch her or I'll kill you!"

They were a couple, she realized. She'd heard of these deadly husband-and-wife teams in Unit 29155. Sham marriages that sometimes turned into love, that sometimes even led to children. This man loved his partner, or at the very least he cared about her. The proof was in the anguish in his voice, the desperation of his fight. "Stop it!" Amanda said, with equal desperation, because the more he talked, the harder this would be. "Shut up! Stop talking!"

• • •

It happened all at once. Charlie, Hacker, and Seppanen burst through the door. The police swarmed the courtyard. Mary reached into her coat and pulled out a gun.

She aimed at Baraath, her eyes glittering with rage. She had

Mary raised her gun and aimed right at him. And here he was, paralyzed again. Charlie felt a vague sense of absurdity. Really? *Again?* Had he learned nothing? But he didn't have the strength to run, to move, to fight. So maybe this was good. He was going to die. Maybe he deserved to die.

With one hand Mary held her bleeding stomach. With the other she held the gun. Her finger was on the trigger, and her finger was squeezing the trigger, and—

And Charlie's head snapped back, falling, shattering the glazed crust of snow. His vision filled with darkness. A total darkness, on the inside rather than outside. He no longer had eyes, because to have eyes implied the ability to open those eyes. And even if he *could* open his eyes, he understood that this darkness wouldn't vanish. It was thick and immovable. It was a limb-sucking mud, tugging him closer to the surface of the earth, to the primordial warmth that lay beneath this frozen snow. It wasn't so bad, actually. For the first time in days (in weeks? in years?), his mind was quiet. He couldn't move, but if immobility was the price of such peaceful silence, maybe it was okay.

It lasted for one second, two seconds, three seconds. Possibly longer.

And then a glimmer. A thin gold interruption to the black. The gold blossomed, beautiful and menacing, like barbed wire strung across the ceiling of his eyelids. Oh. He had eyelids again. If he wanted to, he could open them. His ears were working, too. He heard the night above him, full of gunfire. He was pinned to the ground. He felt pressure, but not pain. He tried to move, and discovered the body atop him. He lifted his head slightly. "Hacker," he grunted. "Hacker. Come on. Get up."

His movement caused snow to slip down the back of his collar. Cold water trickled down his neck. Hacker's weight was making it hard to breathe. Charlie struggled for several seconds, and finally, with a heave, he managed to shift Hacker enough to sit up.

The starry sky and the moonlight. Glistening white snow pitted with blood. Three Russians slumped lifeless against the stone wall. Awad's skinny form, his glassy eyes. Policemen sprawled across the snow, groaning in pain, moving gingerly, or not moving at all. In the middle of the courtyard, the crumpled form of a woman.

The two surviving Russians were running toward her, returning fire from the surviving police. One of them kept firing while the other bent down and lifted Mary into his arms. Her head lolled back, her body limp and light as a rag doll.

Seppanen, blood gushing from his forehead, was leading the charge after the Russians, yelling wildly, squeezing off shot after shot. The Russians were outnumbered. But the air, by now, was clouded with gunpowder. Ears were ringing. Eyes were stinging from sweat and blood. It was hard to see.

They were getting away.

That was the last thing Charlie saw.

· · ·

When the boat finally pulled away from shore, Semonov and Chiara were in mute shock. Bram wasn't speaking, either. He gunned the engine with angry abandon, taking the waves at hard angles, sending cold spray over the bow.

Amanda sat alone, her elbows on her knees, her head in her hands.

It was late. The Russians had been bleeding badly from the gunshots, and the care she had taken in binding those wounds had cost them valuable time. The boat wouldn't make it back to Helsinki before dawn. So they would have to return to the island near Primorsk, to set up camp again, to wait through the day for the next nightfall.

Another twenty hours in Russian waters, during which anything might happen.

· · ·

When Charlie woke up in the hospital in Helsinki, his head was dense with pain. An IV was taped to the vein in his left arm. He was surrounded by thin white curtains. He tried to make a noise, but his throat was too dry.

Anyway, no one could hear him. Beyond the curtain lay the rest of the emergency room. Doctors and nurses shouting for backup, sprinting patients toward surgery, applying paddles to chests. Charlie tried to sit up, but the pain tore through his head. He leaned over the railing of the bed and vomited.

A minute later, a nurse whipped the curtain open. She noticed the vomit and disappeared, reappearing with a cup of ice chips and a metal basin. She pointed at Charlie's mouth, placed the basin on his lap. He couldn't remember a word of Finnish. He said raspily: "Hacker. Benjamin Hacker? Hacker?"

She shook her head, uncomprehending. A janitor came to mop up the mess.

He lay back. His vision was blurry. It was easier to keep his eyes closed, to stop fighting the pain, to slip back inside this relentless skull pressure. He must have slept, because, later, he was aware of waking up. The noisy chaos had subsided into regular beeps and low murmurs. And there, at the foot of his bed, staring at him, was the station chief.

"Seven people dead," Jack said. "Ten if you count the Russians. Seven people dead and six more in critical condition." Charlie swallowed, opened his mouth, but Jack held up his hand. "Don't talk right now. They tell me you have a concussion. We'll get into it later. Jesus Christ, Cole. What did I just say? Stop fucking trying to fucking *talk*."

Charlie ignored him. "Hacker?" he croaked. "Hacker?"

Jack jerked his head. One short, final, unmistakable motion.

• • •

They set up camp in the same place, in the clearing deep within the island forest. Dawn was approaching. The air was cold. Chiara was wrapped in an aluminum heat blanket, but she couldn't stop shivering. When Semonov asked if they could build a fire, Amanda shook her head. "I'm sorry," she said. "The smoke is too risky. But I'll make us some coffee."

A few minutes later, with the help of a butane stove, Amanda handed each of them a small metal cup of coffee. Then she poured a third cup for Bram, who was leaning against a distant tree, ostensibly guarding the camp. She stood next to him, gazing in the same direction.

After a minute, Bram said: "Did I ever tell you about Jalalabad?" She shook her head.

"My buddy and I were headed back to base. We passed this cute kid. Eight, maybe nine years old. It was a market day. The square was crowded. I turned around and my buddy was a dozen yards back, squatting down, talking to the kid. But the kid was wearing a vest."

Her heart thumped. "Jesus," she said.

"I know this isn't Afghanistan." He closed his eyes. "But sometimes everything feels like Afghanistan."

In the clearing Semonov and Chiara sat huddled on a log, her head tilted on his shoulder. Eventually Amanda drew a breath and said: "Did I ever tell you about my friend Jakob?"

Now Bram shook his head.

"I met him in Moscow, in my twenties. I'd been traveling, and I'd been drinking a lot, and I was kind of lost, but then I met Jakob, and I decided to stay. He was a good friend. A good influence. He was a dissident, and he was so smart, and he was so *brave*. I was happy in Moscow. I said, 'Maybe I'll even move here.' But Jakob said, 'No. No, Amanda. This isn't the place for you. You have to figure out what you want to do with your life.' "

How strange to be talking about Jakob. How unfamiliar his name was in her mouth.

"I guess I knew he was right, because that's when I was starting to realize that I wanted to do this. Apply to the agency, I mean. I dreaded telling him. The FSB made his life hell. He didn't think highly of the CIA, either. So I said to him, 'I know what you're thinking. That they're a bunch of heartless murderers.' And Jakob was quiet for a while, then he said: 'You can live your life any way you like, Amanda. But if you don't want to be heartless, then don't be heartless.' "

After a stretch of silence, Bram said: "What happened to Jakob?"

She shook her head. From this, Bram seemed to understand. The whole story was too much for her to speak aloud—the midnight arrest, the slow starvation in a prison cell—but he could see the outline. "Oh," he said. "I'm sorry."

There was a bird's warbling melody, and the soft rush of wind through tall pines. There was the sense of being her forty-one-year-old self, here on this island, and also of being her twenty-two-year-old self, there in Moscow, reeling in the hours after Jakob's arrest. Jakob's other friends were devastated, too—but they weren't shocked, they weren't *scared*, because this kind of loss ran in their blood. But she was scared. So she left. And often it felt like everything that had happened in the nineteen years since was an attempt to repair that leaving.

She looked over at Bram. His head was leaning back against the tree, his gaze tilted up to the sky. The branches made a moving pattern against the translucent dawn. She settled back against her tree and did the same. They would never talk about what had happened on the beach, but they had said what needed saying.

CHAPTER TWENTY-THREE

Charlie was discharged from the hospital with a bandage-wrapped torso, a bottle of painkillers, and instructions to rest. Jack drove them back to the station in silence. The route took them along the harbor, where the setting sun scattered gold coins across the water. Charlie held his bloody coat in his lap. Hacker was dead. And nothing, no words or actions, could ever put this right.

When they arrived at the station, Jack had him wait in the conference room. Charlie sat with his head in his hands, palms pressed against his eyes. It hadn't even been twenty-four hours since Hacker died. (Since Hacker was killed. Since Charlie *got* Hacker killed.) Head down, Charlie noticed his belt. He looked up. He noticed the brass light fixture on the ceiling. He noticed the chair he was sitting in. Belt, ceiling, chair. He should do it. Stand up. Do it. It would be better for everyone.

But you know you won't, a voice in his head taunted him. *Because you're a coward. You've always been a coward.*

When Jack reappeared, he was holding a cup of coffee and a sandwich. He slid them across the table. "Drink," he said. "Eat. Direct order. I need you to focus right now."

Charlie forced himself to swallow the bitter coffee, chew the dry bread. Jack said: "It looks like the people in critical condition are going to pull through. That's the good news. That's the only goddamn good news in this whole clusterfuck. Now listen to me, Cole. You got played. And a whole lot of people died last night because you got played."

"I need to talk to them," he said. "Hacker's parents."

"No."

"I need to tell them. I need to—"

"You need *nothing*, you selfish bastard. These poor people just lost their son. You call them and you start crying and suddenly you're making it about *you*."

"Seppanen. At least let me talk to Seppanen."

Five Finns had been killed. A bloodbath. Seppanen would be furious, and Charlie wanted that fury. He wanted to be shouted at, punched, shot, anything. He wanted to *not* be in this clean and quiet room, with his coffee and his sandwich, with his living, breathing lungs.

"Pull it together, Cole," Jack barked. "Flagellate yourself if you want, but do it on your own time. We're exposed. This is a *major fucking problem*. Got it? We need to figure out what happened so it doesn't get worse. This whole thing was a trap. Sorsa lied to you, he tricked you, and that means our people are in danger."

Charlie shook his head vehemently. "Sorsa didn't know anything about Särkkä. I made that part up. Sorsa didn't lie to me. *I* lied. I made it up because of her. Mary. Remember when I told you that she tried to recruit me, back in 1985?"

Jack narrowed his gaze. "But you knew who she was."

"Nope. I was clueless. She came up to me in the grocery store and she flirted with me and one day she took me home and then she—"

"You're a goddamn CIA agent," he interrupted. "You *had* to know."

"I thought she was just some secretary. She—"

"Stop." Jack stood up. "Stop talking. Right now."

"I don't know why. Loneliness, I guess. Vanity, too. This pretty young secretary." Charlie grimaced. "I took the bait. I fell for it. It's so much worse than you realize."

Jack was now pacing back and forth. "No. No. That isn't going to work."

"It's my fault. It's *my* fault. I've spent the last three years under her thumb, and I wanted to escape. I wanted payback. But I got it wrong. She didn't want to kill Baraath. We could have done something. We could have arrested the Russians and stopped the exchange, but I decided to push our luck."

"No," Jack shouted. "That's not what happened."

Charlie blinked, baffled. "Aren't you listening to me?"

"Yes, Cole. Yes, I am fucking listening to you. And now you listen to me." He shook his head. "That isn't what happened. Okay? Mary tried to recruit you. Sure. But you saw through it. And then, later, you wanted revenge, and it became emotional, and you lost sight of things, and stretched the truth, and it ended in disaster."

Belatedly, Charlie began to see what was happening.

"No," he said. "No! That's not—"

"That's not *what*? I'm trying to save whatever tiny scrap of dignity this station has left, because you destroyed the rest of it. I'm trying to protect the others from your rot. What the fuck is *wrong* with you, Cole? It's not enough to destroy yourself? You want to destroy the rest of us, too?"

"She won! I'm telling you, she beat me! This was my fault. This was *my fault.* This has nothing to do with the rest of you!"

"Shut up, Cole! Just shut the fuck up! You have no idea how serious this is. So listen to me. *Listen to me.* We're dealing with a heap of shit. I don't have time for this moaning and groaning. So here's what's going to happen. I'm going to sit down, and you'll have exactly three minutes. You can waste those three minutes talking about how guilty you feel. Or you can use those three minutes to tell me how to stop the bleeding. Which operations you've compromised. Which agents we need to pull from the field. Got it?"

Jack took a deep breath. Then he sat down and clasped his hands.

After a few seconds of silence, his expression of rage dissolved into perfect calm. Charlie stared at him. This man was a sociopath. He was kidding, right? One of his deputies had just confessed to spying for the Russians for the past *three years*. Jack glanced at his watch. "Two minutes and fifty-five seconds," he said. "Fifty-four. Fifty-three."

Maybe he wasn't kidding.

Of every outcome he had imagined, Charlie had utterly failed to imagine this.

"Charlie," Jack said placidly. "I'm trying to keep our people safe. I'm asking for your help with that. I know you want to do the right thing."

"I don't . . ." But his voice was breaking. He couldn't accept this. He couldn't accept the idea that this, the worst thing he had ever done, was going to be swept under the rug.

But maybe Jack was right. Maybe he knew best. What was Charlie going to trust in this moment? His own instinct, which had gotten him here? Or the instinct of the man in charge, the man who had never done anything half as despicable as what Charlie had done?

.   .   .

He spent the night in the conference room, slumped over the table. After his confession he'd slept in fits, dreaming of arrest, of metal cuffs digging into flesh. Now it was morning, and Jack was there, sliding another cup of coffee across the table, and he was saying: "Here's what's going to happen."

Charlie would be shipped back to Langley. He would be transferred out of the Directorate of Operations, shelved in a dull desk job where he would never again have contact with a foreign agent, where he would no longer have the power to get anyone killed, where he would be kept far away from any valuable intelligence. He would spend the rest of his life within the prison of the agency, because Jack wasn't going to let Charlie unleash his stupidity on the rest of the world, but he would be nothing more than a bureaucrat. This was the agreement; this was his punishment.

The Helsinki newspapers were already writing about Särkkä. The Americans would let leak that one of their own, a man named Charlie Franklin, had been killed in the firefight. If Mary had told anyone at the KGB about Charlie, they would believe him dead, too. And given that Mary had been killed on Särkkä, this meant that only two people in the world knew about what Charlie had done, and both of them were sitting in this room.

"That's right, isn't it?" Jack said. "I hope to God you weren't stupid enough to tell anyone else about this. You didn't tell Helen, did you?"

Meekly, Charlie shook his head.

"Good," Jack said. "Maurice is here. I called him yesterday. He's going to help you get through this. You'll see, Charlie. It's going to be okay."

Maurice had come straight from the airport. He offered to call a taxi to take them home, but Charlie shook his head. He'd rather walk. They passed several blocks in silence. "Was it a trap, then?" Maurice eventually asked. "Was she expecting you?"

"No. Nothing about it was a trap. Mary didn't know we were there. And she didn't want to kill Baraath. That was never her plan."

"So then what—"

"It was me. I waited too long. Awad must have told Baraath about our conversation. And maybe Baraath was glad. The Afghans could get their weapons, we could make our arrests, they could keep their money. Baraath was probably wondering when we were going to come out. So he provoked us into coming out. I kept waiting," Charlie said. "I wanted to be right."

"Oh, Charlie."

Another stretch of silence.

Then Maurice said: "But Mary was killed, in the end?"

In Charlie's mind, a movie of that night. Mary crumpled in the snow. The other people on Särkkä had seen her carried limply onto the boat, seen the boat roar away from the dock. But then what? In one version of the movie: the Russians check her pulse, find it stopped, confer among themselves. They turn the boat out to sea, and her body plunges into the water. In another version of the movie: the Russians check her pulse, find it persisting, confer among themselves. They continue to shore. At the Soviet embassy, a doctor tends to her wounds. She lives. She goes back to Moscow.

But Jack had decided that she was dead. And even if she wasn't, the man named Charlie Franklin was dead. Jack had decided that this would suffice.

They were almost home. He found that he couldn't look at Maurice.

PART VII

WHAT CANNOT BE SAID MUST BE WEPT

CHAPTER TWENTY-FOUR

In the end, the boat made it back to Helsinki without incident. Amanda accompanied the Semonovs on their flight to Washington, where they would be formally debriefed. After that, they would be released into their life in New York, where a modest apartment and a well-padded bank account awaited them. The agency had pulled some strings, arranging a job for Chiara at a publishing house. Semonov would be kept on in a fashion, working as a translator and a loosely defined friend of the agency.

At Langley, the day after the Semonovs had been safely delivered, Director Gasko congratulated Amanda on a job well done. "Seems like you're on a hot streak," he said. "Although, I'll admit, I'm surprised you wanted to pull such a productive asset from the field. I got the sense he was really hitting his stride in Moscow."

"Actually, sir. About that."

On the flight back from Helsinki, she debated the order of operations. Did she owe it to her father to talk to him first, to hear what he had to say before involving the agency? But if she did, could she trust him not to run? *He's a different kind of person*, Maurice had said. And she wanted to believe this. The man she knew—who dressed up as a pirate to hand out candy on Halloween, who cared so tenderly for his garden, who cajoled Lucy into barking hello on their Sunday phone calls—could he really wake up every day and decide to betray his country?

But of course he could. Anyone could. And so she had no choice but to talk to Gasko first.

Amanda continued: "We had strong evidence the GRU was beginning to suspect the asset. So we had to move fast, and get him out. Komarovsky had warned Senator Vogel about the possibility of leaks. He claimed there was a mole in the agency, which was why the senator kept the intelligence from us."

"Ah. And Bob fell for that old chestnut?"

"The thing is, Komarovsky actually gave him a name. Apparently the senator thought there was some credence to this possibility. And so, last year, when all of this began, I decided to . . . see about that credence. I know I should have told you sooner. But this situation . . . It was delicate."

He arched an eyebrow. "You know the person?"

"Well, yeah. You could say that."

While mentally rehearsing, Amanda had decided that she would admit to wrongdoing—she *had* done wrong, after all—but that she would stop short of apologizing. What she had done could very well result in a demotion, or transfer, or even firing. But the more she thought about it, the more she wondered: *Do I really regret this? Am I really sorry for this? If I rewound the tape, would I have done things differently?* And if not, then why would she say otherwise?

After she spoke her father's name, Gasko's expression flattened into unreadability, followed by several seconds of silence. Then he said: "I suppose you considered that this was just a provocation. That your father's name was deliberate misinformation. For you, personally."

"I did, but Vogel had written down my father's name long before I ever got involved. I should have recused myself the moment I found out, but I couldn't. I had to see if there was anything to it."

She took a deep breath. The only thing to do was to get on with it: to tell him the story of what happened in Helsinki, the honeypot, the trapping and leveraging, how the infamous Särkkä bloodbath was the fruit of his betrayal. And had it ended at Särkkä? Or was he, in fact, still working as a Russian mole? Amanda wasn't sure. Her father had over thirty years to come clean. The fact that he hadn't was, obviously, cause for suspicion. Then again, Charlie Cole wasn't much more than a PR flak these days. He had no access to classified intelligence. If he was a mole, he wasn't a very *useful* mole.

"So I'd put the odds at fifty-fifty," she said. "But, obviously, I'm not objective. Someone else needs to take it from here. But before that happens, I'd like to ask for something. I want the chance to talk to him first. To be the one to bring him in. I can wear a wire so that you know nothing strange is afoot. Actually, I *want* to wear a wire."

Gasko stared at her. It was awfully rich of her to make these demands. After concealing the truth for so long, how could Gasko be certain of her loyalties? He didn't owe her anything. The longer the silence lasted, the more she was tempted to cave, to say, *Never mind, bad idea, I'll see myself out,* but she kept holding on, and finally, finally, Gasko shook his head.

"Jesus Christ, Cole." He shook his head heavily. "Jesus *Christ.* What a clusterfuck. But you know what? I should have known. The win was too clean. It's *never* this clean. Not when you're dealing with the Russians. Just when you think you've closed out the balance, gotten that fucking ball *out of* the fucking court, it comes right back to fuck you over, doesn't it? There's always another twist to the story."

She blinked. Gasko seemed to assume that she knew what he was talking about. He shook his head again. Then: "You said fifty-fifty? You mean that?"

"Oh—well, yeah. Yes. I do."

"Okay. Fine. If it's fifty-fifty, I'm okay with you going to talk to him. But I'm taking you at your word, Cole. If the odds are actually, say, ninety-ten that he's their man, well, then, obviously this move is a whole lot riskier. But yeah, we'll do the wire. And backup in case he tries to run. I'm taking you at your word—you've been *killing* yourself this past year, I can see that, Cole; if anyone's earned that trust it's you—but just because I trust you doesn't mean I think you're necessarily capable of putting a bullet in your old man if the situation demands. No offense." He smiled grimly. "You're tough, but you're not *that* tough."

·   ·   ·

In Helsinki, Jack told Charlie to come up with an explanation. He was burned out, he missed his family, he wanted to return to America. "Or whatever," he said. "I don't give a shit. Point is, you're being transferred out of the DO at your request. At *your* request. This was your decision and no one can think otherwise. Got it?"

Thus began the strangest time in his life. It was hard in a way that was different from Helsinki. He had endured his time with Mary by imagining that he might someday free himself from the lie. But this lie, the one he was currently living, would be with him for the rest of his life. And yet—

And yet the world kept spinning. When he returned to the States in February 1990, he didn't have anywhere to live, but Raines, his friend from college, had an extra room in his apartment in Fairfax. He was completing a neurosurgery fellowship at a nearby hospital, and his wife had just filed for divorce, too, and didn't these two sorry bachelors both need the company?

At Langley he was a beginner again, learning the politics and procedures for a completely different branch of the agency. Not to mention the broader changes at the agency, because the Cold War was over. The Soviet Empire was fracturing. The KGB was dissolving. Russia and America were becoming friends. Friends? What movie was he living in? He ate microwave dinners, wore mismatched socks, left the toilet seat up. In time, Raines was the one who shook him out of his pathetic malaise. He told Charlie that if he ever wanted to get laid again, he really needed to lose that weight. So he started playing tennis as a guest at Raines's club. A group played a few mornings a week, and while they were a little starchy, these doctors and lawyers and professors and the like, they were nice enough, and Charlie knew that this was good for him, meeting people beyond the hothouse of the CIA.

On weekends he took the train to New York. He spent every Saturday with Amanda, taking her to the Central Park Zoo and the Temple of Dendur and the Mister Softee trucks that dotted the neighborhood. In August, he requested a week off work. He and Amanda went to stay with his parents in Greenwich. His father was frostily silent, Charlie having proven to be a quitter, therefore letting down the Cole lineage. His mother was silent, too, but more out of fear of contradicting her husband. Charlie found, to his surprise, that he didn't really care. He wasn't here for himself; he was here for Amanda, and Amanda was delighted by deep summer in the suburbs, by the lush green lawns and cicada song, by the crinkle-cut french fries from the snack bar at the town pool.

He often wondered why no one said anything. His father was right, after all. People like Charlie didn't go through those years of training and dues-paying just to *quit*. But in the decades that followed, no one in his life asked the most obvious question: What happened in Helsinki?

The silence felt like a conspiracy, or maybe like a test. There were moments when he came close. In 1991, when Maurice moved to New York City, and Charlie was convinced that Maurice and Helen were finally going to become A Thing, and he realized that he had to tell Helen before Maurice did; but then it turned out Helen had fallen in love with Sidney Wilson, and that Maurice and Helen really were just friends. In 1993, during the dedication ceremony for Hacker's star, when Charlie met Hacker's mother and father, and told them how much he had loved their son, and said it was his fault, and began to cry; but then Hacker's father stepped forward and hugged him, and the strength of his embrace made it so that Charlie could no longer speak. And in 1995, when he testified about Ahmad Baraath before the Senate Committee on Foreign Relations, and Senator Vogel seemed to sense that Charlie was withholding something; but then they adjourned for the day, and he was sent home, and he lost his nerve. And in 2002, when Jack was nominated to become director of the agency, and Charlie was so appalled by this idea that he almost went back to the Senate to volunteer his testimony about what had happened in Helsinki; but then it turned out that Jack had overseen the torture of some Sandinistas in the early 1980s and that was enough to sink his prospects. (A few years later, when Jack died of lung cancer, more stories came out. The Sandinistas, not to mention the Särkkä cover-up, were just the tip of the iceberg.)

And in 2011, when his father died, and Charlie stood up to give the eulogy, and he thought about how satisfying it would be to ruin this distinguished moment with his confession, how satisfying to shock the distinguished people filling the pews of Greenwich's distinguished Christ Church; but then he saw his mother in the first pew, frail and bent with loss, and realized he couldn't do that to her.

And when Amanda decided to join the agency, and he knew how good his daughter would be at this, how this work would both harness and amplify her strengths, and he thought that she ought to know this about her father, ought to know of his mistakes so she was never tempted to do the same; but then he realized that Amanda's love mattered more to him than anything in the world, and risking that love was the one risk he could never take.

And so many years later, when Jenny Navarro found those papers, and the universe was finally sending him the message, telling him to do it, to *just fucking do it*, and he thought about all those times he'd edged right up to the cliff, and he thought that maybe this was it, that maybe it was finally time to stop running.

But he was scared. And he panicked. And in his panic, he called the person he loved most in the world, and only later, only when it was irreversible, did he realize what he had set in motion.

• • •

And now that person was sitting across the street, the engine of her car ticking and cooling in the shade of an oak tree, checking to make sure the recording device concealed beneath her shirt was working. She glanced in the rearview mirror. A Northern Virginia Electric van was parked down the block. Another version of this van was around the corner, covering the back door.

She felt strangely calm about the whole thing. She walked up the redbrick path to the front door and rang the doorbell. Inside, Lucy started barking. A minute later, her father opened the door. "Someone's happy to see you," he said, his finger hooked in Lucy's collar. "Come on in."

Inside, he let go of Lucy's collar and they hugged. The embrace, too, felt strangely normal. Charlie led the way into the kitchen. "Coffee?" he said. "I'll make a fresh pot."

Amanda glanced around the kitchen. She noticed the waffle iron, the mixing bowl, the maple syrup. "Are waffles a regular week-day thing for you?" she asked.

"How about I get this going, and you set the table for us." As he scooped out the coffee grounds, he continued: "I saw you leaving the office last night. I was just pulling out of the parking lot when you came through the door. You hadn't told me you were in town, and you always tell me when you're in town. And, also, it was how you looked."

Laying out the fork and knives, she paused. "How I looked?"

"You looked relieved. So I figured you'd probably gone ahead and done it. And I figured you'd probably want to break the news to me yourself, and that you might be stopping by." His determined smile, she could see, was entirely for her benefit. "Hence the waffles."

Amanda blinked. So he had known. He had always known what she was going to do. She was overcome by a surge of compassion. What must the last twelve hours have been like for him? Forget the last twelve hours. What about the last nine *months*? "Dad," she said, her throat aching. "You must hate me."

"That would be impossible."

"But you . . . You asked me to do it, but I just . . . I couldn't."

"I know. And I never should have asked you."

"You must hate me," she repeated.

"Honey, no. There's nothing you could ever do that would make me hate you."

He was so calm. Maybe he didn't understand the gravity of the situation. There were traitors from the Cold War who were still be-hind bars. Charlie would never survive prison. He was old, he was weak. He would die in prison, just like Jakob. What the fuck! This was *her father*, and she was shipping him off to *prison*? What the fuck was wrong with her!

Charlie saw the horror dawning on her face. "Amanda. *Amanda.* It's okay. Sit down. Take a breath." He steered her toward a chair. "I promise you, it's okay. I think, on some level, I'm actually relieved."

"But, Dad," she said. *"Why?"*

He understood the question she was asking. "I don't know. You'd think three decades would be enough time to figure it out, but I never did. I'm not like you and your mother. I'm not smart enough to understand myself." He turned to the window above the sink. In profile, he looked especially old. The drooping earlobes, the blood on his chin where he'd nicked himself shaving. The waffle iron began to hiss, interrupting his silent contemplation. He shook his head. "It's ready. Are you hungry?"

"Dad, no. This isn't the time for *waffles.*"

"Why not?" He lifted the lid. "If this is my last meal as a free man, I might as well go out with a bang."

She stared at him, wide-eyed, as he ladled out the batter. He looked up. "I'm kidding. Honey! It's only a joke."

The *heh* sound she made came more from fear than amusement. Charlie made the same sound. *Heh. Heh heh heh.* She couldn't tell if he was actually laughing, whether he actually found this amus-ing, or if he was just as terrified as her. But this was so incredibly absurd. Her father, the traitor, her father, the Russian mole, making waffles, cracking jokes about prison, laughing or pretending to laugh. It was so incredibly absurd that it caused her to laugh, this time for real. *This*, she thought, *has got to be the weirdest fucking moment of my life.*

"Yeah, sure," she said. "I'll have a waffle. Why not."

They were quiet again as they waited for it to cook. The sweet fragrance of vanilla, the wisps of steam in the sunlight, the occasional snuffle from Lucy, sleeping in her bed. Amanda would have been happy to sit here for a while, to simply exist in this room with this person she loved, to let the release of the truth sink in—but she was aware, too, that the drivers of the panel vans were listening. And that if she didn't get on with it, they would break through the door and finish this for her. She cleared her throat. "I went to see Maurice the other week. He told me what happened in Helsinki."

Charlie nodded. "I figured you'd talk to him eventually."

"And I told Gasko everything. Mary. Särkkä. I didn't leave anything out."

He lifted the first waffle free. "So, then. Does Gasko think I'm still working for the Russians?"

"I told him the truth. Which is that I . . . that I don't know."

His back was turned to her as he ladled out the next waffle. At her words, he seemed to stiffen. *Oh God*, she thought. *Oh no. No. No.* He was avoiding her gaze on purpose. Writing his script, mapping his escape.

Or was he? When she looked more closely, she saw that his posture had changed. The slightest droop to his neck, the tiniest curve to his spine. This wasn't a man getting ready to flee or fight. This was her father, hunched over the waffle iron, wondering how on earth he was supposed to face her.

Not just the last twelve hours; not just the last nine months. She realized, suddenly, how hard the last thirty-odd years must have been. She felt so sad. And yet her sadness, and his sadness, didn't mitigate the betrayal. The sadness would never bring back the dead. And she knew—she knew because she came from him—that what he was feeling would be a thousand times worse. There was nothing she could offer, no words, no actions, to lessen his pain. And, even if there was, there would be no kindness in that. There are things in life you go through with other people, and there are others you go through alone; and she thought to herself, *Why is it so hard for us to accept this?*

"I'm so sorry." She could barely speak. "Dad. I'm so sorry."

He shook his head, his back still turned. "There's nothing to apologize for."

"No. I mean, I'm sorry you were alone with this for so long."

After a beat, he turned around and gave her a watery smile. "Here we are, in any case."

Charlie slid a plate in front of her. She wasn't hungry in the slightest, but she drowned her waffle in syrup and took a bite. They were crispy on the outside, tender in the middle, reassuringly sweet, the way he knew she liked them.

"Well," he said. "That was nice of them. Letting you bring me in. You can tell them I'm not going to run. Although I assume you have backup, just in case. So how should we do it? Front door, hands up, that sort of thing?"

"I don't think that's necessary."

"Well. Good. That's a testament to how much they trust you. So do you . . ." He cleared his throat. "Do you know what's going to happen when we get there?"

"I don't know. I'm not going to be involved."

"Right. Right. Obviously."

A few minutes later, after Charlie had scraped his picked-at waffle into the trash, rinsed the plates, and loaded the dishwasher, he said: "Honey, before we go, can I ask you a favor?"

He looked across the room to where Lucy was snoozing, her pinkish belly rising and falling, her black fur gleaming in the sun.

He loved her. He loved her in a way that was hard to fathom. Every day, she would bump his leg and gaze at him with those soft black eyes, asking to be fed, to be walked, to have her belly rubbed, to have her ears scratched. And Charlie did those things without fail. From the moment he brought her home, eleven years earlier, they had loved each other. They had kept each other company, which was, he had belatedly learned, often the same thing. He was blinking. "Can you make sure . . ."

But he broke off, unable to continue. He went over and placed his hand on Lucy's soft belly. She lifted her head, blinked sleepily, then lowered her head back to the bed.

Lucy felt no cause for alarm. Why should she? This was the time that Charlie always left in the morning, right as she was beginning her nap. Later, a woman would come to take her for a midday walk. Then she would have her afternoon nap, and before she knew it, he would be walking back through the door. Her senses were aware of what was happening, the lifting of his hand, the retreat of his footsteps, the click of the closing door, the rumble of the starting car, but she felt no sadness at these things. There was no reason to miss what always came back. The sun was warm, and her bed was soft, and her belly was full, and until he returned she would dream an endless dream of rabbits scampering through open fields, and wide blue skies that stretched farther than the eye could possibly see.

CHAPTER TWENTY-FIVE

One morning in June, Moscow traffic was especially slow. Ivan Komarovsky, irritable and underslept, leaned forward and said: "You can't take another route?"

Osipov shook his head. "They're doing construction on the bridge up ahead."

Komarovsky sighed and reached for his phone: still no word from Anya. They'd had a terrible fight the night before, their worst yet. When they left London, back in March, Komarovsky had lied, telling her they'd be gone for a few weeks at most. He kept shunting that date into the future, hoping she would simply accept the situation, but Anya persisted with her questioning. Last night he had finally snapped. They weren't going back to London. They were in Moscow indefinitely. At least until he had sorted things out. *What kinds of things?* she pressed. "That isn't your concern," he'd said coldly.

"Of course it's my concern!" she'd shouted. They had just returned from yet another miserable dinner party. They socialized constantly, far more than in London, Komarovsky believing it was crucial to keep up appearances and show no fear. Anya hated the wives in Moscow, these women who believed they were the junior partners in their marriages, and who scolded Anya whenever she forgot this fact. Cheeks reddening, she yelled: "This is my *life*, Vanya!"

He spent last night in the guest bedroom, tossing and turning against the encroaching tide of guilt. He wanted to tell her the truth, but how? Anya loathed Nikolai Gruzdev and everything he stood for. She had left Russia for a good reason. Yes, she understood that her husband's position required him to interact with Gruzdev from time to time, but to know that he was actually *working* with Gruzdev, actually carrying out his bidding . . . ? He was hoping to make amends over breakfast, but the maid announced that Anya had left for an early appointment with her trainer. Komarovsky had sent her a series of groveling texts. He was so sorry. They could skip the opera that night. They could have dinner at home, and he would explain everything.

This gave him approximately ten hours to come up with a reason why they couldn't return to London, a reason that did *not* involve the fact that the GRU had him under constant surveillance, that they suspected him of continuing to collaborate with the Americans, despite his protestations that he had always remained on their side, despite his insistence that he had never actually trusted Amanda Clarkson, a.k.a. Cole; a reason that did *not* involve the fact that the GRU had taken away his passport and banned him from ever leaving the country.

The Rolls-Royce crawled through traffic. Komarovsky drummed his fingers on his thighs, thinking. Or maybe he should just tell Anya the truth. Because even if he came up with a plausible explanation, would it really matter? London was her home. Her friends, her work, her *life* was in London. No matter what he said, would she really be willing to throw that away in order to stay here, in miserable Moscow? No—of course not—and nor should she. That was the crux of it. This was a sacrifice he didn't *want* her to make.

His phone buzzed. An email from the Pavel Partners office in London, which was running smoothly in his absence. There wasn't really any work for him to do. Komarovsky had rented office space, here in Moscow, simply to have a reason to leave the house each day. He spent most of his day sitting at his desk, fiddling with his model boat kits. He had already progressed to the advanced kits; he was now working on a to-scale model of the 1939 battleship *Bismarck*. As prison sentences went, this was quite mild. Besides, he was an old man. It was good for an old man to slow down. He shook his head, glanced out the car window. Then he frowned. "Osipov?" he said. "Why are you going this way?"

Silence. Komarovsky leaned forward. "Osipov. Where are we going?"

But the driver kept his gaze fixed on the road. Komarovsky felt a prickle on the back of his neck. Up ahead, a group of police officers blocked the entrance to a smaller side street. If a car tried to turn, the police waved them on. The Rolls-Royce slowed down. Osipov applied the turn signal.

The police captain, recognizing Osipov, gestured at his men to clear the traffic cones. The car made the turn. Osipov glanced in the rearview mirror. The cones had been replaced behind them. They would have privacy for what was about to happen. For the briefest moment, in the mirror, his gaze met Komarovsky's gaze.

· · ·

"The driver?" Diane Vogel said, handing Amanda a tepid glass of water. "Why do you ask?"

Amanda knew that her father wasn't, after all, responsible for the Vogel betrayal. She now shared Maurice's belief: that Charlie Cole had done innumerable terrible things, that he had betrayed his country, had spied for the Russians, but it had ended at Särkkä. And she had a hunch about who *was* responsible for the Vogel betrayal, but to confirm that hunch, she had to make a pit stop in New York before returning to Rome.

"Just trying to understand the bigger picture," Amanda said.

"Well, now that you mention it." Diane crossed her arms, leaned against the kitchen counter. "Yes, the driver always went with them."

They were quite attached, she explained. In Davos, Courchevel,

Cannes, Mykonos, everywhere Vogel and Komarovsky met: Osipov was there. He didn't talk much—he was polite but unobtrusive, always blending in with his surroundings—but Diane could tell how much the Komarovskys relied on him. Their errand-runner, their problem-solver, their bodyguard.

Check, Amanda thought. And now onto her next idea.

"And what about Anya?" she asked. "What was your impression of her?"

Diane shrugged. "At first I thought she was just a bimbo. What was I supposed to think? Legs like a supermodel, twenty years younger than her husband. But I was wrong. It was clear right away that she's *smart*. Honestly, were it not for Anya, I think I would have found Ivan somewhat distasteful."

"Meaning, what, she was a good influence on him?"

"Not quite. They stuck to their lanes. Not like me and Bob. Anya knew essentially nothing about his work. She preferred it that way. And Ivan, I think, tried to protect her from the sordid parts. Which is probably where Bob got the idea that he ought to do the same." Diane frowned.

"So what did you mean, then? About Anya?"

"I mean that she changed my impression of Ivan. The fact that he had married *her* specifically. A lot of men like him, they just want an empty vessel. A beautiful pushover. But he didn't. He cuts a certain figure, you know, the flash, the jets, but he's smarter than that. I guess they're both smarter than that."

"And do you think Anya suspected that your husbands were working together?"

"We never talked about it. Honestly, we spent most of our time talking books. She's very well-read. She was probably aware that *something* was happening." Another shrug. "But she grew up poor. I get the sense that she was happy with their life. With the material comforts. She wasn't going to peer under too many rocks. Do you know what I mean?"

• • •

When Amanda returned to Rome, her desk was covered with an avalanche of work. There were payments that needed approving, schedules that needed revising, cables that needed writing. During her long deskbound days, Amanda sometimes thought enviously of Kath, who was on vacation for an undisclosed length of time, in an undisclosed location, finally making up for her interrupted sojourn from the year before. She might be anywhere in the world: hiking through the tropical undergrowth of the Amazon, driving a rusty Jeep across the Saharan dunes, piloting a fishing boat down the Yangtze River, taking another crack at the hell-on-earth of Margaritaville. And this was the point of it, Kath explained. She didn't *want* anyone to know where she was. These escapes belonged to her and her alone.

But this deskbound work, dull as it was, somehow felt appropriate, like a karmic balancing after a year of nonstop action. Besides, the dullness of the work required Amanda's entire attention, and this was good, because it kept her from dwelling too much on what was unfolding in Moscow.

They could have warned Komarovsky about Osipov. But then what? If he suddenly changed his behavior toward his driver, the GRU would know what had happened. Ever since David Hopkins's arrest, the press coverage of the Kremlin scheme had been relentless. Reporters could now scent Gruzdev's direct involvement. Recently there had been speculation about Komarovsky's relationship with Senator Vogel. Of course the GRU already knew about this relationship, but the sting would be different when the betrayal became public. They would, alas, have to make an example of him.

In the murky recesses of her conscience, Amanda sometimes recalled Kath's objections. *They'll kill him. You know they'll kill him, eventually.*

And so, on that June day when the Rolls-Royce disappeared

down the blocked-off street in Moscow, and reappeared an hour later with an empty back seat, everyone knew exactly what had happened. Osipov drove back to the apartment, alone. Before he went inside, he was careful to arrange his face in an expression of distress. Several days later, when Anya finally emerged from the apartment, she was dressed in black and wore wide black sunglasses. The Russian government would never confirm his death, but Anya was too smart not to know.

What kind of person? Amanda asked herself. What kind of person is willing to send a man to his certain death? To make an innocent woman a widow? To take a father away from his children?

Most of the time, when she thought about how she'd handled the situation with her father, she felt okay about it. But other times, she was struck by the glaring fact of it. She, *his own daughter*, had done this to him. Charlie Cole, fired from the only job he'd ever had. No pension. No future. They talked every week, and though she wasn't allowed to know what was happening to him, she could surmise. Her father was an old man. He could very well die behind bars.

What kind of person? Really, sending Komarovsky to his death was the least of it.

·   ·   ·

As if Charlie needed confirmation of how serious the matter was, Gasko had decided to conduct the interrogation himself. On that morning in May, as he gave his no-holds-barred confession, Charlie was struck anew by just how despicable the betrayal was. He expected the first words out of Gasko's mouth to be a raw utterance of disgust.

Instead, Gasko leaned forward, squinted, and said: "This woman. Mary. You said she might have survived. But after Särkkä, you never saw her again?"

"I know how self-serving that sounds, but I'll take a polygraph, I'll do—"

"We'll get to that. So you never saw her again. But do you think you would recognize her if you *did* see her?"

"It's been more than thirty years. But she . . ." Charlie closed his eyes. "She had this scar. A little scar on her chin. Even with makeup, you could see it."

Gasko stood abruptly and left the room. When he returned a few minutes later, he said: "Okay. Thanks for that. We'll see if we can make any headway. In the meantime, I want you to make a list of every agent you ever ran. Every contact, every cutout, every *everything*. We have our records, but I want everything. I want what was on the books, but I especially want what was off the books. Got it?"

Charlie nodded.

"And I want everything you gave to Mary. Everything you remember about her. Every conversation, every scrap of paper, every bit of gossip and pillow talk. We need to start assessing the damage. And don't try to make it look better than it is. Don't bother pretending that you don't remember. And, for the love of God, don't think I'm like that fuckwad Jack. Amanda told me she trusts you, that everything ended back in 1990, and because I trust Amanda, I'm inclined to trust you. But if I sense you're holding anything back, even the *tiniest* thing, that trust is gone. That's when it gets ugly. I'll be back later. Use this." He slapped a pen and paper on the table. "And get to work."

Hours later, when Gasko returned, Charlie had filled several dozen pages with his detailed recollections. Gasko picked up the papers and leafed through them with a neutral expression. "I'm only up to 1988," Charlie explained. "Still have a couple more years to go."

"Good." Gasko sat down. "So. I need you to look at something."

Gasko slid a manila folder across the table. Charlie opened the folder and looked at the photograph. With a magnifying glass, he probably could have identified the scar on her chin, but he didn't need that. He knew right away. "It's her."

"You're certain?"

"Yes."

"*Absolutely* certain?"

"Yes."

"Well." Gasko grimaced. "Well, shit. No wonder."

The photograph was of a sternly attractive woman in her sixties. She wore a black suit jacket, a white silk blouse, a gold necklace. Her hair was styled in an airy Nancy Reagan–style helmet. She was holding a glass of white wine. Her smile was tight and close-lipped. She stood next to an unfamiliar man, a blurry crowd behind them, a party of some kind. "It was taken two years ago," Gasko said. "Right after the Winter Olympics. A reception in honor of the athletes. That's her with the governor of Nizhny Novgorod."

In all these years, Charlie had never allowed himself to wonder about what might have happened to Mary. But here she was—alive. Suddenly he had so many questions.

Gasko drew the folder back across the table. "Her name is Olga Baryamova. She's the widow of Anatoly Baryamov, who was a high-ranking general in the GRU. He died several years ago. While they were married she was, officially, just a homemaker. She spent most of her time raising their children."

"A homemaker?" Charlie shook his head. "Are you *sure*? I guess I just thought that Mary—I mean, Olga—she was so ambitious. It's hard to imagine her stepping back like that."

"Things were different after 1991. The KGB goes under, the FSB is the new game in town, women aren't exactly given priority in the lifeboats. Say what you like about the Soviets, they did have that pseudo-feminism thing going. And bear in mind that I said *officially*. From what we've pieced together, Olga married Anatoly in 1992. At that point he was just a plain old junior lieutenant. After they get together, he has a hell of a rise. A *hell* of a rise. In time, he comes onto our radar as one of the GRU's top commanders. Given what we know about Olga, it could be that she was actually the brains of the operation." Gasko arched an eyebrow. "Could you buy that theory? Lady Macbeth on the Moskva?"

"It wouldn't surprise me." Charlie paused. "How did you say Anatoly died?"

"I didn't. In any case, by the time Anatoly dies, his peers at the GRU have gotten to know Olga, and they're impressed by her, or maybe they've gotten over the whole anti-woman thing, or maybe they think it's a fun novelty to have a woman in their ranks—in any case, they decide to lower the drawbridge. She's back inside. I doubt she has the rank her husband had, but she seems to have the power." Gasko tapped the folder. "These are rarefied circles. Easy to spread rumors among the high and mighty. Doesn't matter whether the rumor is true. A seed of doubt is enough. And maybe, if she gets lucky, someday the seed takes root. The CIA gets wind of it, we give it credence, we investigate, the result is humiliation for us, a prison sentence for Charlie Cole. Olga Baryamova finally has payback for what happened on Särkkä. So here's the idea. Okay? We let her *think* she's gotten lucky."

Charlie blinked. "Pardon me?"

"It's going to hurt. It *has* to. The pain has to be real. But, Charlie, do you want to make this right? Do you want to start making up for everything you did?"

Charlie blinked again.

• • •

In early August, Amanda received last-minute word that Director Gasko was in town, making a pit stop en route to his vacation in Greece. She hurried to tidy her office, then glanced down. She was wearing denim shorts and a loose-fitting guayabera, an old gift from a source in Cartagena. Highly inappropriate attire for a station chief, especially when the boss was visiting, but there was no time to change. The best she could do was grab the brush from her desk drawer and pull it through her hair a few times.

Gasko strode through the bullpen, smiling and gladhanding and clapping newbies on the shoulder. "You're keeping her busy, I hope!" he boomed. "Amanda. Great to see you. Glad I could catch you. Nice shirt. I have one just like it." He sat down and leaned back, surveying her office. "Might help if you got a few pictures in here. A plant, at least. What gives, Cole? This is the office of someone who doesn't think she's going to be around for very long."

Thinking of Kath, she felt a terrible pang. "Décor isn't my strong suit."

"I'll send you a spider plant. You can't screw up a spider plant. So, listen. Don't be nervous. I'm here because I want to reassure you of something."

"Oh," she said, not feeling reassured.

"In the next few days, there's going to be a big story about your father in the *Washington Post*. They won't have everything, but they'll have enough. Spying for the Russians in the eighties. Involvement in the Särkkä episode. Agency unaware of betrayal until earlier this year. Agency administering punishment. Sourced on background, but they'll have enough to print, thanks to a disgruntled employee who decided to call up an old journalist pal. We'll neither confirm nor deny, which obviously won't help. It's going to torch him." Gasko shrugged nonchalantly. "That's all it's gonna take. Clever, right? Kudos to Charlie. He was the one who came up with it. Turns out he learned a few things after all that time in the press office."

"He was—What?" Amanda shook her head. "Sorry. I don't understand."

"It's going to sound scary. It *needs* to sound scary. Okay? The specter of charges, an arrest, prison time, the whole bit. But I don't want you to worry about it. Or worry about him. There's a reason for all of this." He paused, stared at her. "I can't tell you the reason, but there's a reason." Another pause. "You see?"

·   ·   ·

When the article ran in the *Washington Post*, it was enough to send Charlie's neighbors scurrying inside when they saw him watering his garden, and to get him disinvited from his tennis group. It was enough for the chair of the Senate Select Committee on Intelligence to loudly demand hearings. It was enough to make clear that the CIA was distancing itself from Charlie Cole forever; that regardless of arrest or conviction or sentencing, they wanted absolutely nothing to do with him; that he was terminated, pensionless, and dead to them.

But it wasn't enough to put him behind bars.

Charlie had confessed to a litany of misdeeds—disclosing classified information, providing aid and comfort to the enemy—but, for the most part, the statute of limitations on those misdeeds had expired. And his lawyer had made it clear that Charlie would plead the Fifth if asked to take the stand, and without his own self-incriminating testimony, there was insufficient *proof* of the misdeeds. And sure, the Feds could still charge him, but everyone knew the U.S. attorney didn't like taking cases he couldn't win.

So Charlie remained a free man. And after the flurry provoked by the *Post* article eventually died down, he did what he'd sworn he'd never do: he created a Twitter account. He chose a cheesy headshot for his profile, describing himself as *Former assistant communications director for the CIA, now enjoying retirement. Father, dog owner, patriot.* At the top of his page he pinned a tweet that linked to a headline from the Associated Press: U.S. ATTORNEY DECLINES TO PROSECUTE CHARLES COLE. "Glad to have my name cleared," he'd written. "Despite the ongoing #lies from the #CIA I remain proud of my 50 years of service. #GodBlessAmerica."

Charlie started by following a relatively bland roster of accounts: journalists, politicians, think tanks, several Yankees, several famous tennis players, several accounts that only posted pictures of Labrador retrievers. He followed and unfollowed (and followed and unfollowed) the CIA's official account several times over. Gradually, eventually, the roster of his follows became more eclectic. Fringier. Conspiracy-minded pundits. Expat journalists critical of American overreach. Whistleblowers who had found sympathetic reception in other countries. Russia Today. He retweeted all of these with abandon.

Someone had apparently alerted Helen to his feed, because one day she called and said, "I know it's been a hard time, and I know you're going through a lot, but, Charlie, these things you're posting about . . . They *look* a certain way. Do you know what I mean?" And the concern in her voice gave him a stabbing pain in his heart, but he had to shake his head and tell her that *how it looked* didn't matter, that it was the truth, and besides, it wasn't her business.

Helen couldn't know that this was an act. No one could.

• • •

From the other side of the Atlantic, Amanda watched her father undertake this public evolution from bureaucratic functionary to outspoken wingnut. She was, perhaps, the only person in Charlie's life who viewed these developments with pride.

And gratitude, too, that Gasko was willing to make lemonade from lemons. Or, at least, to try. There was no way to know whether it would be worth it. Possibly there was no payoff that could ever conceal the bitter pucker at the heart of the matter. But this was what their kind did. They let the world believe they had been defeated. They donned the disguise of weakness and tried to turn it into strength.

Sometimes this wasn't a good idea. Sometimes you simply had to let the weakness remain a weakness, to let the circle become a line. She thought often—more often that she would have liked—of that conversation with Ambassador Romanoff, in the Rembrandt Room in the Winter Palace. *Certain people were enjoying themselves too much to stop.* And she never wanted to be that kind of person, the one who kept the circle going for its own sake, addicted to the thrill, blind to the harm it could cause.

But she thought, too, of Jakob. Of how that brief friendship had changed her life, and how she never had the chance to tell him this. During that winter in Moscow, Jakob took her to the Bolshoi. He had cheap student tickets, the last row on the last level. At the ballet's climax Amanda began to weep. It was embarrassing, but not surprising. That winter, her skin was thinning. A ballet, a poem, an old couple on a bench. A choir rehearsal in a church. Snowflakes caught in a streetlight. It baffled her, honestly. Why should these things move her? She had no reason to cry; no reason to care so much.

After the curtain fell, she turned to Jakob, drying her eyes, intending to make a joke of it. But he had tears in his eyes, too. At this she started to laugh, and also to cry again. "I don't know what's wrong with me!" she said.

Jakob wasn't laughing. "Nothing," he said gravely.

"It's kind of pathetic, though, isn't it?"

He took her hand. He gripped it hard, as if aware of the brevity of the time that remained. "No, Amanda," he said. "This is what I admire the most about you."

There was a risk to caring too much. The desire to help easily becomes a God complex. But there was a risk to the opposite, too. And sooner or later, you had to pick a side.

Lemons into lemonade. Weakness into strength. In late autumn, she received word that Anya Komarovsky had returned to London. The Russian government refused to give her a straight answer about her husband, and Anya was too much a realist to think she would ever, by staying in Moscow, get blood from that stone. Osipov accompanied her, remaining as her driver and protector. Was it out of personal loyalty? Was it done at the GRU's behest, to keep an eye on the traitor's widow? Probably both. But this move meant Anya was out of immediate danger. If the GRU had suspected her of involvement in her husband's misdeeds, they never would have let her leave.

Anya vastly preferred her life in London. Her loyalty to Russia, like her husband's, was fungible. When she learned what the GRU had done to him, it would create an opening. Delicate, but an opening nonetheless. And, if Amanda was being honest, her roster needed replenishing. Komarovsky was dead. Semonov was out. Anya was right there, ripe for the picking. Amanda began to plan her approach.

It was winter again. Rome was beginning her holiday transformation. The ancient city bedecked in light, a Christmas tree in every piazza, a nativity outside every church. She felt that she was finally getting the hang of this station chief thing. But she was, perhaps, in denial about the loneliness that was creeping back in. Until that day in December, when she heard a knock on the door, and Amanda looked up, and she was flooded with not just happiness, but relief.

"Took you long enough." She smiled. "I was about to call in search-and-rescue."

Kath plopped down in the visitor's chair. "Oh, honey. You think I'd ever let myself be found?"

"Good timing, actually. There's an idea I need to talk to you about."

"Right down to business, huh?"

"Would you have it any other way? So, listen. Anya Komarovsky. She's back in London. And I was thinking—What? What's that look?"

"It's just funny," Kath said with a smile. "The other day, I was thinking the exact same thing."

• • •

The stucco McMansion in suburban Arlington was an easy half-mile detour from the rail-to-trail. Charlie took to biking to their monthly meetings at the safe house, which made it easier for him to go black. If someone tried to follow him on his bike, it would be immediately obvious. Biking had been his idea. As had the leak to the *Post*, and the buffoonish Twitter feed, and, most recently, the desperate overtures to K Street. He'd sent his résumé to the top-tier lobbying shops, all of which bluntly told him to get lost. But it had the intended outcome of establishing in the D.C. grapevine that Charlie Cole was (a) looking for work and (b) in need of money. Now they just had to give it time. There were certain shops that had no such scruples about his reputation. Shops that, in fact, would find great utility in his reputation.

Deep cover was different. Other than their monthly meetings, he and his handler had no communication. They couldn't risk the slightest evidence of an ongoing connection with the agency. The Russians had to think he was out in the cold. They had to think him bitter and resentful, and they had to think it possible that, some-day, with the correct incentive, he might be prepared to act on that resentment.

His friends had stopped calling. Helen had stopped calling. His country club revoked his membership. His neighbors avoided him like the plague. It was a barren life, but it was his to endure. He'd given fifty years of his life to the agency; it would take more than a few months to convince the Russians of the man he had become.

Charlie set arbitrary goals to structure his time. For some rea-son, after all these years, he'd hung on to his college coursebooks. One day he dragged them down from the attic and laid them out across the living room floor. He'd been a mediocre student, had skated by with gentleman's Cs, and couldn't even remember the classes that had required the purchasing of these books. It seemed only right that he now, finally, get around to reading them.

So he cooked for himself and cleaned for himself, he took Lucy on walks and read those old paperbacks, and he watched the world go by. In November, as the weather grew cooler and the country voted in a new president, the oak trees painted the street in a symphony of color. In January, after a blizzard, the children on the block built snowmen in their yards. In April, a group of orioles stopped to visit on their way north. Charlie stood in his living room, watching through his window, wanting to join in that symphony—to lend his scarf to the bare-necked snowmen—to send a picture to Amanda of that bright flash of orange—*I'm turning into such a cliché*, he imagined himself saying, *I even bought binoculars and one of those bird-spotting books*—

Actually, for that last, he didn't have to imagine. Charlie, always slow to a trend, had finally embraced texting. He and Amanda still had their Sunday phone calls, but the spontaneity of their daily WhatsApp exchanges felt somehow more meaningful. Often he wanted to write things like: *I'm sorry for when I wasn't there.* And: *I'm sorry I couldn't protect you from this.* But, for the role he was playing, even this was too much truth. It was better to stick to the present: pictures of birds at the bird feeder, a recipe he thought she might like. The simple pleasure of these exchanges was a revelation. Although he did worry about going overboard. One day, as he was texting her about the shortstop the Yankees had just traded, he thought: *Why am I boring her with this? She doesn't care about the Yankees.*

And then he thought: *I'm telling her this because I love her.*

As much as he wished that they could talk about the work he was now doing, there was comfort in realizing that the nature of their relationship hadn't changed. Their intimacy had always left room for silence. And Amanda had been made aware, in some fashion, of what he was doing, enough not to worry about him. So maybe the nature of their relationship hadn't changed; but, the source of the silence being understood, it had deepened.

Then, before he knew it, it was summer again. It had been more than a year since his confession, and he was still here. He'd put a sizable dent in the unread books, even though it honestly seemed pointless, even though the books often bored him to death. Next up was a volume of John Milton's poetry. That morning, he turned to Sonnet 19 and began reading. *When I consider how my light is spent / Ere half my days, in this dark world and wide—*

But he had to stop. For some reason, there were tears swimming in his eyes.

So he set the book down and decided to go for a ride. Those bike rides were, perhaps, the most crucial ingredient for his sanity. They could be long, forty or fifty miles or more, but they always formed a circle. A loop that returned him to where he had begun. When the ride was over, when he was back in the cool mustiness of his garage, when his heart was pounding and his legs ached from effort, Charlie sometimes lingered, wiping the mud from the frame, greasing the chain, checking the tire pressure, doing things that didn't really need doing, because part of him just wanted to stay out here. Some days, many days, his self-imposed routine simply didn't cut it. He dreaded the quiet emptiness of that house, which hadn't known the presence of another person for over a year. He feared the endless time.

But that was only part of him. Another part of him, the larger part of him, knew that he wasn't meant to resist. The emptiness was the point. It was allowing him to change.

(And later that day he would return to Milton and finish Sonnet 19, and that final line—*They also serve who only stand and wait*—that final line helped make sense of things.)

(And later that year, in the autumn, as the trees were again losing their leaves, he would be asked to lunch by an employee of a lobbying firm with a distinctly pro-Russian bent. He would be invited to share his insights. He would be the recipient of sympathetic smiles. He would embark down a path that would, in time, lead him back to the woman who had once brushed her hand against his in a grocery store.)

So he went back inside his empty house. What would happen was in the future. Charlie didn't know yet whether any of this would work. He only knew that he had made terrible mistakes, and for reasons he didn't understand, and in ways he didn't deserve, he was beginning to believe that this pain might finally reach an end; that even the worst kind of mistake might someday find redemption.

ACKNOWLEDGMENTS

Thank you to my editor, Carina Guiterman, for making me capable of writing the kind of novel I've always wanted to write.

Thank you to my agents, PJ Mark and Stefanie Lieberman, for their warmth, their wisdom, and their steadfast guidance. Thank you to Allison Hunter for her love and her belief.

Thank you to everyone at Janklow & Nesbit, and to everyone at Simon & Schuster, especially Sophia Benz, Hannah Bishop, Lashanda Anakwah, Maggie Southard Gladstone, Brianna Scharfenberg, Danielle Prielipp, Morgan Hart, and Dominick Montalto.

For conversations that have challenged me and inspired me in realms of creativity and beyond, thank you to Emma Brodie, Lily Brooks-Dalton, Nicole Corbett, Jonathan Darman, Sara Faring, Azadeh Moaveni, and Katherine Schafler. For their unwavering love, thank you to my parents, Ed Pitoniak and Kate Barber. For his beautiful heart, for his steadfast honesty, and for telling me to always bet on myself, thank you to my husband, Andrew Bartholomew.

This is a book about a woman making her way through a world that is still mostly dominated by men. I've spent a lot of time in recent years thinking about the women I admire, and the ways in which they raise me up. This book is for two magnificent women in particular: Nellie Pitoniak and Ruth Kim. Nellie and Ruth inspire me, every day, to try and better myself; even as they remind me, too, to accept myself just as I am. They have walked with me through so much. They make my life infinitely better. I love them, and I am lucky to be loved by them in return.

ABOUT THE AUTHOR

Anna Pitoniak is the author of *Our American Friend*, *Necessary People*, and *The Futures*. Before becoming a full-time author, she worked for many years in book publishing, including as a senior editor at Random House. She grew up in Whistler, British Columbia. She graduated from Yale, and lives in New York City and East Hampton.